GENUINE LIES

Nora Roberts

····

Genuine Lies

BANTAM BOOKS TRADE PAPERBACKS
New York

2009 Bantam Books Trade Paperback Edition

Copyright © 1991 by Nora Roberts

Published in the United States by Bantam Books, an imprint of The Random House Publishing Group, a division of Random House, Inc., New York.

BANTAM BOOKS and the rooster colophon are registered trademarks of Random House, Inc.

Originally published in paperback in the United States by Bantam Books, an imprint of The Random House Publishing Group, a division of Random House, Inc., in 1991.

ISBN 978-0-553-38642-4

Printed in the United States of America

www.bantamdell.com

2 4 6 8 9 7 5 3

To Pat and Mary Kay

Thanks for the laughs, and the lunches.

Genuine Lies

Prologue

◆ ◆ ◆ ◆

SOMEHOW, using a combination of pride and terror, she managed to keep her head up and to choke back the nausea. It wasn't a nightmare. It wasn't a dark fantasy she would shake off at dawn. Yet, dreamlike, everything was happening in slow motion. She was fighting to push her way through a thick curtain of water beyond which she could see the faces of the people all around her. Their eyes were hungry; their mouths opened and closed as if they would swallow her whole. Their voices ebbed and flowed like the pounding of waves on rock. Stronger, more insistent, was her heart's jerky beat, a fierce tango inside her frozen body.

Keep moving, keep moving, her brain commanded her trembling legs as firm hands pushed her through the crowd and out onto the courthouse steps. The glare of sunlight made her eyes tear, so she fumbled for her sunglasses. They would think she was crying. She couldn't allow them that dip into her emotions. Silence was her only shield.

She stumbled and felt a moment of panic. She could not fall. If she fell, the reporters, the curious, would leap on her, snarling and snapping and tearing like wild dogs over a rabbit. She had to stand upright, to stand behind her silence for a few yards. Eve had taught her that much.

Give them your brains, girl, never your guts.

Eve. She wanted to scream. To throw her hands up over her face and scream and scream until all the rage, the fear, the grief, emptied out of her.

Shouted questions assaulted her. Microphones stabbed at her face like deadly little darts as the news crews busily tapped the finale of the arraignment for murder of Julia Summers.

"Bitch!" shouted someone whose voice was harsh with hate and tears. "Coldhearted bitch."

She wanted to stop and scream back: *How do you know what I am? How do you know what I feel?*

But the door of the limo was open. She climbed in to be cocooned by cool air, shielded by tinted glass. The crowd surged forward, pressing against the barricades along the curb. Angry faces encircled her; vultures over a still-bleeding corpse. As the car glided away, she looked straight ahead, her hands fisted in her lap and her eyes mercifully dry.

She said nothing as her companion fixed her a drink. Two fingers of brandy. When she had taken the first sip, he spoke calmly, almost casually, in the voice she had come to love.

"Well, Julia, did you kill her?"

Chapter One

♦ ♦ ♦ ♦

SHE WAS A LEGEND. A product of time and talent and her own unrelenting ambition. Eve Benedict. Men thirty years her junior desired her. Women envied her. Studio heads courted her, knowing that in this day when movies were made by accountants, her name was solid gold. In a career that had spanned nearly fifty years, Eve Benedict had known the highs, and the lows, and used both to forge herself into what she wanted to be.

She did as she chose, personally and professionally. If a role interested her, she went after it with the same verve and ferocity she'd used to get her first part. If she desired a man, she snared him, discarding him only when she was done, and—she liked to brag—never with malice. All of her former lovers, and they were legion, remained friends. Or had the good sense to pretend to be.

At sixty-seven, Eve had maintained her magnificent body through discipline and the surgeon's art. Over a half century she had honed herself into a sharp blade. She had used both disappointment and triumph to temper that blade into a weapon that was feared and respected in the kingdom of Hollywood.

She had been a goddess. Now she was a queen with a keen mind and keen tongue. Few knew her heart. None knew her secrets.

"It's shit." Eve tossed the script onto the tiled floor of the solarium, gave it a solid kick, then paced. She moved as she always had, with a thin coat of dignity over a blaze of sensuality. "Everything I've read in the last two months has been shit."

Her agent, a round, soft-looking woman with a will of iron, shrugged and sipped her afternoon cocktail. "I told you it was trash, Eve, but you wanted to read it."

"You said trash." Eve took a cigarette from a Lalique dish and dug into the pockets of her slacks for a book of matches. "There's always something redeeming in trash. I've done plenty of trash and made it shine. This"—she kicked the script again with relish—"is shit."

Margaret Castle took another sip of vodka-laced grapefruit juice. "Right again. The miniseries—"

A snap of the head, a quick glance with eyes sharp as a scalpel. "You know how I detest that word."

Maggie reached for a piece of marzipan and popped it into her mouth. "Whatever you choose to call it, the part of Marilou is perfect for you. There hasn't been a tougher, more fascinating Southern belle since Scarlett."

Eve knew it, and had already decided to take the offer. But she didn't like to give in too quickly. It wasn't just a matter of pride, but a matter of image. "Three weeks location-shooting in Georgia," she muttered. "Fucking alligators and mosquitoes."

"Honey, your sexual partners are your business." And earned a quick snort of laughter. "They've cast Peter Jackson as Robert."

Eve's bright green eyes narrowed. "When did you hear that?"

"Over breakfast." Maggie smiled and settled deeper into the pastel cushions on the white wicker settee. "I thought you might be interested."

Calculating, still moving, Eve blew out a long stream of smoke. "He looks like this week's hunk, but he does excellent work. It might almost make running around in a swamp worthwhile."

Now that she had a nibble, Maggie reeled in her catch. "They're considering Justine Hunter for Marilou."

"That bimbo?" Eve began to puff and pace more rapidly. "She'd ruin the picture. She hasn't the talent or the brains to be Marilou. Did you see her in *Midnight*? The only thing that wasn't flat about her performance was her bustline. Jesus."

The reaction was exactly what Maggie had expected. "She did very well in *Right of Way.*"

"That's because she was playing herself, an empty-headed slut. My God, Maggie, she's a disaster."

"The TV audience knows her name, and . . ." Maggie chose another piece of marzipan, examined it, smiled. "She's the right age for the part. Marilou is supposed to be in her mid-forties."

Eve whirled around. She stood in a patch of sunlight, the cigarette jutting from her fingers like a weapon. Magnificent, Maggie thought as she waited for the explosion. Eve Benedict was magnificent, with her sharp-featured face, those full red lips, the sleekly cropped ebony hair. Her body was a man's fantasy—long and limber, full-breasted. It was clad in a jewel-toned silk, her trademark.

Then she smiled, the famous lightning-quick smile that left the recipient breathless. Tossing back her head, she gave a long, appreciative laugh. "Dead center, Maggie. Goddammit, you know me too well."

Maggie crossed her plump legs. "After twenty-five years, I should."

Eve moved to the bar to pour herself a tall glass of juice from oranges fresh from her own trees. She added a generous splash of champagne. "Start working on the deal."

"I already have. This project is going to make you a rich woman."

"I *am* a rich woman." With a shrug, Eve crushed out her cigarette. "We both are."

"So, we'll be richer." She toasted Eve with her glass, drank, then rattled ice cubes. "Now, why don't you tell me why you really asked me out here today?"

Leaning back against the bar, Eve sipped. Diamonds glinted at her ears; her feet were bare. "You do know me too well. I've got another project in mind. One I've been thinking about for some time. I'll need your help with it."

Maggie arched one thin blond brow. "My help, not my opinion?"

"Your opinion's always welcome, Maggie. It's one of the few that is." She sat in a high-back wicker chair cushioned in scarlet. From there she could see her gardens, the meticulously tended blooms, the carefully trimmed hedges. Bright water fumed up in a marble fountain and glinted in its basin. Beyond was the pool, the guest house—an exact reproduction of a Tudor home from one of her most successful films. Behind a stand of palms were the tennis courts she used at least twice a week, a putting green she had lost interest in, a shooting range she had installed after the Manson murders twenty years before. There was an orange grove, a ten-car garage, a man-made lagoon, and a twenty-foot stone fence to close it all in.

She'd worked for every square inch of her estate in Beverly Hills. Just as she'd worked to turn a smoky-voiced sex symbol into a respected actress. There had been sacrifices, but she rarely thought of them. There had been pain. That was something she never forgot. She had clawed her way up a ladder slippery with sweat and blood—and had been at the top for a long time. But she was there alone.

"Tell me about the project," Maggie was saying. "I'll give you my opinion, and then my help."

"What project?"

Both women looked toward the doorway at the sound of the man's voice. It carried the faintest of British accents, like polish over fine wood, though the man had not lived in England for more than a decade in his thirty-five years. Paul Winthrop's home was southern California.

"You're late." But Eve was smiling easily and holding out both hands for him.

"Am I?" He kissed her hands first, then her cheek, finding them both as soft as rose petals. "Hello, gorgeous." He lifted her glass, sipped, and grinned. "Best damn oranges in the country. Hi, Maggie."

"Paul. Christ, you look more like your father every day. I could get you a screen test in a heartbeat."

He sipped again before handing the glass back to Eve. "I'm going to take you up on that one day—when hell freezes over."

He crossed to the bar, a tall, leanly built male with a hint of muscle beneath his loose shirt. His hair was the color of aged mahogany and was windswept from driving fast with the top of his convertible down. His face, which had been almost too pretty as a boy, had weathered—much to his relief. Eve studied it now, the long, straight nose, the hollowed cheeks, the deep blue eyes with their faint lines that were a woman's curse and a man's character. His mouth was quirked in a grin and was strong and beautifully shaped. It was a mouth she had fallen in love with twenty-five years before. His father's mouth.

"How is the old bastard?" she asked with affection.

"Enjoying his fifth wife, and the tables at Monte Carlo."

"He'll never learn. Women and gambling were always Rory's weaknesses."

Because he planned to work that evening, Paul sipped his juice straight. He'd interrupted his day for Eve, as he would have done for no one else. "Fortunately, he's always had uncanny luck with both."

Eve drummed her fingers on the arm of the chair. She'd been married to Rory Winthrop for a brief and tumultuous two years a quarter of a century before, and wasn't certain she agreed with his son's verdict. "How old is this one, thirty?"

"According to her press releases." Amused, Paul tilted his head as Eve snatched up another cigarette. "Come now, gorgeous, don't tell me you're jealous."

If anyone else had suggested it, she would have raked them clean to the bone. Now Eve merely shrugged.

"I hate to see him make a fool of himself. Besides, every time he takes the plunge, they run a list of his exes." A cloud of smoke veiled her face for a moment, then was whipped up into the current from the ceiling fan. "I detest seeing my name linked with his poorer choices."

"Ah, but yours shines the brightest." Paul lifted his glass in salute. "As it should."

"Always the right words at the right time." Pleased, Eve settled back. But her fingers moved restlessly on the arm of the chair. "The mark of the successful novelist. Which is one of the reasons I asked you here today."

"One of?"

"The other being that I don't see enough of you, Paul, when you're in the middle of one of your books." Again she held out a hand for his. "I might have been your stepmama for only a short time, but you're still my only son."

Touched, he brought her hand to his lips. "And you're still the only woman I love."

"Because you're too damn choosy." But Eve squeezed his fingers before she released them. "I didn't ask both of you here for sentiment. I need your professional advice." She took a slow drag on her cigarette, knowing the value of the dramatic timing. "I've decided to write my memoirs."

"Oh, Christ," was Maggie's first reaction, but Paul merely lifted a brow.

"Why?"

Only the sharpest of ears would have heard the hesitation. Eve always had her lines cold. "Having a lifetime achievement award thrust on me started me thinking."

"That was an honor, Eve," Maggie put in. "Not a kick in the pants."

"It was both," Eve said. "It was fitting to have my body of work honored, but my life—and my work—are far from finished. It did cause me to reflect on the fact that my fifty years in this business have been far from dull. I don't think even someone with Paul's imagination could dream up a more interesting story—with such varied characters." Her lips curved slowly, with malice as well as humor. "There will be some who won't be pleased to see their names and their little secrets in print."

"And there's nothing you like better than to stir the pot," Paul murmured.

"Nothing," Eve agreed. "And why not? The sauce sticks to the bottom and burns if it isn't stirred now and again. I intend to be frank, brutally so. I won't waste my time on a celebrity biography that reads like a press release or a fan letter. I need a writer who won't soften my words or exploit them. Someone who will put my story together as it is, not as some might want it to be." She caught the expression on Paul's face and laughed. "Don't worry, darling, I'm not asking you to take the job."

"I gather you have someone in mind." He took her glass to freshen her drink. "Is that why you sent the Robert Chambers bio over to me last week?"

Eve accepted the glass and smiled. "What did you think of it?"

He shrugged. "It was well done for its kind."

"Don't be a snob, darling." Amused, she gestured with her cigarette. "As I'm sure you're aware, the book received excellent reviews and stayed on the *New York Times* list for twenty weeks."

"Twenty-two," he corrected her, and made her grin.

"It was an interesting work, if one was into Robert's bravado, and machismo, but what I found most fascinating was that the author managed to ferret out a number of truths among the carefully crafted lies."

"Julia Summers," Maggie put in, debating hard and long over another piece of candy. "I saw her on *Today* when she was doing the promotion rounds last spring. Very cool, very attractive. There was a rumor that she and Robert were lovers."

"If they were, she maintained her objectivity." Eve made a circle in the air with her cigarette before crushing it out. "Her personal life isn't the issue."

"But yours will be," Paul reminded her. After setting his glass aside, he moved closer to her. "Eve, I don't like the idea of your opening yourself up. Whatever they say about sticks and stones, words leave scars, especially when they're tossed by a clever writer."

"You're absolutely right—that's why I intend for most of the words to be mine." She waved away his protest, impatiently, so that he saw her mind was already made up. "Paul, without getting on your literary hobby horse, what do you think of Julia Summers professionally?"

"She does what she does well enough. Maybe too well." The idea made him uneasy. "You don't need to expose yourself to public curiosity this way, Eve. You certainly don't need the money, or the publicity."

"My dear boy, I'm not doing this for the money or the publicity. I'm doing it as I do most things, for the satisfaction." Eve glanced toward her agent. She knew Maggie well enough to see that the wheels were already turning. "Call her agent," Eve said briefly. "Make the pitch. I'll give you a list of my requirements." She rose then to press a kiss to Paul's cheek. "Don't scowl. You have to trust that I know what I'm doing."

She walked with perfect poise to the bar to add more champagne to her glass, hoping she hadn't started a ball rolling that would ultimately flatten her.

◆ ◆ ◆

*J*ULIA WASN'T CERTAIN if she'd just been given the world's most fascinating Christmas present or an enormous lump of coal. She stood at the big bay window of her Connecticut home and watched the wind hurl the snow in a blinding white dance. Across the room, the logs snapped and sizzled in the wide stone fireplace. A bright red stocking hung on either end of the mantel. Idly, she spun a silver star and sent it twirling on its bough of the blue spruce.

The tree was square in the center of the window, precisely where Brandon had wanted it. They had chosen the six-foot spruce together, and hauled it, puffing and blowing, into the living room, then had spent an entire evening decorating. Brandon had known where he'd wanted every ornament. When she would have tossed the tinsel at the branches in hunks, he had insisted on draping individual strands.

He'd already chosen the spot where they would plant it on New Year's Day, starting a new tradition in their new home in a new year.

At ten, Brandon was a fiend for tradition. Perhaps, she thought, because he had never known a traditional home. Thinking of her son, Julia looked down at the presents stacked under the tree. There, too, was order. Brandon had a ten-year-old's need to shake and sniff and rattle the brightly wrapped boxes. He had the curiosity, and the wit, to cull out hints on what was hidden inside. But when he replaced a box, it went neatly into its space.

In a few hours he would begin to beg his mother to let him open one—just one—present tonight, on Christmas Eve. That, too, was tradition. She would refuse. He would cajole. She would pretend reluctance. He would persuade. And this year, she thought, at last, they would celebrate their Christmas in a real home. Not in an apartment in downtown Manhattan, but a house, a home, with a yard made for snowmen, a big kitchen designed for baking cookies. She'd so badly needed to be able to give him all this. She hoped it helped to make up for not being able to give him a father.

Turning from the window, she began to wander around the room. A small, delicate-looking woman in an oversize flannel shirt and baggy jeans, she always dressed comfortably in private to rest from being the scrupulously groomed, coolly professional public woman. Julia Summers prided herself on the image she presented to publishers, television audiences, the celebrities she interviewed. She was pleased by her skill in interviews, finding out what she needed to know about others while they learned very little about her.

Her press kit informed anyone who wanted to know that she had grown up in Philadelphia, an only child of two successful lawyers. It granted the information that she had attended Brown University, and that she was a single parent. It listed her professional accomplishments, her awards. But it didn't speak of the hell she had lived through in the three years before her parents had divorced, or the fact that she had brought her son into the world alone at age eighteen. There was no mention of the grief she had felt when she had lost her mother, then her father within two years of each other in her mid-twenties.

Though she had never made a secret of it, it was far from common knowledge that she had been adopted when she was six weeks old, and that nearly eighteen years to the day after had given birth to a baby boy whose father was listed on the birth certificate as unknown.

Julia didn't consider the omissions lies—though, of course, she had known the name of Brandon's father. The simple fact was, she was too smooth an interviewer to be trapped into revealing anything she didn't wish to reveal.

And, amused by being able so often to crack façades, she enjoyed being the public Ms. Summers who wore her dark blond hair in a sleek French twist, who chose trim, elegant suits in jewel tones, who could appear on *Donahue* or *Carson* or *Oprah* to tout a new book without showing a trace of the hot, sick nerves that lived inside the public package.

When she came home, she wanted only to be Julia. Brandon's mother. A woman who liked cooking her son's dinner, dusting furniture, planning a garden. Making a home was her most vital work and writing made it possible.

Now, as she waited for her son to come bursting in the door to tell her all about sledding with the neighbors, she thought of the offer her agent had just called her about. It had come out of the blue.

Eve Benedict.

Still pacing restlessly, Julia picked up and replaced knickknacks, plumped pillows on the sofa, rearranged magazines. The living room was a lived-in mess that was more her doing than Brandon's. As she fiddled with the position of a vase of dried flowers or the angle of a china dish, she stepped over kicked-off shoes, ignored a basket of laundry yet to be folded. And considered.

Eve Benedict. The name ran through her head like magic. This was not merely a celebrity, but a woman who had earned the right to be called star. Her talent and her temperament were as well known and as well respected as her face. A face, Julia thought, that had graced movie screens for almost fifty years, in over a hundred films. Two Oscars, a Tony, four husbands—those were only a few of the awards that lined her trophy case. She had known the Hollywood of Bogart and Gable; she had survived, even triumphed, in the days when the studio system gave way to the accountants.

After nearly fifty years in the spotlight, this would be Benedict's first authorized biography. Certainly it was the first time the star had contacted an author and offered her complete cooperation. With strings, Julia reminded herself, and sunk onto the couch. It was those strings that had forced her to tell her agent to stall.

She heard the kitchen door slam and smiled. No, there was really only one reason she hesitated to grab that golden ring. And he'd just come home.

"Mom!"

"Coming." She started down the hall, wondering if she should mention the offer right away, or wait until after the holidays. It never occurred to her to make the decision herself, then tell Brandon. She stepped into the kitchen, then stood grinning. A step over the doorsill was a mound of snow with dark, excited eyes. "Did you walk or roll home?"

"It was great." Brandon was struggling manfully with his plaid muffler that was knotted and wet around his neck. "We had the toboggan and Will's older brother gave it a really big push. Lisa Cohen screamed and screamed the whole way. When we fell off she cried. And her snot froze."

"Sounds lovely." Julia crouched to work out the mangled knot.

"I went—pow!—right into a snowbank." Icy snow flew as he slammed his gloved hands together. "It was great."

She couldn't insult him by asking if he was hurt. Obviously he was just dandy. But she didn't care for the picture of him flying off a toboggan and into a snowbank. Knowing she would have enjoyed the sensation herself kept her from making the maternal noises that tickled her throat. Julia managed to undo the knot, then went to put on a kettle for hot chocolate while Brandon struggled out of his parka.

When she looked back, he had hung up the dripping parka—he was much quicker about such things than she—and was reaching for a cookie from the wicker basket set out on the kitchen counter. His hair was wet, and was dark, deer-hide blond like hers. Again, like his mother, he was small in stature, something she knew bothered him a great deal. He had a lean little face that had shed its baby fat early. A stubborn chin—again his mother's son. But his eyes, unlike her cool gray, were a rich brandy brown. His only apparent legacy from his father.

"Two," she said automatically. "Dinner's in a couple of hours."

Brandon bit the head off a reindeer and wondered how soon he could talk her into letting him open a present. He could smell the spaghetti sauce that was bubbling on the stove. The rich, tangy scent pleased him, almost as much as it pleased him to lick the colored sugar from his lips. They *always* had spaghetti on Christmas Eve. Because it was his favorite.

This year they would have Christmas in their new house, but he knew exactly what would happen, and when. They would have dinner—in the dining room because tonight was special—then they would do the dishes. His mother would put music on, and they would play games in front of the fire. Later they would take turns filling the stockings.

He knew there wasn't a real Santa Claus, and it didn't bother him very much. It was fun to pretend to *be* Santa. By the time the stockings were filled, he would have talked his mother into letting him open a present. He knew just the one he wanted tonight. The one that was wrapped in silver and green paper, and rattled. He desperately hoped it was an Erector set.

He began to dream of the morning when he would wake his mother before the sun came out. How they would come downstairs, turn on the tree lights, put on the music, and open presents.

"It's an awful long time till morning," he began when she set the mug of chocolate on the counter. "Maybe we could open all our presents tonight. Lots of people do, then you don't have to get up so early."

"Oh, I don't mind getting up early." Julia leaned her elbows on the counter and smiled at him. It was a sharp, challenging smile. The game, they both knew, was on. "But if you'd rather, you can sleep late, and we'll open presents at noon."

"It's better when it's dark. It's getting dark now."

"So it is." Reaching over, she brushed the hair away from his eyes. "I love you, Brandon."

He shifted in his seat. It wasn't the way the game was played. "Okay."

She had to laugh. Skirting the counter, she took the stool beside his, wrapped her stocking feet around the rungs. "There's something I need to talk to you about. I got a call from Ann a little while ago."

Brandon knew Ann was his mother's agent, and that the talk would be about work. "Are you going on tour again?"

"No. Not right now. It's about a new book. There's a woman in California, a very big star, who wants me to write her authorized biography."

Brandon shrugged. His mother had already written two books about movie stars. Old people. Not neat ones like Arnold Schwarzenegger or Harrison Ford. "Okay."

"But it's a little complicated. The woman—Eve Benedict—is a big star. I have some of her movies on tape."

The name meant nothing. He slurped chocolate. It left a frothy brown line above his lip. A young man's first mustache. "Those dumb black and white ones?"

"Some of them are black and white, not all of them. The thing is, to write the book, we'd have to go to California."

He looked up then, his eyes wary. "We have to move away?"

"No." Eyes sober, she put her hands on his shoulders. She understood how much home meant to him. He'd been uprooted enough in his ten years, and she would never do it to him again. "No, we wouldn't move, but we'd have to go there and stay for a few months."

"Like a visit?"

"A long one. That's why we have to think about it. You'd have to go to school there for a while, and I know you're just getting used to being here. So it's something we both have to think about."

"Why can't she come here?"

Julia smiled. "Because she's the star and I'm not, kiddo. One of her stipulations is that I come to her and stay until the first draft is finished. I'm not sure how I feel about that." She looked away, out the kitchen window. The snow had stopped, and night was falling. "California's a long way from here."

"But we'd come back?"

How like him to cut to the bottom line. "Yeah, we'd come back. This is home now. For keeps."

"Could we go to Disneyland?"

Surprised and amused, she looked back at her son. "Sure."

"Can I meet Arnold Schwarzenegger?"

With a laugh, Julia lowered her brow to him. "I don't know. We could ask."

"Okay." Satisfied, Brandon finished off his hot chocolate.

Chapter Two

♦ ♦ ♦ ♦

$\mathcal{I}$T WAS OKAY, Julia told herself as the plane made its final approach into LAX. The house had been closed up, the arrangements had been made. Her agent and Eve Benedict's had phoned and faxed each other continually over the last three weeks. Right now Brandon was bouncing in his seat, impatient for the plane to land.

There was nothing to worry about. But, of course, she knew that she made a science out of worrying. She was biting her nails again, and she was annoyed to have ruined her manicure—especially since she hated the whole process of manicures, the soaking and filing, the agony of indecision over the right shade of polish. Lucious Lilac or Fuchsia Delight. As usual, she'd settled on two coats of clear. Boring but noncommittal.

She caught herself gnawing what was left of her thumbnail and linked her fingers tightly in her lap. Christ, now she was thinking of nail polish like wine. A flirty but substantial shade.

Were they ever going to land?

She pushed up the sleeves of her jacket, then pulled them down again while Brandon stared wide-eyed through the window. At least she'd managed not to pass on her terror of flying.

She let out a long, quiet breath, and her fingers relaxed fractionally as the plane touched down. You lived through another one, Jules, she told herself before she let her head fall back against the seat. Now all she had to do was survive the initial interview with Eve the Great, make a temporary home in the star's guest house, see that Brandon adjusted to his new school, and earn a living.

Not such a big deal, she thought, clipping open her compact to see if she had any color left in her cheeks. She touched up her lipstick, dusted her nose with powder. If there was one thing she was skilled at, it was disguising nerves. Eve Benedict would see nothing but confidence.

As the plane glided to a stop at the gate, Julia took a Tums out of her jacket pocket. "Here we go, kid," she said to Brandon with a wink. "Ready or not."

He hefted his gym bag, she her briefcase. Hands linked, they deplaned, and even before they stepped through the gate, a man in a dark uniform and cap approached. "Ms. Summers?"

Julia drew Brandon a fraction closer. "Yes?"

"I'm Lyle, Miss Benedict's driver. I'll take you directly to the estate. Your luggage will be delivered."

He was no more than thirty, Julia judged as she nodded. And built like a linebacker. There was enough swagger in his hips to make the discreet uniform a joke. He led them through the terminal while Brandon dragged his heels and tried to see everything at once.

The car was waiting at the curb. Car, Julia thought, was a poor term for the mile-long, gleaming white stretch limo.

"Wow," Brandon said under his breath. Mother and son rolled their eyes at each other and giggled as they settled in. The interior smelled of roses, leather, lingering perfume. "It has a TV and everything," Brandon whispered. "Wait till I tell the guys."

"Welcome to Hollywood," Julia said and, ignoring the chilling champagne, poured them both a celebratory Pepsi. She toasted Brandon gravely, then grinned. "Here's mud in your eye, sport."

He chattered all the way, about the palm trees, the skateboarders, the proposed trip to Disneyland. It helped soothe her. She let him switch on the television, but nixed the idea of using the phone. By the time they cruised into Beverly Hills, he'd decided that being a chauffeur was a pretty good job.

"Some people would say that having one's even better."

"Nah, 'cause then you never get to drive."

And it was as simple as that, she thought. Her work with celebrities had already shown her that fame exacted a heavy price. One of them, she decided while she slipped off a shoe and let her foot sink into the deep carpet, was having a chauffeur who was built like a bodyguard.

The next price became apparent as they drove along a high stone wall to an ornate, and very thick iron gate, where a guard, again in uniform, peered out of the window of a small stone hut. After a long buzz, the gate opened slowly, even majestically. And the locks clicked tight behind them. Locked in and locked out, Julia thought.

The grounds were exquisite, graced with lovely old trees and trimmed shrubs that would flower early in the mild climate. A peacock strutted on the lawn, and his hen sent up a scream like a woman. Julia chuckled when Brandon's mouth fell open.

There was a pond dotted with lily pads. Over it arched a fanciful walking bridge. They had left behind, only hours before, the snow and frigid winds of the Northeast and come to paradise. Eve's Eden. She had stepped out of a Currier and Ives print into a Dali painting.

Then the house rose into view, and she was as speechless as her son. Like the car, it was glistening white, three graceful stories in an "E" shape, with lovely shaded courtyards between the bars. The house was as feminine, timeless, elaborate as the woman who owned it. Curved windows and archways softened its lines without detracting from its aura of strength. Balconies, their iron work as delicate as white lace, draped the upper stories. In vivid contrast, trellised flowers in bold colors of scarlet, sapphire, purple, and saffron sliced arrogantly up the white, white walls.

When Lyle opened the door, Julia was struck by the silence. No sound from the world outside the high walls penetrated here. No car engines, belching buses, or squealing tires would have dared to intrude. There was only birdsong, and the seductive whisper of the breeze through fragrant leaves, the tinkle of water from a fountain in the courtyard. Above, the sky was a dreamy blue trimmed with a few powder-puff clouds.

Again she had the dislocated feeling of walking into a painting.

"Your luggage will be delivered to the guest house, Ms. Summers," Lyle told her. He had examined her in the rearview mirror during the long drive, speculating about the best ways to interest her in a quick tussle in his room over the garage. "Miss Benedict asked that I bring you here, first."

She didn't encourage or discourage the gleam in his eye. "Thank you." Julia looked at the curving apron of white marble steps, then tucked her son's hand in hers.

Inside, Eve stepped away from the window. She had wanted to see them first. Had needed to. Julia was more delicate-looking in person than she'd been led to expect from the photographs she'd seen. The young woman had excellent taste in clothes. The trim strawberry-colored suit and subtle jewelry she wore met with Eve's approval. As did the posture.

And the boy . . . the boy had had a sweet face and an air of suppressed energy. He would do, she told herself, and closed her eyes. They would both do very well.

Opening her eyes again, she moved to her nightstand. In the drawer were the pills only she and her doctor knew she needed. There was also a crudely printed note on cheap paper.

LET SLEEPING DOGS LIE.

As a threat, Eve found it laughable. And encouraging. She hadn't yet begun the book, and already people were sweating. The fact that it could have come from several sources only made the game more interesting. Her rules, she thought. The power was in her hands. It was long past time she used it.

She poured water from the Baccarat carafe—swallowed the medication, hated the weakness. After replacing the pills, she walked to a long silver-framed mirror. She had to stop wondering if she was making a mistake. She didn't care to second-guess herself once a decision had been made. Not now. Not ever.

With careful, brutally honest eyes, she checked her own reflection. The emerald-toned silk jumpsuit was flattering. She had done her own makeup and hair only an hour before. Gold glinted at her ears, her throat, her fingers. Assured she looked every bit the star, she started downstairs. She would, as always, make an entrance.

A cool-eyed, beefy-armed housekeeper who called herself Travers, had shown Julia and Brandon into the salon. Tea, they were told, would be forthcoming. They were to make themselves at home.

Julia wondered that anyone could consider such a room in such a house home. Color tumbled into color, streaking and spilling over white walls, white carpet, white upholstery. Pillows and paintings, flowers and porcelain were all dramatic accents against a pristine background. The high ceiling was ornate with plasterwork. The windows were scalloped with teal silk.

But it was the painting, the larger-than-life-size portrait over the white marble fireplace that was the focal point. Despite the drama of the room, the painting dominated . . . and demanded.

Still clutching Brandon's hand, Julia stared up at it. Eve Benedict, nearly forty years before, her beauty staggering, her power awesome. Crimson satin slid off her bare shoulders, draped over her lush body as she stood, laughing down at her audience, not so much with humor as with knowledge. Her hair flowed simply, dark as ebony. She wore no jewelry. Needed none.

"Who is that?" Brandon wanted to know. "Is she like a queen?"

"Yes." Julia bent down to kiss the top of his head. "That's Eve Benedict, and she's very much like a queen."

"Carlotta," Eve said in her rich, whiskey voice as she entered. "From *No Tomorrows.*"

Julia turned and faced the woman. "MGM, 1951," Julia acknowledged. "You played opposite Montgomery Clift. It was your first Oscar."

"Very good." Eve kept her eyes on Julia's as she crossed the room and extended her hand. "Welcome to California, Ms. Summers."

"Thank you." Julia found her hand held in a firm grip while Eve studied her. Knowing the first moments of this relationship would be crucial, she returned the look measure for measure. She saw that both the power and the beauty had aged, and had grown.

With her own thoughts well concealed, Eve looked down at Brandon. "And you are Mr. Summers."

He giggled at that and shot a glance at his mother. "I guess. It's okay to call me Brandon, though."

"Thank you." She had an urge to touch his hair, and repressed it. "You may call me . . . Miss B. for lack of something better. Ah, Travers, always prompt." She nodded as the housekeeper wheeled in the tea tray. "Please sit down, I won't keep you long. I'm sure you'd like to settle in." She took a high-backed white chair and waited until Julia and the boy sat on the couch. "We'll dine at seven, but since I know the food on the plane was ghastly, I thought you'd like a little something."

Brandon, who had been unenthusiastic about tea, noted that the little something included frosted cakes, tiny sandwiches, and a tall pitcher of lemonade. He grinned.

"It's very kind of you," Julia began.

"We'll be spending quite a bit of time together, so you'll find out that I'm rarely kind. Isn't that so, Travers?"

Travers merely grunted and set delicate china plates on the coffee table before she stalked out again.

"I will, however, try to keep you comfortable, because it suits me to have you do a good job."

"I'll do a good job, comfortable or not. One," she said to Brandon as he reached for a second cake. "But your hospitality is appreciated, Miss Benedict."

"Can I have two if I eat two sandwiches?"

Julia glanced down at Brandon. Eve noted that her smile came easily and her eyes softened. "Eat the sandwiches first." When she shifted her attention to Eve, her smile was formal again. "I hope you don't feel obligated to entertain us while we're here. We realize how demanding your schedule must be. As soon as it's convenient, you and I can work out the times best suited to you for interviews."

"Eager to get to work?"

"Of course."

So, she'd been right in her judgment, Eve thought. This was a woman who had been trained—or had trained herself—to push straight ahead. Eve sipped the tea and considered. "All right then, my assistant will give you a schedule. Week to week."

"I'll need Monday morning to take Brandon into school. I'd also like to rent a car."

"There's no need for that." She gave a dismissive wave. "There's a half a dozen in the garage. One will suit. Lyle, my driver, will take the boy to school and back."

"In the big white car?" Brandon asked with his mouth full, his eyes wide.

Eve laughed before sipping her tea. "I think not. But we'll see that you have a ride in it now and again." She noted he was eyeing the tray again. "I once lived with a young boy just about your age. He had a fondness for petits fours."

"Are there any kids here now?"

"No." The shadow came and went in her eyes. She rose then, a swift and casual dismissal. "I'm sure you'd both like to rest before dinner. If you go through the terrace doors and follow the path to the pool, the guest house is just to the right. Shall I have one of the servants show you?"

"No, we'll find it." Julia stood, placing a hand on Brandon's shoulder. "Thank you."

At the doorway Eve paused and turned. "Brandon, if I were you, I'd wrap a few of those cakes in a napkin and take them with me. Your stomach's still on East Coast time."

◆ ◆ ◆

SHE WAS RIGHT. Brandon's first coast-to-coast flight had his system jumbled. By five he was hungry enough that Julia fixed him a light supper from the small but well-stocked kitchen in the guest house. By six, cranky with fatigue and excitement, he nodded off in front of the television. Julia carried him into his bedroom, where one of Eve's efficient servants had already unpacked his things.

It was a strange bed, in a strange room, despite the addition of his Erector set, his books, and the favorite toys that had traveled with them. Still, as always, he slept like a rock, not stirring when she stripped off his shoes and slacks. Once he was tucked in, Julia called the main house to give Travers her apologies and regrets for dinner that evening.

She was weary enough herself to consider slipping into the tempting whirlpool tub or directly into the king-size bed in the master suite. But her mind refused to shut off. The guest house was both luxurious and tasteful, a two-story structure with warm wood trim and cool pastel walls. The curving stairs and open balcony gave it a spacious, informal feel. She much preferred the gleaming oak floors and colorful throw rugs to the acres of white carpet in the main house.

Julia wondered who might have stayed in the guest house, enjoying its own tidy English garden and the warm, scented breezes. Olivier had been a friend of Eve's. Had the great actor brewed tea in the charming country-style kitchen with its bright copper pots and little brick hearth? Had Katharine Hepburn fussed in the garden? Had Peck or Fonda napped on the long, cushy sofa?

Since childhood Julia had been fascinated with the people who made their living on screen or stage. Briefly in her teens she had dreamed of joining them. A crushing shyness had caused her to sweat her way through auditions in high school plays. Desperate desire and determination had won her roles, fed the dream . . . and then there had been Brandon. A mother at eighteen, Julia had changed her course. And she'd survived betrayal, fear, and despair. There were some, she felt, who were meant to grow up early and fast.

Different dreams, she mused as she slipped into a frayed terry-cloth robe. She wrote about actors now, but would never be one. Knowing her child slept safe and content in the next room left no room for regrets. And knowing her own strength and competence would help her give her son a long and happy childhood.

She was reaching up to take the pins from her hair when she heard a knock at the door. Julia glanced down at her faded robe, then shrugged. If this was home for the time being, she had to be able to relax in it.

Julia opened the door to a pretty young blond with lake-blue eyes and a bright smile. "Hi, I'm CeeCee. I work for Miss Benedict. I'm here to look after your son while you have dinner."

Julia lifted a brow. "That's very kind of you, but I phoned my regrets to the main house earlier."

"Miss Benedict said that the little boy—Brandon, right?—was tired out. I'll baby-sit while you have dinner at the main house."

Julia opened her mouth to decline, but CeeCee was already breezing through the door. She was in jeans and a T-shirt, her California-blond hair sweeping her shoulders, her arms full of magazines.

"Isn't this a great place?" she went on in her bubbly champagne voice. "I love cleaning it, and I'll be doing it for you while you're here. You just let me know if you want anything special."

"Everything's perfect." Julia had to smile. The woman vibrated with energy and enthusiasm. "But I really don't think I should leave Brandon on his first night with someone he doesn't know."

"You don't have to worry. I have two little brothers, and I've been baby-sitting since I was twelve. Dustin, the youngest, was a late baby. He's just ten—and a real mega monster." She gave Julia another flashing smile—her even white teeth those of a toothpaste commercial. "He'll be okay with me, Ms. Summers. If he wakes up and wants you, we'll call the house. You're only two minutes away."

Julia hesitated. She knew Brandon would sleep through the night. And the perky blond was exactly the kind of sitter she herself would have chosen. She was being overcautious and overprotective—two things she struggled not to be.

"All right, CeeCee. I'll change and be down in a couple of minutes."

When Julia returned five minutes later, CeeCee was sitting on the couch leafing through a fashion magazine. The television was tuned to one of the bright Saturday-night sitcoms. She glanced up and studied Julia.

"That's a great color on you, Ms. Summers. I want to be a designer, so I pay attention to, you know, tones and lines and material. Not everybody can wear a strong color like that tomato red."

Julia smoothed the jacket she'd paired with black evening pants. She'd chosen it because it gave her confidence. "Thanks. Miss Benedict said informal."

"It's perfect. Armani?"

"You've got a good eye."

CeeCee flipped back her long, straight hair. "Maybe one day you'll wear a McKenna. That's my last name. Except maybe I'll just go by my first. You know, like Cher and Madonna."

Julia found herself smiling, until she glanced back upstairs. "If Brandon wakes up—"

"We'll get along fine," CeeCee assured her. "And if he's nervous, I'll call right away."

Julia nodded, even as she turned the black evening bag over and over in her hands. "I won't be late."

"Enjoy yourself. Miss Benedict gives great dinner parties."

Julia lectured herself during the short walk from house to house. Brandon wasn't a shy or a clinging child. If he did wake up, he would not only accept the baby-sitter, he'd enjoy her. And, she reminded herself, she had a job to do. Part of that job—the hardest part for her—was to socialize. The sooner she began, the better.

The light was softening, and she could smell roses, jasmine, and the damp green smell of leaves freshly watered. The pool was a curving half moon of pale blue fed by an arching fountain at one corner. She hoped pool privileges went along with the guest house, or Brandon would be hell to live with.

She hesitated on the terrace, then decided it would be more correct to go around to the front. She passed yet another gurgling fountain, a hedge of gloriously perfumed Russian olives, then spotted two cars in the drive. One was a late model Porsche in flaming red, the other an old, beautifully reconditioned Studebaker in classic cream. Both meant money.

The antacid pill had dissolved on her tongue by the time she rang the bell at the front door. Travers answered, gave a frigid nod, then led Julia to the salon.

The cocktail hour was in progress. Debussy was playing softly, and the evening garden scent had been captured indoors by a huge bouquet of scarlet roses. The lighting was subtle, flattering. The stage set.

From the doorway Julia quickly surveyed the people in the room. There was a busty redhead in a tiny, glittery black dress who looked miserably bored. Beside her was a tanned Adonis with sunstreaked blond hair—the Porsche.

He was wearing a very correct, very expensive pearl-gray suit and lounged against the mantel as he sipped his drink and murmured to the redhead. A sleek woman in an ice-blue sheath with cropped fawn-colored hair served Eve a flute of champagne. The mistress of the house was stunning in royal blue lounging pajamas piped in chartreuse. And she was smiling at the man beside her.

Julia recognized Paul Winthrop instantly. First, because of his resemblance to his father. And second, from the picture on the dust covers of his books. Like his father, he would always draw eyes and provoke fantasies. His looks weren't as polished as those of the other man in the room, but they were far more dangerous.

He seemed tougher-looking in person, she noted. Less scholarly and more approachable. He, at least, had taken the informal rule to heart and wore slacks and scuffed Nikes with his jacket. He was grinning as he lighted Eve's cigarette. Then he turned, looked at Julia, and the grin vanished.

"It seems your last guest has arrived."

"Ah, Ms. Summers." Eve glided across the room, silks whispering. "I take it CeeCee has everything under control."

"Yes, she's delightful."

"She's exhausting, but that's youth. What will you have to drink?"

"Just some mineral water." A sip of anything stronger, and she knew jet lag would settle her into a coma.

"Nina, dear," Eve called, "we have a teetotaler who needs a Perrier. Julia, let me introduce you around. My nephew, Drake Morrison."

"I've been eager to meet you." He took Julia's hand and smiled. His palm was smooth and warm, his eyes a compelling if slightly tamer version of Eve's bright green eyes. "You're the one who'll dig all Eve's secrets out. Even her family hasn't succeeded in doing that."

"Because it's none of my family's business until I say so." Eve expelled a slow stream of smoke. "And this is—what was your name again, dear? Carla?"

"Darla." The redhead corrected Eve with a pouty lisp. "Darla Rose."

"Charming." Eve's voice held an edgy amusement that put Julia on alert. A few degrees sharper, and it could have rent flesh. "Our Darla is an actress-model. Such a fascinating phrase. More catchy than that lowering term, *starlet*, we used to use. And this is Nina Soloman, my right and left arms."

"Pack mule and whipping boy," the sleek blond said as she handed Julia a glass. There was good humor in the voice and quiet confidence in the bearing. On closer view, Julia noted that the woman was older than she'd first thought. Nearer fifty than forty but with a sleekness that age rolled off. "I'll warn you, you'll need more than mineral water if you work with Miss B. long."

"If Ms. Summers has done her homework, she already knows I'm a professional bitch. And this is my own true love, Paul Winthrop." Eve all but purred as she traced fingers down his arm. "A pity I married the father instead of waiting for the son."

"Anytime you want to take a shot, gorgeous." His voice was warm for Eve. His eyes were cool for Julia. He didn't offer his hand. "Have you done your homework, Ms. Summers?"

"Yes. But I always take the time to form my own opinions."

He lifted his drink and watched as Julia was immediately drawn into small talk. She was smaller than he'd pictured her, more finely built. Despite Darla's flash and Nina's elegance, she was the only woman in the room who could compete with Eve's beauty. Still, he preferred the red-head's blatant show of wares and wants to Julia's cold composure. A man wouldn't have to dig deeply to learn all there was to know about Darla Rose. The aloof Ms. Summers was another matter. But for Eve's sake, Paul intended to find out all there was to learn about Julia.

Julia couldn't relax. Even when they went into dinner and she accepted a single glass of wine, she couldn't force the muscles of her neck and stomach to loosen. She told herself it was her own nerves that had her imagining hostility. There was no reason for anyone in the little group to resent her. Indeed, Drake was going out of his way to be charming. Darla had stopped moping and was packing away stuffed trout and wild rice. Eve was cruising on champagne, and Nina was chuckling over some comment Paul had made about a mutual acquaintance.

"Curt Dryfuss?" Eve put in, catching the end of the conversation. "He'd be a better director if he'd learn to keep his fly zipped. If he hadn't had the leading lady bouncing on him so often during his last project, he might have gotten a decent performance out of her. Onscreen."

"He could have been a eunuch and not gotten a decent performance out of her," Paul corrected Eve. "Onscreen."

"It's all tits and ass these days." Eve skimmed a glance over Darla. Julia took time to hope that she was never on the wrong end of that coldly amused stare. "Tell me, Ms. Summers, what do you think of our current crop of actresses?"

"I'd say it's the same in this as in any generation. The cream rises to the top. You did."

"If I'd waited to rise, I'd still be making B movies with second-rate directors." She gestured with her glass. "I clawed and chewed my way to the top, and I've spent most of my life in a bloody battle to stay there."

"Then I suppose the question would be, is it worth it?"

Eve's eyes narrowed and glittered. Her lips curved. "You're goddamn right it is."

Julia leaned closer. "If you had it to do over again, would you change anything?"

"No. Nothing." She took a quick and deep drink. A headache was beginning to play behind her eyes, and the dull pain infuriated her. "To change one thing is to change everything."

Paul put a hand on Eve's arm, but his eyes were on Julia. Because he didn't bother to disguise it, Julia now could see the source of the hostility she'd been feeling. "Why don't we let the interview wait until working hours?"

"Don't be so snotty, Paul," Eve said mildly. With a laugh, she patted his hand. She turned to Julia. "He disapproves. I'm sure he thinks I'll spill his secrets along with mine."

"You don't know mine."

This time her laugh took on an edge. "My dear boy, there is no secret, no lie, no scandal I don't know. At one time it was thought that Parsons and Hopper were the ones to worry about. But they didn't know how to hold on to a secret until it had ripened." She drank again, as if toasting some private triumph. "How many calls have you fielded in the last two weeks, Nina, from worried luminaries?"

Nina let out a sigh. "Dozens."

"Exactly." Pleased, Eve sat back. In the candlelight, her eyes glittered like the jewels at her ears and around her throat. "It's tremendously satisfying to be the one throwing the shit at the fan. And you, Drake, as my press agent, what do you think about my project?"

"That you're going to make a lot of enemies. And a lot of money."

"I've spent fifty years doing both of those things already. How about you, Ms. Summers, what do you hope to get out of this?"

Julia set her glass aside. "A good book." She caught Paul's look of derision and stiffened. She would have preferred to empty her water goblet into his lap, but relied on dignity. "Of course, I've gotten used to people considering celebrity biographies a long step below literature." Her gaze shifted to meet his. "Just as many people consider popular fiction a bastard form of writing."

Eve threw back her head and laughed; Paul picked up his fork to toy with the remnants of his trout. His clear blue eyes had darkened, but his voice was mild as he asked, "What do you consider your work, Ms. Summers?"

"Entertainment," she said without hesitation. "What do you consider yours?"

He ignored the question and leapt on her answer. "So you believe it's entertaining to exploit the name and the life of a public figure?"

She no longer felt like biting her nails, but pushing up her sleeves. "I doubt Sandburg thought so when he wrote of Lincoln. And I certainly don't believe an *authorized* biography is exploitative of its subject!"

"You're not comparing your work to Sandburg's?"

"Yours has been compared to Steinbeck's." She moved her shoulders carelessly, though her temper was heating fast. "You tell a story based on imagination—or lies. I tell one based on facts and memories. The result of both techniques is that the finished work is read and enjoyed."

"I've certainly read and enjoyed works by both of you," Nina said, stepping in as peacemaker. "I've always been in awe of writers. All I do is compose business correspondence. Of course, Drake has those punchy press releases."

"Which are a mix of truth and lies," he said. He turned to Julia with a smile. "I suppose you'll be interviewing people other than Eve, for a rounded picture."

"That's the usual procedure."

"I'm available. Anytime."

"It looks like Darla's ready for dessert," Eve said dryly and rang for the last course. "The cook made raspberry trifle. You'll take some back to Brandon."

"Oh, yes, your little boy." Satisfied the conversation had cooled, Nina poured more wine. "We were hoping to meet him tonight."

"He was exhausted." Julia snuck a peek at her watch. It succeeded only in reminding her that her body insisted it was past midnight. "I imagine he'll be wide awake by four A.M. and wondering why the sun hasn't come up."

"He's ten?" Nina asked. "You look much too young to have a ten-year-old."

Julia's polite smile was her only comment. She turned to Eve as the last dessert dish was served. "I wanted to ask you what portions of the estate are off limits."

"The boy can have the run of the place. He swims?"

"Yes. Very well."

"Then we won't worry about the pool. Nina will let you know whenever I plan to entertain."

Knowing her duty, Julia forced herself to stay alert until after the meal was finished. Even the single glass of dinner wine had been a mistake, she realized. Desperate for bed, she excused herself, thanking her hostess. It didn't please her at all that Paul insisted on walking her back.

"I know the way."

"There's not much of a moon tonight." He took her elbow and steered her onto the terrace. "It's easy to get turned around in the dark. Or you might fall asleep on your feet and tumble into the pool."

Julia shifted away from him automatically. "I swim very well myself."

"That may be, but chlorine's hell on silk." He pulled a slim cigar from his pocket, and, cupping his hands around a lighter, touched the flame to the end. He'd noticed several things about her that evening, one of which was that she hadn't wanted her child to become dinner conversation. "You could have told Eve you were as exhausted as your son."

"I'm fine." She tilted her head to study his profile as they walked. "You don't care for my profession, do you, Mr. Winthrop?"

"No. But then, this biography is Eve's business, not mine."

"Whether you care for it or not, I'm expecting an interview."

"And do you get what you expect, always?"

"No, but I get what I'm after. Always." She stopped at the door to the guest house. "Thank you for seeing me back."

Very cool, he thought. Very controlled, very slick. He might have accepted her at face value if he hadn't noticed her right thumbnail was chewed down to the quick. In a deliberate test he moved a little closer. While she didn't jerk away, she did shoot up an invisible wall. It would be interesting, he decided, to see if she did the same with all men, or just with him. At the moment, he had only one priority.

"Eve Benedict is the most important person in my life." His voice was low, dangerous. "Be careful, Ms. Summers. Be very careful. You wouldn't want to have me as an enemy."

Her palms had gone damp, and that infuriated her. She coated her temper with ice. "It appears I already have. And what I will be, Mr. Winthrop, is thorough. Very thorough. Good night."

Chapter Three

◆◆◆◆

$\mathcal{B}$Y TEN O'CLOCK on Monday, Julia was ready. She'd spent the weekend with her son, taking advantage of the mild weather by delivering on her promised trip to Disneyland and throwing in the bonus of the Universal tour. He'd acclimated quickly—more quickly than she—to the time change.

She knew they'd both suffered from nerves when they'd walked into his new school that morning. They'd had their interview with the principal before Brandon, looking very small and brave, had gone off to his first class. Julia had filled out dozens of forms, shaken the principal's hand, and had remained composed during the drive home.

Then she'd indulged herself in a long crying jag.

Now, with her face carefully rinsed and made up, her tape recorder and notebook in her briefcase, she rang the bell on the front door of the main house. Moments later, Travers opened the door and sniffed as if in disapproval. "Miss Benedict is up in her office. She's expecting you." So saying, she turned and led the way upstairs.

The office was in the center leg of the "E," with a wide half-moon window making up the front wall. The other three were lined with shelves that held the awards of Eve's long career. The statuettes and plaques were interspersed with photographs and playbills and memorabilia from her movies.

Julia recognized the white lace fan that had been a prop in an antebellum film, the sexy red high-heeled shoes Eve had worn when she'd played an equally scarlet saloon singer, the rag doll she had clung to when she'd starred as a mother searching for a lost child.

She also noted that the office wasn't as tidy as the rest of the house. It was as richly furnished with a combination of antiques and vivid colors. The wallpaper was silk, the carpet deep and soft. But beside the huge rosewood desk where Eve sat were piles of scripts. A coffee machine, its pot already half empty, stood on a Queen Anne table. Stacks of *Variety* littered the floor, and the ashtray beside the phone Eve was barking into overflowed.

"They can take their certificate of honor and shove it." She gestured Julia inside with a smoldering cigarette, then took a deep drag. "I don't give a fuck if it is good press, Drake, I'm not flying out to Timbuktu to sit through a chicken dinner with a bunch of bloody Republicans. It may be the nation's capital, but it's Timbuktu to me. I didn't vote for the sucker, I'm not going to have dinner with him." She gave a snort and tapped the cigarette partially out on the corpses of others. "You handle it. That's what you're paid to do." Hanging up, she waved Julia toward a seat. "Politics. It's for idiots and bad actors."

Julia placed her briefcase beside her chair. "Shall I quote you?"

Eve merely smiled. "I take it you're ready to get to work. I thought we should have our first session in a businesslike atmosphere."

"Wherever you're comfortable." Julia glanced at the mound of scripts. "Rejections?"

"Half of them want me to play somebody's grandmother, the other half want me to take my clothes off." She hefted a foot clad in a red sneaker and gave the pile a shove. It toppled over, an avalanche of dreams. "A good writer's worth a king's ransom."

"And a good actor?"

Eve laughed. "Knows how to turn straw into gold—like any magician." She lifted a brow when Julia took her tape recorder and set it on the coffee table. "What's on and off the record is up to me."

"Naturally." She'd simply make sure to get everything she wanted on the record. "I don't break trusts, Miss Benedict."

"Everyone does, eventually." She waved a long, narrow hand studded with a single, glowing ruby. "Before I begin breaking mine, I want to know more about you—and not just the crap in your press kit. Your parents?"

More impatient than annoyed, Julia folded her hands in her lap. "They're both dead."

"Siblings?"

"I was an only child."

"You never married."

"No."

"Why?"

Though there was a little twist of pain, Julia's voice remained level and calm. "I never chose to."

"As I've been in and out of the institution four times, I can't recommend it, but it seems to me that raising a child alone would be difficult."

"It has its problems, and its rewards."

"Such as?"

The question threw her so that she had to school herself not to squirm. "Such as having only your own feelings to rely on when making decisions."

"And is that problem or reward?"

A faint smile curved Julia's lips. "Both." She took her pad and a pencil out of her briefcase. "Since you can give me only two hours today, I'd like to get started. Naturally I know the background information that's been made public. You were born in Omaha, the second of three children. Your father was a salesman."

All right, Eve decided, they would begin. What she had to learn she would learn as they went along. "A traveling salesman," Eve put in as Julia pressed the record button. "I've always suspected I had several half siblings scattered through the central plains. In fact, I've been approached many times by people claiming relationships, and hoping for handouts."

"How do you feel about that?"

"It was my father's problem, not mine. An accident of birth doesn't equal a free ride." Steepling her fingers, she sat back. "I made my success. On my own. If I were still Betty Berenski from Omaha, do you think any of those people would have bothered with me? But Eve Benedict's a different matter. I left Betty and the cornfields behind when I was eighteen. I don't believe in looking back."

That was a philosophy Julia both understood and respected. She began to feel thrumming excitement—the birth of the intimacy that made her work of this kind so successful.

"Tell me about your family. What it was like for Betty growing up?"

With her head back, she laughed. "Oh, my older sister will be appalled to see in print that I called our father a philanderer. But truth is truth. He hit the road to sell his pots and pans—always sold enough to keep the wolf from the door. He would come back with little trinkets for his girls. Chocolates or handkerchiefs or ribbons. There were always presents from Daddy. He was a big, handsome man with black hair and a mustache and red cheeks. We doted on him. We also did without him five days out of seven."

She plucked up a cigarette and lighted it. "We would do his laundry on Saturdays. His shirts reeked of perfume. On Saturdays my mother always lost her sense of smell. Never once did I hear her question or accuse or complain. She was not a coward, she was . . . quiescent, accepting her lot in life, and her husband's infidelity. I think she knew that she was the only woman he loved. When she died, quite suddenly—I was sixteen—my father was a lost soul. He grieved for her until he died five years later." She paused, leaning forward again. "What do you write there?"

"Observations," Julia told her. "Opinions."

"And what do you observe?"

"That you loved your father, and were disappointed in him."

"What if I told you that's bullshit?"

Julia tapped her pencil against the pad. Yes, there had to be understanding, she thought. And a balance of power. "Then we'd both be wasting our time."

After a moment's silence Eve reached for the phone. "I want fresh coffee."

By the time Eve had instructed the kitchen, Julia had made the decision to steer away from more discussion of family. When she understood Eve better, she would come back to it.

"You were eighteen when you first came to Hollywood," she began. "Alone. Fresh off the farm, so to speak. I'm interested in your feelings, your impressions. What was it like for that young girl from Omaha stepping off the bus in Los Angeles?"

"Exciting."

"You weren't afraid?"

"I was too young to be afraid. Too cocky to believe I could fail." Eve stood and began to stalk the room. "We were at war, and our boys were being shipped off to Europe to fight and die. I had a cousin, a funny kid who joined the navy and went to the South Pacific. He came back in a box. His funeral was in June. In July I packed my bags. I'd suddenly learned that life could be very short, and very cruel. I wasn't going to waste another second of it."

Travers brought in the coffee. "Set it down there," Eve ordered with a gesture toward the low table in front of Julia. "Let the girl pour."

Eve took her coffee black, then leaned against the corner of her desk. Julia scribbled her observations: Eve's strength—revealed in her face, her voice, the lines of her body.

"I was naive," Eve said huskily, "but not stupid. I knew I had taken a step that would change my life. And I understood there would be sacrifices and hardships. Loneliness. You understand?"

Julia remembered lying in a hospital bed at eighteen, a small, helpless baby in her arms. "Yes, I do."

"I had thirty-five dollars when I stepped off the bus, but I didn't intend to go hungry. I had a portfolio stuffed with pictures and clippings."

"You'd done some modeling."

"Yes, and a little theater. Back in those days the studio sent out scouts, more to get publicity than actually do talent searches. But I realized it would be a cold day in hell when a scout got around to discovering me in Omaha. So I decided to go to Hollywood. And that was that. I took a job at a diner, got myself a few spots as an extra at Warner Bros. The trick was to be seen—on the lot, on a set, at the commissary. I volunteered at the Hollywood Canteen. Not selflessly, not because of the GIs, but because I knew I would be rubbing elbows with stars. Causes or good deeds were the last things on my mind. I was concerned with myself, completely. You find that cold, Ms. Summers?"

Julia couldn't think why her opinion would matter, but she considered before she answered. "Yes. I also imagine it was practical."

"Yes." Eve's mouth firmed. "Ambition requires practicality. And it was a heady experience, watching Bette Davis pour coffee, Rita Hayworth serve sandwiches. And I was a part of it. It was there I met Charlie Gray."

♦ ♦ ♦ ♦

THE DANCE FLOOR was packed with GIs and pretty girls. The scents of perfume, aftershave, smoke, and black coffee crowded the air. Harry James was playing, and the music was hot. Eve liked hearing the trumpet soar over the noise and laughter. After a full shift at the diner, and the hours spent dogging agents, her feet were killing her. It didn't help that the shoes she'd bought secondhand were a half size too small.

She made certain the fatigue didn't show in her face. You could never be sure who might drop in, and notice. She was damn certain she'd have to be noticed only once to start the climb.

Smoke hung at the ceiling, curling around the wagon-wheel lights. The music turned sentimental. Uniforms and party dresses drifted together, swayed.

Wondering how soon she could take a break, Eve poured another cup of coffee for another star-struck GI and smiled.

"You've been here every night this week."

Eve glanced over and studied the tall, lanky man. Rather than a uniform, he was wearing a gray flannel suit that didn't disguise his thin shoulders. He had fair hair slicked back from a bony face. Big brown eyes drooped like a basset hound's.

She recognized him, and pumped her smile up a few degrees. He wasn't a big name. Charlie Gray unfailingly played the buddy of the hero. But he was a name. And he had noticed.

"We all do our part in the war effort, Mr. Gray." She lifted a hand to brush a long wave of hair from her eyes. "Coffee?"

"Sure." He leaned against the snack bar while she poured. Watching her work, he pulled out a pack of Luckies and lighted one. "I just finished my shift bussing tables, so I thought I'd come by and talk to the prettiest girl in the room."

She didn't blush. She could have if she'd chosen to, but she opted for the more sophisticated route. "Miss Hayworth's in the kitchen."

"I like brunettes."

"Your first wife was a blond."

He grinned. "So was the second one. That's why I like brunettes. What's your name, honey?"

She'd already chosen it, carefully, deliberately. "Eve," she said. "Eve Benedict."

He figured he had her pegged. Young, stars in her eyes, waiting for that chance to be discovered. "And you want to be in pictures?"

"No." With her eyes on his she took the cigarette from his fingers, drew in, and expelled smoke, then handed it back. "I'm *going* to be in pictures."

The way she said it, the way she looked when she said it, had him revising his first impression. Intrigued, he lifted the cigarette to his lips and caught the faintest taste of her. "How long have you been in town?"

"Five months, two weeks, and three days. How about you?"

"Too damn long." Attracted, as he always was, by a fast-talking, dangerous-looking woman, he glanced over her. She wore a very quiet blue suit made explosive by the body it covered so discreetly. His blood swam a little faster. When his gaze came back to hers and he saw the cool amusement in her expression, he knew he wanted her. "How about a dance?"

"I'll be pouring coffee for another hour."

"I'll wait."

As he walked away, Eve worried that she had overplayed it. Under-played it. She ran every word, every gesture, back through her mind, trying out dozens of others. All the while she poured coffee, flirted with young, soap-scrubbed GIs. Nerves jittered behind each smoldering smile. When her shift ended, she strolled with apparent nonchalance from behind the snack bar.

"That's some walk you've got." Charlie moved beside her, and Eve let out a quiet breath of relief.

"It gets me from one place to the next."

They stepped onto the dance floor, and his arms slipped around her. They stayed around her for nearly an hour.

"Where did you come from?" he murmured.

"Nowhere. I was born five months, two weeks, and three days ago."

He laughed, rubbing his cheek against her hair. "You're already too young for me. Don't make it worse." God, she was like holding sex—pure, vibrant sex. "It's too warm in here."

"I like the heat." She tossed back her head and smiled at him. It was a new look she was trying out, a half smile, lips just parted, eyes slanted lazily under partially lowered lids. From the way his fingers tightened on hers, she figured it worked. "But we could take a drive if you want to cool off."

He drove fast, and a little recklessly, and made her laugh. Occasionally he unscrewed the top on a silver flask of bourbon which he nipped from, and she refused. Bit by bit she let him pry information from her—pieces she wanted him to know. She hadn't yet been able to find an agent, but had talked herself onto a studio lot and was an extra in *The Hard Way* with Ida Lupino and Dennis Morgan. Most of the money she made as a waitress paid for acting classes. It was an investment: She wanted to be a professional, and she intended to be a star.

She asked about his work—not about the glossier stars he worked with, but the work itself. He'd had just enough to drink to feel both flattered and protective. By the time he dropped her off at her boarding-house, he was completely infatuated.

"Honey, you're a babe in the woods. There are plenty of wolves out there who'd love to take a bite."

Eyes sleepy, she laid her head back against the seat. "Nobody takes a bite of me . . . unless I want him to." When he leaned down to kiss her, she waited until his mouth brushed hers, then eased away and opened the car door. "Thanks for the ride." After passing a hand through her hair, she walked to the front door of the old gray building. Turning, she shot him a parting smile over her shoulder. "See you around, Charlie."

The flowers came the next day, a dozen red roses that had the other women in the boardinghouse tittering. As Eve placed them in a borrowed vase, she didn't think of them as flowers, but as her first triumph.

He took her to parties. Eve bartered food coupons, bought material, and sewed dresses. The clothes were another investment. She made certain the gowns were just the slightest bit too small for her. She didn't mind using her body to get what she wanted. After all, it was hers to use.

The huge houses, the armies of servants, the glamorous women in furs and silks, didn't awe her. She couldn't afford to be awed. Evenings at glamour spots didn't intimidate. She discovered that she could learn a lot in the powder room at Ciro's—what part was being cast, who was sleeping with whom, which actress was on suspension and why. She watched, she listened, she remembered.

The first time she saw her picture in the paper, snapped after she and Charlie had dined at Romanoff's, she spent an hour critiquing her hair, her facial expression, her posture.

She asked Charlie for nothing, and kept him at arm's length, though it was becoming difficult to do both. She knew if she even hinted that she wanted him to get her a screen test, he would. Just as she knew he wanted to take her to bed. She wanted the test, and she wanted him as a lover— but she realized the value of timing.

On Christmas Eve, Charlie threw a party of his own. At his request she came early to his big brick mansion in Beverly Hills. The red satin material had cost Eve a week's food allowance, but she thought the dress worth it. It skimmed down her body, cut low at the bust, snug at the hips. She had dared to alter the pattern by slicing a slit up the side—and dared even more by adding a rhinestone pin at the top of the slit, to draw the eye.

"You look delicious." Charlie ran his hands over her bare arms as they stood in the foyer. "Don't you have a wrap?"

Her finances hadn't allowed for one that would have suited the dress. "I'm hot-blooded," she said, and offered him a small package topped with a bright red bow. "Merry Christmas."

Inside was a slim, well-read book of Byron's poetry. For the first time since she'd met him, she felt foolish and unsure. "I wanted to give you something of mine," she explained. "Something that meant some-thing to me." Awkward, she fumbled in her bag for a cigarette. "I know it's not much, but—"

He put a hand on hers to still them. "It's a great deal." Unbearably moved, he released her hands to brush his fingers over her cheek. "It's the first time you've given me a real part of yourself." When he lowered his lips to hers, she felt the warmth and the need. This time she didn't resist when he deepened the kiss, lingered over her mouth. She let herself go with the moment, wrapping her arms around him, experimenting with her tongue. Before, only boys had kissed her. This was a man, experienced and hungry, one who knew what to do with his desires. She felt his fingers slide over the satin, heating the skin beneath.

Oh, yes, she thought, she wanted him too. Timing or not, their desire wouldn't wait much longer. Cautious, she pulled back. "Holidays make me sentimental," she managed to say. Smiling, she rubbed her lipstick from his mouth. He grabbed her wrist, pressed a kiss to her palm.

"Come upstairs with me."

Her heart fluttered, surprising her. He'd never asked before. "Not that sentimental." She struggled to find her balance again. "Your guests will be arriving any minute."

"Fuck the guests."

She laughed, and tucked a hand through his arm. "Come on, Char-lie, you know you want to fuck me. But right now you're going to pour me a glass of champagne."

"And later?"

"There's only now, Charlie. The great big now."

She strolled through a pair of double doors into a sprawling room that held a ten-foot tree glittering with lights and colored balls. It was a man's room, and she liked it for that alone. The furniture straight-lined and simple, the chairs deep and comfortable. A fire was roaring in the huge hearth at one end of the room, and a long mahogany bar was well stocked on the other. Eve slid onto one of the leather barstools and took out a cigarette.

"Bartender," she said, "the lady needs a drink." As Charlie opened and poured champagne, she studied him. He was wearing a tuxedo, and the formal wear suited him. He would never compete with the current leading men. Charlie Gray was no Gable or Grant, but he had solidity and sweetness, and an appreciation for his craft. "You're a nice man, Charlie." Eve lifted her glass. "Here's to you, my first real friend in the business."

"Here's to now," he said, and touched his glass to hers. "And what we make of it." He walked around the bar to take a present from under the tree. "It isn't as intimate as Byron, but when I saw it I thought of you."

Eve set her cigarette aside to open the box. The necklace of icy diamonds shot white fire against a bed of black velvet. In the center, like blood, dripped a huge, hot ruby. The diamonds were shaped like stars, the ruby like a tear.

"Oh. Oh, Charlie."

"You're not going to say I shouldn't have."

She shook her head. "I'd never come up with a shopworn line like that." But her eyes were wet, and there was a lump in her throat. "I was going to say that you have excellent taste. Damn, I can't come up with anything clever. It's stunning."

"So are you." He took the necklace out, let it run through his hands. "When you reach for the stars, Eve, you lose blood and tears. That's something you should remember." He slipped it around her neck and fastened it. "Some women are born to wear diamonds."

"I'm sure I was. Now I'm going to do something very typical." Laughing, she dug in her purse for her compact. After snapping it open, she studied the necklace in the small square mirror. "God. *Goddamn*, it's beautiful." She spun around on the stool to kiss him. "I feel like a queen."

"I want you to be happy." He cupped her face in his hands. "I love you, Eve." He saw the surprise come into her eyes, followed quickly by distress. Biting back an oath, he dropped his hands. "I have something else for you."

"More?" She tried to keep her voice light. She'd known he desired her, that he was fond of her. But love? She didn't want him to love when she couldn't return it. More, she didn't want to be tempted to try. Her hand wasn't completely steady when she picked up her champagne. "You're going to have a hard time topping this necklace."

"If I know you as well as I think I do, this will top it by a mile." From the breast pocket of his dinner jacket he took a piece of paper and set it on the bar beside her.

"January 12, ten A.M., Stage 15." Puzzled, she lifted a brow. "What is this? Clues for a treasure hunt?"

"Your screen test." He saw her cheeks pale and her eyes darken. Her lips trembled open, but she only shook her head. Understanding perfectly, he smiled, but the smile didn't reach his eyes. "Yeah, I thought that would mean more to you than diamonds." And he knew, already, that once he set her on her way, she would sprint beyond him.

Very carefully she folded the paper and tucked it in her bag. "Thank you, Charlie. I'll never forget it."

◆ ◆ ◆

"*I* WENT TO BED with him that night," Eve said quietly. Her voice had thickened, but there were no tears. She no longer shed tears, except on cue. "He was gentle, unbearably sweet, and quite shaken when he discovered he was my first. A woman never forgets the first time. And that memory is precious when the first time is kind. I kept the necklace on while we made love." She laughed and picked up her cold coffee. "Then we had more champagne and made love again. I like to think I gave him more than sex that night, and the other nights of those few weeks we were lovers. He was thirty-two. The studio press had shaved four years off that, but he told me. There were no lies in Charlie Gray."

With a sigh she set the coffee aside again and looked down at her hands. "He coached me for the screen test himself. He was a fine actor, continually underrated in his day. Within two months I had a part in his next movie."

When the silence dragged on, Julia set aside her notebook. She didn't need it. There was nothing about this morning she would forget. "*Desperate Lives,* with Michael Torrent and Gloria Mitchell. You played Cecily, the sultry villainess who seduced and betrayed Torrent's idealistic young attorney. One of the most erotic moments onscreen then, or now, was when you walked into his office, sat on his desk, and pulled off his tie."

"I had eighteen minutes onscreen, and made the best of them. They told me to sell sex, and I sold buckets of it." She shrugged. "The movie didn't set the world on fire. Now it plays on cable at three A.M. Still, I made enough of an impression in it that the studio shoved me right into another tramp part. I was Hollywood's newest sex symbol—making them a mint because I was on a contract player's salary. But I don't resent it, even today. I got quite a bit out of that first movie."

"Including a husband."

"Ah, yes, my first mistake." She gave a careless shrug and a thin smile. "Christ, Michael had a beautiful face. But the mind of a sheep. When we were in the sack, things were fine. Try to have a conversation? Shit." Her fingers began to drum on the rosewood. "Charlie had it all over him as an actor, but Michael had the face, the presence. It still annoys me to think I was stupid enough to believe the jerk had any connection with the men he played onscreen."

"And Charlie Gray?" Julia watched Eve's face carefully. "He committed suicide."

"His finances were a mess, and his career had stalled. Still, it was difficult for anyone to believe it was mere coincidence that he shot himself the day I married Michael Torrent." Her voice remained flat, her eyes calm as they met Julia's. "Am I sorry for it? Yes. Charlie was one in a million, and I loved him. Never the way he loved me, but I loved him. Do I blame myself? No. We made our choices, Charlie and I. Survivors live with their choices." She inclined her head. "Don't they, Julia?"

Chapter Four

♦ ♦ ♦ ♦

YES, THEY DID, Julia thought later. To survive, one lived with choices, but also paid for them. She wondered how Eve had paid.

From Julia's seat at an umbrellaed, glass table on the terrace of the guest house, it looked as though Eve Benedict had reaped only rewards. Working on her notes, she was surrounded by shade trees, the fragrance of jasmine. The air hummed—the distant echo of a lawn mower beyond the stand of palms, the drone of bees drunk on nectar, the whirr of a hummingbird's wings as it fed on a hibiscus nearby.

Here was luxury and privilege. But, Julia thought, the people who shared all this with Eve were paid to do so. Here was a woman who had reached pinnacle after pinnacle, only to be alone. A stiff payment for success.

Yet Julia didn't see Eve as a woman who suffered from regrets, but as one who layered successes over them. Julia had listed people she wanted to interview—ex-husbands, one-time lovers, former employees. Eve had merely shrugged her approval. Thoughtfully, Julia circled Charlie Gray's name twice. She wanted to talk to people who had known him, people who might talk about his relationship with Eve from another angle.

She sipped chilled juice, then began to write.

She is flawed, of course. Where there is generosity, there is also selfishness. Where there is kindness, there is also a careless disregard for feelings. She can be abrupt, cool, callus, rude—human. The flaws make the woman off the screen as fascinating and vital as any woman she has played on it. Her strength is awesome. It is in her eyes, her voice, in every gesture of her disciplined body. Life, it seems, is a challenge, a role she has agreed to play with great verve—and one in which she takes no direction. Any miscues or broken scenes are her responsibility. She blames no one. Beyond the talent, the beauty, that rich, smoky voice or sharp intelligence, she is to be admired for her unflagging sense of self.

"You're not one to waste time."

Julia started, then quickly shifted to look behind her. She hadn't heard Paul approach, had no idea how long he'd been standing reading over her shoulder. Deliberately, she turned her tablet over. The wire binding clicked smartly against the glass.

"Tell me, Mr. Winthrop, what would you do to someone who read your work uninvited?"

He smiled and made himself at home in the chair across from her. "I'd cut off all their nosy little fingers. But then, I'm known to have a nasty temper." He picked up her glass and sipped. "How about you?"

"People seem to think I'm mild-mannered. It's often a mistake." She didn't like him being there. He'd interrupted her work and invaded her privacy. She was dressed in shorts and a faded T-shirt, her feet were bare and her hair was pulled back in an untidy ponytail. The carefully crafted image was shot to hell, and she resented being caught as herself. She looked pointedly at the glass he lifted to his lips again. "Shall I get you one of your own?"

"No, this is fine." Her obvious discomfort amused him, and he liked the fact that she was so easily rattled. "You've had your first interview with Eve."

"Yesterday."

He pulled out a cigar, making it obvious that he intended to settle in. His hands, she noted, were wide at the palm, long of finger. More suited to lifting the silver spoon he'd been born with, she thought, than crafting complex, often grisly murders for the pages of books.

"I realize I'm not sitting in an office with my nose to a grindstone," Julia told him. "But I am working."

"Yes, I can see that." He smiled pleasantly. She'd have to do better than hint to shake him off. "Care to share your impressions of your initial interview?"

"No."

Undaunted, he lighted the cigar, then hooked an arm over the back of the wrought iron chair. "For someone who wants my cooperation, you're very unfriendly."

"For someone who disapproves of my work, you're very pushy."

"Not your work." With his legs stretched out, his feet comfortably crossed at the ankles, he took a slow drag, expelled it. The scent of smoke stung the air, intrusively masculine. It crept around the perfume of flowers like a man's arm around a reluctant woman. "I disapprove only of your current project. I have a vested interest."

It was his eyes, she realized, that gave him his greatest appeal—and, therefore, her greatest problem. Not the color of them, though some women were bound to sigh over that deep, vital blue. It was the look in them, the incredible focus of them that made Julia feel she was not being looked at, but into.

A hunter's look, she decided, and she wasn't about to be any man's prey.

"If you're concerned that I'll write something uncomplimentary about you, don't worry. Your part in Eve's biography probably won't take up more than part of one chapter."

Writer to writer, it would have been an excellent insult if his ego had been on the line. He laughed, liking her better for it. "Tell me something, Jules, is it just me, or all men?"

The use of her nickname threw her almost as much as the question. Like a kiss instead of a handshake. "I don't know what you mean."

"Sure you do." His smile was friendlier, but his eyes still challenged her. "I haven't managed to pull out all the sharp little darts from the first time I met you."

She fiddled with her pen and wished he would just go away. He was entirely too relaxed now, and that made her all the more tense. Men with his degree of self-confidence always left her groping for her own. "As I recall, it was you who launched the first attack."

"Maybe." He rocked back in his chair, watching her. No, he didn't have her measure yet, but he would.

She frowned as he rose to drop the cigar stub in a bucket of sand at the edge of the terrace. His was a dangerous body, she noted, all lean muscle and grace. A fencer's body. Since he was the kind who wouldn't be caged, a smart woman had to deal with him with her imagination behind locked doors. Julia considered herself a smart woman.

"We'll have to negotiate a truce of some kind. For Eve's sake."

"I don't see why. Since you'll be busy, and so will I, I doubt we'll run into each other often enough to need white flags."

"You're wrong." He came back to the table but didn't sit. Instead, he stood beside her, his thumbs hooked in his pockets. "I'll have to keep an eye on you, on Eve's behalf. And, I think, on my own behalf."

Her pen clattered on the glass top. She left it there and laced her nervous fingers together. "If that's some kind of oblique come-on—"

"I like you better this way," he interrupted. "Barefoot and flustered. The woman I met the other night was intriguing, and intimidating."

She was feeling little tugs and pulls she'd been certain she was im- mune to. It was possible, she reminded herself, to feel a sexual attraction for a man you didn't like. It was just as possible to resist it. "I'm the same, with or without shoes."

"Not at all." He sat down again, bracing his elbows on the table, resting his chin on his folded hands as he studied her. "Don't you think it would be deadly boring to wake up every morning of your life as exactly the same person?"

It was the kind of question she enjoyed, one she would have liked to respond to and explore. But with him she was certain any exploration would end on swampy ground. She turned her notepad over, flipping pages until she came to a blank one.

"Since you're here and in the mood to chat, maybe you'd give me that interview."

"No. We'll have to wait for that, see how things go." He knew he was being obstinate, and he enjoyed it.

"What things?"

He smiled. "All manner of things, Julia."

There was the sound of a slamming door and a youthful shout. "My son." Julia hurriedly gathered her notes and stood up. "If you'll excuse me, I have to—"

But Brandon was already racing through the back door onto the terrace. He wore an orange neon cap backward, baggy jeans, a Mickey Mouse T-shirt, and scuffed high-tops. His grin all but split his grubby face.

"I shot two baskets in gym," he announced.

"My hero."

She was reaching for him, and Paul watched her change yet again. There was no cool elegance, no frazzled vulnerability, but pure warmth. It was in her eyes, in her smile as she slid an arm around her son's shoulders. She drew him to her side. The subtle body language said quite clearly: He's mine.

"Brandon, this is Mr. Winthrop."

" 'Lo." Brandon grinned again, showing two gaps in his teeth.

"What position did you play?"

Brandon's eyes lit up at the question. "Point guard. I'm not very tall, but I'm fast."

"I've got a hoop at home. You'll have to come over and show me your moves sometime."

"Yeah?" Brandon all but danced in place while he looked up to his mother for approval. "Can I?"

"We'll see." She tugged on his cap. "Homework?"

"Just some vocabulary and some dumb long division." Both of which he felt duty bound to put off until the last possible minute. "Can I have a drink?"

"I'll get it."

"This is for you." Brandon dug an envelope out of his pocket, then turned back to Paul. "Do you ever get to go and watch the Lakers and stuff?"

"Now and again."

Julia left them to their talk of points scored and games lost. She filled a glass with ice the way Brandon liked it, then added juice. Though it annoyed her, she filled a second for Paul and added a plate of cookies. The rudeness she would have preferred to serve wouldn't set the right example for her son.

After setting the items on a tray, she glanced at the envelope she'd tossed on the counter. Her name was printed on it in big block letters. Frowning, she picked it up again. She'd assumed it was a report from Brandon's teacher. After tearing it open, she read the short message and felt the blood drain from her cheeks.

CURIOSITY KILLED THE CAT.

It was stupid. She read the words again, telling herself they were stupid, but the single sheet of paper shook in her hand. Who would send her such a message, and why? Was it some kind of warning, or threat? She stuffed the paper into her pocket. There was no reason such a silly, shopworn phrase should frighten her.

Giving herself a moment to settle, she lifted the tray and went back outside, where Paul was sitting again, regaling Brandon with some play by play of a Lakers game.

"We saw the Knicks once," Brandon told him. "Mom doesn't get it though. She's pretty good with baseball," he added by way of an apology.

Paul glanced up, and his smile faded the moment he saw Julia's face. "Problem?"

"No. Two cookies, sport," she said when Brandon lunged for the plate.

"Mr. Winthrop's been to lots of games," he told her as he stuffed the first cookie in his mouth. "He's met Larry Bird and everything."

"That's nice."

"She doesn't know who that is," Brandon said in a half whisper. He grinned, man to man, then washed down the cookie with juice. "She's more into girl stuff."

Out of the mouths of babes, Paul thought, he might get some answers. "Such as?"

"Well." Brandon chose another cookie as he thought it over. "You know, old movies where people look at each other all the time. And flowers. She's nuts for flowers."

Julia smiled weakly. "Should I leave you gentlemen to your port and cigars?"

"It's okay to like flowers if you're a girl," Brandon told her.

"My own little chauvinist." She waited until he'd gulped the last of his juice. "Homework."

"But couldn't I—"

"Nope."

"I hate stupid vocabulary."

"And I hate math." She flicked a finger down his nose. "Work on that first, then I'll help you with the vocab."

"Okay." He knew if he talked her into letting it wait until after dinner, he'd lose out on TV. A guy couldn't win. "See you," he said to Paul.

"Sure." Paul waited until the screen door slammed. "Nice kid."

"Yes, he is. I'm sorry, but I have to go in and supervise."

"It'll keep a minute." He rose. "What happened, Julia?"

"I don't know what you mean."

He put a hand under her chin to hold her still. His fingers were warm, firm, the tips roughened from work or some kind of male play. She had to fight back the urge to bolt. "With some people, everything they feel comes right out the eyes. Yours are scared. What is it?"

She didn't like it at all that she wanted to tell him, wanted to share. For more than a decade she had handled her own problems. "Long division," she said carelessly. "Scares the hell out of me."

It surprised him just how keen his disappointment was, but he let his hand drop away. "All right. I don't suppose you've got any reason to trust me at this point. Give me a call, we'll set up that interview."

"I will."

When he walked back toward the main house, she lowered herself into a chair. She didn't need help—his or anyone's—because nothing was wrong. With steady fingers she took the crumpled paper out of her pocket, smoothed it, and read it again.

On a long breath she stood and began to load the tray. Depending on people was always a mistake—one she wouldn't make. But she wished Paul Winthrop had found some other place to spend a lazy hour that afternoon.

◆ ◆ ◆ ◆

WHILE BRANDON SPLASHED in the tub upstairs, Julia poured herself a single, indulgent glass of wine from the bottle of Pouilly Fumé Eve had sent over. Since her hostess wanted her to be comfortable, Julia decided to oblige. But even as she drank the pale golden wine from a crystal glass, she worried about the paper in her pocket.

Had Paul left it for her? She stirred the idea around in her mind, then dismissed it. It was much too indirect a move for a man like Paul Winthrop. In any case, she hadn't a clue how many people had cruised through those big iron gates that day, any one of whom could have dropped the envelope on the stoop.

And she didn't know enough about the people who made their home inside those same iron gates.

Peering through the kitchen window, she could see the lights in the apartment atop the garage. Lyle, the broad-shouldered, slick-hipped chauffeur. Julia had sized him up immediately as a man who thought of himself as the stud of the West. Had he and Eve—No. Eve might indulge herself with men, but never with someone like Lyle.

Travers. The housekeeper skulked around, disapproval tightening her already-pinched mouth. There was no doubt she'd decided to dislike Julia on sight. And, since Julia doubted the woman objected to the scent of her perfume, it was obviously because of the job she'd come to do. Perhaps Travers had thought one cryptic, anonymous note would send her scurrying back to Connecticut. If so, Julia thought as she sipped her wine, the woman was doomed to disappointment.

Then there was Nina. Efficient and chic. Why would such a woman be content to subjugate her life to another? The background information Julia had collected on Nina was sparse. A fifteen-year veteran of Eve's world, she was unmarried, childless. At dinner, she'd unobtrusively managed to keep the peace. Was she worried that the publication of Eve's story would disrupt that peace irrevocably?

Even as Julia thought about her, she spotted Nina coming briskly along the path, carrying a large cardboard box.

Julia pushed the kitchen door open. "Special delivery?"

With a breathless laugh, Nina swung the box through the door. "I told you I was the pack mule." She grunted a bit when she dropped the box onto the kitchen table. "Eve asked me to put this stuff together for you. Photos, clippings, studio stills. She thought it might be helpful."

Instantly curious, Julia flipped open the top. "Oh, yes!" Delighted, she held up an old publicity shot of Eve—sultry, smoldering, wrapped around a spearingly handsome Michael Torrent. She began to root through the box.

To Nina's credit she winced only slightly as Julia destroyed all of her careful filing.

"This is wonderful." Julia lifted out an ordinary snapshot, a bit faded, a bit worn around the edges. Her woman's heart gave a lurch of excitement. "Oh, Christ, it's Gable."

"Yes, taken here, by the pool at one of Eve's parties. That was right before he filmed *The Misfits*. Right before he died."

"Tell her it'll not only help the book, but provide me with enormous entertainment. I feel like a kid in a chocolate factory."

"Then I'll leave you to indulge."

"Wait." Julia forced herself to turn away from the box of goodies before Nina opened the door. "Do you have a few minutes?"

As a matter of habit, Nina checked her watch. "Of course. Do you want to go over some of the pictures with me?"

"No, actually, I'd like an interview. I'll make it short," she added hastily when she saw an evasive expression flicker on Nina's face. "I know how busy you are, and I hate to take any of your time during working hours." Julia smiled, congratulating herself. It was an inspiration to turn the situation around so that she was the one being inconvenienced. "I'll go get my recorder. Please, pour yourself a glass of wine." She hurried out, knowing she'd given Nina no time to agree or refuse.

When she came back, Nina had poured a glass, topped off Julia's, and taken a seat. She smiled, a handsome woman used to juggling her time to suit someone else. "Eve asked me to cooperate, but to tell you the truth, Julia, I can't think of a thing that would be of interest."

"Leave that to me." Julia opened her notebook, switched on the recorder. She recognized a reluctant subject. It only meant she would have to dig with a gentler hand. Keeping the tone light, she asked, "Nina, you must realize how fascinated people would be just to hear Eve Benedict's daily routine. What she has for breakfast, the kind of music she prefers, if she snacks in front of the television at night. But I can find out a lot of that for myself and don't want to take up your time with trivialities."

Nina's polite smile remained in place. "As I said, Eve asked me to cooperate."

"I appreciate it. What I'd like from you are your thoughts about her as a person. As someone who's worked closely with her for fifteen years, you probably know her better than almost anyone."

"I'd like to think that we share a friendship as well as a working relationship."

"Is it difficult to live and work in the same house with someone who, by her own definition, is demanding?"

"I've never found it difficult." Nina cocked her head as she sipped her wine. "Challenging, certainly. Over the years Eve's provided me with many challenges."

"What would you say is the most memorable?"

"Oh, that's easy." Nina laughed. "About five years ago, while she was filming *Heat Wave,* she decided she wanted to throw a party. That doesn't sound unusual. Eve loves a party. But she'd been so enchanted by the location work in Nassau that she insisted the party be set on an island—and she wanted it to come off in two weeks." The memory had her dropping the polite smile for a genuine one. "Have you ever tried to rent an entire island in the Caribbean, Julia?"

"I can't say I have."

"It has its complications—particularly if you want it to have any sort of modern conveniences such as shelter, electricity, plumbing. I managed to find one, a charming little spot about thirty-five miles off the coast of St. Thomas. We flew in generators, in case of tropical storms. Then, of course, there was the logistics of getting the food there, the drink, the china, silver, entertainment. Tables, chairs. Ice." She closed her eyes. "Incredible amounts of ice."

"How did you manage it."

Nina's eyes fluttered open. "By air and by sea. And by the skin of my teeth. I spent three days on the place myself, with carpenters—Eve wanted a couple of cabanas thrown up—with gardeners—she wanted a lusher, more tropical look—and with some very cranky caterers. It was . . . well, one of her most interesting ideas."

Fascinated, letting the whole picture develop in her mind, Julia rested a hand on her chin. "So, how was the party?"

"A roaring success. Enough rum to float a battleship, native music— and Eve, looking like the island queen in a blue silk sarong."

"Tell me something, how does one learn how to rent an island?"

"Trial and error. With Eve, you never know what to expect, so you prepare for everything. I've taken courses in law, accounting, decorating, real estate, and ballroom dancing—among others."

"In all those courses, was there ever any that tempted you to go further, pursue another career?"

"No." There wasn't a hint of hesitation. "I'd never leave Eve."

"How did you come to work for her?"

Nina looked down into her wine. Slowly, she circled her finger around the rim of the glass. "I know it may sound melodramatic, but Eve saved my life."

"Literally?"

"Quite literally." She moved her shoulders as if she were shrugging off any doubts about going on. "There aren't many people who know about my background. I prefer to keep it quiet, but I know Eve's determined to tell the full story. I guess it's best if I tell you myself."

"It usually is."

"My mother was a weak woman, drifted from man to man. We had very little money, lived in rented rooms."

"Your father?"

"He'd left us. I was quite young when she married again. A truck driver who was away as much as he was home. That turned out to be a blessing." The pain in her voice ran deep. Nina began to clench and unclench her fingers on the stem of the glass, still watching the wine as if it might hold a secret. "Things were a little better financially, and it was all right . . . for a while . . . until I wasn't so young anymore." With an effort she raised her eyes. "I was thirteen when he raped me."

"Oh, Nina." Julia felt that icy pain, the kind a woman feels hearing the mention of rape. "I'm sorry." Instinctively she reached out to take Nina's hand. "I'm so sorry."

"I ran away a lot after that," Nina continued, apparently finding comfort in the firm grip of Julia's fingers. "The first couple of times I came back on my own." She gave a wan smile. "No place to go. Other times, they brought me back."

"Your mother?"

"Didn't believe me. Didn't care to believe me. It wouldn't have suited her to think that her daughter was in competition with her."

"That's monstrous."

"Reality often is. Details aren't important," she went on. "I finally ran away for good. Lied about my age, got a job as a cocktail waitress, worked my way up to manager." She began to speak more quickly, not as if the worst was over, but as if she had to get a running start at the rest. "My previous experience had helped me keep myself focused on the job. No dating, no distractions. Then I made a mistake. I fell in love. I was nearly thirty, and it hit me hard."

Something glittered in her eyes—tears or old memories—quickly obscured by her lashes as she lifted the glass to her lips. "He was wonderful to me, generous, considerate, gentle. He wanted to get married, but I let my past ruin that for both of us. One night, angry that I wouldn't give him a commitment, he left my apartment. And he was killed in a car accident."

She drew her hand from Julia's. "I fell apart. Tried to commit suicide. That's when I met Eve. She was researching her role of the suicidal wife in *Darkest at Dawn*. I'd botched the job, hadn't swallowed enough pills, and was in the hospital under observation. She talked to me, listened to me. It may have started as an actress's interest in a character type, but she came back. I've often wondered what she saw in me that made her come back. She asked me if I wanted to waste my life on regrets, or if I wanted to make them work for me. I screamed at her, swore at her. She left me her number and told me to call if I decided to make something of myself. Then she walked out, in that go-to-hell way of hers. In the end I called her. She gave me a home, a job, and my life." Nina drained the rest of the wine. "And that's why I'll rent islands for her, or do anything else she asks me to do."

♦ ♦ ♦ ♦

*H*OURS LATER, Julia was wide awake. The story Nina told her crowded her mind. The private Eve Benedict was so much more complex than the public one. How many people would take a stranger's tragedy and find a way to offer hope? Not just by writing a check. Easy to do when the money was there. Not by making speeches. Words cost nothing. But by opening that most intimate chamber, the heart.

Julia's ambition for the book began to creep along a new path. It was no longer a story she wanted to tell, but one she needed to tell.

As longer-range plans began to form, she thought of the paper still in her pocket. It concerned her more now after Brandon had responded to her casual question by telling her he'd found the envelope lying on the front stoop. She ran her fingers over the page, then withdrew them before she could give in to the urge to take the paper out and read it again. Better to forget it, she told herself.

The night was growing cool. A breeze fragrant with roses ruffled the leaves. In the distance, the peahen screamed. Even though she recognized the sound, still she shuddered. She had to remind herself that the only danger she faced was becoming too used to luxury.

There was little chance of that, she thought, bending to pick up one of her discarded sandals. Julia didn't consider herself the kind of woman who could fit comfortably into minks or diamonds. Some were born for it—she tossed the scuffed leather toward the closet—some weren't.

When she thought of how often she misplaced earrings, or left a jacket crumpled in the trunk of her car, she admitted she was definitely better off with cloth and rhinestones.

Beyond that, she missed her home. The simplicity of it, the basic routine of tidying her own things, shoveling her own walk. Writing about the famous, the glamorous was one thing. Living like them another.

Peeking into Brandon's room, she took another look. He was sprawled on his stomach, his face smashed into his pillow. His latest building project was neatly arranged in the center of the room. All of his miniature cars were lined up in a well-orchestrated traffic jam on his desk. For Brandon, everything had a place. This room, where the famous and powerful must have slept, was now completely her little boy's. It smelled of him—crayons and that oddly sweet, somewhat wild aroma of a child's sweat.

Leaning against the doorjamb, she smiled at him. Julia knew that if she took him to the Ritz or plopped him into a cave, within a day Brandon would have cordoned off his own space and been content. Where, she wondered, did he get that confidence, that ability to make a place of his own?

Not from her, she thought. Not from the man who had conceived the child with her. It was at times like this that she wondered whose blood ran through her to be passed off to her son. She knew nothing about her biological parents, and had never wanted to know—except late at night when she was alone, looking at her son . . . and wondering.

She left his door open, an old habit she had never been able to break. Even as she walked to her own room, she knew she was too restless for bed or for work. After tugging on a pair of sweats, she wandered downstairs, then outside, into the night.

There was moonlight, long silver tapers of it. And quiet, the exquisite quiet she'd learned to prize after her years in Manhattan. She could hear the air breathing through the trees, the fluid ebb and flow that was the song of insects. Whatever the air quality in L.A., here each breath was like drinking flowers and moondust.

She walked past the table where she had sat that afternoon, verbally jostling with Paul Winthrop. It was odd, she thought now, that they had shared her most extensive personal conversation with a man in too long to remember. Yet she didn't think they knew each other any better than they had before.

It was her job to find out more about him—as it pertained to Eve. She was already certain he was the little boy Eve had spoken of to Brandon. The young boy who had liked petits fours. It was difficult for Julia to picture Paul as a child hoping for a treat.

What kind of mother figure had Eve Benedict been? Julia pursed her lips as she considered. That was the angle she needed to explore. Had she been indulgent, careless, devoted, aloof? After all, she had never had a child of her own. How had she reacted to the smattering of stepchildren who had woven in and out of her life? And how did they remember her?

What about her nephew, Drake Morrison? There was a blood tie between them. It would be interesting to talk to him about his aunt, not his client.

It wasn't until she heard the voices that Julia realized she'd wandered deep into the garden. She immediately recognized Eve's whiskey tones and just as immediately noticed a faint difference in them. They were softer, gentler, with the richness that enters a woman's voice when she's speaking to a lover.

And the other voice was as distinctive as a fingerprint. That deep, gravelly rasp sounded as if the vocal cords had been scraped with sandpaper.

Victor Flannigan—the legendary leading man of the forties and fifties, the dashing and dangerous romantic lead in the sixties, and even into the seventies. Now, though his hair had gone white and his face was deeply lined, he still brought sensuality and style to the screen. More, he was considered by many to be one of the finest actors in the world.

He had made a trio of films with Eve, brilliant, fiery films that had provoked a flood of rumors about the fire offscreen. But Victor Flannigan was married to a devout Catholic. Rumors about Eve and him still buzzed from time to time, but neither added the fuel of comment to the flames.

Julia heard the sound of their merged laughter, and knew she was listening to lovers.

Her first thought was to turn quickly and start back to the guest house. Journalist she might be, but she couldn't intrude on so obviously private a moment. The voices were coming closer. Going on instinct, Julia backed off the path and into the shadows to let them pass.

"Have you ever known me to be ignorant about what I was doing?" Eve asked him. She had her arm through his, her head inclined toward his broad shoulder. From the shadows Julia realized she'd never seen Eve look more beautiful or more happy.

"Yes." He stopped and took Eve's face in his hands. He was only a few inches taller than she, but built like a bull, a solid wall of muscle and bulk. His white hair was a mane of silver in the moonlight. "I imagine I'm the only one who could say that and stay alive."

"Vic, darling Vic." Eve stared into the face she had known and loved half of her life. Looking at him now, seeing the age, remembering the youth made tears back up in her throat. "Don't worry about me. I have my reasons for the book. When it's finished . . ." She wrapped her fingers around his wrist, needing badly to feel that strong pump of life from his pulse. "You and I will curl up by the fire and read it to each other."

"Why bring it all back, Eve?"

"Because it's time. It wasn't all bad. In fact"—she laughed and pressed her cheek to his—"since I decided to do it, it's made me think, remember, reevaluate. I've realized how much pleasure there is in just living."

He captured her hands to bring them to his lips. "Nothing in my life has given me more than you. I'll always wish—"

"No." Shaking her head, she cut him off. Julia could see the glint of tears in Eve's eyes. "Don't wish. We've had what we've had. I wouldn't change it."

"Not even the drunken brawls?"

She laughed. "Not one. In fact, sometimes it pisses me off that you let Betty Ford dry you out. You were the sexiest drunk I've ever known."

"Remember the time I stole Gene Kelly's car?"

"It was Spencer Tracy's, God love him."

"Ah, well, we're all Irishmen. You and I drove to Vegas and called him."

"It was more to the point what he called us." She pressed close, absorbing the scents that were part of him. Tobacco, peppermint, and the piney aftershave he'd used for decades. "Such good times, Victor."

"That they were." He pulled away from her, searching her face, finding it fascinating, as always. Was he the only one, he wondered, who knew her weaknesses, those soft spots she hid from a hungry world? "I don't want you hurt, Eve. What you're doing will make a lot of people—a lot of spiteful people—unhappy."

He saw the glitter in her eyes as she smiled. "You were the only one who ever called me a tough old broad and got away with it. Have you forgotten?"

"No." His voice roughened. "But you're *my* tough old broad, Eve."

"Trust me."

"You, yes. But this writer is a different story."

"You'd like her." She leaned against him, shutting her eyes. "She's got class and integrity shouting from her pores. She's the right choice, Vic. Strong enough to finish what she starts, proud enough to do a good job of it. I believe I will like seeing my life through her eyes."

He ran his hand up and down her back and felt the embers start to glow. With her, desire had never aged or paled. "I know better than to try to talk you out of anything once you've made up your mind. Christ knows I gave it my best shot before you married Rory Winthrop."

Her laugh was soft, seductive, as were the fingers she trailed over the back of his neck. "And you're still jealous that I tried to tell myself I could love him the way I love you."

He felt the pang, but it was only part jealousy. "I had no right to hold you back, Eve. Then or now."

"You never held me back." She gripped what she'd always wanted and could never completely have. "That's why no one's ever mattered but you."

His mouth took hers as it had thousands of times, with a rightness and a passion and a quiet despair. "God, I love you, Eve." He laughed when he felt himself harden like iron. "Even ten years ago I'd have had you on your back here and now. These days I need a bed."

"Then come to mine." Hand in hand they hurried off together.

Julia stayed in the shadows for a long time. It wasn't embarrassment she felt, nor was it the tingle of learning a secret. There were tears on her cheeks, the kind that fell when she listened to a particularly beautiful piece of music, or watched a perfect sunset.

That had been love. Enduring, fulfilling, generous. And she realized what she felt beyond the beauty was envy. There was no one to walk in a moonlit garden with her. No one to make her voice take on that musky edge. No one.

Alone, she walked back to the house to spend a restless night in an empty bed.

Chapter Five

♦ ♦ ♦ ♦

THE CORNER BOOTH at Denny's was a far cry from a power breakfast spot, but at least Drake was sure he wouldn't run into anyone he knew. Anyone who mattered. Over his second cup of coffee he ordered a short stack with ham and eggs on the side. He always ate when he was nervous.

Delrickio was late.

Drake laced his cup of coffee with three packs of sugar and checked his Rolex for the third time in five minutes. He tried not to sweat.

If he had dared to risk leaving the table, he would have run into the men's room to check his hair. He passed a careful hand over it to be sure every strand was in place. His fingers walked over the knot of his tie, finding the silk firmly in place. He brushed fussily at the sleeves of the Uomo jacket. His hammered-gold cuff links winked against the crisp ivory linen of his monogrammed shirt.

Image was everything. For the meeting with Delrickio he needed to appear cool, confident, collected. Inside, he was a little boy with jelly knees being led out to the woodshed.

As tough as those beatings had been, they were nothing compared to what would happen to him if he didn't pull off this meeting. At least when his mother had been finished with him, he'd still been alive.

His mother's credo had been spare the rod, spoil the child, and she had wielded that rod while religious fervor glazed her eyes.

Delrickio's credo ran more along the lines of business is business, and he would slice off small vital parts of Drake's body with the same casual skill as a man paring his nails.

Drake was checking his watch for the fourth time when Delrickio arrived. "You drink too much coffee." He smiled as he took his seat. "It's bad for your health."

Michael Delrickio was nearing sixty and took his cholesterol count as seriously as he took the business he had inherited from his father. As a result, he was both rich and robust. His olive skin was pampered by weekly facials and contrasted dramatically with steel-gray hair and a lush mustache. His hands were smooth, with the long, tapering fingers of a violinist. The only jewelry he wore was a gold wedding band. He had a thin, aesthetic face only marginally lined, and deep, rich brown eyes that could smile indulgently at his grandchildren, weep over a soaring aria, or show no expression at all when he was ordering a hit.

Business rarely tapped Delrickio's emotions.

He was fond of Drake, in an avuncular fashion, though he considered Drake a fool. It was that fondness that had caused Delrickio to meet with him personally rather than send someone less fastidious to rearrange Drake's pretty face.

Delrickio waved for a waitress. The restaurant was crowded, noisy with whiny children and the clatter of cutlery, but he got prompt service. Power covered him as neatly as his Italian suit.

"Grapefruit juice," he said in his faintly Bostonian accent. "A bowl of melon balls, very cold, and whole wheat toast, dry. So," he began when the waitress walked away. "You are well?"

"Yes." Drake felt his armpits dampen. "And you?"

"Healthy as a horse." Delrickio leaned back and patted his flat belly. "My Maria still makes the best linguini in the state, but I cut down on my portions, eat only a salad for lunch, and go to the gym three times a week. My cholesterol's a hundred seventy."

"That's wonderful, Mr. Delrickio."

"This is your only body."

Drake didn't want his only body carved like a turkey. "Your family?"

"Wonderful." Always the doting papa, he smiled. "Angelina gave me a new grandson last week. Now I have fourteen grandchildren." It made him misty-eyed. "This is a man's immortality. And you, Drake, you should be married to a nice girl, making babies. It would center your life." He leaned forward, an earnest, concerned father about to impart sage advice. "It's one thing to fuck beautiful women. A man must be a man, after all. But family, there's nothing to replace it."

Drake managed a smile as he lifted his cup. "I'm still looking."

"When you stop thinking with your dick and think with your heart, you'll find." He let out a sigh as their meal was served, then lifted a brow at Drake's and tallied the grams of fat. "Now . . ." Nearly wincing at the syrup Drake puddled over his pancakes, Delrickio daintily forked a melon ball. "You're prepared to pay off your debt."

The bite of ham stuck in Drake's throat. As he fought to swallow it, he felt a thin line of sweat trickle down his side. "As you know, I've had a little downswing. Right now I'm experiencing a temporary cash-flow problem." He soaked his pancakes with more syrup while Delrickio solemnly ate his fruit. "I am prepared to give you ten percent, as good faith."

"Ten percent." Mouth pursed, Delrickio spread a thimbleful of strawberry jam on his toast. "And the other ninety thousand?"

Ninety thousand. The two words rang like hammer blows inside Drake's skull. "As soon as things break for me. All I need is one winner."

Delrickio dabbed his lips with his napkin. "So you've said before."

"I realize that, but this time—"

Delrickio had only to lift a hand to cut off Drake's hurried explanations. "I have an affection for you, Drake, so I'll tell you gambling is a fool's game. For me, it is part of my business, but it disturbs me to see you risk your . . . your health on point spreads."

"I'm going to make it up on the Super Bowl." Drake began to eat quickly, struggling to fill the hole fear left in his gut. "I need only a week."

"And if you lose?"

"I won't." A desperate smile, sweat streaming down his back.

Delrickio went on eating. A bite of melon, a bite of toast, a sip of juice. At the table beside them, a woman settled a toddler into a high chair. Delrickio winked at the child, then returned to the routine— melon, toast, juice. Drake felt the eggs congeal in his stomach.

"Your aunt is well?"

"Eve?" Drake licked his lips. He knew, as few did, that Delrickio and his aunt had had a brief, torrid affair. Drake had never been sure if he could count that in his favor. "She's fine."

"I hear she's decided to publish her memoirs."

"Yes." Though his stomach protested, Drake drank more coffee. "That is, she's brought in a writer from the East to do her authorized bio."

"A young woman."

"Julia Summers. She seems competent."

"And how much does your aunt plan to make public?"

Drake felt a little wave of relief at the turn in the conversation. He slathered butter on a piece of toast. "Who knows? With Eve it depends on the mood of the moment."

"But you'll find out."

The tone had Drake pausing, his knife still in the air. "She doesn't talk to me about that sort of thing."

"You'll find out," Delrickio repeated. "And you'll have your week. A favor for a favor." Delrickio smiled. "That's how it is between friends. And family."

◆ ◆ ◆ ◆

$\mathscr{I}$T MADE HER FEEL YOUNG to dive into the pool. The evening with Victor had made her glow like a girl again. Eve had awakened later than usual, and with a blinding headache. But the medication, and now the cool, clear water, made the pain tolerable.

She swam laps slowly, methodically, taking pleasure in feeling her arms and legs move in precision. It was a small thing, the use of one's body. But she'd learned to appreciate it.

It had been no small thing last night, she thought as she switched to a side stroke. Sex was always incredible with Victor. Passionate or gentle, slow or frantic. God knew they had made love in every possible way over the years.

Last night had been beautiful. Being held after passion had been spent, lying together dozing like two old war horses, waking again to feel him slide into her.

Of all the men, of all the lovers, there was no one like Victor. Because of all the men, of all the lovers, he was the only one who truly had captured her heart.

There had been a time, years and years before, when she had despaired over her feelings for him, when she had cursed and raged and beat her fists against fate for making it impossible for them to be together. That time had passed. Now she could be grateful for every hour they had.

Eve pulled herself out of the pool, shivered as the cool air hit her wet skin, then drew on a long red terry-cloth robe. As if she'd been watching for her cue, Travers hustled out with a breakfast tray and a bottle of moisturizer.

"Did Nina call her?" Eve asked.

Travers sucked air through her nose. The sound was like steam in a kettle. "On her way."

"Good." Eve picked up the bottle, shaking it idly as she watched her housekeeper. "You needn't make your disapproval so obvious."

"I think what I think."

"And know what you know," Eve added with a little smile. "Why blame her?"

Travers busied herself setting up the breakfast on the glossy white table. "Best to send her back and forget the whole thing. Asking for trouble. Nobody'll thank you for it."

With expert fingers Eve spread the moisturizer over her face. "I need her," she said simply. "I can't do this myself."

Travers's lips thinned. "You've done every damn thing you've wanted to do all your life. You're wrong about this."

Eve sat, then popped a raspberry into her mouth. "I hope not. That'll be all."

Travers stomped back toward the house. Still smiling, Eve slipped on sunglasses and waited for Julia. She didn't wait long. From behind the dark lenses, she watched, then made judgments as practical shoes, slim royal blue slacks, a crisp striped blouse came into view. Slightly more relaxed but still cautious, Eve decided, based on body language as well as the clothing.

When, if ever, she wondered, would they forge some kind of trust?

"I hope you don't mind talking out here." Eve gestured to the cushioned chair beside her.

"No, not at all." How many, Julia wondered, had seen that famous face washed of makeup? And how many knew that the beauty was in the complexion and bone structure, not the artifice. "Wherever you're most relaxed suits me."

"I could say the same." Eve poured the juice and lifted a brow when Julia shook her head at the addition of champagne. "Do you ever?" she asked. "Relax?"

"Of course. But not when I'm working."

Thoughtful, Eve sipped her mimosa, and finding it to her liking, sipped again. "What do you do? To relax, I mean?"

Thrown off, Julia stammered, "Well, I . . . I . . ."

"Caught," Eve said with a quick, lusty laugh. "Let me tell you about yourself, shall I? You're enviably young, and lovely. You're a devoted mother whose child is the center of her life, and you're determined to do a good job of raising him. Your work comes second, though you approach it with a ponderous sobriety. Etiquette, propriety, and manners are your bywords, particularly so since there's a tough, passionate woman under all the control. Ambition is a secret vice you're almost ashamed of having. Men are far down on your list of priorities, somewhere, I would think, below folding Brandon's socks."

It took all of Julia's will to keep her face composed. She could do nothing about the flash of heat in her eyes. "You make me sound very dull."

"Admirable," Eve corrected her, and dipped again into the raspberries. "Though the two are sometimes synonymous. The truth is, I'd hoped to get a rise out of you, to shake that awesome composure of yours."

"Why?"

"I'd like to know I'm baring my soul to a fellow human." With a shrug, Eve broke off the end of a flaky croissant. "From your little exchange with Paul over dinner the other night, I detected a good healthy temper. I admire temper."

"Not all of us are in the position to let ours loose." But hers was still smoldering in her eyes. "I'm human, Miss Benedict."

"Eve."

"I'm human, Eve, human enough that being manipulated pisses me off." Julia opened her briefcase to bring out her pad and recorder. "Did you send him to see me yesterday?"

Eve was grinning. "Send who?"

"Paul Winthrop."

"No." Surprise and interest registered clearly, but Julia reminded herself the woman was an actress. "Paul paid you a visit?"

"Yes. He seems concerned about the book, and the way I'll write it."

"He's always been protective of me." Eve's appetite came and went these days. She bypassed the rest of breakfast for a cigarette. "And I'd imagine he's intrigued by you."

"I doubt it's personal."

"Don't." Eve laughed again, but an idea began to brew. "My dear, most women have their tongues hanging out after five minutes with him. He's spoiled. With his looks, his charm, that underlying shimmer of raw sex, it's hard to expect otherwise. I know," she added, drawing in smoke. "I fell for his father."

"Tell me about that." Julia took advantage of the opening and punched record. "About Rory Winthrop."

"Ah, Rory . . . the face of a fallen angel, the soul of a poet, the body of a god, and the mind of a Doberman chasing a bitch in heat." When she laughed again, there was no malice in it, but ripe good humor. "I've always thought it was a pity we couldn't make a go of it. I liked the son of a bitch. Rory's problem was that whenever he got an erection, he felt honor bound not to waste it. French maids, Irish cooks, leading ladies, and spangled bimbos. If a look had Rory getting it up, he felt it was his male duty to stick it somewhere." She grinned, refilling her glass with juice and champagne. "I might have tolerated the infidelity—there was nothing personal about it. Rory's mistake was that he found it necessary to lie. I couldn't stay married to a man who thought me stupid enough to believe pitiful fabrications."

"His unfaithfulness didn't bother you?"

"I didn't say that. Divorce is much too clean and unimaginative a way to pay a man back for screwing around. I believe in revenge, Julia." She savored the word as she savored the zip of champagne. "If I had cared more about Rory, less about Paul, well, let's just say things might have ended more explosively."

Again Julia felt that shimmer of understanding. She had cared too much about a child herself to destroy the father. "Though your relationship with Rory ended years ago, you still have a warm relationship with his son."

"I love Paul. He's the closest I've come to having a child of my own." She waved away the sentiment but lighted a cigarette immediately after crushing one out. How difficult it had been for her to make that statement. "Not your average mother figure," she said with a thin smile. "But I wanted to mother that boy. I was just over forty, right at the point where a woman knows she has virtually no time left to take that turn at the biological bat. And there was this bright, beautiful child—the same age as your Brandon." She drank again, to give herself time to get control over her emotions. "Paul was my only turn at bat."

"And Paul's mother?"

"Marion Heart? A stunning actress—a bit of a snob when it came to Hollywood. After all, she was *theater*. She and Rory bounced the child back and forth between New York and L.A. Marion had a kind of detached affection for Paul, as if he were a pet she had bought on impulse and now had to feed and walk."

"But that's horrible."

It was the first time Eve had heard real emotion in Julia's voice, emotion to match what flashed in her eyes. "There are a great many women in the same situation. You don't believe me," she added, "because of Brandon. But I promise you, not all women embrace motherhood. There was no abuse. Neither Rory nor Marion would have dreamed of harming the boy. Nor was there neglect. There was only a kind of benign disinterest."

"It must have hurt him," Julia murmured.

"One doesn't always miss what one hasn't known." She observed that Julia had stopped taking notes and was listening, just listening. "When I met Paul, he was an intelligent and very self-sufficient child. I couldn't step in and play the doting mama—even if I'd known how. But I could pay attention, and enjoy. The truth is, I often think I married Rory because I was head over heels for his son."

She settled back, enjoying this particular memory. "Of course, I'd known Rory for some time. We traveled in the same circles. There was an attraction, a spark, but the timing had always been off. Whenever I was free, he was involved, and vice versa. Then we made a film together."

"Fancy Face."

"Yes, a romantic comedy. A damn good one. It was one of my best experiences. A sharp, witty script, a creative director, an elegant wardrobe, and a costar who knew how to make those sexual sparks fly. Two weeks into filming, and we were making them fly offscreen."

◆ ◆ ◆ ◆

A LITTLE DRUNK, a lot reckless, Eve strolled into Rory's Malibu beach house. Shooting had run late, and afterward they had hidden themselves away in a dingy diner, swigging beer and gobbling greasy food.

Rory had popped coin after coin in the jukebox so that their laughter and all that sexual teasing had been accompanied by the Beach Boys.

Flower power was making its early noises in California. Most of the other diners were teenagers and college students with hair flowing down the backs of their tie-dyed T-shirts.

A young girl, groggy on pot, slipped love beads around Rory's neck when he dropped two dollars in change into the juke.

They were established stars, but went unrecognized. The kids who patronized the diner didn't spend their money on movies starring Eve Benedict and Rory Winthrop. They spent it on concerts and drugs and incense. Woodstock was only three years and a continent away.

Eve and Rory weren't overly concerned with Vietnam or sitar music.

They had left the diner to roar into Malibu with the top down on his Mercedes, buzzed on beer and anticipation. Eve had timed this night carefully. There was no shoot the next day, so she wouldn't have to worry about puffy eyes. She might have wanted a night of sex, but she was first and last a film star.

She'd made the decision with her eyes open to take Rory as a lover. There were holes in her life, holes she knew would never be filled again. But she could cover them over, at least briefly.

With her hair wildly touseled by the wind, her shoes left behind on the floor of his car, Eve took a quick turn around the living room. High glossy wood ceilings, walls of sheer glass, the sound of the surf. Here, she thought, lowering herself to the rug in front of the huge stone fireplace. Here and now.

She smiled up at him. In the light of the candles he'd hurriedly lit, he looked incredible. Bronze skin, mahogany hair, sapphire eyes. She'd already tasted his mouth, while technicians had crowded around them. She wanted it—and him—without a script or director.

She wanted wild, dangerous sex, to help her forget for a few hours what she would live with for the rest of her life.

He knelt beside her. "Do you know how long I've wanted you?"

There was nothing, she knew, more powerful than a woman about to yield to a man. "No."

He gathered her hair in his hand. "How long have we known each other?"

"Five, six years."

"That's how long." He lowered his head to nip at her lip. "The trouble is I've been spending too much time in London, when I could have been here, making love to you."

It was part of his charm, making a woman believe he thought only of her. In fact, whatever woman he was with at the moment, the fantasy was quite real.

She slid her hands over his face, fascinated with the lines and dips and planes that formed into such staggering male beauty. Physically, Rory Winthrop was perfect. And for tonight, at least, he was hers.

"Then have me now." She accompanied the invitation with a low laugh as she tugged his shirt over his head. In the candlelight her eyes glinted with hunger and promise.

He sensed that she wanted not a dance but a race. Though he might have preferred a bit more romance and anticipation this first time, Rory was always willing to accommodate a woman. That, too, was part of his charm—and part of his weakness.

He dragged at her clothes, delighted, destroyed by the way her nails scraped shallow furrows in his back. A woman's body always excited him, whether slender or full, youthful or ripe. He feasted on Eve's flesh, sinking into her lush curves, seduced by the scents, the textures, groaning as she tore at his slacks to find him hard and ready.

It wasn't fast enough. She could still think. She could still hear the drum of water against sand, her own heartbeat, her own ragged breaths. She wanted the vacuum of sex where there was nothing, nothing but sensation. Desperate, she rolled over him, her body as agile and dangerous as a whip. He had to make her forget. She didn't want to remember the feel of other hands cruising over her, the tastes of someone else's mouth, the scent of someone else's skin.

Escape would be her survival, and she had promised herself that Rory Winthrop would be that escape.

The candlelight danced on her skin as she arched over him. Her hair streamed back, an ebony waterfall. As she took him into her, she let out a cry that was only a prayer. She rode him hard until at last, at last, she found release in forgetfulness.

Spent, she slid bonelessly down to him. His heart jackhammered against hers, and she smiled, grateful. If she could give herself to him, find pleasure and passion with this man, she would heal and be whole again.

"Are we still alive?" Rory murmured.

"I think so."

"Good." He found the energy to run his hands down her back and slowly knead her bottom. "That was a hell of a ride, Evie."

She smiled. No one had ever called her Evie, but she decided she liked the way it sounded in his proper, theater-trained voice. Lifting her head, she looked down at him. His eyes were closed and he wore a foolish grin of pure satisfaction. It made her laugh, and she kissed him, grateful again.

"Want to try for round two?"

His eyes opened slowly. She could see both desire and affection mirrored there. Until that moment she hadn't realized how much she had craved both. Care for me, just for me, she thought, and I'll do my damnedest to care for you.

"Tell you what. I've got a great big bed upstairs, and a great big hot tub out on the upper deck. Why don't we make use of both?"

They did, splashing in the steamy water, tearing up the satin sheets. Like greedy children they fed off each other until their bodies begged for sleep.

It was a hunger of a different kind that awakened Eve just past noon. Beside her Rory was spread out on the enormous bed, facedown in the posture of the half dead. Still floating on the afterglow, she gave him a quick kiss on the shoulder and went off to shower.

There was a choice of women's robes in his closet—either ones he had bought for convenience or that had been left behind by other lovers. Eve chose one in blue silk because it suited her mood, and started downstairs with the idea of fixing them both a light breakfast they could eat in bed.

Eve followed the murmur of a television to the kitchen. A housekeeper, she thought. Better yet. Now she could order breakfast, not cook it. Humming, she dug out the pack of cigarettes she'd slipped into the pocket of the robe.

The last thing she expected to see standing at the kitchen counter was a young boy. From her side view in the doorway, she caught the profound resemblance to his father. The same dark, rich hair, the sweet mouth, the intense blue eyes. As the boy carefully, almost religiously spread peanut butter on a slice of bread, the television across the room switched from commercial to cartoon. Bugs Bunny popped out of his rabbit hole gnawing wryly on a carrot.

Before Eve could decide whether to walk in or to slip quietly away again, the boy's head lifted—like a young wolf scenting the air. As his gaze met hers, he stopped slathering the bread and studied.

In her time Eve had been measured and considered by too many men to count, yet this young boy struck her speechless with his sharp, disconcertingly adult scrutiny. Later, she would laugh it off, but at that moment she felt he had punched straight through the image to the woman beneath, to Betty Berenski, the thirsty, dreamy girl who had forged herself into Eve Benedict.

"Hello," he said in a childish echo of his father's cultured voice. "I'm Paul."

"Hello." She had a ridiculous urge to tidy her hair and smooth down her robe. "I'm Eve."

"I know. I've seen your picture."

Eve felt embarrassed. He looked at her as if she were almost as funny as Bugs outwitting Elmer Fudd. She could tell he knew what went on in his father's bedroom. There was such a cynical curl to his lip.

"Did you sleep well?"

The little shit, Eve thought as embarrassment became amusement. "Very well, thank you." She swept in then, like a queen into a drawing room. "I'm afraid I didn't realize Rory's son lived with him."

"Sometimes." He picked up a jar of jelly and began to coat another piece of bread. "I didn't like my last school, so my parents decided to transfer me to California for a year of two." He fit the two pieces of bread together, matching up the edges. "I was driving my mother crazy."

"Were you?"

"Oh, yes." He turned to the refrigerator and chose a large bottle of Pepsi. "I'm rather good at it. By summer I'll have driven my father crazy, so I'll go back to London. I enjoy flying."

"Do you?" Fascinated, Eve watched him settle himself at the glass-topped kitchen table. "Is it all right if I fix myself a sandwich?"

"Of course. You're making a film with my father." He said it matter-of-factly, as though he expected all of his father's leading ladies to stand in the kitchen on Saturday afternoons in a borrowed robe.

"That's right. Do you like movies?"

"Some of them. I've seen one of yours on the telly. TV." He corrected himself, reminding himself he wasn't in England now. "You were a saloon singer and men killed for you." He took a neat bite of the sandwich. "You have a very pleasant voice."

"Thank you." She looked over her shoulder to assure herself she was having this conversation with a child. "Are you going to be an actor?"

His eyes lit with laughter as he took another bite. "No. If I were going to go into films, it would be as a director. I think it would be satisfying to tell people what to do."

Eve decided against making coffee, plucked another soft drink from the refrigerator, and joined him at the table. Her notion of taking a snack up to Rory and indulging in an afternoon tussle was forgotten. "How old are you?"

"Ten. How old are you?"

"Older." She sampled the peanut butter and jelly and was rewarded by a flash of sensory memory. The month before she had met Charlie Gray, she had lived on peanut butter and jelly sandwiches and canned soup. "What do you like best about California?"

"The sun. It rains a lot in London."

"So I've heard."

"Did you always live here?"

"No, though sometimes it feels like it." She took a long drink of Pepsi. "So, tell me, Paul, what didn't you like about your last school?"

"The uniforms," he said immediately. "I hate uniforms. It's as if they want to make you look alike so you'll think alike."

Because she'd nearly choked, she set the bottle down. "Are you sure you're ten?"

With a shrug he polished off the last of the sandwich. "I'm almost ten. And I'm precocious," he told her with such sobriety she swallowed her chuckle. "And I ask too many questions."

Under the veneer of a smart aleck was the poignant tone of a lonely little boy. A fish out of water, Eve thought, and checked the urge to ruffle his hair. She knew the feeling very well. "People say you ask too many questions only when they don't know the answers."

He gave her another long, searching look with those direct, adult eyes. Then he smiled and became an almost ten-year-old with a missing tooth. "I know. And it makes them crazy when you just keep asking."

This time she didn't resist ruffling his hair. The grin had hooked her. "You're going to go places, kid. But for now, how do you feel about a walk on the beach?"

He stared for a full thirty seconds. Eve would have bet her last dollar that Rory's lovers never spent time with him. She'd also bet that Paul Rory Winthrop desperately wanted a friend.

"Okay." He ran a finger down the Pepsi bottle, making designs in the condensation. "If you want." It wouldn't do to seem too eager.

"Good." She felt exactly the same way, and rose casually. "Just let me find some clothes."

♦ ♦ ♦ ♦

"WE WALKED for a couple of hours," Eve said. She was smiling now, and her cigarette had burned down to the filter, untouched in the ashtray. "Even built sand castles. It was one of the most . . . intimate afternoons of my life. By the time we got back, Rory was awake, and I was head over heels in love with his son."

"And Paul?" Julia asked quietly. She'd been able to picture him perfectly, a lonely little boy fixing a solitary sandwich on a Saturday afternoon.

"Oh, he was more cautious than I. I realized later that he suspected I was using him to get to his father." With a restless movement Eve shifted and took out a fresh cigarette. "Who could blame him? Rory was a very desirable man, powerful in the industry, wealthy—in his own right and also through family."

"You and Rory Winthrop were married before the picture you were working on was released."

"One month after that Saturday in Malibu." For a few moments Eve smoked in silence, looking out over the orange grove. "I admit I went after him, single-mindedly. The man didn't have much of a chance. Romance was his weakness. I exploited it. I wanted that marriage, that ready-made family. I had my reasons."

"Which were?"

Focusing on Julia again, Eve smiled. "For now we'll say Paul was a large part of it. It's true enough, and I don't intend to lie. And at that point in my life I still believed in marriage. Rory could make me laugh, he was—is—intelligent, gentle, and just wild enough to be interesting. I needed to believe it could work. It didn't, but of my four marriages, it's the only one I don't regret."

"There were other reasons?"

"You don't miss much," Eve murmured. "Yes." She tapped out her cigarette with quick, jerky motions. "But that's another story for another day."

"All right. Then tell me what your reasons were for hiring Nina."

Very rarely was Eve thrown off balance. Now, to give herself a moment, she blinked and smiled blankly. "I beg your pardon?"

"I spoke with Nina last night. She told me how you'd found her in the hospital after her attempted suicide, how you'd given her not only a job, but the will to live."

Eve picked up her glass, studied the few remaining inches of champagne and juice. "I see. Nina didn't mention to me that you'd interviewed her."

"We talked when she brought the photos over last night."

"Yes. I haven't seen her yet this morning." Changing her mind, Eve set the glass down again without drinking. "My reasons for hiring Nina were twofold, and more intricate than I care to get into at the moment. I will tell you that I detest waste."

"I'd wondered," Julia persisted, more interested in watching Eve's face than in hearing her answer, "if you'd felt it was a way to pay an old debt? Charlie Gray had committed suicide, and you couldn't do anything to prevent it. This time, with Nina, you could. And did."

A sadness crept into Eve's eyes, lingered. Julia watched the green darken, deepen. "You are very perceptive, Julia. Part of what I did was to pay Charlie back. But since I gained a very efficient employee and a devoted friend, one might say it cost me nothing."

And it was the eyes, not the answer that had Julia reaching out to lay a hand over Eve's before she realized she'd crossed the distance. "Whatever you gained, compassion and generosity are worth more. I've admired you as an actress all my life. In the past few days, I've started to admire you as a woman."

As Eve stared down at their joined hands, tangles of emotion passed across her face. She fought a brief and gritty war to control them before she spoke. "You'll have plenty of time to develop other opinions of me— as a woman—before we're finished. Not all of them will be anything remotely resembling admiration. Meanwhile, I have business to see to." She rose and waved her hand at the recorder. Reluctantly, Julia turned it off. "There's a charity dinner dance tonight. I have a ticket for you."

"Tonight?" Julia shaded her eyes against the sun as she looked up. "I really don't think I can attend."

"If you're going to write this book, you can't do it all from this house. I'm a public figure, Julia," Eve reminded her. "I want you with me, in public. You'll need to be ready by seven-thirty. CeeCee will sit with Brandon."

Julia rose as well. She preferred handling the unexpected on her feet. "I'll go of course. But you may as well know, I don't mingle very well." Irony spiking her words, she added, "I never outgrew that habit of driving people crazy by asking too many questions."

Eve chuckled and, satisfied, strolled toward the house. It was, she was certain, going to be an interesting evening.

Chapter Six

♦ ♦ ♦ ♦

$\mathcal{I}$F THERE WAS ONE THING Julia hated more than being given orders, it was having no choice but to obey them. It wasn't that she couldn't enjoy an evening out, particularly at a glitzy event. If it threatened to make her feel too hedonistic, she could justify it as research. It was being told on the morning of the event that she was expected to attend.

Not asked, not invited. Commanded.

And she'd been human enough to spend a large chunk of time that afternoon fretting over what to wear. Time, she thought now, that should have been spent working. Just as her annoyance with Eve had reached its peak, Nina had knocked on the door, carrying a trio of dresses. Dresses, Julia was told, that Eve had selected personally from her own wardrobe, on the off chance that Julia hadn't packed anything appropriate for a formal party.

Dictatorial, perhaps, but still considerate. And it had been tempting, very tempting, to choose one of the shimmery, glittery gowns. At one point, Julia had spread them out over her bed, thousands of dollars worth of silk and spangles. She'd even weakened enough to try one on, a strapless slither of coral-colored silk. It was only marginally too big in the bust and hips so that she imagined it slicked down Eve's body like rainwater.

In that moment when she stood studying herself in the star's gown, her own skin somehow softer, creamier against the vivid material, she felt enchanted, touched by magic.

If her life had not taken that single turn, would she have made her home in Beverly Hills? Would she have had a closet full of exquisite clothes? Would her face, her name, have drawn gasps from millions of fans as her image flickered across a movie screen?

Maybe, maybe not, she'd thought, and had indulged herself in a few twists and turns in front of the mirror. But her life had taken that other direction, and had given her something much more important, much more lasting than fame.

In the end her practicality had won out. She'd decided it was better to refuse the gowns than to go through the evening pretending she was something she wasn't.

She wore the only evening gown she had brought with her, a simple column of midnight blue with a snug bolero jacket studded with bugle beads. In the two years since she'd bought it, on sale at Saks, she had worn it only once. As she fastened on rhinestone drop earrings, she listened to her son's giggles float up the stairs. He and CeeCee, already fast friends, were deeply involved in a game of Crazy Eights.

Julia took a last inventory of her purse, slipped into pretty and miserably uncomfortable evening shoes, then started down the stairs.

"Hey, Mom." Brandon watched her come down. She looked so nice, so different. It always made him feel proud, and a little funny in the stomach, to realize how beautiful his mother was. "You look really good."

"You look terrific," CeeCee corrected the boy. She shifted from her stomach, where she and Brandon were sprawled on the rug, to her knees. "That's not one of Miss B.'s."

"No." Self-conscious, Julia smoothed her skirt. "I didn't feel right. I'd hoped this would do."

"It does," CeeCee told her with a nod. "Classic elegance. And with your hair swept up like that, you add sex appeal. What more could you ask for?"

Invisibility, Julia thought, but only smiled. "I shouldn't be late. I'm hoping to slip away right after dinner."

"Why? This is a totally big event." CeeCee sat back on her heels. *"Everybody's* going to be there. And it's for a good cause and all too. You know, the Actors' Fund. You should just enjoy yourself. I'll crash in the spare room if I get tired."

"Can we make popcorn?" Brandon wanted to know.

"Okay. Make sure you—" At the knock, she glanced over to see Paul standing at the door.

"Put plenty of butter on it," he finished, and winked at Brandon as he stepped inside.

CeeCee immediately fluffed her hair. "Hi, Mr. Winthrop."

"Hi, CeeCee, how's it going?"

"Fine, thanks." Her twenty-year-old heart went into overdrive. He wore a tux with the casual grace that transmitted instantly into sex. CeeCee wondered if there was a woman alive who wouldn't fantasize about loosening that tidy black tie.

"Eve said you'd be prompt," Paul said to Julia. She looked flustered. He'd already decided that was the way he liked her best.

"I hadn't realized you'd be going. I'd thought I'd be riding with Eve."

"She went with Drake. They had some business." He gave her a slow smile. "It's just you and me, Jules."

"I see." The simple phrase had her tensing all over. "Brandon, bed at nine." She crouched to kiss his cheek. "Remember, CeeCee's word is law."

He grinned, thinking that gave him an opening to talk CeeCee into a nine-thirty bedtime. "You can stay out as long as you want. We don't mind."

"Thank you very much." She straightened. "Don't let him lull you into complacency, CeeCee. He's tricky."

"I've got his number. Have fun." She gave a little sigh as they walked out the door.

Things were not working out according to plan, Julia thought as she crossed to the narrow, graveled drive where Paul's Studebaker was parked. First thing this morning she'd decided to spend a quiet evening working. Then she adjusted to the idea of going out, but actually to do a couple of hours of on-the-spot research, while keeping herself unobtrusively in some corner. Now she had an escort who would probably feel obliged to entertain her.

"I'm sorry Eve imposed on you this way," she began as he opened the car door for her.

"What way?"

"You might have had other plans for the evening."

He leaned on the open door, enjoying the way she slid into the car—one slim knee hooking out through the slit in the dress, shapely calves lifting, an unadored hand tucking the hem of the skirt inside. Very smooth.

"Actually, I had planned to drink too much coffee, smoke too many cigarettes, and wrestle with chapter eighteen. But . . ."

She glanced up, her eyes very serious in the lowering light. "I hate having my work time interrupted. You must feel the same way."

"Yes, I do." Though, oddly enough, he wasn't feeling that way tonight. "Then again, at times like this I have to remind myself it isn't brain surgery. The patient will rest comfortably until tomorrow." After closing the door, he rounded the hood to settle into the driver's seat. "And Eve asks me for very little."

Julia let out a quick breath as the engine sprang to life. As Eve's dress had, this car made her feel like someone else. This time a pampered, mink-wrapped debutante rushing down white marble steps to dash off with her favorite beau for a fast ride. That'll be the day, Julia thought, then said, "I appreciate this. But it wasn't really necessary. I don't need an escort."

"No, I'm sure you don't." He steered the car down the drive that veered off from the main house. "You strike me as the kind of woman who goes very competently single file. Has anyone told you it's intimidating?"

"No." She ordered herself to relax. "Do people find your competence intimidating?"

"Probably." Idly, he switched the radio on low, more for the mood than the music. She was wearing that same scent—old-fashioned romance. The air whipping through the windows offered it to him like a gift. "But then, I enjoy keeping people off balance." He shifted his head just long enough to flick her a glance. "Don't you?"

"I haven't thought about it." Imagining herself having that kind of power made her smile. A good six months out of every twelve she spent virtually alone with Brandon, divorced from people. "This affair tonight," she continued. "Do you go to many of them?"

"A few each year—usually at Eve's instigation."

"Not because you enjoy them?"

"Oh, they're entertaining enough."

"But you'd go because she asked in any case?"

Paul paused briefly, waiting for the gates of the estate to open. "Yes, I'd go for her."

Julia shifted to study his profile, seeing his father, seeing the little boy Eve had described. Seeing someone altogether different. "This morning Eve told me about the first time you met."

He grinned as he drove down the quiet, palm-lined street. "At the beach house in Malibu, over p.b. and j.'s."

"Will you share your first impressions of her?"

His grin faded as he drew a cigar out of his pocket. "Still on the clock?"

"Always. You should understand."

He punched in the lighter, then shrugged. He did understand. "All right, then. I knew a woman had spent the night. There were a few telltale items of clothing strewn around the living room." He caught her look, arched a brow. "Shocked, Jules?"

"No."

"Just disapproving."

"I'm simply imagining Brandon under the same circumstances. I wouldn't want him to think that I . . ."

"Had sex?"

The amusement made her stiffen. "That I was indiscriminate or careless."

"My father was—is—both. By the time I was Brandon's age, I was quite used to it. No lasting scars."

She wasn't so sure about that. "And when you met Eve?"

"I was prepared to dismiss her out of hand. I was quite the little cynic." Comfortable, he blew out smoke. "I recognized her when she walked into the kitchen, but I was surprised. Most of the women my father bedded looked, well, let's say worse for wear the morning after. Eve was beautiful. Of course that was just a physical thing, but it impressed me. And there was a sadness in her eyes." He caught himself and grimaced. "She won't like that. More important to me at that stage of my life was the fact that she didn't find it necessary to coo all over me as so many of them did."

Understanding perfectly, she laughed. "Brandon hates it when people pat his head and tell him what a cute little boy he is."

"It's revolting."

He said it with such feeling, she laughed again. "And you said no scars."

"I considered it more of a curse—until I hit puberty. In any case, Eve and I had a conversation. She was interested. No one can spot false interest quicker than a child, and there was nothing false about Eve. We walked on the beach, and I was able to talk to her in a way I'd never been able to talk to anyone before. The things I liked, didn't like. What I wanted, didn't want. She was amazingly good to me from that first day on, and I developed a monumental crush on her."

"Do you—"

"Hold it. We're nearly there and you've been asking all the questions." He took a lazy last drag, then tapped out his cigar. "Why celebrity bios?"

With an effort, she changed gears. "Because I don't have enough imagination for fiction."

Paul stopped at a light, drumming his fingers on the wheel in time with the music. "That answer was much too smooth to be true. Try again."

"All right. I admire people who not only tolerate but court the spotlight. Since I've always functioned better on the sidelines, I'm interested in the kind of people who thrive on center stage."

"Still smooth, Julia, and only partially true." He let the car drift forward as the light changed. "If it were really true, how do you explain the fact that you once considered a career in acting?"

"How do you know that?" Her voice was sharper than intended and pleased him. It was about time he pierced that slick outer layer.

"I made it my business to know that, and a great deal more." He shot her a look. "I do my research."

"You mean you checked up on me?" Her hands curled into fists in her lap as she struggled with temper. "My background is none of your business. My agreement is with Eve, only Eve, and I resent you poking into my private life."

"You can resent anything you want. And you can also be grateful. If I'd found anything that didn't jive, you'd be out on your sweet ass."

That snapped it. Her head whirled around. "You arrogant son of a bitch."

"Yeah." After pulling up at the Beverly Wilshire, he turned to face her. "Remember, on the drive back, I get to ask the questions." He laid a hand on her arm before she could wrench the door open. "You tear out of here and slam the door, people are going to ask questions." He watched as she strained, fighting for control, and won. "I knew you could do it. By God, you're good."

She took a deep breath, and when her face was composed again, turned to him and spoke calmly. "Fuck you, Winthrop."

His left brow shot up, but he let out a quick laugh. "Whenever you like." He climbed out and handed his keys to the valet. Julia was already on the curb. Paul took her stiff arm and led her inside. "Eve wants you to mingle," he said quietly as they filed through a press of reporters with Minicams. "There will be a lot of people here tonight who'll want to get a look at you, maybe dig out a couple of hints as to what Eve's telling you."

"I know my job," Julia said between her teeth.

"Oh, Jules, I'm sure you do." The comfortable drawl made her blood simmer. "But there are people who enjoy chewing up proper young women and spitting them out."

"It's been tried." She wanted to shake off his arm, but thought it would look undignified, particularly when she saw two reporters making a beeline for them.

"I know," Paul murmured, and deliberately took her other arm to turn her to face him. "I'm not going to apologize for prying, Julia, but you should know that what I found was admirable, and more than a little fascinating."

The contact was too intimate, almost an embrace, and she wanted to be free. "I don't want your admiration, or your fascination."

"Regardless, you have both." Then he turned a very charming smile toward the camera.

"Mr. Winthrop, is it true that Mel Gibson's been signed to play the lead in the screen version of *Chain Lightning*?"

"You'd do better to ask the producers—or Mr. Gibson." Paul urged Julia along while the reporters circled.

"Is your engagement to Sally Bowers off?"

"Don't you think that's an indelicate question when I'm escorting a beautiful woman?" As more reporters crowded in, Paul's smile remained friendly, though he felt Julia begin to tremble. "That engagement was a product of the press. Sally and I aren't even the proverbial good friends. More like passing acquaintances."

"Can we have your name?"

Someone stuck a mike under Julia's nose. She tensed, then struggled to relax. "Summers," she said calmly. "Julia Summers."

"The writer who's doing Eve Benedict's biography?" Before she could answer, other questions were hurled and kicked in her direction.

"Buy the book," she suggested, relieved when they moved into the ballroom.

Paul leaned down to speak quietly in her ear. "Are you all right?"

"Of course."

"You're shaking."

She cursed herself for it, then stepped aside, out from under his protective arm. "I don't like being crowded."

"Then it's a good thing you didn't come with Eve. You'd have been hemmed in by more than half a dozen of them." After signaling to a passing waiter, he took two glasses of champagne from the tray.

"Shouldn't we find our table?"

"My dear Jules, no one sits yet." He touched his glass to hers before sipping. "That's no way to be seen." Ignoring her shrug of protest, he slipped an arm around her waist.

"Must you always have a hand on me?" she asked under her breath.

"No." But he didn't remove it. "Now, tell me, whom would you like to meet?"

Since temper didn't make a dent, she tried ice. "There's no reason for you to entertain me. I'll be perfectly fine on my own."

"Eve would have my hide if I left you alone." He steered her through the laughter and conversation. "Particularly since she's decided to try her hand at heating up a romance."

Julia nearly choked on frothy champagne. "Excuse me?"

"You must realize she's got it into her head that if she throws us together often enough, we'll stick."

Julia looked up, inclined her head. "Isn't it a shame we have to disappoint her."

"Yes, it would be a shame."

It was obvious his intentions clashed with Julia's. She saw the challenge in his eyes, felt the sudden charge in the air. And hadn't a clue how to respond to either. He continued to smile as his gaze lowered to her mouth, lingered there, the look as physical as a kiss.

"I wonder what would happen—" A hand clamped Paul's shoulder.

"Paul. Son of a bitch, how'd they manage to drag you out here?"

"Victor." Paul's smile warmed as he grasped Victor Flannigan's hand. "It just took a couple of beautiful women."

"It always does." He turned to Julia. "And this is one of them."

"Julia Summers, Victor Flannigan."

"I recognized you." Victor took Julia's offered hand. "You're working with Eve."

"Yes." She remembered clearly the devotion, the intimacy she'd witnessed in the moonlit garden. "It's a pleasure to meet you, Mr. Flannigan. I've admired your work tremendously."

"That's a relief, especially if I manage a footnote in Eve's biography."

"How is Muriel?" Paul asked, referring to Victor's wife.

"A bit under the weather. I'm stag tonight." He held up a glass full of clear liquid and sighed. "Club soda and I tell you, these affairs are hell to get through without a couple of belts. What do you think of the gathering, Miss Summers?"

"It's too soon to tell."

"Diplomatic." Eve had told him as much. "I'll ask you again in a couple of hours. Christ knows what they'll serve. Too much to hope it'll be steak and potatoes. Can't stand that damn French stuff." He caught the understanding glint in Julia's eyes and grinned. "You can take the peasant out of Ireland, but you can't take the Irish out of the peasant." He winked at Julia. "I'll be by to claim a dance."

"I'd be delighted."

"Impressions?" Paul asked when Victor wandered off.

"So often an actor seems smaller offscreen. He only seems bigger. At the same time, I think I'd feel comfortable sitting in front of a fire with him playing canasta."

"You have excellent powers of observation." He put a finger on the side of her jaw to move her face to his. "And you've stopped being angry."

"No, I haven't. I'm saving it."

He laughed and this time swung a friendly arm around her shoulder. "Christ, Jules, I'm beginning to like you. Let's find our table. Maybe we'll eat before ten."

◆ ◆ ◆ ◆

"Goddammit, Drake, I detest being nagged." Eve's voice was impatient as she took her seat at the table, but her face was placid. She didn't choose to have the rumormongers muttering over the fact that she was sniping with her press agent.

"I wouldn't have to nag if you'd give me a straight answer." Unlike his aunt, Drake was no actor and scowled into his drink. "How am I supposed to promote something when you won't give me anything to go on?"

"There's nothing to promote at this point." She lifted a hand in salute to familiar faces at an adjoining table and shot a smile at Nina, who was laughing with a group in the center of the room. "In any case, if people know what's going to be in the book, there won't be any anticipation—or sweaty palms." Just thinking of it made her smile, and mean it. "Concentrate on pumping up this project I'm doing for television."

"The miniseries."

She winced at the word—she couldn't help it. "Just spread the news that Eve Benedict is doing a television *event*."

"It's my job to—"

"To do as I tell you," she finished. "Keep that in mind." Impatient, she finished off her champagne. "Get me another glass."

With an effort, he controlled a flurry of sharp words. He, too, knew the value of public image. Just as he knew the killing edge of Eve's temper. Seething, he rose, then spotted Julia and Paul crossing the ballroom. Julia, he thought, and his eyes cleared of resentment. He would get the information Delrickio had requested. She was the source he could tap.

"Ah, here you are." Eve lifted both hands. Julia took them, felt the slight tug and realized she was expected to lean over and kiss Eve's cheek. Feeling more than a little foolish, she complied. "And Paul." Well aware curious eyes had turned their way, Eve repeated the ceremony with her former stepson. "What a staggering couple you two make." She shot a glance over her shoulder. "Drake, make sure we all have more champagne."

Glancing up, Julia caught the tightening of his lips, the quick and lethal glint in his eye. Then it was replaced by a dazzling smile. "Nice to see you, Paul. Julia, you look lovely. Just hang on while I play waiter."

"You do look lovely," Eve said. "Has Paul been introducing you around?"

"I didn't see much need for it." Settling back, Paul scanned the room. "Once they see she's sitting with you, they'll figure it out and introduce themselves."

He was exactly right. Before Drake returned with the wine, people began to trickle over. All through dinner, Eve sat like a queen granting audience as other luminaries table-hopped, always making their way to her throne. As crème brûlée was served, a thin-haired, amazingly fat man waddled over.

Anthony Kincade, Eve's second husband, had not weathered well. In the past two decades he had put on so much weight that he resembled an unsteady mountain crammed into a tux. Each wheezing breath caused an avalanche of flab to jiggle over his stomach. The journey across the room had turned his face the bright pink of a two-day sunburn. Jowls waggled, and his trio of chins swayed in tandem.

He'd gone from being a husky, literate director of major films to an obese, wheedling director of minor ones. Most of his wealth had been amassed in the fifties and sixties in real estate. Lazy at heart, he was content to sit on his comfortable portfolio and eat.

Just looking at him made Eve shudder to think she'd been married to him for five years.

"Tony."

"Eve." He leaned heavily on her chair, waiting for air to fight its way into his lungs. "What's this crap I hear about a book?"

"I don't know, Tony. You tell me." She remembered what fine eyes he'd once had. Now they were buried under layers of flesh. His hand pressed on the back of her chair—a thick meat patty with five stubby sausages. Once those hands had been big and bruising and demanding. They had known and enjoyed every inch of her body. "You know Paul and Drake." She reached for a cigarette to coat some of the bile in her throat with smoke. "And this is Julia Summers, my biographer."

He turned. "Be careful what you write." With his breath back, his voice had a hint of the full-throated power of his youth. "I for one have enough money and enough lawyers to keep you in court for the rest of your life."

"Don't threaten the girl, Tony," Eve said mildly. It didn't surprise her that Nina had come to the table to stand silently at her other side, ready to protect. "It's rude. And remember"—she deliberately aimed a stream of smoke toward his face—"Julia can't write what I don't tell her."

He clamped a hand on Eve's shoulder, hard enough to have Paul starting out of his chair before Eve waved him down again. "Dangerous ground, Eve." Kincade sucked in another spoonful of air. "You're too old to take risks."

"I'm too old not to take them," she corrected him. "Relax, Tony, I don't intend for Julia to write a word that isn't the sterling truth." Though she was quite sure her shoulder would ache in the morning, she lifted her glass. "A good dose of honesty never hurt anyone who didn't deserve it."

"Truth or lies," he murmured. "It's a long-standing tradition to kill the messenger." With that, he left them, weaving his way through the crowd.

"Are you all right?" Nina murmured. Though she kept a placid smile on her face as she leaned over, Julia could see the concern in her eyes.

"Of course. Jesus, what a disgusting slug." Eve tossed back champagne and grimaced at her crème brûlée. The visit had ruined her appetite. "Hard to believe that thirty years ago he was a vital, interesting man." A glance at Julia made her laugh. "My dear child, I can see those literary wheels turning. We'll talk about Tony," she promised, patting Julia's hand. "Very soon."

The wheels were turning. Julia sat silently through the after-dinner talks, the comedy act, the glossy production number. Anthony Kincade hadn't been annoyed by the possibility that Eve would reveal their private marital secrets. He'd been furious. And threatening. And there was little doubt in her mind that his reaction had pleased Eve enormously.

The reactions of the men at the table had been just as telling. Paul had been ready to haul Kincade off by his flabby nape. The man's age and health would have made no difference. The flash of violence had been very real and very shocking when it had sprung from a man sipping champagne from a tulip glass and wearing a tux.

Drake had watched, taking in every detail. And he had smiled. Julia had the impression that he would have continued to sit, continued to smile if Kincade had wrapped his beefy fingers around Eve's throat.

"You're thinking too much."

Julia blinked, then focused on Paul. "What?"

"You're thinking too much," he repeated. "We'll dance." Rising, he pulled her to her feet. "I've been told when I've got my arms around a woman she finds it hard to think at all."

"How did you manage to tuck that ego in your tux without it showing?"

He joined other couples on the dance floor, then gathered Julia close. "Practice. Years of practice." He smiled down at her, pleased by the way she fit into his arms, excited by the fact that the dress dipped in the back, low enough so he could slide his hand up and touch her flesh. "You take yourself too seriously." She had the loveliest jaw, he thought. Very firm, slightly pointed. If they had been alone, he would have given himself the pleasure of taking a couple of gentle nips at it. "When you're living in fantasyland, you should go with the flow."

There was no dignified way she could tell him to stop skimming those fingers over her back. There was certainly no safe way to admit what the sensation was doing to the inside of her body. Like tiny electric currents, they set off a charge that had her blood sizzling.

She knew what it was to want. And she didn't choose to want again.

"Why do you stay here?" she asked. "You could write anywhere."

"Habit." He glanced over her shoulder toward their table. "Eve." When she started to speak again, he shook his head. "More questions. I must not be doing this right, because you're still thinking." His solution was to draw her closer so that she was forced to turn her head to avoid his mouth. "You remind me of taking tea on the terrace of an estate in the English countryside. Devon, I think."

"Why?"

"Your scent." His lips teased her ear and sent out shock waves. "Erotic, ethereal, cunningly romantic."

"Imagination," she murmured, but her eyes were drifting closed. "I'm none of those things."

"Right. A hardworking single parent with a practical bent. Why did you study poetry at Brown?"

"Because I enjoyed it." She caught herself before her fingers could tangle in the tips of his hair. "Poetry is very structured."

"Imagery, emotion, and romance." He drew back far enough to look at her, close enough that she could see her reflection captured in his eyes. "You're a fraud, Jules. A complex, fascinating fraud."

Before she could think of a response, Drake strolled up and tapped Paul's shoulder. "You don't mind sharing the wealth, do you?"

"Yes, I do." But he backed off.

"How are you settling in?" Drake asked as he picked up the rhythm of the dance.

"Fine." She felt an immediate sense of relief and wondered that she could have forgotten how different one man's arms could be from another's.

"Eve tells me you're making considerable progress. She's had an amazing life."

"Yes, putting it on paper will be a challenge."

He moved her gracefully across the floor, smiling and nodding at acquaintances. "What angle are you shooting for?"

"Angle?"

"Everyone has an angle."

She was sure he did, but merely tilted her head. "Biographies are pretty straightforward."

"The tone, then. Are you going for a year-by-year foray into the life of a star?"

"It's early to say, but I think I'll be taking the obvious approach, writing about the life of a woman who chose a demanding career and made herself a success, a lasting success. The fact that Eve is still a major force in the industry after nearly fifty years speaks for itself."

"So you'll concentrate on the professional end."

"No." He was digging, she realized, carefully but deep. "Her professional and personal lives are interlinked. Her relationships, marriage, family, are all vital to the whole. I'll need not only Eve's memories, but documented facts, opinions, anecdotes from people she was or is close to."

A different tack, he decided. "You see, Julia, I have a problem. If you could keep me abreast of the book, the content, as you went along, I'd be able to plan the press releases, the hype, and promotion." He offered her a smile. "We all want the book to be a hit."

"Naturally. I'm afraid there's little I can tell you."

"But you will cooperate as the book takes shape?"

"As much as possible."

She dismissed the conversation as the night wore on. There was still enough starry-eyed girl inside Julia to be rattled when she was asked by Victor to dance, and by other of the flesh-and-blood counterparts to the shadows that flickered on movie screens.

There were dozens of impressions and observations she wanted to write down before the evening faded to a dream. Sleepy, more relaxed than she'd thought possible, she slipped back into Paul's car at two A.M.

"You enjoyed yourself," he commented.

She lifted a shoulder. She wasn't going to let that trace of amusement in his voice spoil her evening. "Yes, why not?"

"That was a statement, not a criticism." He glanced toward her and saw that her eyes were half closed and there was a slight smile on her lips. The questions he'd wanted to ask seemed inappropriate. There would be other times. Instead, he let her doze through the ride.

By the time he pulled up in front of the guest house, she was sound asleep. With a little sigh, Paul took out a cigar and sat smoking, and watching her.

Julia Summers was a challenge. Hell, she was a paradox. There was nothing Paul liked better than tugging on the threads of a mystery. He'd intended to get close to her, to make certain Eve's best interests were protected. But . . . He smiled as he pitched the cigar out of the window. But there was no law that said he couldn't enjoy the proximity while he was at it.

He brushed a hand over her hair, and she murmured. He traced a fingertip down her cheek, and she sighed.

Thrown off by the stirring in his gut, he pulled back, tried to think it through. Then, as had been his habit most of his life, he did what he wanted to do. He covered her mouth with his as she slept.

Soft and lax in sleep, her lips yielded beneath his, slipped apart as he traced their shape with his tongue. Now he tasted her sigh as well as heard it. The punch of sensation slapped into his system, leaving him straining for more. His hands itched to touch, to take, but he curled them into fists and contented himself with her mouth.

There were some rules that weren't meant to be broken.

She was dreaming, a glorious, heavenly dream. Floating down a long, quiet river. Drifting with the current, dozing on cool blue water. The sun rained down on her in golden streams, warm, healing, compassionate.

Her mind, hazy with fatigue and wine, gave only minimal effort to clearing the mists. It was much too comfortable in dreams.

But the sun heated, the current quickened. Excitement bounced like tiny red-tipped sparks along her skin.

Her mouth moved under his, then parted on a groan so that he was invited in. Without hesitation he slid his tongue over hers and was driven half mad by her lazily seductive response. With a quiet oath he nipped her bottom lip. Julia shot awake, stunned and stirred.

"What the hell do you think you're doing?" She pushed herself back in the seat and shoved at him in one indignant move. When the heel of her hand connected with his breast bone, he realized how much stronger she was than she appeared to be.

"Satisfying my curiosity. And getting us both in trouble."

She snatched the purse off her lap but managed not to smash it into his face. Words were better. "I had no idea you were so desperate, or so lacking in conscience. Forcing yourself on a woman while she sleeps takes a special kind of perversion."

His eyes narrowed, flashed, and darkened. When he spoke, his voice was deceptively mild. "It was a long way from force, but you may have a point." Putting his hands on her shoulders, he hauled her against him. "But you're awake now."

This time his mouth wasn't soft or seducing, but hot and hard. She could taste the anger, the frustration. And desire shot like a bullet through her.

She needed. She'd forgotten what it was like to really need. To thirst for a man the way one thirsted for water. Her defenses in shambles, she was assaulted by sensations, longings, desires. The barrage left her weak enough to cling to him, hungry enough to plunge greedily into the kiss and take.

Her arms were around him, binding them together like rope. Her mouth—God, her mouth was urgent and frantic and hot. He could feel the quick, helpless tremors that coursed down her body, hear her shuddering breaths. He forgot to be angry, and frustration was ripped apart by edgy blades of passion. That left only desire.

His fingers dived into her hair, curled tight. He wanted her here, in the front seat of the car. She made him feel like a teenager fumbling for skill, like a stallion quivering to mate. And like a man rushing headlong over the verge of safety into the unknown.

"Inside." He could hear his own blood pump as his mouth raced over her face. "Let me take you inside. To bed."

When his teeth scraped lightly down her throat she nearly cried out with need. But she struggled back. Responsibility. Order. Caution. "No." She called out years of restraint, spiced with painful memories, and resisted. "This isn't what I want."

When he cupped her face in his hands, he realized he, too, was trembling. "You lie very poorly, Julia."

She had to regain control. Her fingers closed around her purse like wires as she stared at him. He looked dangerous in the moonlight. Compelling, reckless. Dangerous.

"It's not what I intend to have," she said. She reached for the door handle and jerked twice before she managed to unlatch it. "You've made a mistake, Paul." She streaked across the narrow patch of lawn and into the house.

"There's no doubt about that," he murmured.

Inside, Julia leaned against the door. She couldn't go racing upstairs in this state. Taking quiet deep breaths to settle her jackhammering heart, she turned off the light CeeCee had left burning for her and started upstairs. A peek in the spare bedroom showed her that CeeCee was asleep. In the room opposite, she looked in on her son.

That was enough to calm her, enough to assure her she had made the right choice in turning away. Needs, however tumultuous, would never be enough to make her risk what she'd built. There would be no Paul Winthrops in her life. No smooth lovers who excited, enticed, and walked away. She took a moment to tuck up Brandon's covers and smooth them before going into her own room.

The shaking started again, and she swore, tossing her purse toward the bed. It slipped off, spilling its contents. Though she was tempted to kick them around the room, she knelt and retrieved the compact, the comb, the slim wallet.

And the folded paper.

Odd, she thought. She didn't remember putting any paper inside. Once she opened it, she was forced to use the bed as a brace in order to rise.

LOOK BEFORE YOU LEAP.

Leaving the scattered contents of her purse on the floor, she sat on the bed. What the hell was this? And what the hell was she going to do about it?

Chapter Seven

◆ ◆ ◆ ◆

JULIA SAW BRANDON off to school, grateful he was tucked inside the discreet black Volvo with Lyle behind the wheel. Brandon would be safe with him.

Of course there was nothing to worry about. She'd told herself that over and over through the restless night. A couple of foolish anonymous notes couldn't hurt her—and certainly couldn't hurt Brandon. But she'd feel better once she'd gotten to the bottom of the whole business. Which was something she intended to do right away.

Her thoughts veered to how odd she felt watching her little boy drive off to his own world of classrooms and playgrounds where her control didn't reach.

When the car was out of sight, she shut the door on the early morning chill. Julia could hear CeeCee cheerfully singing along with the radio as she tidied the kitchen. Happy sounds—the rattle of dishes and the young, enthusiastic voice competing with the spice of Janet Jackson's. Julia didn't like to admit they bolstered her for the simple reason they meant she wasn't alone. She carried her half-empty cup into the kitchen for a refill of coffee.

"That was a great breakfast, Ms. Summers." Her hair scooped back in a bouncy ponytail, CeeCee wiped the counter with a damp cloth while her foot tapped the next top forty hit. "I just can't imagine someone like you cooking and all."

Still sleepy-eyed, Julia tipped more coffee in her cup. "Someone like me?"

"Well, famous and everything."

Julia grinned. It was comfortably easy to shrug off the vague weight of concern. "Almost famous. Or maybe famous by association after last night."

All big blue eyes and fresh-scrubbed face, CeeCee sighed. "Was it really great?"

Two women in a sunny kitchen, and neither of them were talking about a star-studded benefit. But of a man.

Julia thought of dancing with Paul, of waking up, unbearably stirred, with his mouth hot on hers. And yes, feeling that demand snap from him into her with a beat much more primal than any recorded music. "It was . . . different."

"Isn't Mr. Winthrop just totally gorgeous? Every time I talk to him, my mouth gets dry and my palms get wet." She closed her eyes as she rinsed the cloth clean. "Too wild."

"He's the kind of man it's difficult not to notice," Julia said, her voice wry with her own understatement.

"You're telling me. Women go crazy for him. I don't think he's ever brought the same one here twice. Stud city, you know?"

"Hmm." Julia had her own opinion of a man who would flit so arbitrarily from woman to woman. "He seems devoted to Miss Benedict."

"Sure. I guess he'd do about anything for her—except settle down and give her the grandchildren she wants." CeeCee tossed back her wispy bangs. "It's funny to think of Miss B. as a grandma."

Funny wasn't the word that came to Julia's mind. It was more like *incredible*. "How long have you worked for her?"

"Technically just a couple of years, but I've been underfoot as long as I can remember. Aunt Dottie used to let me come over on weekends, and during the summer."

"Aunt Dottie?"

"Travers."

"Travers?" Julia nearly choked on her coffee, trying to equate the stern-mouthed, suspicious-eyed housekeeper with the expansive CeeCee. "She's your aunt?"

"Yeah, my dad's big sister. Travers is like a stage name. She did some acting back in the fifties, I think. But never really hit. She's worked for Miss B. forever. Kind of weird when you figure they were married to the same man."

This time Julia had the sense to lower the coffee cup before attempting to drink. "Excuse me?"

"Anthony Kincade," CeeCee explained. "You know, the director? Aunt Dottie was married to him first." A glance at the clock had her straightening from her slouch against the counter. "Wow, I've got to go. I've got a ten o'clock class." She bolted toward the living room to gather up books and bags. "I'll be here tomorrow to change the linens. Is it okay if I bring my little brother? He really wants to meet Brandon."

Julia nodded, still trying to catch up. "Sure. We'd be glad to have him over."

CeeCee shot a grin over her shoulder as she raced for the door. "Tell me that after he's been around for a couple of hours."

Even as the door slammed, Julia was sharpening her thoughts into calculations. Anthony Kincade. That bitter mountain of flesh had been husband to both the glamorous Eve and the monosyllabic housekeeper. Curiosity sent her bolting through the living room, into her temporary office and to her reference books. For a few minutes she mumbled and swore to herself, trying to locate what never seemed to be in the last place she'd left it.

She would get organized, she would, she swore to whatever saint watched over distracted writers. Right after she satisfied her curiosity, she'd spend an hour—okay, fifteen minutes—putting everything in order.

The vow apparently worked. With a crow of triumph she pounced. She found the listing quickly in *Who's Who*.

Kincade, Anthony, she read. Born Hackensack, N.J., November 12, 1920 . . . Julia skipped over his accomplishments, his successes and failures. Married Margaret Brewster, 1942, two children, Anthony Jr. and Louise, divorced 1947. Married Dorothy Travers, 1950, one child, Thomas, deceased. Divorced 1953. Married Eve Benedict, 1954. Divorced 1959.

There were two more marriages, but they didn't interest Julia; it was too fascinating to speculate about the peculiar triangle. Dorothy Travers— and the name set off a faint bell in Julia's head—had been married to Kincade for three years, and had bore him a son. Within a year of the divorce, Kincade had married Eve. Now Travers worked as Eve's housekeeper.

How could two women who had shared the same man share the same house?

It was a question she intended to ask. But first she was going to show the anonymous notes she'd received to Eve, hope for a reaction, and perhaps an explanation. Julia pushed the reference book aside, her bargain with the long-suffering saint already forgotten.

Fifteen minutes later Travers opened the door of the main house. Studying the woman's set, dissatisfied face and paunchy build, Julia wondered how she could have attracted the same man as the stunning, statuesque Eve.

"In the gym," Travers muttered.

"Excuse me?"

"In the gym," she repeated, and led the way in her reluctant style. She turned into the east wing and headed down a corridor with many intricate wall niches, each filled with an Erte statue. To the right was a wide arched window that opened onto the central courtyard, where Julia saw the gardener, Wayfarers and headphones in place, delicately clipping the topiary.

At the end of the hall were thick double doors painted a bold teal. Travers didn't knock, but swung one open. Immediately the hallway was filled with bright, bouncy music and Eve's steady curses.

Julia would never have called the room by the lowly name *gym*. Despite the weight equipment, the slant boards, the mirrored wall and ballet barre, it was elegant. An exercise palace, perhaps, Julia mused, studying the high ceiling painted with streamlined art deco figures. Light broke through a trio of stained glass skylights in refracting, rainbow colors. Not a palace, Julia corrected herself. A temple erected to worship the smug-faced god of sweat.

The floor was a glossily polished parquet, and a gleaming smoked-glass wet bar, complete with refrigerator and microwave, took up another wall. Music cartwheeled out of a high-tech stereo system flanked by potted begonias and towering ficus trees.

Standing beside Eve as she lay on a weight bench doing leg curls was Mr. Muscle. Temporarily mesmerized, Julia let out a long breath as she looked at him. He had to be nearly seven feet—a Nordic god whose bronze body bulged out of an incredibly brief unitard. The single white band stretched low on his gleaming chest, snaked down his hips, rode high and tight over a very muscular set of buns.

His golden blond hair was pulled back in a ponytail, his ice-blue eyes smiling approval as Eve's curses turned the air a deeper, much hotter blue.

"Fuck this, Fritz."

"Five more, my beautiful flower," he said in precise, musical English that had images of cool lakes and mountain streams dancing in Julia's mind.

"You're killing me."

"I make you strong." As she huffed her way through the last of the curls, he laid a huge hand on her thigh and squeezed. "You have the muscle tone of a thirty-year-old." Then he gave her bottom an intimate little rub.

Dripping sweat, Eve collapsed. "If I ever walk again, I'm going to kick you right in your enormous crotch."

He laughed, patted her again, then grinned over at Julia. "Hello."

Barely, she managed to swallow. Eve's last comment had lured Julia's gaze down so that she'd seen for herself the adjective hadn't been an exaggeration. "I'm sorry. I don't want to interrupt."

Eve managed to open her eyes. If she'd had the energy, she would have chuckled. Most women got that slack-jawed, dazed look after their first load of Fritz. She was glad Julia wasn't immune. "Thank God. Travers, pour me something very cold—and put some arsenic in it for my friend here."

Fritz laughed again, a deep, cheerful sound that bounded easily over Eve's creative curses. "You drink a little, then we work on your arms. You don't want the skin hanging down like turkey's."

"I can come back," Julia began as Eve turned over.

"No, stay. He's almost through torturing me. Aren't you, Fritz?"

"Almost done." He took the drink Travers offered and downed it in one gulp before she had shuffled out the door. While Eve mopped her face with a towel, he studied Julia. The look in his eyes made her uneasy. Brandon's took on the same light when he was offered a nice, pliant lump of modeling clay. "You have good legs. You work out?"

"Well, no." A dastardly admonition in southern California, she realized. People had been hanged for less. She was wondering if she should apologize, when he crossed to her and began to feel her arms. "Hey, look—"

"Skinny arms." Her mouth fell open when he ran his hands over her stomach. "Good abs. We can fix you up."

"Thank you." He had fingers like rods of iron, and she didn't want to rile him. "But I really don't have time."

"You must make time for your body," he said so seriously, she swallowed the nervous laugh. "You come on Monday, I start you off."

"I really don't think—"

"An excellent idea," Eve put in. "I hate to be tortured alone." She grimaced as Fritz set the weights on the Nautilus for her arm work. "Have a seat, Julia. You can talk to me and take my mind off my misery."

"Monday, my ass," Julia muttered.

"I beg your pardon?"

She smiled as Eve got in the next position for pain. "I said I wonder if the weather will last."

Eve, who had heard her very well the first time, merely lifted a brow. "That's what I thought you said." Once she was settled, Eve took a cleansing breath and began to pull the weights toward the center of her body, and out. "You enjoyed yourself last night?"

"Yes, thank you."

"So polite." She shot a grin at Fritz. "She wouldn't swear at you."

Julia watched Eve's muscles bunch and strain. Sweat was popping out again. "Oh yes I would."

Eve laughed even as the effort slicked wet down her flesh. "You know the trouble with being beautiful, Julia? Everyone notices the least little flaw—they relish finding them. So you have to maintain." Straining at the tense and flow of her own muscles, she sucked in air and puffed it out. "Like a religion. I'm determined to do the best I can for the body God and the surgeons have given me. And not give anyone the satisfaction of saying she was beautiful—once." She broke off to swear for a moment while her arms throbbed. "Some people claim to be addicted to this. I can only think they're very, very sick. How many more?" she asked Fritz.

"Twenty."

"Bastard." But she didn't slacken pace. "What are your impressions from last night?"

"That a very high percentage of the people there cared as much about the charity as they did the publicity. That new Hollywood will never have quite the same class as old Hollywood. And that Anthony Kincade is an unpleasant and potentially dangerous man."

"I wondered if you'd be easily dazzled. Apparently not. How many more, you son of a bitch?"

"Five."

Eve swore her way through them, panting like a woman in the last throes of childbirth. The more vicious her oaths, the wider Fritz's grin. "Wait here," she ordered Julia, then groaned to her feet and disappeared through a door.

"She is a lovely woman," Fritz commented. "Strong."

"Yes." But when she tried to imagine herself pumping iron as she cruised toward seventy, Julia shuddered. She'd damn well take her flab and like it. "You don't think all this might be too much, considering her age?"

He lifted a brow as he glanced toward the door where Eve had gone. He knew if she had heard that, she would do a great deal more than swear. "For someone else, yes. Not for Eve. I am a personal trainer. This program is for her body, for her mind. For her spirit. All three are strong." He moved toward one of the windows. Beside it was a massage table and a shelf cluttered with oils and lotions. "For you I design something different."

That was a subject she wanted to veer away from. And quickly. "How long have you been her personal trainer?"

"Five years." After choosing his oils, he used the remote to change the music. Now it was classical, soothing strings. "She has brought me many clients. But if I had only one, I would want Eve."

He said her name almost reverently. "She inspires loyalty."

"She is a great lady." He passed a tiny bottle under his nose and reminded Julia of the bull, Ferdinand, smelling flowers. "You're writing her book."

"Yes, I am."

"You be sure to say she is a great lady."

Eve came back in, wrapped in a short white robe, her hair damp, her face pink and glowing. Without a word she walked over to the table, stripped as carelessly as a child, and stretched out on her stomach. Fritz draped a sheet modestly over her hips and went to work.

"After hell comes heaven." Eve sighed. She propped her chin on her fists and her eyes glowed into Julia's. "You may want to include that I put myself through this hideous business three times a week. And while I hate every minute of it, I know it's kept my body looking good enough that Nina has to turn down an annual offer from *Playboy,* and my endurance up so that I can endure a ten- or twelve-hour shoot without collapsing. In fact, I'm stealing Fritz away when I go to Georgia on location. The man has the best hands on five continents."

He blushed like a boy at the compliment.

While Fritz used those hands to knead and relax Eve's muscles, Julia centered the conversation on health, exercise, and daily routine. She waited, patient, while Eve slipped back into her robe and exchanged a very warm, very intimate kiss with her trainer. Julia thought of the scene she'd witnessed in the garden and wondered how a woman so obviously in love with one man could flirt so blatantly with another.

"Monday," he said with a nod at Julia as he tugged on sweats. "I start your program."

"She'll be here," Eve promised before Julia could politely decline. She was grinning as Fritz hefted his gym bag and strode out the door. "Consider it part of your research," Eve advised. "Well, what did you think of him?"

"Was I drooling?"

"Only a little." Eve flexed her limbered muscles, then slipped a pack of cigarettes from her robe pocket. "Christ, I'm dying for one of these. I don't have the heart—or maybe it's the nerve—to smoke around Fritz. Fix us another drink, will you? Heavy on the champagne in mine."

While Julia rose to obey, Eve took a deep, hungry drag. "I can't think of another man in the world I'd give these up for, even for a few hours." She blew out another stream of smoke as Julia offered a glass. Her laugh was quick and rich, as if at a private joke. "The longer I know you, the easier you are to read, Julia. Right now you're struggling not to be judgmental, wondering how I justify an affair with a man young enough to be my son."

"It's not my job to be judgmental."

"No, it's not, and you're bound and determined to do your job. Just for the record, I wouldn't attempt to justify it, but merely to enjoy it. As it happens, I'm not having an affair with that fabulous slice of beefcake, because he's quite obstinately gay." She laughed and sipped again. "Now you're shocked and telling yourself not to be."

Uncomfortable, Julia shifted and sipped her own drink. "The purpose of this is for me to explore your feelings, not for you to explore mine."

"It works both ways." Eve slipped off the table to curl like a cat into a deeply cushioned rattan chair. Every movement was sinuously feminine, seductive. It occurred to Julia that young Betty Berenski had chosen her name well. She was all woman—as ageless and mysterious as the first. "Before this book is finished, you and I will know each other as well as two people are able to. More intimately than lovers, more completely than parent and child. As we come to trust each other, you'll understand the purpose."

To put things back on the level she preferred, Julia took out her recorder and pad. "What reason would I have not to trust you?"

Eve smiled through a veil of smoke. Secrets, ripe as plums for picking, glistened in her eyes. "What reason indeed? Go ahead, Julia, ask the questions that are buzzing around in that head of yours. I'm in the mood to answer them."

"Anthony Kincade. Why don't you tell me how you came to marry him, and how his second wife went from making B movies to working as your housekeeper?"

Rather than answering, Eve smoked and considered. "You've been questioning CeeCee."

There was a trace of annoyance in the statement, enough to give Julia a tug of satisfaction. Maybe they would reach a level of trust and intimacy, but it would be on equal terms. "Talking to her, certainly. If there was something you didn't want her to tell me, you neglected to mention it to her." When Eve remained silent, Julia tapped her pencil on her pad. "She commented this morning that she'd often spent time here as a child, visiting her Aunt Dottie. Naturally, it came out who Aunt Dottie was."

"And you took it from there."

"It's my job to follow up information," Julia said mildly, not only registering the growing irritation, but relishing it. Petty perhaps, she reflected, but satisfying to know that she'd finally chipped under that glossy guard.

"You had only to ask me."

"That's precisely what I'm doing now." Julia tilted her head, and the angle was as much a challenge as a pair of raised fists. "If you wanted to keep secrets, Eve, you chose the wrong biographer. I don't work with blinders on."

"It's my story." Eve's eyes sliced like twin green scythes. Julia felt the keen edge and refused to dodge.

"Yes, it is. And by your own choice, it's mine too." She had her teeth into it now, her jaws snapped tight, like a wolf's over a fleshy bone. Her will rose up to tangle with Eve's, muscles flexed. Nerves smoldered like bright embers in her stomach. "If you want someone who'll bow when you pull the strings, we'll stop this now. I'll go back to Connecticut and we'll let our lawyers hash it out." She started to rise.

"Sit down." Eve's voice quivered with temper. "Sit down, dammit. You made your point."

With an acknowledging nod, Julia settled again. Surreptitiously she slipped a hand into her pocket and thumbed free a Tums from its roll. "I'd prefer to make yours, but that won't be possible if you block me whenever I touch on something that discomfits you."

Eve was silent a moment, silent while temper faded into grudging respect. "I've lived a long time," she said at length. "I'm used to doing things my own way. We'll see, Julia, we'll see if we can find a way to merge your way with mine."

"Fair enough." She slipped the tablet onto her tongue, hoping that it and the small victory would soothe her jittery stomach.

Eve lifted the glass to her lips, sipped, and prepared to open a long-locked and rusted door. "Tell me what you know."

"It was simple enough to check out the fact that Dorothy Travers was Kincade's second wife, whom he divorced only months before marrying you. I couldn't quite place her at first, but I've remembered she made a dozen or so Bs in the fifties. Gothics and horror films mostly, until she dropped out of sight. I can only assume now, to work for you."

"Nothing's quite as straight-lined as that." Though it continued to irritate that she hadn't stated the connection first, Eve shrugged and expanded. "She came to work for me a few months after Tony and I finalized our divorce. That would be, Christ, over thirty years ago. You find that strange?"

"That two women could have a lasting and close relationship for three decades after being in love with the same man?" Tension was crowded aside by interest. "I suppose I do."

"Love?" Eve smiled as she stretched luxuriously. She always felt luxurious after a session with Fritz. Purged, pumped, and primed. "Oh, Travers may have loved him briefly. But Tony and I married for mutual lust and ambition. An entirely different thing. He was rather gorgeous in those days. A big, strapping man, and more than a little wicked. When he directed me in *Separate Lives,* his marriage was falling apart."

"He and Travers had a child who died."

Eve hesitated, then sipped her drink. Perhaps Julia had pushed her into a corner, but there was only one way to tell the story. Her way. "The loss of the child destroyed the foundation of their marriage. Travers couldn't, wouldn't forget. Tony was determined to. He'd always been completely self-absorbed. It was part of his charm. I didn't know all the details when we began to see each other. It—our affair and resulting marriage—was a minor scandal at the time."

Julia had already made a note to look up back issues of *Photoplay* and the *Hollywood Reporter*.

"Travers wasn't a big enough star to warrant a lot of sympathy or outrage. You find that arrogant," Eve observed. "It's simply truthful. That small triangle took up some space in a few columns, then was forgotten. People took it much more personally when Taylor scooped Eddie Fisher up from under Debbie Reynolds." Finding that amusing, she tapped out her cigarette. "Actually I may or may not have been the straw that broke the back of their marriage."

"I'll ask Travers."

"I'm sure you will." She made a fluid gesture with her hands, then settled again. "It's unlikely she'll speak to you, but go right ahead. For the moment, it might be helpful if I started at the beginning, my beginning with Tony. As I said, he was a very attractive man, dangerously so. I had a great deal of respect for him as a director."

"You met when you made *Separate Lives*?"

"Oh, we'd run into each other before—as people do in this small ship of fools. But a movie set, Julia, is a tiny, intimate world, divorced from reality. No, immune to it." She smiled to herself. "Fantasy, however difficult the work, is its own addiction. Which is why so many of us delude ourselves into believing we've fallen desperately in love with another character in that shiny bubble—for the length of time it takes to create a film."

"You didn't fall for your costar," Julia said. "But your director."

Her lashes lowered, hooding her eyes as she took herself back. "It was a difficult movie, very dark, very draining. The story of a doomed marriage, betrayal, adultery, and emotional breakdown. We'd spent all day on the scene where my character had finally acknowledged her husband's infidelity and is contemplating suicide. I was to strip down to a black lace slip, carefully paint my lips, dab on perfume. Turn on the radio to dance, alone. Open a bottle of champagne and drink, in candlelight, while I swallow one sleeping pill after another."

"I remember the scene," Julia murmured. In the brightly lit room smelling of sweat and perfumed oils, it played vividly through her mind. "It was terrifying, tragic."

"Tony wanted excitement, almost an exaltation along with despair. Take after take, he was never satisfied. It felt as though my emotions were being ripped out, raw and bleeding, then ground to dust. Hour after hour, that same scene. After I looked at the rushes, I saw that he'd gotten exactly what he'd wanted from me. The exhaustion, the rage, the misery, and that light that comes in the eyes from hatred."

She smiled then, in triumph. It had been, and was still, one of her finest moments onscreen. "When we wrapped, I went to my dressing room. My hands were shaking. Shit, my soul was shaking. He came in after me, locked the door. God, I remember how he looked, standing there, his eyes burning into mine. I screamed and wept, spewed out enough venom to kill ten men. When he grabbed me, I struck him. And I drew blood. He ripped my robe. I scratched and bit. He pulled me to the floor, tearing that black lace slip to shreds, still never, never saying a word. Good Jesus, we came together like a pair of wild dogs."

Julia had to swallow. "He raped you."

"No. It would be easier to lie and say he did, but by the time we landed on the floor of the dressing room I was more than willing. I was manic. If I hadn't been willing, he would have raped me. There was something incredibly exciting in knowing that. Perverted," she added as she lit another cigarette, "but damned arousing. Our relationship was twisted, right from the start. But for the first three years of our marriage, it was the best sex I've ever had. It was almost always violent, almost always on the edge of something unspeakable."

Laughing a little, she rose to fix herself another drink. "Well, after my five years of marriage to Tony, nothing, no one, will shock me again. I had considered myself quite knowledgeable. . . ." Lips pursed, Eve poured champagne to within a breath of the rim, then poured a glass of the same for Julia. "It's lowering to admit I went into that marriage as innocent as a lamb. He was a connoisseur of the deviant, of things that weren't even spoken of back then. Oral sex, anal sex, bondage, S and M, voyeurism. Tony had a closetful of wicked little toys. I found some of them amusing, some of them revolting, and some of them erotic. Then there were the drugs."

Eve sipped enough of the drink to keep the wine from lapping over the glass as she walked. Julia took the second glass when it was offered. Right here, right now, it didn't seem so odd to drink champagne before lunch.

"Tony was way ahead of his time on drugs. He enjoyed hallucinogenics. I dabbled in them myself, but they never held much appeal for me. But in all things Tony was a glutton, and he overused. Food, drink, drugs, sex. Wives."

This memory was ripping at her, Julia realized, and discovered she wanted to protect. They'd had their war of wills, but she disliked when victory caused pain. "Eve, we don't have to go into all this now."

Making the effort, Eve shrugged off the tension, lowering herself into a chair as lithely as a cat curling on a rug. "How do you go into a pool of cold water, Julia? Inch by inch or all at once."

A smile fluttered over her lips, into her eyes. "Headfirst."

"Good." Eve took another sip, wanting a clean taste in her throat before she dived. "The beginning of the end was the night he locked me to the bed. Velvet handcuffs. Nothing we hadn't done before, enjoyed before. Shocked?"

Julia couldn't imagine what it would be like—to be that helpless, to put herself totally in the hands of another. Was bondage synonymous with trust? Nor could she imagine a woman like Eve willing to subjugate herself. Still, she shrugged. "I'm not a prude."

"Of course you are. That's one of the things I like best about you. Under all that sophistication beats the heart of a puritan. Don't be annoyed," Eve said with a dismissive wave. "It's refreshing."

"And I thought it was insulting."

"Not at all. Shall I warn you, young Julia, that when a woman tumbles to a man sexually, really tumbles, she will do things that would make her tremble with shame in the light of day? Even as she pants to do them again." She sat back regally, cupping the glass in both hands. "But enough womanly wisdom—you'll find out for yourself. If you're lucky."

If she was lucky, Julia thought, her life would go on just as it was. "You were telling me about Anthony Kincade."

"Yes, I was. He liked, ah, I suppose we'll call them costumes. That night he wore a black leather loincloth and a silk mask. He was putting on weight by that time, so a bit of the effect was lost. He lit candles, black ones. And incense. Then rubbed oil over my body until it was glistening and throbbing. He did things to me, wonderful things, stopping just short of giving me release. And when I was half mad for him—Christ, for anyone—he got up and opened the door. He let in a young boy."

Eve paused to drink. When she spoke again, her voice was cold and flat. "He couldn't have been more than sixteen, seventeen. I remember swearing at Tony, threatening, even pleading while he undressed that child. While he touched him with those wickedly clever hands. I discovered that even after nearly four years of being married to a man like Tony, I was still innocent in some things, still capable of being appalled. Because I couldn't stand to watch what they were doing to each other, I closed my eyes. Then Tony brought the boy to me and told him to do what he wanted, while he watched. I realized that the boy was far less innocent than I. He used me in every possible way a woman can be used. While the boy was still in me, Tony knelt behind him, and . . ." Her hand wasn't steady as she lifted her cigarette, but her voice was curt. "And we had a three-way fuck. It went on for hours, with them endlessly switching positions. I stopped swearing, pleading, crying, and started planning. After the boy left and Tony let me go, I waited until he fell asleep. I went downstairs and got the biggest carving knife I could find. When Tony woke up, I was holding his cock in one hand, the knife in the other. I told him if he ever touched me again, I would castrate him, that we were going to get a quick, quiet divorce and that he was going to agree to give me the house, all its contents as well as the Rolls, the Jag, and the little hideaway we'd bought in the mountains. If he didn't agree, I was going to whack him off right then and there like he'd never been whacked off before." Remembering the way he'd looked, the way he'd babbled made her smile. Until she glanced over at Julia.

"There's no need for tears," she said quietly as they streamed down Julia's cheeks. "I got my payment."

"There is no payment for that." Her voice was husky with a rage she could only imagine. Her eyes shone with it. "There couldn't be."

"Maybe not. But seeing it in print, at least there'll be revenge. I've waited for it long enough."

"Why?" Julia brushed tears away with the back of her hand. "Why did you wait?"

"The truth?" Eve sighed and finished off her drink. Her head was beginning to throb, and she bitterly resented it. "Shame. I was ashamed that I had been used that way, humiliated that way."

"You'd been used. You had nothing to be ashamed of."

The long black lashes fluttered down. It was the first time she had spoken of that night—not the first time she'd relived it, but the only time she hadn't relived it alone. It hurt still; she hadn't known it could. Nor had she known how cooling, how healing unconditional compassion could be.

"Julia." The lashes lifted again, and beneath them her eyes were dry. "Do you really believe there's no shame in being used?"

Faced with that, Julia could only shake her head. She, too, had been used. Not so hideously, not so horribly, but she understood that shame could nip at the heels like a dog for years. And years. "I don't know how you stopped yourself from using the knife, or using the story."

"Survival," Eve said simply. "At that point of my life I didn't want the story to come out any more than Tony did. Then there was Travers. I went to see her a few weeks after the divorce, after I'd discovered several reels of film Tony had hidden. Not only of him and me in various sexual stunts, but of him and other men, of him and two very young girls. It made me realize that my entire marriage had been a sickness. I think I went to her to prove to myself that someone else had been fooled, taken in, seduced. She was living alone in a little apartment downtown. The money Tony was ordered to pay her every month barely covered the rent after her other expenses. Those other expenses being the institutional care for her son."

"Her son?"

"The child Tony insisted that the world believe was dead. His name is Tommy. He's seriously retarded, an imperfection Tony refused to accept. He prefers to consider the child dead."

"All those years?" A new kind of rage worked in Julia now, had her pushing up out of the chair, striding to one of the windows where the air might be cleaner. "He turned his back on his son, kept it turned all these years?"

"He isn't the first or last to do that, is he?"

Julia turned back. She recognized the sympathy, the understanding, and automatically closed off. "That choice was mine as well, and I wasn't married to Brandon's father. Travers was married to Tommy's."

"Yes, she was—and Tony already had two perfectly healthy and perfectly spoiled children by his first wife. He chose not to acknowledge a child with flaws."

"You should have sliced his balls off."

"Ah, well." Eve smiled again, pleased to see anger rather than unhappiness. "My chance for that is lost, at least literally."

"Tell me about Travers's son."

"Tommy's nearly forty. He's incontinent, can't dress himself or feed himself. He wasn't expected to live to adulthood, but then, it's his mind, not his body."

"How could she have said her own son was dead?"

"Don't condemn her, Julia." Eve's voice had gentled. "She suffered. Travers agreed to Tony's demands because she was afraid of what he might do to the child. And because she blames herself for Tommy's condition. She's convinced the, let's say, unhealthy sexual practices under which the boy was conceived are to blame for his retardation. Nonsense, of course, but she believes it. Maybe she needs to. In any case, she refused what she considered charity, but agreed to work for me. She's done so for more than three decades, and I've kept her secret."

No, Julia thought, she didn't condemn her. She understood too well the choices a woman alone had to make. "You've kept it until now."

"Until now."

"Why do you want this made public?"

Eve settled back in her chair. "There's nothing Tony can do to the boy, or to Travers. I've seen to that. My marriage to him is part of my life, and I've decided to share that life—without lies, Julia."

"If he becomes aware of what you've told me, of the possibility of it being published, he'll try to stop you."

"I stopped being afraid of Tony a lifetime ago."

"Is he capable of violence?"

Eve moved her shoulders. "Everyone's capable of violence."

Saying nothing, Julia reached into her briefcase and brought out the pair of notes. She handed them to Eve. On reading them, Eve paled a little. Then her eyes darkened and lifted.

"Where did you get these?"

"One was left on the front stoop of the guest house. The other was slipped into my bag sometime last night."

"I'll take care of it." She pushed them into the pocket of her robe. "If you receive more, give them to me."

Slowly, Julia shook her head. "Not good enough. They were meant for me, Eve, so I'm entitled to some answers. Am I to consider them threats?"

"I'd consider them more pitiful warnings issued by a coward."

"Who could have left one on the stoop?"

"That's something I have every intention of finding out."

"All right." Julia had to respect the tone, and the gleam in Eve's eyes. "Tell me this. Is there anyone besides Anthony Kincade who would be unnerved enough about this biography to write these notes?"

Now Eve smiled. "Oh, my dear Julia. There are indeed."

Chapter Eight

♦ ♦ ♦ ♦

EVE DIDN'T OFTEN THINK of Tony, and that period of her life when she had enslaved herself to the darker side of sex. It had been, after all, only five years out of her sixty-seven. She had certainly made other mistakes, done other deeds, enjoyed other pleasures. It was the book, the project she had instigated, that had her reviewing her life in segments. Like pieces of film in an editing room. But with this drama she wasn't about to let any clips end up on the cutting-room floor.

All of it, she thought as she downed medication with mineral water. Every scene, every take. Damn the consequences.

She rubbed the center of her forehead where the pain seemed to gather tonight like a bunched fist. She had time, enough time. She would make sure of it. Julia could be trusted to do the job—had to be trusted. Closing her eyes a moment, Eve willed the medication to kick in and gloss over the worst of the pain.

Julia. . . . Concentrating on the other woman eased her as much as the drugs she took in secret. Julia was competent, quick-witted, packed with integrity. And compassion. Eve still wasn't certain how she felt about seeing those tears. She hadn't expected empathy, only shock and perhaps disapproval. She hadn't expected to have her own heart twisted.

That was her own arrogance, she reflected. She'd been so certain she could direct the writing of the script and have all the characters take up their assigned roles. Julia. . . . Julia and the boy didn't quite fit the parts Eve had cast them in. How the hell could she have anticipated she would begin to care where she had expected only to use?

Then there were the notes. Eve spread them out on her dressing table to study them. Two for her, and two for Julia, so far. All four were in the same block letters, all four trite sayings that could be construed as warnings. Or threats.

Hers had amused her, even encouraged her. After all, she was far beyond the point where anyone could hurt her. But the warnings to Julia changed things. Eve had to find out who was writing them, and put a stop to it.

Her hard, coral-colored nails tapped on the rosewood table. So many people didn't want her to tell her tales. Wouldn't it be interesting, wouldn't it be plain good fun to put as many of those people as possible under the same roof at the same time?

At a knock on her bedroom door Eve swept all of the notes into a drawer of the dressing table. For now they were her secret. Hers and Julia's.

"Come in."

"I've brought you some tea," Nina said as she walked in with a tray. "And a few letters you need to sign."

"Just set the tea by the bed. I've got a couple of scripts to look at yet tonight."

Nina set the Meissen pot and cup on the nightstand. "I thought you were taking some time off after the miniseries."

"Depends." Eve took up the pen Nina had brought and dashed her looping signature on the letters without bothering to read them. "Tomorrow's schedule?"

"Right here." Always efficient, Nina opened a leather-bound day book. "You have a nine o'clock appointment at Armando's for the works, one o'clock lunch at Chasen's with Gloria DuBarry."

"Ah, yes, hence the works at Armando's." Eve grinned and opened a pot of moisturizer. "Wouldn't want the old bat to spot any new wrinkles."

"You know you're very fond of Miss DuBarry."

"Naturally. And since she'll be eyeing me over her scrawny salad, I have to look good. When two women of a certain age dine together, Nina, it's not only for comparisons, but for reassurance. The better I look, the more relieved Gloria will be. The rest?"

"Drinks with Maggie at four. Polo Lounge. Then you're entertaining Mr. Flannigan here for dinner, at eight."

"See that the cook prepares manicotti."

"Already done." She closed the book. "And she's making zabaglione for dessert."

"You're a treasure, Nina." Eve studied her own face as she swooped the cream up over her throat, her cheeks, her brow. "Tell me, how soon can we put together a party?"

"Party?" Frowning, Nina opened the book again. "What sort?"

"A large sort. An extravagant sort. Say, two hundred people. Black tie. An orchestra on the lawn, dinner and dancing under the stars. Gushers of champagne—oh, and a few well-heeled members of the press."

Even as she did mental calculations, Nina flipped through the book. "I suppose if I had a couple of months—"

"Sooner."

Nina let out a long breath as she thought of frantic calls to caterers, florists, musicians. Well, if she could rent an island she could do a black tie in under two months. "Six weeks." She noted Eve's expression and sighed. "All right, three. We'll slide it in right before you leave for location."

"Good. We'll go over the guest list Sunday."

"What's the occasion?" Nina asked, still scribbling in the book.

"The occasion." Eve smiled as she sat back. In the lighted mirror of the dressing table her face was strong, stunning, and smug. "We'll call it an opportunity to relive and revive memories. An Eve Benedict retrospective. Old friends, old secrets, old lies."

Out of habit Nina walked over to pour the tea Eve had forgotten. It wasn't done in the manner of an employee, but as a longtime relation used to caring for others. "Eve, why are you determined to stir up trouble this way?"

With the deft skill of an artist, Eve dabbed lotion around her eyes. "Life's so deadly dull without it."

"I'm serious." Nina set the cup on the dressing table, among Eve's lotions and creams. The scent of the room was pure female, not floral or fussy, but mysterious and erotic. "You know—well, I've already told you how I feel. And now . . . Anthony Kincade's reaction the other night really worried me."

"Tony's not worth a moment's worry." She patted Nina's hand before picking up her tea. "He's slime," she said mildly, drawing in the subtle scent and taste of jasmine. "And it's more than past time someone told what perversions he's tucked in that monstrous body of his."

"But there are other people."

"Oh, yes, there are." She laughed, thinking of several with pleasure. "My life's been a crazy quilt of events and personalities. All those clever half truths, genuine lies, threading through a fascinating cover, intersecting, linking. The interesting thing is, when you pull one thread, the whole pattern changes. Even the good you do has consequences, Nina. I'm more than ready to face them."

"Not everyone is as ready as you."

Eve sipped her tea, watching Nina over the rim of the cup. When she spoke again, her voice was kinder. "The truth isn't nearly as destructive when it hits the light as a lie that's hidden in the dark." She squeezed Nina's hand. "You shouldn't worry."

"Some things are better left alone," Nina insisted.

Eve sighed and set the tea aside. "Trust me. I have reasons for doing what I'm doing."

Nina managed a nod and a thin smile. "I hope so." She picked up her day book again and started out. "Don't read too late. You need your rest."

After the door shut, Eve looked at her reflection again. "I'll have plenty of rest, soon enough."

♦ ♦ ♦ ♦

JULIA SPENT most of Saturday huddled over her work. Brandon was entertained by CeeCee and her young brother, Dustin, referred to by his sister as "mondo brat." He was the perfect compliment for Brandon's more internal nature. He said whatever he thought the instant it struck his brain. Without a shy bone in his body, he had no trouble asking, demanding, questioning. Where Brandon could play for hours in absolute and often intense silence, Dustin believed it wasn't fun unless it was loud.

From her office on the first floor, Julia could hear them bashing and banging in the upstairs bedroom. Whenever it came too close to destructive, CeeCee would shout out from whatever space she was dusting and tidying.

It wasn't easy to balance the everyday sounds of children playing, the hum of a vacuum cleaner, the bright beat of the music on the radio with the vileness of the story Julia transcribed from tape.

She hadn't expected ugliness. How to handle it? Eve wanted the unvarnished truth published. Her own insistence on it was the hallmark of her work. Still, was it necessary, or even wise, to dredge up things so painful and so damaging?

It would sell books, she thought with a sigh. But at what cost? She had to remind herself that it wasn't her job to censor, but to tell the story of this woman's life, good and bad, tragedy and triumph.

Her own hesitation annoyed her. Whom was she protecting? Certainly not Anthony Kincade. As far as Julia was concerned, he deserved much, much more than the embarrassment and disgrace the written story would bring to him.

Eve. Why did she feel this need to protect a woman she barely knew and didn't yet understand? If the story was written as Eve had retold it, she wouldn't emerge undamaged. Hadn't she admitted to being attracted to that darker, graceless aspect of sex? To being a willing, even eager participant up until that last terrible night. Would people forgive the queen of the screen for that, or for dabbling in drugs?

Perhaps they would. More to the point, Julia mused, Eve didn't seem to care. There had been no apology in the retelling, nor any bid for sympathy. As a biographer, it was Julia's responsibility to tell the story, and to add insights, opinions, feelings. Her instincts told her that Eve's marriage to Kincade had been one of the experiences that had forged her into the woman she was today.

The book would not be complete or truthful without it.

She forced herself to listen to the tape one more time, making notes on tone of voice, pauses, hesitations. She added her own recollections on how often Eve had sipped from her glass, lifted her cigarette. How the light had come in through the windows, how the smell of sweat had lingered.

This part had to be told in Eve's voice, Julia decided. Straight dialogue, so that the matter-of-fact tone would add poignancy. She spent almost three hours on this chapter, then went into the kitchen. She wanted to divorce herself from the scene, the memory that was so vivid it seemed too much her own. Since the kitchen was spotless, she couldn't lose herself in the mindless task of cleaning, so she opted to cook.

Domestic chores never failed to soothe her. During the first few weeks after she'd discovered she was pregnant, Julia had spent endless hours with a cloth and lemon oil patiently, persistently, polishing furniture and woodwork. Of course, clothes had been scattered around her room, shoes lost in the closet. But the furniture had gleamed. Later, she had realized that the monotony of the simple chore had saved her from more than one bout of hysteria.

It was then she had decided, quite calmly, against abortion or adoption, both of which she had seriously, painfully considered. More than ten years later, she knew the choice, for her, had been the right one.

Now she put together one of Brandon's favorite dishes. Homemade pizza that he had come to take for granted. The extra time and trouble helped her deal with the guilt she often felt during those weeks she was away on tour, and more, for all the times when a book was so involving and immediate that she could do no better than a quick combination of soup and sandwich.

She set the dough aside to rise and began to make the sauce. While she worked she thought of her home in the East. Would her neighbor remember to knock the snow off the yews and junipers? Would she be back in time to start sweet peas and larkspur from seed? Could she manage this spring to get that puppy Brandon so desperately wanted?

Would the nights be as lonely when she returned as they were beginning to be here?

"Something smells good."

Startled, she glanced toward the kitchen doorway. There was Paul, leaning comfortably against the jamb, his hands in the pockets of snug, faded jeans, a friendly smile on his face. Instantly she was as tense as he was relaxed. Perhaps he had already forgotten the fevered embrace enjoyed at their last meeting. But it had left a mark on Julia.

"CeeCee let me in," he said when Julia remained silent. "I see you've met Dustin, the crown prince of chaos."

"It's nice for Brandon to have a friend his own age." Stiffly, she went back to stirring the sauce.

"Everyone needs a friend," Paul murmured. "I know that look." Though her back was to him, she heard the smile in his voice as he came into the room. "You're waiting for an apology for my . . . ungentlemanly behavior the other night." Casually, he brushed fingertips down the length of her neck, exposed as her hair was swept up in an untidy bun. "I can't accommodate you there, Jules."

She shrugged off his hand in a move she knew was bad tempered. "I'm not looking for an apology." Her brows were drawn together as she glanced over her shoulder. "What are you looking for, Paul?"

"Conversation, companionship." He leaned closer to the pot and sniffed. "Maybe a hot meal."

When he turned his head, his face was inches from hers. There were twin lights of humor and challenge in his eyes. Damn him, that quick spear of heat jabbed right into her midsection.

"And," he added, "whatever else I can get."

She jerked her head around. The spoon clanged against the pot. "I'd think all of those things would be available to you elsewhere."

"Sure. But I like it here." In a move too smooth to be threatening, he put his hands on the stove, effectively caging her. "It's good for my ego to see just how nervous I make you."

"Not nervous," she said, having no compunction about the lie. "Annoyed."

"Either way. It's a reaction." He smiled, amused by the knowledge that she would go on stirring the sauce from now until Armageddon rather than turn and chance being caught in his arms. Unless he made her mad enough. "The problem with you, Jules, is you're too uptight to take a kiss at face value."

Her teeth set. "I am not uptight."

"Sure you are." He sniffed at her hair, deciding it was every bit as enticing as the bubbling herbs. "I did my research, remember? I couldn't find one man you've been linked to seriously in the past decade."

"My personal life is just that. However many men I've chosen to include in that life is none of your damn business."

"Exactly. But it's so fascinating that the number is zero. My dear Julia, don't you know there's nothing more tempting to a man than a woman who holds her passion on a choke chain? We tell ourselves we'll be the one to make her lose her grip." Adroitly, he touched his mouth to hers in a brief, arrogant kiss that infuriated rather than stirred. "I can't resist."

"Try harder," she suggested, and nudged him aside.

"I thought about that." There was a bowl of plump green grapes on the counter. He plucked one and popped it into his mouth. It wasn't the taste he wanted, but it would do. For now. "Trouble is, I like giving in to impulse. You have such pretty feet."

With a cookie sheet in one hand she turned to stare at him. "What?"

"Whenever I stop by unexpectedly, you're barefoot." He leered at her feet. "I had no idea that naked toes could be arousing."

She didn't mean to laugh—certainly didn't want to. But it bubbled out. "If it'll help things, I'll start wearing thick socks and heavy shoes."

"Too late now." She began to grease the sheet in deft, housewifely moves he found incredibly seductive. "I'd only fantasize about what's underneath. Are you going to tell me what you're making?"

"Pizza."

"I thought that came frozen or in a cardboard box."

"Not around here."

"If I promise not to nibble on your very attractive toes, will you ask me to lunch?"

She considered, weighing the pros and cons as she preheated the oven, then sprinkled flour on a wooden board. "I'll ask you to lunch if you agree to answer a few questions honestly."

He sniffed the sauce again, then gave in to temptation and sampled a bit from the wooden spoon. "Done. Do we get pepperoni?"

"All that and more."

"I don't suppose you'd have a beer."

She began to knead the dough, and he lost track of the question. Though her fingers were deft as a grandmother's, they didn't make him think of sturdy old women, but of clever young ones who knew where to touch, and how. She said something, but it passed through his brain without comprehension. It had started as a joke, but now he couldn't quite understand how watching her perform some ancient female ritual could make his mouth dry.

"Did you change your mind?"

He brought his eyes from her hands to her face. "What?"

"I said CeeCee stocked a lot of cold drinks in the fridge. I'm pretty sure there's a beer."

"Right." After clearing his throat, he opened the refrigerator. "Do you want one?"

"Hmm. No. Something soft maybe."

He took out a bottle of Coors and a bottle of Pepsi. "Hooking up any interviews?"

"Here and there. I talk regularly with Eve, of course. And I've spoken with Nina, bounced a few questions off Fritz."

"Ah, Fritz." Paul took a quick chug. "The Viking god of health. What'd you think?"

"I thought he was sweet, dedicated, and gorgeous."

"Gorgeous?" Brows knit, he lowered the bottle again. "Christ, he's built like a freight train. Do women really find all those hulking muscles appealing?"

She couldn't resist. Turning back to him briefly, she smiled. "Honey, we love being taken by a strong man."

He drank again, scowling a bit, and resisted the urge to test his biceps. "Who else?"

"Who else what?"

"Who else have you talked to?"

Pleased with his reaction, she went back to work. "I have a few appointments next week. Most of the people I've been able to contact are being very cooperative." She smiled to herself as she spread the dough. "I think they're banking on pumping me for information rather than vice versa."

That was exactly what he was doing—rather, what he'd intended to do before she'd distracted him. "And how much will you tell them?"

"Nothing they don't already know. I'm writing Eve Benedict's biography, with her authorizaton." It was easier now, Julia realized, since they were over the awkward hump of what had happened between them. With her hands busy and children upstairs, she felt her confidence return. "Maybe you could tell me a little about some of the people I'll be seeing."

"Such as?"

"Drake Morrison's first on my list for Monday morning."

Paul took another swig of beer. "Eve's nephew—only nephew. Her older sister had the one child, two stillborn children after, then took up religion in a big way. Eve's younger sister never married."

The information dissatisfied. "Drake's her only blood relative. That's public stuff."

He waited until she'd finished patting the dough into place and ladled on the sauce. "Ambitious, personable. Drawn to slick clothes, cars, and women. In that order, I'd say."

Lifting a brow, she looked around. "You don't like him very much."

"I have nothing against him." He took out one of his slim cigars while she rooted through the refrigerator. Relaxed again, he could slide into the simple appreciation of looking at long legs in brief shorts. "I'd say he does his job well enough, but then, Eve's his major client and she's not exactly a hard sell. He's enamored of the finer things, and sometimes finds himself in awkward pinches because of his weakness for gambling." He caught Julia's look and shrugged. "It's not what you'd call a secret, though he is discreet. He also favors the same bookie as my father does when he's in the States."

Julia decided to let that lie until she had more time and had done more research. "I'm hoping to get an interview with your father. Eve seems fond of him still."

"It wasn't a bitter divorce. My father often refers to their marriage as a short run in a bloody good play. Still, I don't know how he'd feel about discussing the staging with you."

She diced green peppers. "I can be persuasive. Is he in London now?"

"Yes, doing *King Lear*." He took one of the thin slices of pepperoni before she could arrange it on top of the pizza.

She nodded, hoping she wouldn't have to make a transatlantic flight. "Anthony Kincade?"

"I wouldn't get too close." Paul blew out smoke. "He's a snake that bites. And it's a well-known secret that he prefers young women." He toasted Julia with the bottle. "Watch your step."

"It pays more to watch the other guy's step." She copped a piece of pepperoni herself. "How far do you think he'd go to keep portions of his private life from being revealed?"

"Why?"

She chose her phrasing carefully as she heaped on mozzarella. "He seemed very disturbed the other night. Even threatening."

He waited a beat. "It's hard to give an answer where you're asked half the question."

"You just answer the part you're asked." She slid the pizza in the oven, then hit the timer.

"I don't know him well enough to have an opinion." Watching her, Paul tapped out his cigar. "Has he threatened you, Julia?"

"No."

Eyes narrowed, he stepped closer. "Has anyone?"

"Why should they?"

He only shook his head. "Why are you biting your nails?"

Guilty, she dropped her hand to her side. Before she could evade him, he took her by the shoulders. "What sort of things is Eve talking to you about? Who is she involving in this trek down memory lane? You won't tell me," he said softly. "And I doubt Eve will either." But he'd find out, he thought. One way or another. "Will you come to me if there's trouble?"

That was the last thing she wanted to be tempted to do. "I'm not anticipating any trouble I can't deal with."

"Let me put it another way." His fingers moved down her arms, massaging gently. Then they tightened, pulling her against him as his mouth came to hers.

He held her there, deepening the kiss before her brain could register the order to snap away. Her hands fisted at her sides, barely resisting the urge to grab on, to cling. Even while she struggled to hold something back, her mouth surrendered to the assault and answered his.

There was heat and hunger, passion and promise. The backs of her eyes stung as her emotions scrambled out of hiding to revel in the chance for freedom. God, she wanted to be needed like this. How could she have forgotten?

More shaken than he cared to admit, he slid his lips from hers to nuzzle her throat. Incredibly soft. Enticingly firm. Added to the texture, the flavor, the scent, was that quick and faint tremor he found outrageously arousing.

He thought about her too often. Since that first taste he had craved more. She was the only woman he was afraid he would beg for.

"Julia." He murmured her name as he brushed his lips over hers again. Softer now, persuasive. "I want you to come to me. I want you to let me touch you, to show you what it could be like."

She knew what it could be like. She would give herself. Content with his conquest, he would walk away whistling and leave her shattered. Not again. Never again. But his body felt so tempting against her. If she could convince herself she could be as tough as he, as immune to hurts and disappointments, then perhaps she could take her pleasure and walk away whole.

"It's too soon." It didn't seem to matter that her voice was unsteady. It was foolish to pretend he didn't affect her. "Too fast."

"Not nearly soon or fast enough," he muttered, but stepped away. Damned if he'd beg—for anyone, for anything. "All right. We'll slow down for the moment. Seducing a woman in the kitchen with a trio of kids upstairs isn't my usual style." He went back for his beer. "You . . . change things, Julia. I believe I'd be better off to think this through as carefully as you." He took a sip, then slammed the bottle aside. "Like hell I would."

Before he had taken a step toward her, stomping feet sounded on the stairs.

Chapter Nine

♦♦♦♦

GLORIA DUBARRY WAS at an awkward age for an actress. Her official bio listed that awkwardness at fifty. Her birth certificate, under the name of Ernestine Blofield added five dangerous years to that mark.

Heredity had been kind enough that she had required only minor tucks and lifts to maintain her ingenue image. She still wore her honey-blond hair in the short, boyish style that had been copied by millions of women during her heyday. Her gamine face was offset by huge and guile-less blue eyes.

The press adored her—she made sure of it. Always, she had graciously granted interviews. A press agent's dream, she had been generous with pictures of her one and only wedding, had shared anecdotes and snapshots of her children.

She was known as a loyal friend, a crusader of the right charities, Actors and Others for Animals being her current project.

In the rebellious sixties, mainstream America had placed Gloria on a pedestal—a symbol of innocence, morality, and trust. They had kept her there, with Gloria's help, for more than thirty years.

In their one and only film together, Eve had played the carnivorous older woman who had seduced and betrayed the innocent and long-suffering Gloria's weak-willed husband. The roles had capped the image for each. Good girl. Bad woman. Oddly enough, the actresses had become friends.

Cynics might say the relationship was aided by the fact that they had never been forced to compete for a role—or for a man. It would have been partially true.

When Eve strolled into Chasen's, Gloria was already seated, brooding over a glass of white wine. There weren't many who knew Gloria well enough to see past the placid expression to the dissatisfaction beneath. Eve did. It was, she thought, going to be a long afternoon.

"Champagne, Miss Benedict?" the waiter asked after the women had exchanged quick cheek pecks.

"Naturally." She was already reaching for a cigarette as she sat and gave the waiter a slow smile as he lighted it for her. It pleased her to know she was looking her best after her morning session. Her skin felt firm and taut, her hair soft and sleek, her muscles limber. "How are you, Gloria?"

"Well enough." Her wide mouth tightened a little before she lifted her glass. "Considering how *Variety* gutted my new movie."

"The bottom line's the box office line. You've been around too long to let the opinion of one snot-nosed critic worry you."

"I'm not as tough as you." Gloria said it with the hint of a superior smirk. "You'd just tell the critic to—you know."

"Get fucked?" Eve said sweetly as the waiter placed her champagne on the table. Laughing, she patted his hand. "Sorry, darling, not you."

"Eve, really." But there was a chuckle in Gloria's voice as she leaned closer.

The prim little girl caught giggling in church, Eve thought with some affection. What would it be like, she wondered, to actually believe your own press?

"How's Marcus?" she asked. "We missed you both at the benefit the other night."

"Oh, we were sorry to miss it. Marcus had the most vile headache. Poor dear. You can't imagine how difficult it is, being in business these days."

The subject of Marcus Grant, Gloria's husband of twenty-five years, always bored Eve. She made some noncommittal noise and picked up her menu.

"And the restaurant business has to be the worst," Gloria went on, always ready to suffer her husband's woes—even when she didn't understand them. "The health department's always snooping around, and now people are crabbing about cholesterol and fat grams. They don't take into account that Quick and Tasty's practically fed middle-class America single-handedly."

"The little red box on every corner," Eve commented, describing Marcus's fast-food chain. "Don't worry, Gloria, health conscious or not, Americans will always go for the burger."

"There is that." She smiled at the waiter. "Just a salad, tossed with lemon juice and pepper."

The irony of that would escape her, Eve thought, and ordered chili. "Now . . ." Eve picked up her glass again. "Tell me all the gossip."

"Actually, you head the list." Gloria tapped her short clear-coated nails against the wineglass. "Everyone's talking about your book."

"How satisfying. And what do they say?"

"There's a lot of curiosity." Stalling, Gloria switched from wine to water. "More than a little resentment."

"And I was hoping for fear."

"There's that too. Fear of being included. Fear of being excluded."

"Darling, you've made my day."

"You can joke, Eve," she began, then clammed up as the bread was served. She broke off a corner of her roll, then crumbled it in her plate. "People are worried."

"Specifically?"

"Well, it's no secret how Tony Kincade feels. Then I heard that Anna del Rio was muttering about libel suits."

Eve smiled as she slathered butter on a roll. "Anna's a delightful and innovative designer, God knows. But is she so stupid to believe the general public cares what she snorts in the back room?"

"Eve." Flushed and embarrassed, Gloria gulped her wine. Her gaze darted nervously around the room as she checked to see if anyone could hear. "You can't go around saying things like that. I certainly don't approve of drugs—I've done three public service announcements—but Anna's very powerful. And if she uses a bit now and then, recreationally—"

"Gloria, don't be any more stupid than necessary. She's a junkie with a five-thousand-dollar-a-day habit."

"You can't know—"

"I do know." For once Eve was discreet enough to pause as the waiter returned to serve their food. At her nod, their glasses were refilled. "Exposing Anna might save her life," Eve continued, "though I'd be lying if I claimed to have any altruistic motive. Who else?"

"Too many to count." Gloria stared at her salad. As she did for any role, she had rehearsed this lunch for hours. "Eve, these people are your friends."

"Hardly." Her appetite healthy, Eve dug into the chili. "For the most part, they are people I've worked with, attended functions with. Some I've slept with. As for friendship, I can count on one hand the people in this business I consider true friends."

Gloria's mouth moved into the pout that had charmed millions. "And do you count me?"

"Yes, I do." Eve enjoyed another spoonful before she spoke again. "Gloria, some of what I'll say will hurt, some might heal. But that's not the point."

"What is the point?" Gloria leaned forward, her big blue eyes intense.

"To tell my story, all of it, no wavering. That includes the people who have walked in and out of that story. I won't lie for myself or for anyone."

Reaching out, Gloria clamped her fingers around Eve's wrist. Even that move had been practiced, but in rehearsal Gloria's fingers had been soft and pleading. In the performance they were strong and urgent, hardened by genuine emotion. "I trusted you."

"With good cause," Eve reminded her. She'd known it was coming, was sorry it couldn't be avoided. "You had no one else to go to."

"Does that give you the right to take something so private, so personal, and destroy me with it?"

With a sigh, Eve used her free hand to lift her drink. "As I tell the story, there will be people and events that interlink, that will be impossible to delete. If I left one part out to protect one person, the whole business collapses."

"How could what I did all those years ago have possibly affected your life?"

"I can't begin to explain," Eve murmured. There was a pain here, a surprising one, one the medication wouldn't touch. "It will all come out, and I hope with all my heart you'll understand."

"You'll ruin me, Eve."

"Don't be ridiculous. Do you really believe that people will be shocked or appalled by the fact that a naive twenty-four-year-old girl who fell unwisely in love with a manipulative man chose to have an abortion?"

"When that girl is Gloria DuBarry, yes." She snatched her hand back. It hovered by the wine a moment, then veered toward the water. She couldn't afford to get sloppy in public. "I made myself an institution, Eve. And dammit, I believe in what I've come to stand for. Integrity, innocence, old-fashioned values and romance. Do you know what they'll do to me if it comes out that I had an affair with a married man, had an abortion, all the while I was filming *The Blushing Bride?*"

Impatient, Eve pushed aside the chili. "Gloria, you're fifty-five years old."

"Fifty."

"Christ." Eve yanked out a cigarette. "You're loved and respected—all but canonized. You have a wealthy husband who—lucky you—isn't in the movie business. You have two lovely children who have gone on to live very tidy, very normal lives. Some people probably believe they were conceived immaculately, then found under a cabbage leaf. Does it really matter at this stage—when you are an institution—if it's revealed that you actually had sex?"

"In the bounds of marriage, no. My career—"

"You and I both know that you haven't had a decent part in over five years." Gloria bristled, but Eve held up a hand for silence. "You did good work, and will do more yet, but the business hasn't been the focus of your life for quite some time. Nothing I can say about the past is going to change what you have now, or will have."

"They'll slap my face on all the tabloids."

"Probably," Eve agreed. "It might just get you an interesting part. The point is, no one is going to condemn you for facing a difficult situation and making something of the rest of your life."

"You don't understand—Marcus doesn't know."

Eve's brow shot up in surprise. "Why the hell doesn't he?"

The pixie face flushed, the guileless eyes hardened. "Damn you, he married Gloria DuBarry. He married the image, and I've made certain that image has never been marred. Not even a whiff of scandal. You'll ruin that for me. You'll ruin everything."

"Then I'm sorry. Truly. But I don't feel responsible for the lack of intimacy in your marriage. Believe me, when I tell the story, it will be told honestly."

"I'll never forgive you." Gloria plucked her napkin off her lap and tossed it on the table. "And I'll do anything and everything to stop you."

She made her exit dry-eyed, petite and elegant in her white Chanel suit.

Across the room a man lingered over his lunch. He'd already taken half a dozen pictures with his palm-size camera and was satisfied. With any luck, he would finish his day's work and get home in time to watch the Super Bowl.

◆ ◆ ◆ ◆

DRAKE WATCHED the game alone. For once in his adult life he didn't want a woman within arm's reach. He didn't want any pouty blond sprawled on his sofa sulking because he paid more attention to the game than to her.

He watched from the game room of his cedar and stone home in the Hollywood Hills. The big-screen TV where the teams had already kicked off and received dominated one wall. Surrounding Drake were the adult toys he used to compensate for those his mother had denied him during childhood. A trio of pachinko machines, a billiard table, a bronze-backed basketball hoop, state of the art in pinball, arcade, and sound systems. His library of videotapes topped five hundred, and there was a VCR in every room of the house. A guest would be hard put to find reading material other than racing forms or trade magazines, but Drake had other entertainment to offer.

In the room beyond, sexual toys were stacked—from the sublime to the ridiculous. He'd been taught from an early age that sex was a sinful thing, and had long since decided in for a penny, in for a pound. In any case, a few visual aids increased his appetites.

Though he had only a passing taste for drugs himself, he kept a stash of pills and powders to trot out if a party threatened to become dull. Drake Morrison considered himself a conscientious host.

He'd refused more than a dozen Super Bowl parties for that Sunday. To him, it wasn't a game flickering on the screen, something to be enjoyed and hooted over with friends. It was life and death. He had fifty big ones riding on the outcome, and couldn't afford to lose.

Before the first quarter had ended, he'd gulped down two Becks and a half bag of chips dripping with guacamole. With his team up by a field goal, he relaxed a little. His phone rang twice, but he let his machine do the talking, convinced it was bad luck to leave his perch even to urinate during the game, much less to answer the phone.

Two minutes into the second quarter and Drake was feeling smug. His team was holding the line like bulls. Personally, he detested the game. It was so . . . physical. But the need to bet was unrelenting. He thought of Delrickio and smiled. He would pay the Italian bastard back, every penny. He wouldn't have to sweat when he heard the cool, polite voice over the phone.

Then maybe he'd take a quick winter vacation. Down to Puerto Rico to play in the casinos and fuck a few high-class broads. He'd deserve it after pulling himself out of this hole.

With no help from Eve, he thought and reached for a fresh beer. The old bitch refused to lend him another dime—just because he'd had a run of bad luck. If she knew he was still dealing with Delrickio . . . Well, he didn't have to worry there. Drake Morrison knew how to be discreet.

Anyway, she didn't have any right being so tight-assed with her money. Where the hell was it going to go after she croaked? All she had was her sister, and she didn't have any use for her. That left Drake. He was her only blood tie, and he'd spent his entire adult life knotting himself around her neck.

He was brought back to the game with a thud when the tight end on the opposing team sprinted thirty-five yards for a touchdown.

He felt his little bubble burst—as if a balloon had lodged then exploded in his throat. And reached for another handful of chips. Crumbs scattered over his shirt and lap as he stuffed them into his mouth. Didn't matter, he told himself. It was only a three point spread. Four, he corrected himself, wiping his hand across his mouth as the kick sailed through the posts.

He'd get it back. There was plenty of time.

◆ ◆ ◆ ◆

IN HIS BEACH HOUSE in Malibu, Paul huddled over his keyboard. The book was giving him trouble—more than he'd expected. He was determined to get past his current block. He often looked at writing that way. One wall to scale after the next. He didn't enjoy it—and it was the greatest pleasure of his life. He hated it and loved it in much the same way he'd learned some men felt about their wives. Writing a story was something he had to do—not for the money; he had plenty—but in the same way he had to eat or sleep or empty his bladder.

Leaning back, he stared at the screen, at the little white cursor that blinked after the last word he'd written.

The word was *murder*.

It gave him a great deal of satisfaction to create thrillers, complicating the lives of the characters that grew inside him. Most of all, he liked to watch them balance life and death in their hands. At the moment he just didn't seem to care enough.

Too many distractions, he admitted, and glanced over his shoulder at the television that was blaring out the action in the third quarter of the big game. He knew it was childish to have the set on and pretend to watch. The truth was he didn't even care for American football. But he was sucked in, year after year, by the Super Bowl. He'd even picked his team, vindicating his weakness by rooting for what he considered the underdog—since they'd been behind by three in the first quarter.

The game was certainly a distraction, but it wasn't what had been keeping him from falling into his work over the past couple of weeks. That distraction was certainly more fascinating than a bunch of men with padded shoulders dragging each other to the ground. A cool-eyed, long-legged blond named Julia.

He wasn't even sure what he wanted from her. Besides the obvious. Getting his hands on her was a pleasant enough fantasy—particularly with her remoteness and bursts of passion sending out such mixed and irresistible signals. But if that was all it was, why wasn't he able to dismiss her from his mind as he had been able to dismiss others when it was time to settle in to work?

Perhaps it was her complexity that nagged at him. She was slickly professional, quietly domestic. Ambitious and retiring. He'd already discovered that rather than aloof, she was shy. Cautious rather than cynical. Yet she had been bold enough, brave enough, to cross a continent with her young son and take on the vagaries of one of Hollywood's legends.

Or was it hungry enough? he wondered.

He could fill in some of the blanks himself since he had dipped into her background. He knew she had been raised by two professionals, had survived a broken home, a teenage pregnancy, and the loss of both parents. Despite the vulnerabilities he'd seen, she was tough. She'd had to be.

Christ, he realized with a laugh. She reminded him of Eve. Perhaps it was because of Brandon, so unlike the boy he had been.

Eve hadn't mothered him in the traditional sense, Paul knew. But she had saved him. Even though she had been his father's wife such a short time, she had changed Paul's direction. She'd given him the attention he'd so desperately craved, praise he'd stopped expecting, criticism that had mattered. Most of all, she'd given him an uncomplicated love.

Brandon was being raised that way, so how could he not be an appealing child? Odd, Paul thought, he'd never considered himself a man who particularly enjoyed children. He liked them well enough, found them amusing and often interesting, and certainly necessary for the preservation of the human race.

But he actually liked being around the kid. He'd felt comfortable the day before, eating pizza and swapping basketball stories. He was really going to have to see about taking the kid to a game. And if the mother came along, so much the better.

He glanced back at the television long enough to see the underdog was now behind by three going into the fourth quarter. Paul gave a fleeting thought to all the money that would be lost and won over the next fifteen minutes, then went back to work.

◆ ◆ ◆ ◆

DRAKE WAS on the edge of his seat. The rug beneath him was scattered with crumbs from the chips and pretzels he'd been steadily devouring. Fuel to feed that gnawing pit of fear in his gut. He was into his second six-pack of beer, and his eyes were red-rimmed and glazed—like a man's who was suffering from a hideous hangover. But he didn't take them off the screen.

Four minutes and twenty-six seconds to go, and he was up by three. His team had muscled its way to a touchdown, but had blown the extra point.

They were going to do it. They were going to put him in the black. Drake stuffed a handful of pretzels into his mouth. His Ralph Lauren sport shirt was soaked with sweat and beneath it his heart hammered.

His breath short and fast, he toasted the gladiators on the screen with a half-empty beer, then bolted up in shock, as if the defensive lineman had kicked him in the groin. The opposing receiver caught a long pass and sailed unmolested into the end zone.

The ball was spiked. The crowd went wild.

Three minutes and ten, and his life passed before his eyes.

They were assholes, he thought, swilling his dry throat with beer.

They'd fumbled twice in the last ten minutes. Even he could do better. Pussies. He chugged beer, noshed chips, and prayed.

Bit by bit, they marched their way down the field. With every yard gained, Drake inched closer to the edge. His eyes were watering when they hit a solid defensive wall on the seventeen.

"One fucking touchdown!" he shouted, springing up to pace at the two-minute warning. His legs felt like rusty springs.

Fifty thousand dollars. He walked back and forth, cracking his knuckles as the commercial droned on. He couldn't bear to think what Delrickio would do if he didn't come up with the rest of the money. With his hands shaking, he pressed them to his eyes.

How could he have done it? How could he have taken fifty thousand and bet it on a stinking game when he owed the mob ninety?

Then the game was back, and so was his desperation. Drake didn't sit now, but stood in front of the six-foot screen. The quarterback's eyes seemed to stare into his. Desperation into desperation. There were grunts. The snap. Big, sweaty men scrambled on the screen inches from Drake's face.

Three-yard gain. Time out.

Drake began to bite his nails.

The teams formed again. It seemed the same to him. What was the difference? he thought desperately. What was the fucking difference?

Quarterback sack. Six-yard loss.

He began to blubber now as the time dripped away. A grown man sobbing in a room full of toys. The need to urinate became so intense, he could only dance from foot to foot. With less than a minute to go, the defense held. Fourth and two. Run, pass, or punt. After an excruciating time-out where Drake raced to the john to relieve his aching kidneys, they opted to run. Hulking uniforms formed a mountain of grass-stained color.

He panted as the players pushed and shoved, as refs jumped in to pull hot heads apart. Drake wanted them to tear at each other, to draw blood. More tears welled in his eyes as the measurement was taken.

"Please, please, please," he chanted.

Short, inches short of the down. Miles short of hope. When the ball changed hands, the game was virtually over.

Drake stood, weeping as the crowd cheered. Big men took off helmets to show grimy faces of triumph or sorrow.

More than one life was changed when the clock ran out.

Chapter Ten

◆◆◆◆

*J*ULIA HOBBLED into the circular reception area of Drake Morrison's office at ten o'clock sharp for her appointment. She struggled to keep from wincing as she crossed to the center reception counter and announced herself to the slick-looking brunette who seemed to be in charge.

"Mr. Morrison's expecting you," she said in a silky contralto that was bound to make male clients salivate over the phone. If that didn't do the trick, the forty-inch bust that was holding a cubic zirconia captive in its admirable cleavage should finish the job. "If you'd just have a seat for a few moments."

There was nothing Julia wanted more. With a long and quiet sigh, she settled onto one of the sofas and pretended to be absorbed in *Premiere* magazine. She felt as though she had been beaten slowly, methodically, with a foam-coated baseball bat.

A one-hour session with Fritz and she was ready to beg for mercy—hopefully from a fully prone position.

He was kind-eyed, encouraging, flattering, and, she was sure, the real Conan.

Julia remembered to turn a page of the magazine while the receptionist answered the phone in her best Lauren Bacall. From profile, her amazing bust made Dolly Parton look prepubescent. Curious, Julia sneaked a peek, and noted that neither male in the reception area was salivating.

Settling back gingerly, she let her mind drift.

Despite the aches, it had been an interesting morning. Apparently women became more expansive when they shared torture. Eve had been friendly and amusing—particularly when Julia had forgotten dignity long enough to pant out a stream of oaths during the last of the dreaded crunchies.

And it was hard, if not impossible, to retain a professional distance when two exhausted women were naked and sharing the showers.

They hadn't discussed people during this session, but things. The gardens Julia discovered Eve was so fond of. The music she preferred, her favorite cities. It hadn't occurred to Julia until later that it had been less of an interview and more of a chat. And that Eve had learned more about Julia than Julia about Eve.

The more discomfort she had suffered, the more comfortable Julia had been with talking about herself. It had been easy to describe her home in Connecticut, how good she felt the move from New York had been for Brandon. How much she hated flying and loved Italian food. How terrified she'd been at her first book-signing with people crowded around.

And what was it Eve had said when she'd confessed to being frightened by public appearances?

"Give them your brains, girl, never your guts."

Remembering, Julia smiled. She liked that.

Cautiously, she shifted. When her thigh muscles shrieked in chorus, she didn't quite hold back the whimper. The men across from her flicked a glance over the tops of their magazines, dismissed her, then went back to reading. To take her mind off her multiple aches, she speculated about them.

A couple of actors hoping for representation by one of the big guns? No, she decided. Actors would never go looking for a publicity manager together. Not even if they were lovers.

It wasn't fair to label them gay because they weren't drooling over Dolly Bacall. Maybe they were loyal and faithful family men who never looked at women other than their wives.

And maybe she was sitting across from two dead guys.

An IRS team waiting to audit Drake's books, she decided. Much closer to the mark. The men had the cool, unsympathetic, and ruthless looks she expected from IRS agents—or Mafia hit men. Did they have calculators or .32s tucked beneath those trim black jackets?

That had her grinning for a moment, until one of them looked over and caught her studying them. Julia had reason to hope her own books were in good order.

A glance at her watch showed her she'd already been waiting ten minutes. The double white doors with Drake's name prominently displayed were firmly closed. Staring at them, she wondered what was keeping him.

◆ ◆ ◆

INSIDE HIS OVERDECORATED ecru and emerald office, as spiffy and obsessively trendy as the reception area, Drake kept his trembling hands linked on the glossy surface of his desk. He looked as though his body had shrunk to the size of a child, dwarfed by the custom-made leather executive chair.

Behind him was a window with its view of L.A. from high up in Century City. It always pleased him that at any whim, he could see in a glance the panorama the producers of *L.A. Law* had made famous.

He kept his back to it now, his eyes downcast. He hadn't slept the night before until jittery panic had sent him hunting up a couple of Valium and the brandy bottle.

"I've come to you personally," Delrickio was saying, "because I feel we have a relationship." When Drake merely nodded, Delrickio's lips tightened, only briefly, in disgust. "You understand what would happen now if I did not have this personal connection with you?"

Because he felt this demanded an answer, Drake wet his lips. "Yes."

"Business can be influenced by friendship only to a point. We are at that point. Last night you were unlucky. I can sympathize, friend to friend. But as a businessman, my priority must be my own profit and loss. You, Drake, are costing me money."

"It shouldn't have happened." Drake's emotions threatened to surface again, swam in his eyes. "Up until the last five minutes . . ."

"That is neither here nor there. Your judgment was poor, and your time is up." Delrickio rarely raised his voice and didn't do so now. His words boomed and echoed in Drake's head, nonetheless. "What do you intend to do?"

"I—I can get you another ten thousand in two, maybe three weeks."

His eyes masked by the downsweep of his lashes, Delrickio took out a roll of peppermint Life Savers, thumbed one free, and laid it on his tongue. "That's far from satisfactory. I expect the rest of the payment in one week." He paused, waggling his finger. "No, because we are friends, in ten days' time."

"Ninety thousand in ten days?" Drake reached for the Waterford carafe on his desk, but his hands shook too badly for him to pour. "That's impossible."

Delrickio's face remained impassive. "When a man owes a debt, a man pays. Or takes the consequences. A man who doesn't pay his debts may find himself becoming clumsy—so clumsy he slams his hand in a door and crushes his fingers. Or he may become so distracted by his obligations that he is careless when he shaves—so that he slices his face . . . or his throat. In the end he may become so disheartened that he will throw himself out of a window." Delrickio glanced at the wide pane at Drake's back. "Like that one."

Drake's Adam's apple pressed against the square knot in his tie when he swallowed the ball of fear in his throat. His voice came out like the whine of air from a leaky balloon. "I need more time."

Delrickio sighed like a disappointed father who had just been shown a poor report card. "You ask me for a favor, and yet you haven't granted me the one I asked you."

"She wouldn't tell me anything." Drake reached for a handful of sugared almonds from the Raku bowl on his desk. "You know how unreasonable Eve can be."

"Indeed I do. But there must be a way."

"I tried pumping the writer." Drake caught the faint glimmer of light at the end of a dark tunnel, and sprinted. "In fact, I'm working on bringing her around. She's in the outer office right now."

"So." Delrickio's brow lifted, the only sign of interest.

"I've got her pegged," Drake hurried on, taking the journey in frantic leaps and bounds. "You know, the lonely career-type who needs a little romance. Two weeks, and she'll be eating out of my hand. Everything Eve tells her, I'll know."

Delrickio's lips curved slightly as his finger brushed his mustache. "You have a reputation with the ladies. In my youth I enjoyed one myself." When he rose, Drake could all but feel the wave of relief slick down his clammy skin. "Three weeks, *paisan*. If you bring me useful information, we will arrange a longer-term loan. And to show your good faith, ten thousand in one week. Cash."

"But—"

"It's a very good deal, Drake." Delrickio moved to the door, turned. "Believe me, you would not get such consideration from others. Don't disappoint me," he added, brushing at his cuff. "It would be a shame if your hand was so unsteady while you shaved that you damaged your face."

When he stepped out, Julia saw a distinguished man of perhaps sixty. He had the sleek, glossy look of wealth and power heightened by dramatic good looks that had aged to distinction. The two other men rose. The man exiting Drake's office bowed slightly to Julia showing her by the look in his eyes that he had not forgotten what it was to appreciate a young, attractive woman.

She smiled—the gesture from him was so courtly and old-fashioned. Then he moved off, flanked by the two silent men.

Another five minutes passed before the receptionist answered her buzzer and showed Julia into Drake's office.

He was struggling to recover. He hadn't dared another Valium, but had gone into the adjoining bath and vomited up most of the terror. After splashing water on his face, a quick swishing of Scope around his sour-tasting mouth, and smoothing his hair and suit, he greeted Julia with the Hollywood handshake, a buss on the cheek.

"So sorry to keep you waiting," he began. "What can I get you? Coffee? Perrier? Juice?"

"Nothing, I'm fine."

"Make yourself comfortable and we'll chat." He glanced at his watch, wanting her to see that he was a busy man with a lot on his plate. "How are you settling in with Eve?"

"Very well, actually. I had a session with Fritz this morning."

"Fritz?" He went blank for a minute, then sneered. "Oh, yes, the exercise queen. Poor darling."

"I enjoyed it. And him," she said, her voice cool.

"I'm sure you're a trooper. Tell me, how's the book going?"

"I think we can be optimistic."

"Oh, you've got a best-seller, no doubt about it. Eve tells a fascinating story—though I'd have to wonder if her memory wouldn't be slanted. Still, the old girl's one in a million."

Julia was dead sure Eve would pop him right in the caps if he referred to her as "the old girl" to her face. "Are you speaking as her nephew or her press agent?"

He chuckled as his fingers snuck into the almonds. "Both, absolutely. I won't hesitate to say that having Eve Benedict for an aunt has added spice to my life. Having her for a client has iced the cake."

Julia didn't bother to comment on the mixed metaphors. Something, or someone, had Drake shaking in his alligator shoes. The distinguished-looking man with the silver hair and courtly manners? she wondered. Not her business—unless it pertained to Eve. She filed the question away.

"Why don't you start by telling me about your aunt? We'll get to your client later." She took out her recorder, lifting a brow until he nodded his permission. When her notebook was balanced on her knee, she smiled. Drew was scooping up almonds into one hand, then plucking them out of his palm one at a time, popping them into his mouth like bullets. Pop, crunch, gulp. She wondered if he ever missed a step and swallowed one whole. The idea forced her to look away a moment on the pretext of cuing the tape. "Your mother is Eve's older sister, correct?"

"That's right. There were three Berenski girls. Ada, Betty, and Lucille. Of course, Betty was already Eve Benedict by the time I was born. She was an established star, a legend even. She was certainly a legend back in Omaha."

"Did she come back home for visits?"

"Only twice that I remember. Once when I was about five." He licked the light dusting of sugar off his fingers and hoped he looked properly pained. It was a sure bet a single mother with a young son would sympathize with what he was about to say. "You see, my father deserted us. It crushed my mother, as you can imagine. I was too young to understand then. I just wondered why my father didn't come home."

"I'm sorry." She did sympathize. "That must have been very difficult."

"It was incredibly painful. Something I doubt I've ever completely gotten over." Drake hadn't given the old man a passing thought in more than twenty years. Taking out a monogrammed handkerchief, he dried off his fingers. "He simply walked out and never came back. For years I blamed myself. Perhaps I still do." He paused as if to regain his composure, turning his head slightly to profile and gazing broodingly out of the plate glass that shielded him from the morning's smog. Nothing, he was certain, got to a woman quicker than a sob story told bravely. "Eve came, though to be honest she and my mother never saw eye to eye. She was very kind in her no-nonsense way, and made certain we always had enough. My mother eventually took a part-time job in a department store, but it was Eve's contribution that kept a decent roof over our heads. She saw to it I got an education."

Though Julia wasn't fooled by the little show he was putting on for her benefit, she was interested in the story. "You said they didn't see eye to eye. What do you mean?"

"Well, I can't say what happened when they were girls. I get the impression that all three sisters competed for their father's attention. He was away quite a bit. Some sort of salesman. From what my mother has said, they often lived hand to mouth, and Eve was never content. It could have been more basic than that," he said with a smile. "I've seen pictures of them, all three of them together when they were young. I don't imagine it was easy for three beautiful women to live under the same roof."

Julia blinked and nearly lost her train of thought. Did the man have any idea how much he glinted? she wondered. The gold band on his Rolex, the gleam of his caps, the mousse in his hair.

"I—ah." She glanced hurriedly down at her notes, unaware that he preened, certain her attraction to him was distracting her. "So Eve left."

"Yes, and the rest is history. My mother married. I've heard gossip that my father had been in love with Eve. My mother wasn't particularly young when she married, and I believe there were many years of struggle before she finally became pregnant. Are you sure I can't get you anything?" he asked as he rose to go to the neatly stocked bar at the side of the room.

"No, nothing. But please, go ahead."

"Well then, in any case, I turned out to be the one and only." As he spoke he poured sparkling water over ice. He would have preferred a drink, but felt sure Julia would disapprove of such habits before lunch. As he sipped, he angled his head, treating her to his other profile. "Lucille devoted her life to traveling. I think she even lived in a commune for a few years. Very sixties. She was killed in a railway accident in Bangladesh or Borneo or some out of the way place, about ten years ago, I guess." He passed over his aunt's life and death with barely a shrug.

Julia scribbled a note. "I take it you weren't close?"

"To Aunt Lucille?" He started to laugh this off, then disguised it with a cough. "I don't think I saw her more than three or four times in my life." He didn't add that she had always brought him some fascinating toy or book. Or that she had died with little more than the clothes on her back and pocket change. No inheritance for Drake, no fond memories of Lucille. "She never seemed—well, particularly real to me, if you know what I mean."

Julia softened a bit. It wasn't fair to judge the man as callous because he lacked affection for an aunt he barely knew. Or because he was a preening peacock with an overindulged sense of his own sexual attraction. "I suppose I do. Your family was scattered."

"Yes. My mother kept the small farm she'd bought with my father, and Eve . . ."

"What was it like for you, meeting her for the first time?"

"She was always larger than life." He perched on the edge of the desk to enjoy the view of Julia's legs. Exploiting her would be anything but a painful experience. And, to be fair, he intended to see she enjoyed herself as well. "Beautiful, of course, but with that quality so few women have. Innate sensuality, I suppose. Even a child could see it, if not recognize it. I believe at that time she was married to Anthony Kincade. She arrived with mountains of luggage, red lips, red nails, what was surely a Dior suit, and the ubiquitous cigarette perched in her fingers. She was, in a word, fabulous."

He sipped, surprised at how vivid the memory was. "I recall one scene right before she left. Arguing with my mother in the kitchen of the farmhouse. There Eve was, puffing smoke and pacing over the cracked linoleum while my mother sat at the table, red-eyed and furious."

◆ ◆ ◆ ◆

"*For* CHRISSAKE, Ada, you've put on thirty pounds. It's no wonder Eddie ran off with some tacky little waitress."

Ada's dissatisfied mouth thinned. Her skin looked like day-old porridge. "There'll be no taking of the Lord's name in my house."

"And little of anything else unless you pull yourself together."

"I'm a woman without a husband, all but penniless, with a boy to raise."

Eve waved her cigarette so that smoke zigzagged in the air. "You know very well money won't be a problem. And there are women all over the world without husbands. Sometimes all to the good." She plunked her palms down on the wooden table, the cigarette jutting through her fingers. "Listen to me, Ada. Mama's gone, Daddy's gone. Lucille too. Even that lazy shit you married's gone. They're not coming back."

"I won't have you speak about my husband—"

"Oh, shut up." Eve rammed a fist onto the table so the little plastic rooster and hen salt and pepper shakers rattled and fell. "He isn't worth you defending, and by God he isn't worth your tears. What you've been given is a new chance, a fresh start. We're out of the fucking fifties, Ada. We're going to have a president who's not in his dotage in the White House come January. Women are going to start trading in their aprons. There's a change in the air, Ada. Can't you taste it? It's coming."

"Had no business electing a Catholic, a papist. It's a national disgrace is what it is." Her chin jutted out. "Anyways, what's it got to do with me?"

Eve only closed her eyes, knowing Ada would never taste the change, savor the cool, fresh flavor of it, not through her own bitterness. "Clean house, Ada," she murmured. "Bring the boy and come back to California with me."

"Why in God's green earth would I do that?"

"Because we're sisters. Sell this godforsaken place, move to a place where you can get a decent job, have a social life, where the boy can have a life."

"Your kind of life." Ada sneered, her red-rimmed eyes filled with resentment and envy. "Posing on the screen half naked so's anyone with change jingling in their pocket can watch. Marrying and divorcing on your whim, and giving yourself to any man who winks at you. I'll keep my boy here, thank you very much, where he can grow up with decent values and under God's plan."

"Do what you want," Eve said wearily. "Though why you'd think God would plan for you to be a bitter, dried-up woman before you're forty is beyond me. I'll send you money for the boy. It's up to you what you do with it."

♦ ♦ ♦ ♦

"OF COURSE she took the money," Drake went on. "Spouting off about wickedness, godlessness, and so on while she cashed the check." He shrugged, too used to the taste of bitterness on his tongue to notice as it spread. "As far as I know, Eve still sends her a check every month."

It disturbed Julia that she sensed no gratitude. She wondered if Drake realized how very much he was his mother's son. "If you'd had such little contact with her while you grew up, how did you come to work for her?"

"The summer I graduated from high school, I hitchhiked to L.A. with thirty-seven dollars in my pocket." He grinned, and for the first time Julia thought she could see a trace of his aunt's charm. "It took me nearly a week to get ahold of her once I got here. It was quite an adventure for me. She picked me up herself in this little dive in East L.A. Walked into this greasy taco joint wearing a drop-dead dress and stiletto heels that could impale a man through the heart. I'd caught her on her way out to some party. She crooked her finger at me, turned around, and walked out. I was after her like a shot. She didn't ask me a single question on the way back to her house. When we got there, she told me to take a bath and to shave off the excuse for a beard I was wearing. And Travers served me the best meal I'd had in my life."

Something stirred inside him with the memory—a fondness he'd all but forgotten under the layers of ambition and greed.

"And your mother?"

The stirring died away. "Eve dealt with her. I never asked. She put me to work with the gardener, then shoved me into college. I apprenticed with Kenneth Stokley, her assistant at the time. Nina came along just before Eve and Kenneth had a falling-out. When she decided I had potential, Eve put me on as her press agent."

"Eve has very little family," Julia commented. "But she's loyal and generous with those she does have."

"Yes, in her way. But relation or employee, you toe the line." He set the drink aside, remembering it best to gloss over any dissatisfaction. "Eve Benedict is the most generous woman I know. Not all of her life has been easy, but she's made it work. She gives those around her the inspiration to do the same. In short, I adore her."

"Would you consider yourself a kind of surrogate son to her?"

His teeth flashed in a smile that was too smug to be affectionate. "Absolutely."

"And Paul Winthrop. How would you describe his relationship with Eve?"

"Paul?" Drake's brows drew together. "There's no blood tie there, though she's certainly fond of him. You might consider him one of her entourage, one of the attractive younger men Eve likes to surround herself with."

Not only no gratitude, Julia reflected, but a thin little streak of nastiness. "Odd, I would have thought Paul Winthrop very much his own man."

"He certainly has his own life, his own successes, as far as his writing career." Then he smiled. "But if Eve snaps her fingers, you can bet your last dollar Paul will jump. I've often wondered . . . strictly off the record?"

"Of course." She hit the stop button on the recorder.

"Well, I've wondered if they've ever indulged in a more intimate sort of relationship."

Julia stiffened. More than a thin streak, she realized. Under all that gloss, Drake Morrison was eaten up by nastiness. "She's more than thirty years older than he."

"Age difference wouldn't stop Eve. That's part of her mystique, and her continuing charm. As for Paul, he may not marry them as his father does, but he has the same weakness for beautiful women."

Finding the subject distasteful, Julia closed her notebook. She had all she wanted from Drake Morrison for the moment. "I'm sure Eve will tell me if she decides their relationship warrants space in the book."

He tried to pry the slight opening wider. "She tells you such personal matters? The Eve I know keeps things to herself."

"It's her book," Julia commented as she rose. "It would hardly be worthwhile if it wasn't personal. I hope you'll talk to me again." She offered a hand and tried not to wince when he took it and raised it to his lips.

"Just name the time and place. In fact, why don't we have dinner?" He kept her hand, brushing his thumb lightly over her knuckles. "I'm sure we can find more to talk about than Eve—however fascinating she is."

"Sorry. The book's taking up nearly all my time."

"You can't work every night." He slid his hand up her arm to toy with the pearl stud at her ear. "Why don't we get together at my place, informally? I have a number of clippings and old photos you might be able to use."

As a variation on showing off etchings, it didn't take much creativity. "I try to make it a policy to spend the evenings with my son—but I'd love to see the clippings, if you wouldn't mind sending them over."

He let out a half laugh. "Apparently I'm being too subtle. I'd like to see you again, Julia. For personal reasons."

"You weren't being too subtle." She picked up her recorder and put it into her briefcase. "I'm just not interested."

He managed to keep his hand light on her shoulder. Pulling a mock grimace, he pressed the other to his heart. "Ouch."

That did the job of making her laugh, and making her feel ungracious. "I'm sorry, Drake, that wasn't very smooth. I should have said that I'm flattered by the offer, and the interest, but the timing's off. Between the book and Brandon, I'm much too busy to think about a social life."

"That's a little better." He kept his hand on her shoulder as he walked her to the door. "How about this? I'm probably the best one to help you with this project. Why don't you show me your notes as you go, or what you've drafted so far? I might be able to fill in some blanks for you, suggest a few names, even jog Eve's memory. While I'm doing that . . ." His gaze roamed slowly over her face. "We could get to know each other better."

"That's very generous." She put her hand on the door, struggling not to be irritated when he casually set his palm against the door to keep it closed. "If I run into any snags, I may take you up on it. But since it's Eve's story, I'll have to check with her." Her voice was mild and friendly as she tugged open the door. "Thank you, Drake. Believe me, I'll call you if I need something from you."

She smiled to herself as she passed out of the reception area. Julia was damned sure something was already up. And that Drake Morrison was right smack in the middle of it.

Chapter Eleven

◆ ◆ ◆ ◆

$\mathcal{J}$ULIA SLIPPED OUT of her shoes and walked barefoot into her office. The freesia the gardener had chivalrously given to her the afternoon before brought the delicacy of early spring to the cluttered room. When she rapped her bare toe against a stack of research books stacked on the floor, she swore only halfheartedly. She really was going to get this all tidied up. Soon.

Following habit, she took her day's tapes out of her briefcase to file them in the desk drawer. Her mind was on a cool glass of wine, perhaps a quick dip in the pool before Brandon got home from school. But it snapped back quickly as she stared into the drawer and lowered herself into the chair.

Someone had been there.

Very slowly, she walked her fingers over the tops of the tapes. None were missing, but they were out of order. One of the few things she was compulsively organized about was her interviews. Labeled and dated, the tapes were always filed alphabetically. Now their order was random.

Yanking open another drawer, she pulled out her typed draft. A quick glance reassured her that all her pages were there. But she felt, she *knew* someone had read them. She slammed the drawer closed and opened another. All of her things, she thought, all of them had been riffled. But why?

A bubble of panic sent her racing upstairs. She had very little of great value, but the few pieces of her mother's jewelry were important to her. As she scrambled into the bedroom, she cursed herself for not asking Eve to put the boxes into her safe. Surely she had one. But she also had a security system. Why in hell would anyone break into the guest house to steal a handful of heirlooms?

Of course, they hadn't. As the relief washed over her, Julia could call herself an idiot. The single strand of pearls and matching drop earrings, the diamond studs, the gold brooch in the shape of the scales of justice. They were all there, undisturbed.

Because her legs were weak, she sat on the edge of the bed, clutching the old jewelry boxes to her breast. It was foolish, she told herself, to have such a desperate attachment to things. She rarely wore any of those pieces, only occasionally took them out to look at them.

But she had been twelve when her father had given her mother the brooch. A birthday present. And she remembered how delighted her mother had been. She had worn it at every case she had tried, even after the divorce.

Julia made herself stand and replace the boxes. It was possible she had misarranged the tapes herself. Possible, but unlikely. Yet it was just as unlikely that anyone would breach Eve's security in broad daylight and make themselves at home in the guest house.

Eve, Julia thought with a short laugh. Eve herself was the most likely candidate. They hadn't had a session in three days. Curiosity and arrogance might have made her want to go through the work.

And that would have to be corrected.

She started downstairs again, intending to look through the tapes once more before phoning Eve. Before she'd reached the bottom, Paul was rapping on the front door.

"Hi." He opened it himself and strode in without invitation.

"Make yourself at home."

The tone had him tilting his head. "Problem?"

"Why, no." She stood where she was, feet braced apart, chin angled for a dare. "Why should it be a problem for people to waltz in? After all, it's not my house. I only happen to be living here."

He lifted his hands, palms out. "Sorry. I suppose I've been living with California casual for too long. Want me to go out and try again?"

"No." She slapped the word out at him. There was no way he was going to make her feel foolish. "What do you want? You've caught me at a bad time, so you'll have to make it fast."

He didn't have to be told it was a bad time. Her expression seemed so calm—she was good at that—but her fingers were busy twisting together. It made him only more determined to stay. "Actually, I didn't come to see you. I came to see Brandon."

"Brandon?" The instant warning bells had her arms dropping stiffly to her sides. "Why? What do you want with Brandon?"

"Loosen up, Jules." He settled on the arm of the sofa. He liked it there—really liked it, he realized. There was something about the way she'd inhabited the cool comfort of the guest area and had made it her own. A kind of charming untidiness, he mused, that spread Julia everywhere. The odd earring on the Hepplewhite table, the pretty high heels tilting against each other where they'd been stepped out of, a scribbled note, a china bowl full of rose petals and rosemary.

If he went into the kitchen, he'd find more of her there. And upstairs, in the bath, in the child's room, in the room where she slept. Just what would he find of Julia in Julia's most private space?

He looked back at her and smiled. "I'm sorry, did you say something?"

"Yes, I said something." She blew out a stream of impatience. "I said what do you want with Brandon?"

"I'm not planning to kidnap him or take him off to show him my newest copy of *Penthouse*. It's man business." When she stomped down the rest of the stairs, he grinned. "Had a rough one?"

"A long one," she said. "He's not home from school yet."

"I can wait." His gaze flickered down, then back. "You're barefoot again. I'm so glad you didn't disappoint me."

She shoved her nervous hands into the pockets of her suit jacket. He should have to register that voice with the police, she thought uneasily. Or maybe with medical science. It could put a woman into a coma—or bring her straight out of one, terminally aroused.

"I really am busy, Paul. Why don't you simply tell me what you want to talk to Brandon about?"

"You really are quite the mother. It's admirable. Basketball," he told her. "The Lakers are in town Saturday night. I thought the kid would get a kick out of going to the game."

"Oh." Her face was a study in contradictions. Pleasure for her son, concern, doubt, amusement. "I'm sure he would. But—"

"You can check with the cops, Jules. I don't have a rap sheet." Idly, he plucked one of the rose petals from the bowl and rubbed it between his thumb and forefinger. "As a matter of fact, I have three tickets, if you want to tag along."

So that was it, she thought, disappointed. It wasn't the first time a man had tried to use Brandon to get to her. Well, Paul Winthrop was in for his own disappointment, she decided. He'd opened himself up for a night with a ten-year-old, and that's what he'd get.

"It's not my game," she said mildly. "I'm sure you and Brandon would do better without me."

"Okay," he said so easily, she only stared. "Don't feed him. We'll catch something at the arena."

"I'm not sure—" She broke off at the sound of a car.

"Looks like school's out," Paul commented, and tucked the petal into his pocket. "Don't let me keep you. I'm sure Brandon and I can work out the details."

She held her ground as her son burst through the front door, book bag swinging. "I didn't miss one on the spelling test."

"Way to go, champ."

"And Millie had her babies. Five of them." He glanced at Paul. "Millie's the guinea pig from school."

"I'm relieved, for Millie's sake, to hear that."

"It was kinda gross." Brandon couldn't help but relish it. "She looked sick and all, and just was lying there breathing real fast. Then these little wet things came out. And there was blood too." He wrinkled his nose. "If I were a lady, I wouldn't do it."

Paul had to grin. He reached out and tugged the bill of Brandon's cap over his eyes. "Lucky for us they're made of sterner stuff."

"I'm pretty sure it had to hurt." He looked at his mother. "Does it?"

"You bet." Then she laughed and swung an arm over his shoulder. "But sometimes we get lucky, and it's worth it. I've almost decided you are." Since it didn't seem quite the time for a discussion on sex education and childbirth, she gave him a quick squeeze. "Mr. Winthrop came to see you."

"Really?" As far as Brandon could remember, it was the first time an adult had ever done so. Especially a male adult.

"It so happens," Paul began, "the Lakers are in town Saturday."

"Yeah, they're playing the Celtics. It'll be maybe like the biggest game of the whole season, and . . ." A thought wiggled into his brain, such a huge and stunning one, he gaped.

Paul's lips curved as he saw the wild hope in the boy's eyes. "And it so happens I've got a couple of extra tickets. Wanna go?"

"Oh, wow." His eyes threatened to pop out of his head. "Oh, wow. Mom, please." As he turned to grab her around the waist, his entire face was suffused with urgent pleading. *"Please."*

"How could I say no to someone who aced his spelling test?"

Brandon let out a whoop as he hugged her. Then to Paul's astonishment, the boy spun around and launched into his arms. "Thanks, Mr. Winthrop. This is the best. Really the best."

Rocked by the spontaneous show of affection, Paul patted Brandon's back, then nudged aside the book bag that was pressing into his kidneys. It had cost him nothing, he thought. He bought two season tickets every year as a matter of course, and had wangled the third from a friend who would be out of town. As Brandon grinned up at him, his face beaming with excitement and gratitude, Paul wished he'd had to slay a few dragons for the seats, at the very least.

"You're welcome. Listen, I've got one extra. Is there anyone you know who'd like to go with us?"

It was almost too much. Like going to sleep in August and waking up on Christmas morning. Brandon stepped back, suddenly unsure if it was cool for a guy to hug another guy. He didn't know. "Maybe Mom."

"Already declined, thank you," she said.

"Jeez, Dustin would really go nuts."

"Dustin already is nuts," Paul said. "Why don't you go give him a call, see if he can make it?"

"No kidding? Great!" He bolted into the kitchen.

"I don't like to interfere in man business." Julia unbuttoned her suit jacket. "But do you know what you've got yourself into?"

"Boys' night out?"

"Paul." She couldn't help but be kindly disposed to him now—not after seeing Brandon's face. "If I have this right, you were an only child, you've never been married or had any children of your own."

His gaze wandered down to her fingers that were still toying with the buttons of her jacket. "So far."

"Ever baby-sit?"

"Excuse me?"

"I thought not." On a sigh, she slipped out of the jacket and tossed it over the back of a chair. She was wearing a brick-colored sleeveless leotard, and Paul was delighted to see that as well as terrific legs, she had great shoulders. Smooth, creamy, and athletic. "Now, for your opening act, you're going to take two ten-year-old boys to a professional basketball game. Solo."

"It's not like a trek into the Amazon, Jules. I'm a reasonably competent man."

"I'm sure you are—under normal circumstances. Circumstances are never normal with ten-year-olds. It's a very big arena, isn't it?"

"So?"

"I'm going to have a lot of fun imagining you with two wild-eyed little boys."

"If I do a good job, will you treat me to a post-game . . . drink?"

She had both hands on his shoulders now, and a terrific urge to slide her fingers into his hair. "We'll see," she murmured. Her eyes changed, darkened. Going with impulse, she started to lower her head.

"He can go!" Brandon shouted from the kitchen doorway. "His mom says it's okay, but she has to talk to you to be sure he's not making it up."

"Right." Paul kept his eyes on Julia's. Even if he'd been across the room, he could have seen the desire turn to astonished embarrassment. "I'll be back."

Julia blew out a short breath. What the hell had she been thinking of? Wrong question, she decided. She hadn't been thinking at all, just feeling. And that was always dangerous.

Sweet Lord, he was attractive, appealing, sexy, charming. He had all those qualities that tempted a woman to make mistakes. It was a very good thing that she knew the pitfalls.

She smiled as she heard Brandon's excited voice pipe in counterpoint to Paul's deeper, wryer tones. Cautious or not, she couldn't help but like him. She wondered if he had any idea how he had looked when Brandon had swooped into his arms. That blank astonishment, then the slow pleasure. It was entirely possible that she'd misjudged him, that he'd asked the boy to the game without any ulterior motives.

She'd wait and see.

Now she'd better start thinking about dinner. She glanced toward the mantel to check the time on the antique ormulu clock. It was gone. Baffled, she stared, then the color drained out of her face.

She hadn't been wrong. There had been someone in the house. Struggling not to panic again, she made a careful search of the living room. Besides the clock, there was a Dresden figurine, a pair of jade candlesticks, and three of the miniature antique snuff boxes that had been in the display cabinet.

Keeping a mental account, she hurried into the dining room. There, too, she found several small, valuable pieces missing. There had been an amethyst butterfly that would fit in the palm of her hand, and had probably been worth several thousand dollars. A set of salt cellars from the Georgian period.

When was the last time she had seen any of these things? She and Brandon invariably used the kitchen or the terrace for meals. A day, a week? Two weeks? She pressed a hand to her churning stomach.

There could be a simple explanation. Maybe Eve had decided to remove the pieces herself. Clinging to that, she went back into the living room to find Brandon and Paul seated, discussing plans for the big night.

"We're going to go early," Brandon told her. "So we can meet some of the guys in the locker room."

"That's great." She forced a smile. "Listen, why don't you get yourself a snack, and we'll deal with your homework a little later?"

"Okay." He leapt up and shot Paul another grin. "See you."

"You'd better sit down," Paul advised when they were alone. "You're white as a sheet."

She only nodded. "There are some things missing from the house. I need to call Eve right away."

He was up, taking her arm. "What things?"

"The clock, antique boxes. Things," she snapped, afraid she would babble. "Valuable things. The tapes—"

"What about them?"

"They're misfiled. Someone . . ." She forced herself to take a long, deep breath. "Someone's been here."

"Show me the tapes."

She led the way into the office off the living room. "They're mixed," she told him as she opened the drawer. "I always file them alphabetically."

After nudging her into the chair, he looked for himself. "You've been busy," he murmured, noting the names and dates. "Any chance you've been working late and jumbled them yourself?"

"Almost none." She caught his doubtful glance around the disordered room. "Listen, I know how it looks, but the single thing I'm obsessive about is keeping my interviews in precise order. It's part of my work pattern."

He nodded, accepting. "Could Brandon have played with them?"

"Absolutely not."

"I didn't think so." His voice was mild, but there was something flickering in his eyes, something dangerous, when he looked at her again. "All right, Julia, is there anything on these tapes you wouldn't want someone to hear before publication?"

She hesitated, then shrugged. "Yes."

His lips tightened before he closed the drawer. "Obviously you're not going to expand on that. Are any of the tapes missing?"

"They're all there." A sudden thought had more color washing out of her cheeks. Snatching the tape recorder out of her briefcase, she grabbed a tape at random. A moment later a thin, nasal voice entered the room.

"My opinion of Eve Benedict? A tremendously talented actress and an enormous pain in the ass."

Julia let out a little sigh as she hit stop.

"Alfred Kinsky," she explained. "I interviewed him Monday afternoon. He directed Eve in three of her early films."

"I know who he is," Paul said dryly.

Nodding, she slipped the tape back in its plastic case, but held on to it. "I was afraid someone might have erased the tapes. I'll still have to check them all, but . . ." She dragged a hand through her hair, loosening pins. "It wouldn't make sense. I could always reinterview. I'm not thinking. I'm not thinking," she said to herself, then put the tape down to press her fingers to her eyes. "Someone came in here to steal. I've got to call Eve. And the police."

Paul clamped a hand on her wrist as she reached for the phone. "I'll call her. Relax. Go pour yourself a brandy."

She shook her head.

Paul punched in the number for the main house. "Then pour me one—and leave the bottle out for Eve."

However much she might resent the order, it was something to do. Julia was replacing the stopper in the decanter when Paul strode into the living room.

"She's on her way. Have you checked your personal things?"

"My jewelry. A few pieces I have from my mother." She handed him the snifter. "It's all there."

He swirled the brandy, watching her as he sipped. "It's absurd for you to feel responsible."

She was pacing, couldn't stop. "You don't know how I feel."

"Julia, I can all but see the thoughts in your head. I'm responsible, she's thinking. I should have prevented it." He sipped again. "Don't these lovely shoulders of yours get tired carrying the problems of the world around?"

"Back off."

"Ah, I keep forgetting. Julia handles the wrath of the world alone."

She turned on her heel and marched into the kitchen. He heard her murmur to Brandon, then the slam of the screen door. Sent the child out to play, he presumed. However rattled she might be, she would protect her son first. When Paul walked into the kitchen, she was standing with her hands braced on the sink, staring through the window.

"If you're concerned about the value of the missing pieces, I can promise you they're insured."

"That's not really the point, is it?"

"No, it's not." After setting the brandy aside, he moved behind her to massage her rigid shoulders. "The point is your space has been invaded. This is, after all, your space while you're here."

"I don't like knowing someone could walk in here, look through my work, select a few expensive trinkets, and stroll out again." She pushed away from the sink. "Here comes Eve."

Eve rushed in with Nina one step behind. "What the hell is all this?" she demanded.

Braced, Julia told her as quickly and clearly as possible what she had discovered.

"Son of a bitch" was Eve's only comment as she moved from the kitchen into the living room. Her gaze sharpened as it swept the room, noting the spaces where items were missing. "I was damn fond of that clock."

"Eve, I'm so sorry—"

With an impatient wave of her hand, she cut off Julia's apology. "Nina, check the rest of the place against your inventory list. Paul, for Christ's sake, pour me a brandy."

Since he was already doing so, he only lifted a brow. She took the glass and drank deep.

"Where's the boy?"

"I sent him outside to play."

"Good." She drank again. "Where have you set up your office?"

"In the den, through here."

Eve had already swept in to yank open drawers before Julia could speak again. "So, you claim someone's gone through the tapes."

"That's not what I claim," Julia said evenly. "That's what I say."

The faintest hint of amusement touched Eve's lips. "Don't get up on your high horse, girl." After brushing a finger over the tops of the tapes, she let out a quick laugh. "Well, well. Busy little beaver, aren't you? Kinsky, Drake, Greenburg, Marilyn Day. Good Christ, you've even gotten to Charlotte Miller."

"Isn't that what you hired me for?"

"It certainly is. Old friends, old enemies," she murmured. "All tidily filed. I'm sure dear Charlotte gave you an earful."

"She respects you almost as much as she dislikes you."

Eve glanced up sharply, then let out a full-throated laugh as she dropped into the chair. "You're a cool-handed bitch, Julia. By God, I like you."

"I'll return both compliments, Eve. But more to the point, what do we do now?"

"Hmm. You haven't got any cigarettes around here, do you? I left without mine."

"Sorry."

"Never mind. Where the hell's my brandy? Ah, Paul." She smiled and patted his cheek when he crossed over to hand it to her. "How convenient that you were here in our moment of crisis."

He let the sly inference pass. "Julia is naturally upset at having the house broken into, her work pawed over. And, perhaps not so naturally, feels responsible for the loss of your property."

"Don't be ridiculous." Eve dismissed it all with a negligent wave, then sat back, eyes closed, to think. "We'll check with the guard at the gate. There may have been some deliveries, some repairmen—"

"The police," Julia interrupted. "They should have been called."

"No, no." Already planning, Eve swirled her brandy. "I think we can handle this incident with more delicacy than the police."

"Eve?" Nina stepped into the doorway, a clipboard in her hand. "I think I've got the bulk of it."

"Estimate?"

"Thirty, maybe forty thousand. The amethyst butterfly." Her eyes filled with concern. "I'm sorry. I know you were fond of it."

"Yes, I was. Victor gave it to me nearly twenty years ago. Well, I think the wise thing to do is take inventory at the main house. I'd like to know if we've had any sticky fingers there as well." After finishing off the brandy, she rose. "I'm very sorry, Julia. Paul was perfectly right to use that censoring tone to inform me you're upset by all this. You can be sure I'll speak with security personally. I dislike having my guests disturbed."

"May I speak to you a moment privately?"

Eve merely gestured her assent as she perched on the edge of the desk. Julia closed the door behind Paul and Nina. "I am sorry you've been upset, Julia," Eve began. While she drummed the fingers of one hand on the desk, the others rubbed a small circle at her temple. "If I've appeared to make light of it, it's because I'm infuriated that anyone would dare."

"I think you should reconsider calling the police."

"Public figures have very little privacy. Forty thousand dollars worth of knickknacks aren't worth finding my face plastered all over supermarket tabloids. It's much more interesting to find it there because I've had an affair with a thirty-year-old body builder."

Julia opened the drawer and took out a tape. "On this are your recollections of your marriage with Anthony Kincade. Someone might have dubbed it, Eve. Someone surely might leak the information to him."

"And?"

"He frightens me. And it frightens me to think of what he might do to prevent this story from becoming public."

"Tony is my worry, Julia. There's nothing he can do to hurt me, and nothing I would permit him to do to hurt you. Unconvinced?" She held up a finger, lifted her voice only slightly. "Nina, dear?"

The door opened in less than ten seconds. "Yes, Eve?"

"Take a letter, please. To Anthony Kincade—you'll find his current address?"

"Yes." Nina flipped over a page on the clipboard and began scribbling in shorthand.

"Dearest Tony." She laced her fingers slowly, almost as if in prayer. The malice was back in her eyes. "I hope this finds you in the poorest of health. Just a quick, chatty note to let you know I'm progressing with the book by leaps and bounds. I know how interested you are in this project. You may be aware that several people are quite concerned about the content—so concerned that there have been hints and rumbles about trying to put a stop to it. Tony, you of all people should know how poorly I react to pressure. To save you any trouble, in case you've considered inducing some of your own, I'm writing to let you know that I'm seriously considering Oprah's offer to come on her show and gossip my bio. If there's any interference from your neighborhood, darling, I'll snap up her offer, and titillate the audience with a couple of memoirs from our fascinating years together. I believe that little slice of prepromotion, on network television, might sell gobs of advance copies. As ever. Eve."

Smiling, Eve lifted a hand. "That should send the cocksucker into apoplexy."

Unsure whether she wanted to laugh or scream, Julia sat on the desk as well. "I admire your guts if not your strategy."

"Only because you don't fully understand my strategy." She squeezed Julia's hand. "You will eventually. Now, take a hot bubble bath, drink some wine, let Paul talk you into bed. Believe me, the combination will work wonders for you."

Julia laughed, shook her head. "Maybe the first two."

Eve surprised them both by putting an arm around Julia's shoulder. It was a gesture of comfort and support, and, undeniably, of affection. "My dear Jules—isn't that what he calls you?—any woman can have the first two. Come to the house, tomorrow, ten o'clock. We'll talk."

"Eve?" Nina interrupted. "You have your first wardrobe fitting for the miniseries tomorrow morning."

"Right. Check with Nina," Eve said as she started for the door. "She knows my life better than I."

Nina waited until Eve glided out. "I know how upsetting this must be. You've only to say the word and we can move you and Brandon into the main house."

"No, no, really. We're fine here."

Nina's slim brows knit with doubt. "If you change your mind, it can be done quickly and without fuss. In the meantime, is there anything I can do for you?"

"No. I appreciate your offer, but to tell the truth, I feel better already."

"You call the house." Nina reached out to take Julia's hand. "If you're uneasy during the night. If you just want someone to talk to."

"Thanks. I can't feel uneasy knowing you're there."

"Two minutes away," Nina added, giving Julia's fingers a final squeeze.

Alone, Julia reorganized her tapes. It was a small gesture, and useless at that point, but it eased her mind. Picking up Eve's empty brandy snifter, she started toward the kitchen. The aroma of cooking had her hesitating, sniffing the air, then continuing on. At the kitchen doorway she could only stare at the sight of Paul Winthrop slaving over a hot stove.

"What are you doing?"

"Making dinner. Rotini with tomato and basil."

"Why?"

"Because pasta's good for the soul—and it's impossible for you not to invite me for dinner when I'm cooking it." He picked up a bottle of Burgundy he had breathing on the counter, poured some into a glass. "Here."

She took it, holding it in both hands, but not drinking. "Are you any good?"

His grin flashed. Since her hands were occupied, he took advantage by wrapping his arms around her waist. "At what in particular?"

It felt wonderful, too wonderful, to be held at that particular moment. "At rotini with tomato and basil."

"I'm terrific." He bent closer, then sighed. "Don't jerk, you'll spill the wine." Patient, he slid one hand up to cup her neck, which served the dual purpose of holding her still and making about a dozen nerve endings sizzle. "Relax, Jules. A kiss isn't terminal."

"It is the way you do it."

His lips were curved when they met hers. "Better and better," he murmured, nuzzling. "Tell me, do I set off the same kind of explosions in you as you do in me when I do this?" He scraped his teeth over her ear, then tugged on the lobe.

"I don't know." But she felt her legs dissolve from the knees down. "I'm out of practice as far as explosions go."

His fingers tightened on the back of her neck before he forced them to relax. "That was exactly the right thing to say to make me suffer." He leaned back to study her face. The gray of her irises had deepened, warmed to a rich smoke by whatever fires she fought down behind them. Was it his imagination, or had her scent intensified, heightened by the blood that rushed under her skin? It was a pity, Paul thought, a goddamn pity he had scruples. "You've got some color again. When you're upset your skin goes as pale as glass. It makes a man determined to fix things for you."

The backbone he'd melted so effectively stiffened again. "I don't need anyone to fix things for me."

"Which makes a certain kind of man all the more determined. Vulnerability and independence. I hadn't realized what a devastating combination they could be."

Struggling for a light tone, she brought the wine to her lips. "Well, in this case it's getting me dinner."

Still watching her, he took the glass from her and set it aside. "We could both have a lot more."

"Maybe." She stared into his eyes, dark and brilliantly blue. And very close. It was much too easy to see herself in them. Much too easy to wonder. "I'm not sure I can handle even a little more."

Whether that was true or not, he could see she believed it. "Then it looks like we'll have to progress by stages."

Because it seemed safer than the meltdown she'd just experienced, she cautiously agreed. "I suppose."

"The next stage would be for you to kiss me."

"I thought I had."

He shook his head. There was a challenge to the gesture, a not entirely friendly one. "I kissed you."

Julia deliberated and told herself to act like a grown-up. An adult didn't have to take up every dare tossed her way. Then she sighed.

Softly, she touched her lips to his. It took only an instant for her to realize this stage could be a tumultuous one. Still, she gave herself another moment, kept her lips warm against his, absorbing the thrill of risk.

"I need to call Brandon in," she said as she stepped back. She wanted plenty of time to think before moving on to the next stage.

Chapter Twelve

♦ ♦ ♦ ♦

$\mathcal{M}$ICHAEL DELRICKIO RAISED ORCHIDS in a fifteen-hundred-square-foot greenhouse attached to his Long Beach fortress by a wide breezeway. He took his hobby very seriously and belonged to the local garden club, contributing not only financially but often giving informative and amusing lectures on the family Orchidales. One of his greatest triumphs was his creation of a hybrid he'd named the Madonna.

It was an expensive hobby, but he was a very rich man. Many of his business enterprises were legal, and he paid taxes—more perhaps than many men in his particular bracket. Delrickio courted no trouble from the IRS, an institution he respected.

His business ranged from shipping, theatrical and restaurant supply, real estate, catering, prostitution, gambling, electronics, extortion to computers. He was owner of or partner in several liquor stores, clubs, boutiques—and he even had a piece of a heavyweight boxer. In the seventies, after resistance on his part brought on by personal distaste, Delrickio Enterprises dipped its toe into the drug trade. He considered it an unfortunate sign of the times that this area of his conglomerate was so profitable.

He was a loving husband who handled his extramarital affairs with taste and discretion, a doting father who had raised his brood of eight with a firm and fair hand, and an indulgent grandpapa who had difficulty refusing his grandchildren anything.

He wasn't a man to make mistakes, and when he did, he admitted them. Eve Benedict had been one of his mistakes. He had loved her in a wild, fevered way that had made him both indiscreet and foolish. Even now, fifteen years after their affair, he remembered what it had been like to have her. Remembering could still arouse him.

Now, as he puttered around his orchids, babying them, cooing to them, he waited for Eve's nephew. For all his faults, the boy was okay. Delrickio had even permitted Drake to date one of his daughters. Of course, Delrickio wouldn't have allowed anything serious to come of it. A hybrid was fine, even desirable in horticulture—but not in grandchildren.

Michael Delrickio believed in like to like, which was one of the reasons he had never forgiven himself for becoming mesmerized by Eve. Or her, for doing the mesmerizing.

And because he saw the fault in himself, he was more patient with Eve's worthless nephew than business dictated.

"Godfather."

Delrickio straightened from his stance over a trio of spider orchids. Young Joseph was at the doorway. He was a handsome, solid brute who liked to lift weights and spar at the gym Delrickio had an interest in. The son of one of his wife's cousins, Joseph had been in the family business for nearly five years. Delrickio had had him trained by his own first lieutenant, knowing the boy was not too bright, but loyal and eager to please.

Muscle didn't have to be intelligent, only tractable.

"Yes, Joseph."

"Morrison is here."

"Good, good."

Delrickio dusted off his hands on the white bib apron he wore when he was working with his flowers. His youngest daughter had made it for him, painting on the snowy material a clever caricature of her smiling papa with a garden spade in one hand and a curvy, sexy woman-size orchid with long, feminine legs draped around him.

"Bring him in here. Your cold sounds better." He was a good, concerned employer.

Joseph shrugged, more than a little embarrassed to have a physical flaw. "I feel fine."

"Still congested. You eat lots of Teresa's soup. Fluids, Joseph, to wash the poisons out. Your health is everything."

"Yes, Godfather."

"And stay close, Joseph. Drake may need some incentive."

Joseph grinned, nodded, and slipped away.

♦ ♦ ♦ ♦

IN THE SPACIOUS PARLOR, Drake sat in a comfy wing chair and drummed his fingers on his knees. When the rhythm failed to soothe him, he cracked his knuckles. He wasn't sweating yet, or not badly. At his feet was a briefcase containing seven thousand dollars. It was short of the mark, and Drake cursed himself for that. He'd had fifteen after fencing

Eve's goodies. Though he understood he'd been thoroughly ripped off in the exchange of merchandise for cash, it had been enough. That is, until his trip to the track.

He'd been so sure, so fucking sure that he could finesse the fifteen into thirty, even forty. The pressure would have been off for a while. He'd pored over the racing form, calculating his bets carefully. He'd even had a bottle of Dom Pérignon chilling at home, along with a snazzy little brunette keeping the sheets warm.

Instead of marching back in triumph, he'd lost half of his investment.

But it was going to be all right. He cracked his knuckles again. Pop. Pop. Pop. It was going to be just fine. Along with this seven thousand, he had three dubbed tapes in the briefcase.

It had been so easy, he remembered. Bagging up a few choice items—things Eve wouldn't miss. The old girl never wandered down to the guest house more than once or twice a year. Besides, she had so much, no one could remember where everything was kept. He figured it had been pretty clever of him to bring the blank tapes along. He'd have gotten more than three copied—but he'd heard someone coming in the back door.

Drake smiled to himself. That was a little more insurance. He'd been able to hide in the storage closet and watch the person go through the tapes, listen to them. That might come in handy down the road.

"He's ready for you," Joseph said, and led the way to the greenhouse.

Drake followed, feeling superior. Thugs, he thought derivisely. The old man surrounded himself with thugs. Soft brains and well-defined bodies in Italian suits that wouldn't show the bulge from a shoulder holster. A smart man could always outwit a goon.

Oh, Christ, they were going into the greenhouse. Behind Joseph's back, Drake rolled his eyes. He hated the place, the moist heat, the filtered light, the jungle of flowers he was expected to show interest in. Knowing the drill, he fixed a smile on his face as he entered.

"I hope I'm not interrupting."

"Not at all." Delrickio checked some soil with his thumb. "Just tending my ladies. I'm pleased to see you, Drake." He nodded to Joseph, and the other man melted away. "Pleased that you're prompt."

"I appreciate you seeing me on a Saturday."

Delrickio waved the thought away. Though his temperature control was the best on the market, he checked one of the six thermometers he had stationed throughout the long room. "You're always welcome in my home. What have you brought me?"

Smug, Drake set the case on a work table. After opening it, he stepped back to let Delrickio inspect the contents.

"I see."

"Ah, I'm a little short on the payment." He smiled, a young boy confessing to squandering his allowance. "I think the tapes might make up the difference."

"Do you?" was all Delrickio said. He didn't bother to count the money, but moved on to examine a particularly fine example of an *Odontoglossum triumphans.* "How short?"

"I have seven thousand." Drake felt his armpits begin to leak and told himself it was the humidity.

"So, your opinion is the tapes are worth one thousand apiece?"

"I—ah . . . It was difficult to copy them. Risky. But I knew how interested you were."

"Interested, yes." He took his time, moving from plant to plant. "So, after weeks of work, Ms. Summers has only three tapes?"

"Well, no. Those were all I could copy."

Delrickio moved from plant to plant, examining, cooing, scolding his little darlings. "How many more?"

"I'm not sure." Drake loosened the knot in his tie and licked his lips. "Maybe six or seven." He figured it was time to improvise. "She's been on such a tight schedule, we haven't had a lot of time to spend together, but we're—"

"Six or seven," Delrickio interrupted. "So many, but you bring me only three, and a partial payment." Delrickio's voice was growing softer. A bad sign. "You disappoint me, Drake."

"Getting the tapes was dangerous. I was almost caught."

"This, of course, is not my problem." He sighed. "I will give you some points for initiative. However, I will require the rest of the tapes."

"You want me to go back, to break in again?"

"I want the tapes, Drake. The method of getting them is up to you."

"But I can't do it. If I were caught, Eve would have my head on a platter."

"I would suggest you not get caught. Don't disappoint me again. Joseph."

The man slid into the doorway, filled it.

"Joseph will show you out, Drake. I'll hear from you soon, yes?"

Drake could only nod, relieved to step out into the breezeway, where the temperature dropped considerably. It took Delrickio only a moment to give his order. He held up a finger, bringing Joseph into the room. "A small lesson," he said. "Don't mark his face, I'm fond of him."

Drake gained confidence with each step. It hadn't been so bad, really. The old man was a pushover, and he'd find a way to copy the other tapes. Delrickio might even forgive the rest of the debt if he managed it fast enough. When it came down to it, Drake figured he'd been damn clever.

It surprised him when Joseph took his arm and yanked him off the path into a grove of pear trees. "What the fuck—"

It was all he got out as a fist the size and weight of a bowling ball rammed into his gut. The air whooshed out of his lungs as he doubled over, his breakfast threatening to follow.

The beating was passionless, methodical, and effective. Joseph held Drake upright with one beefy hand and used the other to bruise and batter, keeping the area confined to the sensitive internal organs. Kidneys, liver, intestines. In less than two minutes, with only the sound of Drake's wheezing grunts to punctuate the thud of fist against flesh, he was done and let Drake slide limp to the ground. Knowing words weren't needed to get the point across, he walked away in silence.

Drake struggled to breathe as hot tears swam down his face. Breathing was agony. He didn't understand this kind of pain, the kind that radiated out even to the fingertips. He vomited under the pear blossoms, and only terror that someone would come back to beat him again forced him up on watery legs to lurch to his car.

◆ ◆ ◆

NEVER AGAIN would Paul consider parenting a natural function in life. It was incredibly hard, exhausting, and intricate work. He may have been playing substitute daddy for only one evening, but by halftime he felt as though he'd run the Boston marathon on one leg.

"Can I—"

Paul merely lifted a brow before Dustin could finish. "Kid, if you eat one more thing, you'll explode."

Dustin slurped at his jumbo Coke and grinned. "We haven't had popcorn yet."

The only thing they'd missed, Paul thought. The boys had to have cast-iron stomachs. He glanced down at Brandon, who was holding his Lakers cap in his hands, studying the autographs he'd gotten on its bill before the game. Looking up, the boy flushed, grinned, and settled the cap back on his head.

"This is the best night of my whole life," he said with a simplicity and a certainty that men have briefly, and only in childhood.

Since when did I get a marshmallow for a heart? Paul wondered. "Come on. We'll hit the concessions one more time."

They watched the last half with their fingers greasy and their eyes trained on the action. The score seesawed, causing emotional outbursts from the crowd and the players. A basket missed, a rebound snatched, and the noise level rose like a river. One battle under the hoop resulted in a right cross, and an ejection.

"He clothes-lined him!" Brandon shouted, scattering popcorn. "Did you see it?" Impassioned, he scrambled to stand on his seat as the boos echoed in the auditorium. "They threw out the wrong guy."

Since Paul was having such a good time watching Brandon's reaction, he missed some of the pushy-shovy on the court. The boy was bouncing on the seat, slicing the Laker pennant through the air like an ax. Sprinkling his face was the sweat of the righteous.

"Shit," he said, then caught himself and shot Paul a sheepish look.

"Hey, don't expect me to wash your mouth out with soap. I couldn't have said it better myself."

As they settled down to watch the foul shot, Brandon hugged the small victory to himself. He'd said shit, and been treated like a man. He was awfully glad his mother hadn't been around.

◆ ◆ ◆ ◆

JULIA WAS WORKING LATE. Through tapes and transcripts she was back in the postwar forties, when Hollywood had glittered with its brightest stars and Eve had been a blazing comet. Or as Charlotte Miller had stated, a ruthless, ambitious piranha who'd enjoyed devouring the competition.

No love lost there, Julia mused as she leaned back from the keyboard. Charlotte and Eve had vied for many of the same roles, had been romanced by many of the same men. Twice they had been up for the Oscar at the same time.

One particularly valiant director had guided them through a movie together, a period piece set in prerevolutionary France. The press had gleefully reported the squabbles over close-ups, dressing rooms, hairdressers, even the amount of cleavage to be shown. The Battle of the Boobs had amused the public for weeks—and the movie had been a smash.

The joke around town was that the director had been in therapy ever since. And of course, neither actress spoke *to* the other, only *about* the other.

It was an interesting bit of Hollywood lore, particularly since when pressed, Charlotte wasn't able to fault Eve's professional skills. Even more interesting to Julia was Charlotte Miller's brief involvement with Charlie Gray.

To refresh her own memory, Julia replayed a portion of Charlotte's tape.

"Charlie was a delightful man, full of fun and excitement." Charlotte's crisp, almost staccato voice warmed slightly when she spoke of him. Like her beauty, it had hardened a bit with time, but was still distinctive and admirable. "He was a much finer actor than he was ever given credit for. What he lacked was the presence—the leading-man dash the studios and the public demanded in those days. Of course, he wasted himself on Eve."

There was a chorus of quick high barks that made Julia smile. Charlotte owned a trio of cranky Pomeranians who had the run of her Bel Air mansion.

"There are my babies, my sweet babies." Charlotte cooed and clucked. Julia recalled that she had fed caviar from a Baccarat bowl placed right on the Aubusson rug to the yipping balls of fur.

"Don't be greedy, Lulu. Let your sisters have their share. What a sweet girl. What a good girl. Mommy's baby. Now, where was I?"

"You were telling me about Charlie and Eve." Julia heard the suppressed laughter in her taped voice. Luckily, Charlotte hadn't noticed.

"Yes, of course. Well, he completely lost his head over her. Dear Charlie had poor judgment when it came to women, and Eve was unscrupulous. She used him to get a screen test, kept him dangling until she'd landed that part in *Desperate Lives* with Michael Torrent. If you recall, she was cast as a slut for the film, and the casting was superb." She'd given a sniff as she'd fed her greedy dogs bits of salmon. "He was completely devastated when she and Michael became lovers."

"Isn't that when your name began to be linked with his?"

"We were friends," Charlotte said primly. "I'm happy to say I gave Charlie a shoulder to cry on, and by attending certain functions and parties with him, helped him save face. That's not to say Charlie wasn't a little bit in love with me, but I'm afraid he believed Eve and I were of a kind. Which we most certainly were not and are not. I enjoyed him. Consoled him. He was also having trouble around that time, financial trouble due to one of his ex-wives. There was a child, you see, and the ex-wife insisted that Charlie pay through the nose so the baby could be raised in high style. Charlie, being Charlie, paid."

"Do you know what happened to the child?"

"I can't say that I do. In any case, I did what I could for Charlie, but when Eve married Michael, he went over the edge." There was a long pause, then a sigh. "Even in death, Charlie boosted Eve's career. The fact that he had killed himself for love of her made headlines, and created a legend. Eve, the woman men would kill themselves for."

The legend, Julia mused. The mystique. The star. Yet the book wasn't about those things. It was personal, intimate, honest. She picked up a pen and scrawled on a legal pad.

EVE
THE WOMAN

And there, Julia thought, was her title.

She began to type, and was soon lost in a story that as yet had no end. Over an hour passed before she stopped, reaching for a watered-down Pepsi with one hand and opening her drawer with another. Wanting to check a minor detail from the pages she'd already drafted, she leafed through them. When a small square of paper fell out and landed on her lap, she could only stare at it.

As fate would have it, the sheet had fallen faceup. The boldly printed words leered at her.

BETTER SAFE THAN SORRY.

Julia sat very still, ordering herself not to give in to a quick clutch of fear. They were ridiculous, even laughable, these clichéd aphorisms. It was someone's poor idea of a joke.

But whose? And she'd looked through those pages just the other day, after the break-in. Hadn't she?

Straining for calm, she closed her eyes and rubbed the glass, damp with condensation, against her cheek. She hadn't found it then—that was the only explanation. Whoever had gone through the tapes had planted it there.

She didn't want to believe, couldn't bear to believe that someone had come back after the security had been tightened. After she'd started locking the doors and windows whenever she left the house.

No. Julia picked up the note and crumpled it in her hand. It had been there for days, waiting for her to find it. The very fact that she had shown no reaction was bound to discourage the author.

Yet she found it impossible to stand inside, alone in the quiet house with darkness pressing on the windows. Without giving herself time to think, she ran upstairs and changed into her bathing suit. The pool was heated, she reminded herself. She'd take a quick swim, stretch her muscles, relax her mind. She tossed her frayed terry robe over her shoulders, and a towel around her neck.

Steam was rising out of that deep blue water when she shucked her robe. She shivered once, sucked in her breath, dove. She cut through the water, swam deep, imagining all her tension floating up on the surface to become as insubstantial as the steam climbing into the air.

Fifteen minutes later, she rose up in the shallow end, hissing through her teeth as the chill air hit her wet skin. And she felt wonderful. Laughing to herself, rubbing her arms, she started to haul herself from the water, starting when a towel landed on her head.

"Dry off," Eve suggested. She was sitting at the round table on the tiled apron. A bottle and two glasses stood in front of her. In her hand was a fat white geranium she'd plucked from her own beds. "And let's have a drink."

Automatically Julia scrubbed the towel over her hair. "I didn't hear you come out."

"You were busy shooting for the Olympic record." She passed the geranium under her nose before laying it aside. "Haven't you ever heard of a leisurely swim?"

With a grin, Julia straightened up and reached for her robe. "I was on the swim team in high school. I always did the last leg of the relays. And I always won."

"Ah, competitive." Eve's eyes glittered approval as she poured two glasses of champagne. "Let's drink to the victor."

Julia sat, accepted the glass. "Do we have one yet?"

This brought a rich burst of laughter. "Oh, I like you, Julia."

Mellowed, Julia touched her glass to Eve's. "I like you too."

There was a pause while Eve lit a cigarette. "So, tell me." She blew out smoke that vanished into the dark. "What brings you out for a not so leisurely swim?"

Julia thought about the note, then dismissed it. The mood here was much too easy to spoil. And, if she were honest, it hadn't been only the note that had sent her out. It had been loneliness, the crushing weight of an empty house.

"The house was too quiet. Brandon went out for the evening."

Eve smiled as she lifted the glass to them. "So I heard. I ran into your young son yesterday on the tennis courts. He has the makings of an excellent serve."

"You . . . you played tennis with Brandon?"

"Oh, very impromptu," Eve said, and crossed her bare feet at the ankles. "And I much preferred his company to the machine that shoots tennis balls at me like fuzzy cannonballs. In any case, he told me that the men were having a night out at the big game. You needn't worry," she added. "Paul may be a bit reckless from time to time, but he won't let the boy get drunk and pick up women."

Julia might have laughed if she hadn't felt so transparent. "I'm not used to him being out at night. That is, sleepovers at a friend's and that sort of thing, but . . ."

"But not him being out with a man." She tapped her cigarette in an ashtray fashioned like a swan. "Were you hurt very badly?"

Julia stopped brooding into her drink and straightened her shoulders. "No."

Eve merely arched a brow. "When a woman has told as many lies as I have, she recognizes one easily. Don't you feel it's destructive to pretend?"

After a moment Julia drank deeply. "I feel it's constructive to forget."

"If you can. But you live with a reminder every day."

Very deliberately Julia refilled her glass, topped off Eve's. "Brandon doesn't remind me of his father."

"He's a beautiful child. I envy you."

The annoyance Julia had started to build faded. "You know, I believe you do."

"Oh, I do." She rose quickly and began to shed the emerald lounging pajamas, dropping the silk carelessly to the tiles. "I'm going for a quick dip." Naked, her milk-white flesh glowing in the starlight, she crushed out the cigarette. "Be a darling, Julia, and fetch me a robe out of the bath house." With this, she dove headfirst into the dark water.

Amused, intrigued, Julia obeyed, choosing a long thick robe of navy velour. She offered it, and a matching towel, to Eve as the woman stepped back out of the pool, shaking herself like a dog—one with a top pedigree.

"Christ, there's nothing like swimming naked under the stars." Chilled and invigorated, she slipped her arms into the robe. "Unless it's swimming naked under the stars with a man."

"Sorry I don't qualify."

With a long and pleased sigh, Eve sunk into her chair, lifted her glass. "Ah, to men, Julia. Believe me, some of them are almost worth it."

"Worth something," Julia agreed.

"Why didn't you ever name Brandon's father?"

It was a sneak attack, Julia thought, but found herself more weary than annoyed. "I didn't do that to protect Brandon's father. He wasn't worthy of loyalty or protection. My parents were."

"And you loved them very much."

"I loved them enough to try to keep from hurting them more than I had. Of course I couldn't fully understand what it must have done to them to have their seventeen-year-old daughter tell them she was pregnant. But they never shouted or berated, they never judged or blamed— unless they blamed themselves. When they asked who the father was, I knew I could never tell them because it would have ripped the wound open further instead of letting it heal."

Eve waited a moment. "You've never been able to talk about it with anyone?"

"No."

"Talking about it can't hurt them now, Julia. If there was ever someone who isn't in the position to judge another woman's behavior, it's me."

Julia hadn't expected Eve's offer or her own pressing need to take her up on it. It was the right time, the right place, and the right woman, Julia realized.

"He was a lawyer," Julia began. "Not so surprising. My father took him into the firm right after he passed the bar. He thought Lincoln showed tremendous potential for criminal law. And though my father would never have said it, never even have consciously thought it, he'd always wished for a son—one to sort of carry on the Summers name in the hall of justice."

"And this Lincoln fit the bill."

"Oh, beautifully. He was ambitious and idealistic at the same time, dedicated, eager. It pleased my father tremendously that his protégé was climbing right up the ladder."

"And you," Eve asked. "You were attracted to ambition and idealism?"

After a moment's thought, Julia smiled. "I was just attracted. I did some clerical work for my father during my senior year—after school, evenings, Saturdays. I'd missed him after the divorce, and it was a way to spend more time around him. But I started spending it around Lincoln."

She smiled to herself. When she thought back, it was hard to condemn the young girl who had been so hungry for love and romance.

"He was a striking man—elegant. Tall and blond, always so polished, with this trace of sadness in his eyes."

Eve gave a quick laugh. "Nothing seduces a woman quicker than a trace of sadness in the eyes."

Julia heard her own laugh with some amazement. Odd, she hadn't realized that something that had seemed so tragic could have its light side after time had ripened it. "I thought it was Byronic," Julia said, and laughed again. "And of course it was all the more exciting and dramatic because he was older. Fourteen years older."

Eve's eyes widened. She let out a long, quiet breath before she spoke. "Christ, Julia, you should have been ashamed of yourself, seducing the poor bastard. A girl of seventeen is lethal."

"And the first time one comes sniffing around Brandon, I'll shoot her between the eyes. But . . . I was in love," she said airily, and realized the absurdity of it. "He was this dashing, dedicated, deserving older man—and married," she added. "Though, of course, his marriage was over."

"Of course," Eve said dryly.

"He started asking me to do a little extra work for him. My father had given him his first really important case, and he wanted to be fully prepared. There would be all these long, meaningful looks over cold pizza and law books. Accidental brushes of the hand. Quiet, longing sighs."

"Jesus, I'm getting hot." Eve propped a hand on her chin. "Don't stop now."

"He kissed me in the law library, right over the State vs. Wheelwright."

"Romantic fool."

"Better than Tara and Manderley combined. Then he was leading me over to the couch—this big, overstuffed couch in burgundy leather. I was telling him that I loved him, and he was telling me that I was beautiful. It didn't occur to me until later what those differences meant. I loved him, and he thought I was beautiful. Well," she said as she sipped. "The deed's been done for less lofty motives."

"And the one who does the loving is usually the one to be hurt."

"In his way, he paid." Julia made no objections when Eve refilled their glasses. It felt good, damn good, to sit out in the night, drink a little too much, and talk to an understanding woman. "We were lovers for a week on that big, ugly couch. One week in a person's life is so little, really. Then he told me, very kindly, very honestly that he and his wife were going to make another go of it. I caused one hell of a scene. Scared him to death."

"Good for you."

"It was satisfying, but short-lived. He was out of the office for the next couple of weeks, trying the case. He won, of course, and began his very illustrious career with my father strutting around like a proud papa with a pocketful of cigars. So when I discovered I wasn't just late, I wasn't just out of sorts or coming down with the flu, but I was pregnant, I didn't go to my father, or to my mother. I went to Lincoln, who had been told by his newly reconciled wife that she, too, would be delivering a little bundle of joy."

Eve's heart broke a little, but she kept her tone matter-of-fact. "Our boy'd been very busy."

"Very busy. He offered to pay for the abortion, or to handle an adoption. It never occurred to him that I would keep the baby. Actually, it hadn't occurred to me either. And I realized as he took on this thorny little problem in his very organized, very dedicated way, that I'd never been in love with him at all. When I finally made my choice, and told my parents about the pregnancy, he had months to sweat out whether or not I would point the finger. That's nearly enough punishment for a man who had nudged a girl, a starry-eyed but very willing girl, into being a woman."

"Oh, I doubt that's enough," Eve said. "But then, you have Brandon. That, I think, is justice."

Julia smiled. Yes, she thought. It had been the right time, the right place, and the right woman. "You know, Eve, I think I might try my hand at skinny-dipping before I go in."

Eve waited until Julia had peeled out of her suit and jumped into the steamy water. She allowed the silent tears to come, then brushed them away before they could be caught in the glint of starlight.

♦ ♦ ♦ ♦

WARM, dry, Julia relaxed in front of the late news. The house was as empty as it had been before she'd dashed off for the pool, but she didn't feel so uncomfortable in it now. Whatever came of the book, she knew she would always be grateful to Eve for that hour by the water.

The nasty little fingers of tension were gone from the base of her neck and spine. She was so relaxed, so purged, she could almost shut her eyes and drift off to sleep.

But she sprang up, heart thundering, at the sound of an approaching car. The headlights speared through the window, slashed across the room. She had her hand on the telephone before she heard the car door open, and slam shut. With her fingers poised to punch 911, she peeked through the blinds. When she recognized Paul's Studebaker, she let out a nervous laugh. By the time she met him at the front door, she had herself under control.

Brandon was sleeping nuzzled against his shoulder. For one instant, seeing Paul in the glow of the front porch light, her child safe in his arms, she felt a longing, a need she couldn't afford to recognize. Julia shoved the need aside and reached for her son.

"He's zonked," Paul said unnecessarily, shifting enough to keep the boy to himself. "There's some more stuff in the car. I'll carry him up if you'll get it."

"All right. It's the first door on the left." Shivering a little, she dashed out to the car. The "stuff" included three rolled-up posters, a pennant, an official NBA jersey, a full color program, and a souvenir mug filled with buttons, pens, and key chains. As she gathered it all up, she caught the faint whiff of stale sickness and bubble gum. With a shake of her head she walked back inside as Paul came downstairs.

"Plenty of willpower, right?"

He shoved his hands in his pockets and shrugged. "They ganged up on me. If you're interested, we won, 143 to 139."

"Congratulations." She dumped Brandon's trophies on the couch. "Who got sick?"

"Nothing gets by a mother. Dustin. I was unlocking the car. He said—wow, that was rad, or words to that effect. And threw up on his shoes. He'd almost recovered by the time I got him home."

"And Brandon?"

"An iron constitution."

"You?"

On a short, heartfelt moan, he dropped down on the steps. "I could really use a drink."

"Help yourself. I'll run up and check on Brandon."

Paul snagged her wrist as she started to pass. "He's fine."

"I'll check," she said, and continued up.

She found him tucked in, still wearing his cap. A look under the covers showed her Paul had taken the time, and the care, to remove the boy's shoes and jeans. Leaving him sleeping, she went down to find Paul holding two glasses of wine.

"I figured you wouldn't make me drink alone." He passed her the glass, tapped his against it. "To motherhood. You have my undying respect."

"Put you through the paces, did they?"

"Eight times," he said, and sipped. "That's how often two ten-year-olds need to use the john during a basketball game."

She laughed and sat on the sofa. "I can't say I'm sorry I missed it."

"Brandon says you're pretty good with baseball." He pushed the loot to the edge of the couch and sat beside her.

"Pretty good."

"Maybe you'll come along for the Dodgers."

"I'll think about it, if we're still in town."

"April's not so far away." He tossed an arm over the back of the couch and let his fingers play with her hair. "And Eve's led a long and eventful life."

"So I'm learning. And on the subject of the book, I'd like that interview as soon as possible."

His fingers wandered through her hair and onto her neck. "Why don't you come to my place, say tomorrow night? We can have dinner, privacy, and . . . discuss things."

The curling in her stomach was part fear, part temptation. "I've always felt business was best done in a business setting."

"We have more than business between us, Julia." He took the glass out of her hand, set it aside next to his. "Let me show you."

Before he could, she put both hands on his chest. "It's getting late, Paul."

"I know." He took one of her hands by the wrist, bringing her fingers to his mouth to nibble. "I love watching you get stirred up, Julia." He stroked his tongue down her palm, then back. "There's such a battle going on in your eyes over what you like, and what you think's best for you."

"I know what's best for me."

When she curled her hand into a fist, he contented himself with scraping his teeth over her knuckles. He smiled. "And do you know what you like?"

This, she thought. She liked this very much. "I'm not a child who overindulges in what feels good. I know the consequences."

"There are some indulgences that are worth the consequences." He took his hands to her face and held it still. The taut thread of impatience she felt in his made him only more seducing. "Do you think I pursue every woman I'm attracted to so single-mindedly?"

"I have no idea."

"Then let me tell you." He dragged her head back with a roughness that surprised and excited. "You do something to me, Julia. I haven't been able to get a fix on it, and I haven't been able to change it. So I've decided not to try, just to take things as they come."

His mouth was a breath from hers. She could feel herself being drawn in, helplessly, to a place she was afraid to go. "It takes two people."

"That's right." His tongue flicked out to trace the shape of her lips. And she began to tremble. "We both know if I pushed this right now, we'd make love the rest of the night." She would have shaken her head, but his mouth closed over hers. He was right, absolutely and completely right. And so was the taste of his lips.

"I want you, Julia, and fair means or foul, I will have you. I prefer it to be fair."

Her breath was coming too fast, the need leaping too high. "And what I prefer doesn't count."

"If that were true, we'd already be lovers. I feel something for you, some dangerous thing, some volatile thing. God knows what's going to happen when I let it loose."

"Are you interested in how I feel?"

"That's something I've given a great deal of thought to, maybe too much thought to, over the past few weeks."

She needed distance, quickly, and was grateful he didn't prevent her from rising. "I've also given this situation a lot of thought, and realize I should be honest from the start. I like my life as it is, Paul. I've worked very hard to establish the right kind of routine, environment, for my son. I won't risk that, not for anyone or anything."

"I can't see how a relationship with me would endanger Brandon."

"Maybe it wouldn't. That's something I'd have to be sure of. I've balanced my life very carefully, very deliberately. Casual sex isn't on my list."

He was up quickly, dragging her into his arms. By the time he jerked her back, she was weak and staggering. "Does that strike you as casual, Julia?" he asked, giving her a quick shake. "Is that something you can add to a scale or jot down on a list?"

Furious, he released her to snatch up his wine. This was not the way he'd intended to begin, or end, the evening with her. Control had always been so simple before. He was afraid it would never be simple again—not around Julia.

"I won't be forced to feel, or be bullied into an affair."

"You're absolutely right. This time, at least, I'll apologize." Calmer, he smiled. "That's thrown you off, hasn't it? Which may be the best way to handle you, Jules. The unexpected disarms you." He traced a finger down her cheek, which was now very pale. "I didn't mean to frighten you."

"You didn't."

"I scared you to death, not my usual way with women. You're different," he murmured. "Maybe that's what I'm trying to cope with." Taking her hand, he kissed her fingers gently. "At least I'll go home confident that tonight you'll think of me."

"Since I'll be working for another hour, I'm afraid I won't."

"Oh, you'll think of me," he told her as he strolled to the door. "And you'll miss me."

She nearly smiled when he closed the door behind him. The hell of it was, he was right.

Chapter Thirteen

••••

$\mathscr{I}$T WAS GOOD to be back in harness again. For Eve, there was nothing quite like filming to jolt the mind and body to full alert. Even preproduction work was its own kind of arousal, a long and incredible foreplay to the climax of performing for the camera.

This kind of lovemaking involved hundreds of people, and it pleased her when she recognized some of the faces. The grips, the gaffers, the property men, the sound crew, even those assistants to the assistants. She didn't think of them so much as family, but as participants in an orgy of work that, if done well, could result in intense satisfaction.

She had always been cooperative and patient with the technicians she'd worked with—unless they were slow, incompetent, or lazy. Her ease and lack of arrogance had earned her the affection of crews for half a century.

As a matter of professional pride, Eve would tolerate hours of makeup and hairdressing without complaint. She detested the whiners. She was never late for a wardrobe fitting or rehearsal. When necessary—and it had often been necessary—she would stand in the blazing sun or shiver in the rain while a shot was being reset.

There were some directors who considered her difficult to work with, for she was not a complacent puppet who danced at the pull of a string. She questioned, argued, insulted, and challenged. By her own count, she had been right as often as wrong. But there was no director, no honest one, who would label her unprofessional. When action was called, Eve Benedict hit her marks. She was usually the first off book, with her lines fully memorized—and when the lights were on and the cameras rolling, she slipped into character as effortlessly as a woman might step into a bubble bath.

Now, after nearly a week of last-minute meetings, script changes, photo sessions, and fittings, she was ready for some meat. She sat, smoking and silent, while her wig was arranged. Today they would rehearse, full costume, the ball scene where Eve's character, Marilou, met Peter Jackson's Robert.

Due to a scheduling conflict, the prior blocking and choreography had been done with Jackson's stand-in. Eve knew the actor was in the studio now. Several of the females on set had been murmuring about him.

When he walked in, she understood why. The dynamic sexuality she'd seen onscreen was as much a part of the real man as the color of his eyes. The tux showed off his broad-shouldered build to perfection. Since he'd be required to go shirtless through much of the film, Eve imagined that beneath silk and studs he had the chest for it. His rich blond hair was unstyled and added a touch of little-boy appeal. His eyes, heavy lidded and tawny, added straight sex.

Eve knew his bio listed him at thirty-two. It could be true, she thought, getting her first good look at him.

"Miss Benedict." He stopped beside her, smooth voice, silky manners, sexuality purring in neutral. "It's a pleasure to meet you. An honor to have the chance to work with you."

She extended a hand, and wasn't disappointed when he lifted it gallantly to his lips. A scoundrel, she thought, and smiled. Maybe those weeks in Georgia wouldn't be so trying after all. "You've done some interesting work, Mr. Jackson."

"Thank you." When he grinned, Eve thought—oh, yes, a scoundrel. The kind every woman needs in her life at least once. "I have to confess, Miss Benedict. When I learned you'd accepted the part of Marilou, I was torn between ecstasy and terror. I still am."

"It's always gratifying to keep a man on the point between ecstasy and terror. Tell me, Mr. Jackson . . ." She picked up another cigarette and tapped it gently against the dressing table. "Are you good enough to convince the audience that a virile, ambitious man could be completely seduced by a woman nearly twice his age?"

His eyes never left hers as he took a book of matches, striking one, letting the flame flare, then leaning close to touch it to the end of the cigarette. "That, Miss Benedict, will be"—over the small, hot fire, the look held—"effortless."

She felt the quick tug, the frisson of animal excitement. "And are you a method actor, darling?"

"Absolutely." He blew the match out.

◆ ◆ ◆ ◆

HER BODY might have been tired, but her mind was very much alert when Eve returned home. The tingle, the one she felt whenever anticipating an affair, kept the blood moving. Peter Jackson, she was sure, would make an interesting and inventive lover.

Starting up the stairs, she called, "Nina dear, ask the cook to fix me some red meat. I feel like a carnivore."

"Would you like it brought up?"

"I'll let you know." Eve lifted a brow when she saw Travers on the landing.

"It's Mr. Flannigan," Travers told her. "He's waiting in the back parlor. He's been drinking."

Eve hesitated only a moment, then continued up. "Have the cook serve up two portions of red meat, Nina. We'll take it in the parlor. And light a fire, dear, will you?"

"Of course."

"Tell Victor I'll be with him directly."

She took nearly an hour, selfishly, needing the time to gird herself for whatever trouble waited. There had always been trouble waiting with Victor.

Victor Flannigan was still as married as he had been a lifetime before. He could not, or would not, leave his wife. Over the years Eve had battled, raged, wept, and ultimately accepted that unmovable wall of matrimony as seen through the eyes of Victor's church. She could not give him up, this man who had made her weep as no other man had.

Christ knew she'd tried, Eve thought as she slipped on a scarlet silk robe. Marrying again and again—taking lovers. It didn't matter. With her head back, her eyes closed, she spritzed perfume down the column of her neck, then slowly fastened the ornate gold frogs so that the scent would breathe its warm breath through the silk.

She had been Victor Flannigan's woman since the first day she'd met him. She would die Victor Flannigan's woman. There were worse fates in life.

She found him pacing in the parlor, a glass of whiskey in his hand. He filled the room as he filled his suit. With arrogance and style. She'd always felt it was only men who lacked the latter who made the former unpalatable.

He could have come upstairs, confronted her in the bedroom with whatever was troubling him. But Victor had always respected her work without question, and her privacy when she'd requested it.

"I should have known you'd fall off the wagon and land on my doorstep." Her voice was mild, without censure.

"I'll pay tomorrow." Even as he gulped another shot of fire, he wished he could set the glass aside. "Irish genes, Eve. All Irishmen love their mothers and a good glass of whiskey. My mother's dead, God rest her. But there'll always be whiskey." He took out a cigarette because the act forced him to put the glass down for a moment.

"I'm sorry I kept you." She walked to the bar and opened the compact refrigerator. It took only a moment for her to decide to open a full bottle of champagne rather than a split. It looked like a long night. "I wanted to wash the day's work off."

He watched as she competently opened the bottle so that the cork eased out with a muffled pop. "You look beautiful, Eve. Soft, sexy, sure."

"I am soft, sexy, and sure." She smiled as she poured the first glass. "Aren't those three reasons you love me?"

With a jerk, he turned his back to stand before the fire Nina had kindled. Between the flames and the liquor, he imagined he could see his life pass before his eyes. In nearly every frame of the long, long film, there was Eve.

"Christ, I do love you. More than any sane man should. If all I had to do was kill to have you, it would be easy."

It wasn't his drinking that disturbed her, but the desperate tone in his voice she knew had nothing to do with Irish genes or Irish whiskey. "What is it, Victor? What's happened?"

"Muriel's been hospitalized again." The thought of his wife sent him back for the glass of whiskey, and the bottle.

"I'm sorry." Eve laid a hand over his, not to stop him but to offer as she always had—always would—all the comfort she could. "I know what hell it is for you, but you can't continually blame yourself."

"Can't I?" He poured and drank deliberately, with desperation and without enjoyment. Eve knew he wanted to get drunk. Needed to. And the hell with tomorrow's payment. "She still blames me, Eve, and why shouldn't she? If I had been there, if I had been with her when she went into labor instead of off in London shooting a fucking movie, we might all be free today."

"That was almost forty years ago," Eve said impatiently. "Isn't that enough penance for any God, for any church? And your being there wouldn't have saved the baby."

"I'll never be sure." And because of that, he'd never found absolution. "She laid there for hours before she managed to call for help. Goddammit, Eve, she should never have gotten pregnant in the first place, not with her physical problems."

"It was her choice," Eve snapped. "And it's an old story."

"The beginning of everything—or the end of it. Losing the baby broke her until she was as delicate mentally as she was physically. Muriel's never gotten over the loss of the child."

"Or let you. I'm sorry, Victor, but it hurts me, it infuriates me to watch her make you suffer for something that was beyond your control. I know she's not well, but I find her illness a poor excuse for ruining your life. And mine," she added bitterly. "By God, and mine."

He looked at her, troubled gray eyes seeing the pain in hers and the wasted years between them. "It's hard for a strong woman to sympathize with a weak one."

"I love you. I hate what she's done to you. And to me." She shook her head before he could speak. Again her hands reached out to cover his. This ground had been well trod. It was fruitless to drag their heels over it again. "I'll survive. I have and will. But I'd like to believe that before I die I'd see you happy. Truly happy."

Unable to answer, he squeezed her fingers, drawing what he needed from the contact. After forcing himself to take several long breaths, he was able to tell her the worst of his fears. "I'm not sure she'll pull out of this one. She took Seconal."

"Oh, God." Thinking only of him, she wrapped her arms around him. "Oh, Victor, I'm so sorry."

He wanted to burrow against her, against that soft sympathy—and the want sliced at him because he could still see his wife's colorless face. "They pumped her out, but she's in a coma." He scrubbed at his face, but couldn't wipe away the weariness. "I've had her transferred, discreetly, to Oak Terrace."

Eve saw Nina come to the door, and shook her head. Dinner would wait. "When did all this happen, Victor?"

"I found her this morning." He didn't resist when Eve took his arm and led him to a chair. He settled there, before the fire, with his lover's scent and his own guilt hammering at his senses. "In her bedroom. She'd put on the lace peignoir I'd bought her for our twenty-fifth anniversary, when we'd tried, again, to put things back together. She'd made up her face. It's the first time I'd seen her in lipstick for over a year." He leaned forward, burying his head in his hands while Eve massaged his shoulders. "She was clutching the little white booties she'd knitted for the baby. I thought I'd gotten rid of all those things, but she must have hidden them somewhere. The bottle of pills was beside the bed, with a note."

Behind them the fire crackled, full of life and heat.

"It said that she was tired, that she wanted to be with her little girl." He sat back, groping for Eve's hand. "The worst of it was, we'd argued the night before. She'd gone out to meet someone, she wouldn't tell me who. But whoever it was had gotten her stirred up about your book. When she got home she was wild, in a dangerous rage. I was to stop you, I had to stop you. She would not have her humiliations and tragedies put into print. The only thing she'd ever asked of me was that I keep my sinful relationship private and spare her the pain of exposure. Hadn't she honored her vows? Hadn't she nearly died trying to give me a child?"

And hadn't she chained a man to her in a loveless, destructive marriage for nearly fifty years? Eve thought. She could feel no sympathy, no guilt, and no regret for Muriel Flannigan. And beneath the love she felt for Victor was a resentment that he should wish her to.

"It was an ugly scene," he continued. "With her damning my soul and yours to hell, calling on the Virgin for strength."

"Good Christ."

He managed a wan smile. "You have to understand, she means it. If anything's kept her alive these past years, it's been her faith. It's even kept her calm most of the time. But the book, the idea of it, sent her over the edge into a seizure."

He closed his eyes a moment. The image of his wife writhing on the floor, her eyes rolled back, her body bucking, made his skin clammy.

"I called for the nurse. She and I were able to give Muriel the medication. When we finally got her to bed, she was quiet, weepy, apologetic. She clung to me awhile, begging me to protect her. From you. The nurse sat up with her until dawn. Sometime after that and before I checked on her at ten, she took the pills."

"I'm very sorry, Victor." She had her arms around him now, her face pressed to his, rocking, rocking, as she would a small child. "I wish there was something I could do."

"You can." He put his hands on her shoulders, pulling her back. "You can tell me that whatever you have written, you won't include our relationship."

"How can you say such a thing?" She jerked away, amazed that after all these years, after all the pain, he could still hurt her.

"I have to ask you that, Eve. Not for myself. God knows not for myself. For Muriel. I've taken enough from her. We've taken enough from her. If she lives, this would be more than she could survive."

"For nearly half of my life Muriel has held the upper hand."

"Eve—"

"No, dammit." She swooped back to the bar to slop champagne in her glass. Her hands were shaking. By God, she thought, there wasn't another man on earth who could make her tremble. She wished she could have hated him for it. *I've* taken from *her?* Her voice cut the air between them like a scalpel, separating it into two equal parts that could never, never make one whole. "My God, what a crock. She's been your wife, the woman you've felt obligated to spend Christmas with, the woman you've had in your home night after night while I've been forced to live with whatever's left over."

"She's my wife," he said quietly while shame gnawed at him. "You're the woman I've loved."

"Do you think that makes it easier, Victor?" How much easier, she wondered bitterly, was it to swallow a handful of pills? To end all pain, to erase all mistakes instead of facing them. "She had your name, carried your child inside her in front of the world. And I have your secrets, your needs."

It shamed him that he'd never been able to give her more. It ripped at him that he'd never been able to take more. "If I could change things—"

"You can't," she interrupted. "And neither can I. This book is vital to me. Something I cannot and will not turn away from. To ask me to do so is to ask me to turn away from my life."

"I'm only asking you to keep our part of it ours."

"*Ours?*" she repeated on a laugh. "Yours, mine, and Muriel's. Plus all the others we've taken into our confidence over the years. Trusted servants and friends, self-righteous priests who lecture and absolve." She made an effort to beat back the worst of her anger. "Don't you know the saying that a secret can be kept by three people only if two of them are dead?"

"It doesn't have to be made public." He rose, snatching at his glass. "You don't have to put it in print and sell it at any bookstore . . . or supermarket!"

"My life is public, and you've been a part of that life for nearly half of it. Not for you, not for anyone will I censor it."

"You'll destroy us, Eve."

"No. I thought that once, a long time ago." The last of the anger drained out of her as she looked down into the bubbles dancing in her glass, and remembered. "I've come to believe I was wrong then. The decision I made was . . . incorrect. I might have liberated us."

"I don't know what you're talking about."

She smiled secretively. "Right now it only matters that I do."

"Eve." He tried to bury his own anger as he crossed to her. "We're not children any longer. Most of our lives are behind us. The book won't make any difference to you or to me. But for Muriel, it could be the difference between a few years of peace, or of hell."

And what of my hell? The question raced through her mind, but she wouldn't voice it. "She's not the only one who's had to live with loss and pain, Victor."

His face ruddy with emotion, he restrained himself from moving any closer. "She might be dying."

"We're all dying."

The muscles in his jaw worked. At his sides his big hands closed into fists. "Christ, I'd forgotten how cold you can be."

"Then it's best you remember." Yet she put a hand over his and it was warm and soft and loving. "You should go to your wife, Victor. I'll still be here when you need me."

He turned his hand over, held hers tight for a moment, then left.

Eve stood for a long time in a room that smelled of woodsmoke and whiskey and packed-away dreams. But when the decision was made, she moved quickly.

"Nina! Nina, have someone bring my meal to the guest house."

Eve was already to the terrace doors before Nina rushed into the room. "To the guest house?"

"Yes, and right away. I'm starving."

♦ ♦ ♦ ♦

BRANDON WAS in the middle of building a very intricate space port. The television flickered in front of him, but he'd lost interest in the sitcom. The idea of building a floating walkway between the docking area and the lab had just come to him.

He sat on the living room rug, Indian-style, dressed in his faded and much-loved Batman pajamas. Scattered around him were a variety of action figures.

At the knock, he looked up and peered at Eve through the terrace doors. His mother had given him repeated instructions not to open the door to anyone, but he certainly knew that didn't include their hostess.

He scrambled up to throw the latch. "Hi. Do you want to see my mom?"

"Yes, eventually." She'd forgotten how appealing a freshly scrubbed, pajamaed child could be. Beneath the scent of soap lurked that wild forest smell that was boy. Her fingers itched with a surprising urge to ruffle his hair. "And how are you, Master Summers?"

He giggled and grinned. She often called him that if they happened to pass on the estate. Over the last weeks, he'd come to like her in a distant way. She had the cook send over frosted cakes and pastries which Julia meted out. And she often waved or called out to him when his mother or CeeCee watched him at the pool.

"I'm okay. You can come in."

"Why, thank you." She swept inside, silk robe swirling.

"My mom's on the phone in her office. Should I get her?"

"We can wait until she's done."

Not quite sure what to do with her, Brandon stood and shrugged. "Should I get you something—like to eat or drink? We've got brownies."

"That sounds delightful, but I haven't had my dinner yet. It's on its way." She dropped onto the sofa and took out a cigarette. It occurred to her that this was the first time she'd had an opportunity to talk to the boy alone in what could be considered his home. "I suppose I should ask you the usual questions about school and sports, but I'm afraid I have little interest in either." She glanced down. "What are you doing there?"

"I'm building a space port."

"A space port." Intrigued, she set the cigarette aside, unlit, and leaned forward. "How does one go about building a space port?"

"It's not so hard if you've got a plan." Willing to share, he sat on the rug again. "See, these things hook together, and you've got all kinds of pieces so you can make layers and curves and towers. I'm going to put this bridge between the docking bay and the lab."

"Very wise, I'm sure. Show me."

When Nina arrived five minutes later with a tray, Eve was sitting on the floor with Brandon, struggling to link plastic pieces together. "You should have had one of the servants bring it." Eve gestured to the coffee table. "Just set it down there."

"I wanted to remind you that you have a six-thirty call."

"Don't worry, dear." Eve let out a little crow of triumph as the pieces clicked. "I'll get my beauty sleep."

Nina hovered, hesitated. "You won't let your dinner get cold?"

Eve made a few agreeable noises and continued to build. Brandon waited until the terrace doors closed, then whispered, "She sounded like a mother."

Eve glanced up, brows lifted high, then let out an uproarious laugh. "My God, child, you're absolutely right. One day you'll have to tell me about yours."

"She hardly ever yells." Brandon's mouth pursed as he worked out the engineering of the bridge. "But she worries all the time. Like I might run out in the street and get hit by a car, or eat too much candy, or forget my homework. And I hardly ever."

"Get hit by a car?"

His chuckle was quick and appreciative. "Forget my homework."

"A mother's meant to worry, I'd guess, if she's a good one." She lifted her head, smiled. "Hello, Julia."

Julia only continued to stare, wondering what to make of the fact that Eve Benedict was sitting on the floor playing with her son and discussing motherhood.

"Miss B. came to see you," Brandon supplied. "But she said she could wait until you were off the phone."

In an absent and automatic gesture, Julia switched off the television. "I'm sorry I kept you waiting."

"No need." This time Eve gave in to the urge and stroked Brandon's head. "I've been beautifully entertained." She rose, suffering only minor aches in her joints from squatting on the floor. "I hope you don't mind if I eat while we talk." She gestured to the covered tray. "I haven't had time for dinner since returning from the studio, and I have a story to tell you."

"No, please, go right ahead. Brandon, tomorrow's a school day."

It was the signal for bedtime, and he sighed. "I was going to build this bridge."

"You can build it tomorrow." After he'd gotten reluctantly to his feet, she cupped his face. "It's a first class space port, pal. Just leave everything here." She kissed his forehead, then his nose. "And don't forget—"

"To brush your teeth," he finished, and rolled his eyes. "Come on, Mom."

"Come on, Brandon." Laughing, she gave him a quick squeeze. "Lights out in ten."

"Yes, ma'am. Good night, Miss B."

"Good night, Brandon." She watched the boy climb the stairs before turning back to Julia. "Is he always so obedient?"

"Brandon? I suppose he is." She smiled as she rubbed a day's worth of tension away from the base of her neck. "Then again, he knows there are only a handful of rules I'm unlikely to bend."

"Lucky you." Eve lifted the top off the tray and examined her steak Diane. "I remember when many of my friends and associates were raising young children. As a guest, you were often subjected to the whining, the crabbing, the tantrums and tears. It quite put me off children."

"Is that why you never had any of your own?"

Eve took the napkin out of its porcelain ring, spread the square of rose-colored linen over her lap. "You could say it is why I spent a great deal of time wondering why anyone would. But I didn't come here to-night to speak of the mysteries of parenting." She chose a delicate spear of asparagus. "I hope it's convenient for you to talk now. And here."

"Yes, of course. If you'll give me time to see to Brandon and get my recorder."

"Go ahead." Eve poured some herb tea from the pot on the tray and waited.

Though she appreciated the tastes and textures, she ate mechanically. She required fuel to give her best on the set in the morning. She never gave less than her best. By the time Julia settled in the chair opposite her, she was halfway through the meal.

"I should tell you that I had a visit from Victor tonight, which is why I decided to talk now, while it's so much on my mind. His wife attempted suicide this morning."

"Oh, my God."

Eve lifted her shoulders and sliced at the meat. "It isn't the first time. Nor, if medical science pulls Muriel through, is it likely to be the last. God seems to protect fools and neurotics." She slipped the slice between her lips. "You find me unfeeling."

"Unmoved," Julia said after a moment. "There's a difference."

"Indeed there is. I feel, Julia. Indeed I feel." She went back to the tea, wondering how much it would take to ease the ache in her throat. "What other reason could there be for me to give so many years of my life to a man I could never really have?"

"Victor Flannigan."

"Victor Flannigan." With a sigh, Eve covered the tray and sat back with a goblet of chilled water. "I have loved him, and have been his lover, for thirty years. He is the only man I have ever made a sacrifice for. The only man to give me lonely nights, the kind of nights a woman spends in tears, in despair, in hope."

"Yet you've married twice in the past thirty years."

"Yes. And taken and enjoyed lovers. Being in love with Victor didn't mean I had to stop trying to live. That was, is, Muriel's way. Not mine."

"I wasn't asking you to justify, Eve."

"No?" She skimmed her fingers through her hair, then drummed them on the arm of the couch. Julia might not ask, Eve realized, but Julia's eyes did. "I would not try to hold him by martyring myself. And, I'll admit, I tried to forget him by filling myself with other men."

"And he loves you."

"Oh, yes. Our feelings for each other are very closely matched. That's part of the tragedy, and the glory of it."

"If that's true, Eve, why is he married to someone else?"

"An excellent question." After lighting a cigarette, she sank back into the pillows on the couch. "One I've asked myself countless times over the years. Even when I knew the answer, I still asked. His marriage to Muriel was already on shaky ground when we met. I don't say that to gloss over adultery. I say it because it's true." She expelled smoke in a hurried puff. "I wouldn't give a damn if I had been the reason Victor had fallen out of love with his wife. But that had already happened before I came along. He stayed with her because he felt responsible, because her faith made it impossible for her to condone divorce. And because they lost a child, a daughter, at birth. That loss was something Muriel never adjusted to—or never allowed herself to adjust to.

"Muriel was always delicate physically. Epilepsy. No," Eve said, smiling, "there's never been any whisper or hint that Victor's wife is an epileptic. Of course there's no stigma attached to the illness now."

"But there was a stigma a generation ago," Julia put in.

"And Muriel Flannigan is the kind of woman who clasps such things to her bosom and revels."

Julia frowned. "You're saying she uses her illness to provoke sympathy."

"My dear, she uses it as cleverly, as calculatingly, and as cold-bloodedly as a general uses his troops. It's her shield against reality, and she's spent a lifetime dragging Victor behind that shield with her."

"It's hard to drag a man anywhere he doesn't want to go."

Eve's lips tightened for a moment, then she smiled brittlely. "Touché, darling."

"I'm sorry, I'm making judgments. It's only . . ." Because I care about you. She blew out an impatient breath. If anyone could muddle through on her own, it was Eve. "I shouldn't be," she finished. "You know the players better than I."

"Well put," Eve murmured. "The three of us have indeed been players in an endless script. The other woman, the long-suffering wife, and the man torn between his heart and conscience." She whipped up a cigarette, then stared into space without lighting it. "I offer sex, and she responsibility, and she plays so astutely. How often she conveniently neglects to take the medication that would control the illness—usually when there is some crisis to be faced, some decision to be made."

Julia held up a hand. "I'm sorry, Eve, but why would he tolerate it? Why would anyone allow themselves to be used year after year?"

"What's the stronger motivator, Julia? Tell me using your practical brain. Is it love, or is it guilt?"

It took her only a moment to see the clearest answer. "A combination of both would outweigh any other emotion."

"And such a desperate woman knows just how to wield that combination." She let out an impatient huff of breath to clear the bitterness from her voice. "Victor has seen to it that Muriel's illness has been kept secret. She insists on it—fanatically. Since the miscarriage, her mental health has been unstable at best. We both knew, we both accepted, that while Muriel lived, he could never be mine."

This wasn't the time for censor or criticism, Julia realized. Like the hour they had spent by the pool, it was a time for understanding. "I'm so sorry. I can see I only believed myself in love with a man who could never belong to me. But still there was terrible pain. I can't even imagine what it would be like to love someone so long, and so hopelessly."

"Never hopelessly," Eve corrected Julia. She had to strike the match three times before it flared. "Always hopefully." She expelled a slow stream of smoke. "I was older than you when I met him, but still young. Young enough to believe that miracles happened. That love conquered all. Now I'm not young, and though I know better, I wouldn't change my life. I can look back at those first giddy months with Victor and be grateful. So very grateful."

"Tell me," Julia said.

Chapter Fourteen

••••

"I SUPPOSE I was still smarting from my disillusionment with Tony—or myself," Eve began. "It was a couple of years after the divorce, but I was still raw. I'd moved out of the house Tony and I had shared—the house I'd forced him to sign over to me. But I'd hung on to it. I enjoy dabbling in real estate," she said with a casualness that skimmed over more than twenty million in prime properties. "Why don't you have some tea?" she suggested. "It's still warm and Nina brought two cups."

"Thanks."

"I'd just bought this estate," she went on as Julia helped herself. "I was having some remodeling and redecorating done, so it's safe to say my life was in a state of flux."

"Not your professional one."

"No." Eve smiled through the mist of smoke. "But things had changed. It was the early sixties, and the faces had changed, become younger. Garbo was retired and in seclusion, James Dean was dead. Monroe would be in a matter of months. But more than those two wasted youths, that one defiant and suppressed talent, was the changing of the guard. Fairbanks, Flynn, Power, Gable, Crawford, Hayworth, Garson, Turner. All those beautiful faces and magnificent talents were being replaced, or certainly challenged by other faces, other talents. The classy Paul Newman, the young, dashing Peter O'Toole, the ethereal Claire Bloom, the gamine Audrey Hepburn." She sighed again, knowing the guard had changed yet again. "Hollywood is a woman, Julia, forever charging after youth."

"Yet it celebrates endurance."

"Oh, yes. Yes, it does indeed. When I met Victor on the set of our first movie together, I was not yet forty. Neither fish nor fowl—no longer quite young, not yet eligible for the label of endurance. Hell, I hadn't even had my eyes done yet."

Julia had to grin. Where else but Hollywood would people measure their lives by their cosmetic surgery? "The movie was *Dead Heat*. It brought you your second Academy Award."

"And it brought me Victor." Lazily, Eve curled her legs up on the couch. "As I was saying before I started to ramble, I was still sore from my last marriage. Distrustful of men, though I certainly knew they had their uses and was never shy about utilizing them. I was pleased to be making this movie—particularly since Charlotte Miller had wanted the part desperately, and I'd beaten her to it. And because I'd be working with Victor, who had a tremendous reputation as an actor—stage and screen."

"You must have met him before."

"No, actually I hadn't. I imagine we'd attended some of the same functions, but our paths hadn't crossed. He was often in the East doing theater, and when here in California, he didn't socalize often, unless one counts the habitual drunken forays with a group of his male companions. We met on set. It happened so fast. Comet fast."

Lost in her thoughts, Eve ran a finger up and down the lapel of her robe. Her eyes were narrowed, concentrated, as if against some nagging pain. "People speak of love at first sight casually, humorously, wistfully. I don't believe it happens often, but when it does it's irresistible and dangerous. We said all the polite things strangers in the same profession say to each other at the start of an important project. But beneath all that was fire. How clichéd, but how true."

She rubbed absently at her temple. "Do you have a headache?" Julia asked. "Can I get you something?"

"No. It's nothing." Eve dragged deep on the cigarette and willed her mind beyond the pain, back into memory. "It all went very well initially. The plot of the movie was basic—I was a tough broad who'd inadvertently gotten herself mixed up with the mob. Victor was the cop assigned to protect me. What made the movie better than that was the sum of its parts. Gritty dialogue, moody sets and lighting, solid directing, a treasure chest of a supporting cast, and yes, the chemistry between the stars."

"I can't tell you how many times I've seen that film." Julia smiled, hoping to ease some of the pain she saw in Eve's eyes. "Each time I do, I find something new, something different."

"A small, shiny gem in my crown," Eve said, gesturing with the cigarette. "Do you recall the scene where Richard and Susan are hiding out in a grubby hotel room—he waiting for orders, she looking for a way out? They're arguing, insulting each other, fighting the attraction they've felt from the beginning. He the good, solid Irish cop believing in only right and wrong; she the girl from the wrong side of the tracks who lived in all the shades between black and white."

"I remember it very well. I caught it on television one night when I was baby-sitting. I would have been oh, fifteen, maybe sixteen, and I had a monster crush on Robert Redford. After the movie I tossed him aside like an old shoe and fell desperately in love with Victor Flannigan."

"How flattered he would be." To clear some of the emotion from her voice, Eve sipped at the water. "And how disappointing for Mr. Redford."

"I think he got over it." She gestured with her cup. "Go on, please. I shouldn't have interrupted."

"I enjoy it more when you do," Eve murmured, then rose to wander the room as she spoke. "What most don't remember about that scene in that long-ago movie, even those involved at the time, was that it wasn't played the way it was written. Victor changed the moves, and our lives."

♦ ♦ ♦ ♦

"Quiet on the set."

Eve took her place, mentally gearing up.

"Roll film."

She ignored the dollies, the booms, the technicians. Tossed up her chin, eased her weight onto one foot, pouted out her lower lip. Became Susan.

"Scene twenty-four, take three." The clapper slapped together.

"And . . . action."

"You don't know anything about me."

"I know everything about you, sweetheart." Victor loomed over her, fury and frustration in eyes that had been mild only seconds before. "You figured out when you were twelve that your looks would take you anywhere you wanted to go. And you went, taking the easy road and leaving a trail of men behind."

The close-up would come later. She knew the medium shot wouldn't capture the frost in her eyes, or the sneer on her lips. But she used them, the same way a good carpenter uses a hammer. To drive the point home. "If that were true, I sure as hell wouldn't be here in this dump with a loser like you."

"You walked into this." He stuck his hands in his pockets and rocked back on his heels. "Eyes wide. Women like you always have their eyes wide. You'll get yourself out too. That's your style."

Turning, she poured a drink from the bottle on the scarred chest of drawers. "It's not my style to turn my friends over to the cops."

"Friends." On a laugh he pulled out a cigarette. "You call it friendship when someone's out to slit your throat? Your choice, honey." The cigarette dangled from the corner of his mouth, his eyes squinted against the smoke that curled up between them. "You make the right choice—for you. And you'll get paid for it. The D.A.'ll slip you a few for the information. A woman like you . . ." He pulled the cigarette out of his mouth, blew smoke in a cloud. "You'd be used to getting paid for a favor."

She slapped him, forgetting to pull her punch at the last minute. His head jerked back, his eyes narrowed. Slowly, watching her, he dragged on the cigarette again. Eve drew her arm back a second time, wincing a little when his fingers clamped over her wrist. She was braced for the shove they'd rehearsed, prepared to slam hard into the chair behind him.

Instead, he tossed the cigarette to the floor. Her look of surprise, of knowledge, of panic, was captured on film forever as he dragged her into his arms. When his mouth crushed against hers, she struggled. Not so much against the arms that banded her against him, but against the explosions rocketing furiously inside her that had nothing to do with Susan and everything to do with Eve.

She might have staggered if he hadn't held her upright. It was terrifying to feel her legs go weak, to hear her blood roar. When he freed her she was fighting for each breath. Her skin had a pallor that needed no trick of lighting or makeup. Her lips trembled open. Her eyes glittered with tears, then with rage. She remembered her line only because it so completely suited her own feelings.

"You bastard. Do you think that's all it takes to have a woman fall at your feet?"

He grinned, but it didn't diffuse the passion or the violence in the air. "Yeah." Now he shoved her. "Sit down and shut up."

"Cut—print it. Jesus, Vic." The director was up, striding onto the set. "Where the hell did that come from?"

Bending, Victor picked up the smoldering cigarette, took a drag. "Just seemed like the thing to do."

"Well, it worked. Christ almighty, it worked. Next time the two of you get a brainstorm, fill me in. Okay?" He turned back to the cameras. "Let's shoot the close-ups."

She got through another three hours of shooting. That was her job. Not by a flicker did she reveal how shaken she was. That was her pride.

In her dressing room she exchanged Susan's clothes for her own. Shed Susan's problems for her own. Her throat was raw so she accepted the tall glass of iced tea from her on-set assistant.

"Susan smokes too much," she said with a half laugh. "Go on home. I'm just going to sit for a while and quiet down."

"You were terrific today, Miss Benedict. You and Mr. Flannigan are wonderful together."

"Yeah." God help her. "Thanks, darling. Good night."

"Good night, Miss Benedict. Oh, hello, Mr. Flannigan. I was just saying how well things went today."

"That's good to hear. Joanie, isn't it?"

"Oh, yes, sir."

"Good night, Joanie. See you tomorrow."

He stepped inside, and Eve remained seated and braced, watching him in the dressing table mirror. She relaxed fractionally when he left the door open. It wasn't, she realized, going to be a repeat of her initiation with Tony.

"I thought I should apologize." But there wasn't a hint of regret in his voice. Eve kept her eyes on his reflection, wondering when she'd get over this weakness for cocky actors. Casually she lifted a brush and began to pull it through her shoulder-length hair.

"For your brainstorm?"

"For kissing you when it had nothing to do with acting. It's something I've wanted to do since the first day we met."

"Now you have."

"And now it's worse." He dragged a hand through his hair, hair that was still dark with only the faintest hint of gray at the temples. "I'm a little past the age for playing games, Eve."

After setting the brush aside, she reached for the glass again. "No man ever is."

"I'm in love with you."

The ice clinked together when her hand shook. Very carefully she set the glass down. "Don't be ridiculous."

"I have to be because it's true. The first minute we were together."

"There's a difference between love and lust, Victor." She sprang up, snatching the canvas bag she habitually carried to the studio. "I'm not terribly interested in lust at the moment."

"How about a cup of coffee?"

"What?"

"A cup of coffee, Eve. In a public place." When she hesitated, he grinned—and the grin was nearly a sneer. "You're not afraid of me, are you, sweetheart?"

She had to laugh. It was Richard challenging Susan. "If I was afraid of anything," she said, in character, "it wouldn't be a man. You're buying."

They sat for almost three hours, eventually ordering meat loaf to go with the coffee. Victor had chosen a harshly lit diner with laminated tables and hard plastic booths that turned the average derriere to stone in ten and a half minutes. The floor was a dingy gray that would never bleach white again, and the waitresses talked in shrieks.

Obviously, Eve thought, this wasn't going to be a seduction.

He talked of Muriel, of his marriage, of its failure, of his obligations. He did not, as she had half expected, start with the line that his wife didn't understand him, or that his marriage was an open one. Instead, he admitted that in her way, Muriel loved him. That more than love, there was a desperate need in her to pretend the marriage was intact.

"She's not well." He toyed with the blueberry pie he'd ordered to top off the meal. It tasted like something his mother might have baked—a million years ago in the stifling kitchen on the fifth floor apartment on East 132nd Street. His mother, he thought fleetingly, had been an incredibly bad cook. "Not physically or emotionally. I'm not sure she'll ever be, and I can't leave her until she is. She doesn't have anyone else."

As a woman who had not so long ago escaped a ruinous marriage, she tried to empathize with Victor's wife. "It must be difficult for her, your work, the traveling, and the hours involved."

"No, actually, she enjoys it. She loves the house, and the servants are well trained to care for her. If she needs care. Actually, she would be self-sufficient but she often forgets to take her medication, and then . . ." He shrugged. "She paints. Very well, too, when the mood's on her. That's how I met her. I was your typical starving young actor, and I took a job modeling for an art school to earn enough to eat."

She forked a bite of his pie and grinned. "Nude?"

"Yeah." Her smile eased out one of his own. "I was a bit on the thin side then. After a session, Muriel showed me a sketch she'd done of me. One thing led to the other. She was what we'd have called a bohemian. Very forward-thinking and free-spirited." His smile faded away. "She's changed. The illness—the baby. Things changed her. She was diagnosed less than a year after we were married, and gave up completely on the dream of making art her career. Replaced it by making a career out of the religion we'd both rebelled against. I was sure I could shake her out of it. We were young, and I was positive nothing really terrible could happen to us. But it did. I began to get parts, we began to have money. Muriel began to become what she is today: a frightened, often angry, unhappy woman."

"You still love her."

"I love the rare, the very rare glimpses of that young bohemian who so enchanted me. If she were to come back, I don't think the marriage would hold. But we'd part as friends."

Eve suddenly felt tired, overwhelmed by the smell of grilling onions, the taste of coffee that was too hot and too strong, the hard, headachy colors that surrounded them. "I don't know what you expect me to say, Victor."

"Maybe nothing. Maybe I just need you to understand." Reaching across the table, he took her hand. When she looked down she saw that she was completely enveloped by him, completely covered, completely caught. "I was twenty-two when I met her. Now I'm forty-two. We might have made it all work if the fates hadn't been against us. I'll never know. But I knew when I looked at you. I knew you were the woman I was meant to spend my life with."

She felt the truth of it, the terrifying truth of it pass from his heart to hers. As cleanly, as quickly as a flower is sliced from its stem, the bright corner where they sat was cut off from the rest of the world.

Her voice was unsteady as she drew her hand away. "You've just spent a great deal of time explaining to me why that's not possible."

"It's not, but that doesn't stop me from knowing it's what should be. I'm too Irish not to believe in destiny, Eve. You're mine. Even if you get up and walk away, that won't change."

"And if I stay?"

"Then I'll give you whatever I can for as long as I can. It's not only sex, Eve, though Christ knows I want you. It's needing to be there when you first open your eyes in the morning. Sitting on some sunny porch together listening to the wind. Reading by the fire. Sharing a beer at a baseball game." He took a careful breath. "It's been nearly five years since Muriel and I have been together as husband and wife. I haven't been unfaithful—not in those five years or all the years we've been married. I don't expect you to believe me."

"Maybe that's why I do believe you." She got shakily to her feet, but held out a hand to keep him from rising as well. "I need time, Victor, and so do you. Let's finish the movie, then see how we feel."

"And if we feel the same?"

"If we feel the same . . . we'll see what destiny has in store for us."

♦ ♦ ♦ ♦

"*And* when the movie was over, we felt the same." Eve still had the glass in her hand. There were tears running unnoticed down her cheeks. "Destiny has run us a long, hard course."

"Would you change it?" Julia asked quietly.

"Parts of it, God, yes. But as a whole—it would hardly matter. I would still be here, exactly as I am today. And Victor would still be the only man." She laughed, brushing a tear away with her index finger. "The only man who could bring me to this."

"Is love worth it?"

"It's worth everything." She shook off the mood. "I'm becoming maudlin. Christ, I could use a drink, but I indulged earlier and the camera picks up every bloody swallow." She sat again. Leaning back, she shut her eyes and fell silent so long, Julia wondered if she slept. "You've made a happy home here, Julia."

"It's your home."

"Mmm. My house. It's you who's put flowers in the watering can, dropped your shoes on the floor, lit the candles on the mantel, put pictures of a smiling boy on the table by the window." Her eyes opened lazily. "I think it must take a clever woman to make a happy home."

"Not a happy woman?"

"But you're not. Oh, content certainly. Satisfied with your work, fulfilled in motherhood, pleased with your abilities and willing to sharpen them. But happy? Not quite."

Julia leaned over to press the stop button on the recorder. Something told her this wouldn't be a conversation she'd enjoy replaying later. "Why wouldn't I be happy?"

"Because you're carrying around a wound, never quite healed, from the man who conceived Brandon with you."

The mild, interested tone of her voice sharpened like ice. "We've already discussed Brandon's father. I hope I won't regret that."

"I'm not discussing Brandon's father, but you. You were used and set aside, at a very early age. That's kept you from looking for another kind of fulfillment."

"It may be difficult for you to understand, but not all women measure fulfillment by the number of men in their lives."

Eve merely arched a brow. "Well, it seems I pierced the skin. You're quite right. But the woman who measures it that way is as foolish as the one who refuses to admit that a certain man might enhance her life." She stretched long and limberly. "Julia darling, the recorder is off. It's only we two. Can you tell me, woman to woman, that you're not attracted, intrigued, titillated with Paul?"

After inclining her head, Julia folded her hands on her lap. "If I were attracted to Paul, would it be any of your business?"

"Hell no. Who wants to know only her own business? You of all people understand the desperate need in all of us to know everyone else's."

Julia laughed. It was hard to stay annoyed with such good-natured honesty. "I'm not a star, so fortunately my secrets are my own." Because she was enjoying herself, she propped her feet on the coffee table. "The truth is, they're not terribly interesting. Why don't you tell me why you're trying to hook up Paul and me?"

"Because when I see you together, something strikes me as right. And knowing him much better than I know you at this point, I'm able to judge his reaction. You fascinate him."

"Then he's easily fascinated."

"Quite the contrary. As far as I know—and I say so with all proper modesty—I've been the only woman to do so until you."

"Modesty, hell." Lazily, Julia rubbed the bottom of her foot over an itch on her instep. "You don't have a self-effacing bone in your body."

"Bingo."

Surrendering to a sudden craving for the brownies, Julia rose and went into the kitchen to fetch the plate heaped with the dark chocolate squares. She set them on the coffee table. Both women studied them warily, then dived.

"You know," Julia said with her mouth full, "he said the other day that I remind him of you."

"Did he?" Eve licked chocolate off her fingers, savoring. "Writer's imagination? Or instinct?" At Julia's puzzled look, she shook her head. "Christ, I have to get out of here before I eat another one."

"If you will, I will."

With no little regret, Eve resisted. "You don't have to be shoved into costume in the morning. But let me leave you with one small thought. You asked if I would change anything in my relationship with Victor. The first and most important change I would make is so very simple." She leaned forward, eyes intense. "I wouldn't wait until the movie was finished. I wouldn't waste a day, not an hour, not a moment. Take what you want, Julia, and damn caution. Live, enjoy. Feed ravenously. Or the biggest regret you'll have at the end of your life is wasted time."

◆ ◆ ◆

*L*YLE JOHNSON TOOK A PULL from a bottle of Bud and mechanically pressed the channel changer on the remote. It was a lousy night for television. He was stretched out on his unmade bed wearing only a pair of baby-blue net bikinis. That way, if he decided to get up and fetch another beer from the fridge, he'd be able to admire his body when he passed the mirror. He was damn proud of his build, and had a particular fondness for his penis—which he'd been told by a number of lucky females was a sight to behold.

All in all, Lyle was satisfied with his life. He got to drive the big bitching limo for a movie star. Maybe Eve Benedict wasn't Michelle Pfeiffer or Kim Basinger, but for an old broad, she was put together fine. In fact, Lyle would have been willing to share his amazing, world-renowned penis with her. But the lady was strictly business.

Still, he had it pretty good. His apartment over the garage was bigger and better than the dump in Bakersfield where he'd spent his childhood and dissatisfied adolescence. He had a microwave, cable TV, and someone to change the sheets and dig the place out once a week.

The snotty little maid, CeeCee, had turned down a trip to paradise on those nice fresh sheets. Didn't know what she was missing. Her loss was someone else's gain as far as Lyle was concerned. He'd been able to talk plenty of other, more friendly, ladies into his bed.

Still, it pissed him off that she'd threatened to go to Miss B. if he'd copped another feel.

Lyle settled on MTV, and since he was bored brainless, decided to get up and sneak a joint out of his stash. He had his ten neatly rolled buddies wrapped in plastic and hidden in a box of Quaker Oats. Miss B. had a strict policy on drugs. You use, you lose. She didn't mean just the hard stuff either, and had made that perfectly clear when she'd hired him.

Since the night was mild, he decided to do one better. Pulling on a pair of sweats, he gathered up the beer, the joint, and a pair of binoculars. At the last minute he turned the sound on the TV up so he could hear it on the roof.

With the binoks slung around his neck, the joint clamped in his mouth, and the beer hooked in two fingers, he made the climb easily enough.

Settled on his perch, he lit up. From there he could see most of the estate. Overhead was a canopy of stars and a sliver of moon. The mild breeze carried the mixture of scents from the garden, and the summery tang of grass mown by the gardener just that afternoon.

The old girl lived high, and he respected that. She had it all—the pool, the tennis courts, all the fancy trees. Lyle had fond memories of the putting green Miss B. no longer had any interest in. He'd snuck a waitress onto the estate one eventful evening and had fucked her brains out on the cool, clipped grass. What had she said her name was? he wondered as he held marijuana smoke in his lungs. Terri, Sherri? Shit, whatever it had been, she'd had a mouth like a suction cup. Maybe he should look her up again.

Idly, he swiveled the binoculars toward the guest house. Now, that was one fine piece of work in there. Real quality. Too bad that cute little ass of hers was so tight. She was cold as a witch's tit too.

And careful. He hadn't once been able to catch her doing anything interesting with the shades up. He'd been able to spot her going past a lighted window, bundled in a robe, or covered in a baggy sweatshirt. But when she undressed, down came the shades. Since Lyle had been playing peek-a-boo for weeks, he was wondering if Miss Julia Summers ever took off her clothes at all.

Now, Miss B. wasn't so particular. Lyle had seen her strip down to the skin before, and he'd be the first to compliment her on how well preserved she was.

Tonight there were lights on in the guest house. A guy could hope. Anyway, Lyle was looking at this Peeping Tom business as a job. A man in his position, with his ambitions, could always use some extra cash. Maybe if Julia had been friendlier he would have turned down the proposition that he spy on her. He laughed to himself as he began to cruise on the combo of Bud and grass. And maybe not. The pay was good; the work was a breeze.

All he had to do was pass along the comings and goings in the guest house, write down Julia's routine, and keep a record of her outside appointments. Even that wasn't hard. The woman was so tied up in her kid, she never left the estate without leaving word where she'd be.

Easy work. Good pay. What else could you ask for?

Lyle perked up when her bedroom light came on. He caught a glimpse of her. She was still dressed in a sweater and slacks. She was pacing, distracted. Hope bloomed in horny Lyle's chest. Maybe she was distracted enough to forget to close the blinds. She paused, was nearly centered in the window as she reached up to draw the band from her hair.

"Oh, yeah. Come on, baby. Keep going." Chuckling to himself, he held the binoks with one hand and slipped the other down his pants, where he was already firming up nicely.

He'd always heard patience was rewarded. He believed it now when Julia dragged the sweater over her head. Underneath she was wearing some thin, lacy things. A camisole. Tap pants. Lyle prided himself on knowing the correct name in ladies' lingerie.

He murmured encouragement to her as he primed his own pump. "Come on, baby, don't stop now. That's the way. Ditch those pants. Oh, Christ. Look at those legs."

He let out a groan when the blinds came down, but he still had his imagination. By the time Julia's lights blinked out, Lyle had shot himself to the moon.

Chapter Fifteen

♦ ♦ ♦ ♦

"THE PLACE is really hopping." CeeCee slipped into the kitchen, where Julia was preparing a late afternoon snack for Brandon and Dustin.

"I can hear the commotion." That alone had caused Julia to ruin two nails and eat her way through a half a roll of Tums. "It's taken all my wiles to keep the boys from running over and getting in the middle of it."

"It was nice of you to take Dustin to the park."

"They keep each other busy." And to keep herself busy, Julia arranged fruit and vegetable slices on a tray in a way she hoped disguised nutrition. "I like watching them together."

Because she'd come to feel as comfortable in this kitchen as in her own, CeeCee chose an apple crescent. "If you want a real show, you should go next door. You should see the flowers! Man, truckloads of them. And there are all these people jumbling around, speaking in different languages. Miss Soloman's running around trying to coordinate all of them, and they just keep coming."

"Miss Benedict?"

"She's being buffed and waxed by a team of three," CeeCee said with her mouth full. "The phone hasn't quit ringing all day. There was this guy in a white suit who actually started crying because some quail eggs hadn't arrived yet. That's when I left."

"Good thinking."

"Really, Julia, Miss. B.'s given some knockout parties, but this is the ultimate. Like she's pulling out all the stops because she's afraid she'll never give another one. Hell, Aunt Dottie told me she was having those quail eggs and some kind of mushrooms flown in all the way from Japan or China or someplace over there."

"I'd just say Miss B. is indulging herself."

"Big time." CeeCee popped a cube of cheese in her mouth.

"I feel guilty that you're going to miss it because you're watching Brandon."

"Hey, I don't mind." Anyway, she planned to sneak the boys into the shrubbery to watch for an hour or so. "Half the fun's seeing everybody go crazy putting it all together. Did you get a new dress?" she asked casually, trailing behind as Julia walked out to call the boys.

"No, I meant to, but it slipped my mind. Hey up there. Snacks in the kitchen." With the sound of clammering feet and war whoops, the boys streaked down the stairs and zapped into the kitchen. "I'll put something together," she told CeeCee. "Maybe you can help me decide."

CeeCee grinned and stuck her hands in the pockets of her cutoffs. "Sure. I love playing closet. Want to do it now?"

Julia looked at her watch and sighed. Time was running out. "I suppose I should. You can't get ready for a bash like this in less than two hours."

"You don't sound excited. I mean, this is shaping up to be *the* Hollywood party this year."

"I do better at birthday parties. The kind with pin the tail on the donkey and twenty-five revved-up kids cramming in cake and ice cream."

"Tonight you're not a mom," CeeCee said, giving Julia a little nudge up the stairs. "Tonight you're on Eve Benedict's A list." At the sound of a knock on the door, CeeCee jumped, then blocked Julia's path. "No, no. I'll get it. You go on up. I'll bring it."

"Bring what?"

"I mean, I'll see who it is. Go ahead. And if you're wearing a bra, take it off."

"If I'm . . ." But CeeCee was already rushing off. Shaking her head, Julia headed for the bedroom. Listlessly, she began to paw through her closet. There was the old reliable blue silk, but she'd worn that when she and Paul . . . It was her own fault she'd chosen to pack more business suits than finery. There was always basic black, she thought, and pulled out a simple number that had served her well for five years. She smiled to herself as she laid it on the bed. CeeCee would probably gag. Julia dove back into the closet.

"My choices," she said when she heard CeeCee come in, "are pitifully limited. But with a little ingenuity, who knows?" She turned. "What's that?"

"Delivery." CeeCee set the box she carried on the bed, then stepped back. "I guess you should open it."

"I didn't order anything." Since the box was unmarked, Julia shrugged and ripped at the packing tape.

"Here, let me." Impatient, CeeCee grabbed a nail file from the nightstand and raked through.

"I'd love to see you on Christmas morning." Julia blew the hair out of her eyes and opened the top. "Tissue paper," she said. "My favorite." But her laugh changed to a gasp of astonishment when she lifted the paper aside.

The shimmer of emerald silk, the dazzle of rhinestones. Hardly breathing, Julia gently slid the dress from the box. It was long, slim, and spectacular, a slither of silk that would sleek over the body like air. The high neck was topped with a banded collar that glittered with stones and was repeated at the cuffs at the end of long, snug sleeves. The back dropped off to nothing from shoulder to waist.

"Oh, my," Julia managed to get out.

"There's a card." With her bottom lip caught in her teeth, CeeCee handed it over.

"From Eve. She says she'd appreciate it if I'd wear this tonight."

"What do you think?"

"I think she's put me in an awkward position." Reluctantly, Julia laid the dress on the box, where it glittered up at her. "I can't possibly accept this."

CeeCee looked down at the dress, then back at Julia. "You don't like it?"

"Don't like it? It's fabulous." Giving in to temptation, Julia ran her hand along the skirt. "Stunning."

"Really?"

"And outrageously expensive. No." She wavered. "I don't suppose I'd have to worry about it respecting me in the morning."

"Huh?"

"Nothing." Julia caught herself and spread a layer of tissue paper over the dress. The rich emerald shimmered through, beckoning. "It isn't right. It's very generous of her, but it's just not right."

"The dress isn't right?"

"No, for heaven's sake, CeeCee, the dress is perfectly beautiful. It's a matter of ethics." She knew she was groping. She wanted that dress, wanted to feel it slide over her and change her into something, someone, elegant. "I'm Eve Benedict's biographer, and that's all. I'd feel better—" That was a lie. "It would be more appropriate for me to wear something of my own."

"But it is yours." CeeCee grabbed the dress and held it in front of Julia. "It was made for you."

"I'll admit it's my style, and certainly seems to be my size—"

"No, I mean it *was* made for you. I designed it for you myself."

"You made it?" Stunned, she turned full circle so she could study the dress held against her in the mirror.

"Miss B. asked me to. She wanted you to have something special for tonight. And she likes surprises. I had to go through your closet." CeeCee began to wipe her damp palms on her cutoffs when Julia remained silent. "I know it was sneaky. But I needed to get the fit right. You like rich colors, so I thought the emerald was a good choice, and the style . . . I figured I'd try for subtly sexy. You know, classy but not prim or anything." Running out of steam, CeeCee sank to the bed. "You hate it. It's okay," she hurried on when Julia turned around. "I mean, I'm not like sensitive or anything. I understand if it's not really your type."

Julia held up a hand, realizing CeeCee was getting her second wind. "Didn't I say it was beautiful?"

"Yeah, sure, but you didn't want to hurt my feelings."

"I didn't know you'd made it when I said that."

CeeCee pursed her lips as that sunk in. "Right."

Julia laid the dress aside again and placed her hands on CeeCee's shoulders. "It's an incredible dress, the most terrific dress I've ever had."

"Then you're going to wear it?"

"If you think I'm passing up the chance to wear a McKenna original, you're crazy." She laughed as CeeCee bounced up and hugged her.

"Miss B. told me I could pick out some accessories too." Running full steam, she spun around to tear at the tissue paper until she unearthed a velvet pouch. "This rhinestone clip. I thought you'd wear your hair up, you know?" She demonstrated by sweeping up her own. "And snap this in. And the earrings. Shoulder dusters." Eyes bright with excitement, she held them out. "What do you think?"

Julia jingled the long, glittery drops in her hand. She'd never thought of herself as the shoulder-duster type. Feather duster, maybe. But since CeeCee did, Julia was willing to risk it for one night. "I think I'm going to knock them dead."

Two and a half hours later, after a long, indulgent female ritual of creams, oils, powders, and perfumes, Julia let CeeCee help her into the dress.

"Well?" Julia started to turn to the mirror, but CeeCee grabbed hold.

"Not yet. First the earrings."

While Julia clipped them on, CeeCee fussed with her hair, tugged at the skirt of the dress, adjusted the collar.

"Okay. You can look." Stomach jittering, CeeCee took a long breath and held it.

One glance told Julia the dress lived up to its promise. The dazzle of rhinestones added dash to the long, cool lines. The high collar and long, tight sleeves hinted at dignity. While the back hinted at something else altogether.

"I feel like Cinderella," Julia murmured. She turned and held out her hands to CeeCee. "I don't know how to thank you."

"That's easy. When people start asking you about your dress, be sure to tell them you discovered a hot new designer. CeeCee McKenna."

♦ ♦ ♦ ♦

JULIA'S FEELINGS of panic had escalated several notches when she walked to the main house. The setting was perfect.

An ocean of flowers set off by a trio of ice sculpture mermaids. Linen-covered tables as white as the rising moon, groaning under the weight of elegant food, champagne enough to swim in, the twinkle of starry lights strung through the trees.

There was a glamorous mixing of the old and the new, Hollywood's tribute to youth, and to endurance. Julia thought it was epitomized by Victor Flannigan and Peter Jackson. Eve's long and enduring love and—if the looks exchanged were anything to go by—her latest flirtation.

Jewelry glittered, outsparkling the fairy lights. The fragile scents of roses, camellias, magnolias, wafted around perfumed flesh. Music floated over laughter, and the ubiquitous dealing that used galas as handily as boardrooms.

More stars than a planetarium, Julia mused, recognizing faces familiar to the screen, small and large. And with the addition of producers, directors, writers, and the press, power enough to light any major city.

And this is Hollywood, she thought. Where fame and power arm-wrestle on a daily basis.

She spent over an hour mingling, making mental notes and wishing it wouldn't have been bad form to haul out her tape recorder. Needing a breather, she slipped away from the crowd to listen to the music at the edge of the garden.

"Hiding out?" Paul asked.

Her smile came too quickly, so quickly she was grateful her back was to him. Because he enjoyed the view, he was glad of it himself.

"Catching my breath," she said. She told herself she had not been waiting for him, had not been looking for him. Or wishing for him. "Are you fashionably late?"

"Just late. Had a good run going in chapter seven." He offered her one of the two glasses of champagne he held. Looking at her, he wondered why it had seemed so urgent that he sweat out those last few pages. She smelled like a garden at dusk, and looked like sin. "Why don't you fill me in?"

"Well, personally, I've had my hand kissed, my cheek bussed, and, in one unfortunate case, my ass pinched." Her eyes laughed over the rim of her glass. "I've dodged, evaded, and avoided a number of pointed questions about my work on Eve's book, tolerated numerous stares and whispers—relevant to the same, I'm sure—and interrupted a small, nasty quarrel between two stunning-looking creatures over someone named Clyde."

He slid a finger down the earring that brushed one silky shoulder. "Busy girl."

"So you can see why I wanted to catch my breath."

Absently, he nodded as he scanned the clusters of people over terrace and lawn. They reminded him of the most elegant of animals set out to graze in an expensive zoo. "When Eve does it, she does it all the way."

"It's been a terrific party so far. We have quail eggs and button mushrooms from the Far East. Truffles and pâté from the French countryside. Salmon from Alaska, lobster from Maine. And I believe the artichoke hearts were imported from Spain."

"We have much more than that. Do you see that man? The frail-looking one with thin white hair. He's leaning on a cane and attended by a redhead who's built like a—"

"Yes, I see him."

"Michael Torrent."

"Torrent?" Julia took a step forward to get a better look. "But I thought he'd retired to the Riviera. I've been trying to contact him for a month to set up an interview."

Experimentally, Paul traced a fingertip down her spine, pleased when he felt her quick tremor. "I like your bare back almost as much as your bare feet."

She would not be distracted—even if he'd lit a line of fire down her spine. She eased a cautious inch away. His mouth quirked. "We were talking about Torrent," she said. "Why do you suppose he'd come all this way for free food and champagne?"

"Obviously he thought an invitation to this particular party was worth a trip. And there?"

Before she could tell Paul to stop playing with her fingers, she focused on the man he was watching. "I know Anthony Kincade is here. I don't understand why Eve invited him."

"If you don't, you should."

"Well, two of her husbands—"

"Three," Paul corrected her. "Damien Priest just stepped onto the terrace."

Julia recognized him instantly. Though he was the only one of Eve's husbands who hadn't been in films, he was a celebrity in his own right. Before his retirement at thirty-five, Priest had been one of the top money winners in professional tennis. A Wimbledon champion, he had also racked up wins in all the other Grand Slam tourneys.

Tall and rangy, Priest had a long reach and a wicked backhand. He had a gut-slamming sexuality a woman noticed instantly. Seeing him now, with his arm tucked around the waist of a young woman, Julia understood why Eve had married him.

His marriage to Eve had generated acres of print. He had been nearly twenty years her junior when they had eloped to Las Vegas. Though their marriage had lasted only one tumultuous year, it had given the tabloids fodder for months after.

"Three out of four," Julia murmured, wondering how she could work it to her advantage. "Your father?"

"Sorry. Not even this could tear him away from a performance of *Lear*." Paul sampled the champagne and thought how much he'd have liked to sample the taste of Julia's long, smooth back. "Though I am under orders to report anything of interest."

"Hopefully there will be."

"Don't borrow trouble." He laid a hand on her arm. "Other than the husbands, I could point out any number of ex-lovers, old rivals, and displeased friends."

"I wish you would."

He only shook his head. "There are also plenty of people here who would probably be very happy to see this entire book business disappear."

Irritation sparkled in her eyes. "Including you."

"Yes. I've had a long time to think about you having someone break in and go through your work. Maybe it was just idle curiosity, but I doubt it. I told you from the beginning I didn't want Eve hurt. I don't want you hurt either."

"We're both big girls, Paul. If it helps ease your mind, I can tell you that what Eve has told me so far is sensitive, certainly personal, perhaps uncomfortable for certain people. I really don't think any of it could be considered threatening."

"She isn't finished yet. And she—" Even as his eyes narrowed, his fingers tightened on the stem of the glass.

"What is it?"

"Another of Eve's Michaels." His voice had cooled, but it was nothing compared to the ice in his eyes. She wondered the air around them didn't crackle. "Delrickio."

"Michael Delrickio?" Julia tried to pick out the man Paul was staring at. "Should I know him?"

"No. And if you're lucky, you'll live the rest of your life without knowing him."

"Why?" As she asked, she recognized the man she had seen come out of Drake's office. "Is he that distinguished-looking man with silver hair and a mustache?"

"Looks can be deceiving." Paul passed her his half-full glass of wine. "Excuse me."

Ignoring the people who called his name or reached out to lay a hand on his arm, Paul made a direct line for Delrickio. It might have been the expression in his eyes or the barely suppressed fury in his stride that had several backing off—and the burly Joseph moving closer. Paul sent one long, challenging glance toward Delrickio's muscle, then trained his eyes on the don. With only the barest flicker of his eye, Delrickio had Joseph standing aside.

"Well, Paul. It's been a long time."

"Time's relative. How did you slither through the gate, Delrickio?"

Delrickio sighed and chose one of the delicate lobster puffs from his plate. "You still have trouble with respect. Eve should have let me discipline you all those years ago."

"Fifteen years ago I was a boy, and you were a slimy smear on the boot heel of humanity. The difference now is I'm no longer a boy."

Rage was something Delrickio had long since learned to control. It snapped at him now, dug in its teeth, and was whipped back in a matter of seconds. "Your manners dishonor the woman who opened her house to us tonight." With care and deliberation, he chose another hors d'oeuvre. "Even enemies must respect neutral territory."

"This has never been neutral territory. If Eve invited you here, she made an error in judgment. The fact that you're here tells me you have no conception of the word *honor.*"

The raw anger flared again. "I'm here to enjoy the hospitality of a beautiful woman." He smiled, but his eyes burned. "As I have done often in the past."

Paul made a quick move forward. Joseph moved simultaneously. By slipping his hand inside his jacket, he turned the barrel of the .32 automatic he carried into the flesh beneath Paul's armpit.

"Oh!" Julia stumbled and spilled a full glass of champagne over Joseph's shiny Gucci loafers. "Oh, I'm terribly sorry. How awful. Really, I don't know how I could be so clumsy." Fluttering and smiling, she whipped Joseph's handkerchief from his pocket, then squatted at his feet. "I'll dry them off for you before it spots."

The commotion she was causing had a ripple of laughter moving through the nearby huddle of people. Smiling artlessly at Joseph, she lifted her hand, giving him little choice but to help her to her feet—and position her between himself and Paul.

"I seemed to have soaked your handkerchief."

He muttered something and stuffed it into his pocket.

"Haven't we met before?" she asked him.

"A tired line, Julia." Eve glided up beside her. "It almost ruins the effect of you kneeling at the man's feet. Hello, Michael."

"Eve." He took her hand, lifting it slowly to his lips. The old need churned in him, darkened his eyes. If Paul hadn't told Julia they had been lovers, she would have known it then, by the snapping in the air. "More beautiful than ever."

"You're looking . . . prosperous. I see you're making old acquaintances—and new. You remember Paul, of course. And this is my charming, if clumsy, biographer, Julia Summers."

"Miss Summers." He brushed his lips and mustache over her knuckles. "I'm delighted to meet you, at last."

Before she could reply, Paul had an arm around her waist and was pulling her to his side. "Why the hell is he here, Eve?"

"Now, Paul, don't be rude. Mr. Delrickio's a guest. I wondered, Michael, have you had a chance to speak with Damien yet? I'm sure the two of you have a lot of old times to talk over."

"No."

Eve's eyes glittered, as cold as the stars at her throat. She laughed. "You might be interested, Julia, that I met my fourth husband through Michael. Damien and Michael were—would you say you were business associates, darling?"

There was no one who had touched his life who could bait him as successfully as Eve Benedict. "We had—common interests."

"What a clever way of putting it. Well, Damien retired a champion, and all got what they wanted. Oh, except for Hank Freemont. Such a tragedy. Do you follow tennis, Julia?"

There was something here, something old and unpleasant beneath the scent of flowers and perfume. "No, I'm afraid I don't."

"Well, this was about fifteen years ago. How time flies." She took a delicate sip of champagne. "Freemont was Damien's chief competitor— even his nemesis. They went into the U.S. Open as first and second seeds. The betting was high as to who would come out on top. But to make it short, Freemont overdosed. A cocaine and heroine injection—a speedball, I believe they call it. It was tragic. But then Damien romped his way to the championship. Those with money on him did very nicely." Slowly, carmine-tipped nails gleaming, she ran a finger around the rim of her champagne flute. "You're a gambler, aren't you, Michael?"

"All men are."

"And some are more successful than others. Please don't let me keep you from mingling, or enjoying the buffet, the music, old friends. I hope we have a chance to speak again before the evening ends."

"I'm sure we will." He turned and saw Nina standing a few feet away. Their eyes met, held. Hers dropped first before she turned and rushed inside the house.

"Eve," Julia began, but she only shook her head.

"Christ, I need a cigarette." Then she turned her smile up a hundred candlepower. "Johnny darling, how delightful of you to come." She was moving off to be embraced and kissed.

Julia gave up on that source and turned to Paul. "What was that all about?"

He reached down to take her hands. "You're shaking."

"I feel as though I just witnessed a bloodless coup. I—" She bit her tongue as Paul took two fresh glasses from a passing waiter.

"Three slow sips," he ordered.

Because she needed to calm down, she obeyed. "Paul, did that man have a gun at your heart?"

Though he smiled at her, the amusement in his eyes was offset by something more dangerous, more deadly. "Were you saving me with a glass of champagne, Jules?"

"It worked," she said sharply, then sipped again. "I want you to tell me why you spoke to that man that way, who he is, and why he brought an armed bodyguard to a party."

"Have I had a chance to tell you how beautiful you look tonight?"

"Answers."

Instead, he set his glass down on a wrought iron table and cupped her face in his hands. Before she could evade—or even decide if she wished to—he was kissing her with a great deal more passion than was wise in public. And beneath it she tasted a bitter, smoldering anger.

"Stay away from Delrickio," he said quietly, then kissed her again. "And if you want to enjoy the rest of the evening, stay away from me."

He left her there to turn inside the house in search of something stronger than champagne.

"Well, it's been quite a show so far."

Jolted, Julia let out a long sigh as Victor patted her shoulder. "I just wish someone had given me a script."

"Eve often prefers ad-lib." He glanced around, shaking the ice in his glass of club soda. "Christ knows she likes to stir the pot. She's managed to bring out nearly all the players tonight."

"I don't suppose you'll tell me who Michael Delrickio is."

"A businessman." Victor smiled down at her. "Would you like to walk in the garden?"

She would simply have to find out on her own. "Yes, I would."

They left the terrace and crossed the lawn through the shadows and twinkling lights. The orchestra was playing "Moonglow" as they moved into the perfumed air. Julia remembered that weeks before she had seen Victor and Eve stroll through this same garden, under the same moon.

"I hope your wife is recovering." She saw from his expression that she'd made the move too quickly. "I'm sorry, Eve mentioned that she was ill."

"You're being diplomatic, Julia. I'm sure she told you more than that." He gulped club soda and fought against the siren call of whiskey. "Muriel is out of immediate danger. The recovery, I'm afraid, will be a long and difficult one."

"It can't be easy for you."

"It could be easier, but Eve won't let it." With weary eyes he looked down at Julia. The way the moonlight slanted over her face struck some chord in him he couldn't identify. Tonight the garden was meant for young men and women. And he was feeling old. "I know Eve has told you about us."

"Yes, but she didn't have to. I saw you here one night a few weeks ago." When he stiffened, she laid a hand on his arm. "I wasn't spying. Just in the wrong place at the wrong time."

"Or the right place at the right time," he said grimly.

Julia nodded, and took the time while he lighted a cigarette to choose her words. "I know it was private, but I can't be sorry. What I saw were two people deeply in love. It didn't shock me or send me rushing to my typewriter to report it. It touched me."

His fingers relaxed fractionally, but his eyes remained cold. "Eve has always been the best part of my life, and the worst. Can you understand why I need to keep what we've had private?"

"Yes, I can." She let her hand fall away. "As I can understand why she needs to tell it. However much I might sympathize, my first obligation is to her."

"Loyalty is admirable. Even when it's misplaced. Let me tell you something about Eve. She's a fascinating woman, one of incredible talent, of deep feelings, of unrelenting strengths. She is also a creature of impulse, one who makes huge life-altering mistakes because of a moment's passion. She will come to regret this book, but by then it may be too late." He tossed the cigarette onto the path and crushed it out. "Too late for all of us."

Julia let him go. There was no comfort or reassurance she could offer. However much she might sympathize, her allegiance was to Eve. Suddenly weary, she sank down on a marble bench. It was quiet there. The band had switched to "My Funny Valentine," with the female vocalist crooning. Eve was definitely in an old-fashioned mood. Taking advantage of the solitude and soothing music, Julia tried to reconstruct and evaluate what she had seen and heard thus far.

As her thoughts drifted, Julia became aware of other voices, farther off in the shrubbery. At first she was annoyed. She wanted only fifteen minutes of peace. Then, as she caught the tone, she was curious. Definitely a man and a woman, she thought. And definitely an argument. Eve perhaps? she wondered, and debated whether to stay or go.

She heard an oath, sharp and Italian, then a stream of harsh words in the same language, followed by a woman's bitter weeping.

Pressing her fingers at her temples and circling them, Julia rose. Leaving was definitely the best course.

"I know who you are."

She saw a woman in shimmering, virginal white stagger onto the path. Julia recognized Gloria DuBarry immediately. Though the weeping had stopped abruptly, the petite and very drunk actress had approached from the opposite direction.

"Miss DuBarry," Julia said, and wondered what the hell she was supposed to do now.

"I know who you are," Gloria repeated, and stumbled forward. "Eve's little snitch. Let me tell you something, if you print one word about me, one single word, I'll sue your ass right off."

The virgin queen was drunk as a skunk, Julia noted, and bruising for a fight. "Maybe you should sit down."

"Don't touch me." Gloria slapped Julia's hand away, then gripped her arms, nails digging in. She leaned in, and Julia winced more from her breath than her manicure. It wasn't champagne on Gloria's breath, but high-grade scotch.

"You're doing the touching, Miss DuBarry," Julia pointed out.

"Do you know who I am? Do you know what I am? I'm a fucking institution." Though she weaved as she threw out the words, her fingers were like wires. "Mess with me and you're messing with motherhood, apple pie, and the goddamn American flag."

Julia made one attempt to drag Gloria's hands from her arms and found the small woman surprisingly strong. "If you don't let go of me," Julia said between her teeth, "I'm going to knock you down."

"You listen to me." Gloria gave Julia a shove that nearly sent her over the marble bench. "If you know what's good for you, you'll forget whatever she's told you. It's all lies, all cruel, vicious lies."

"I don't know what you're talking about."

"You want money?" Gloria spat out. "Is that it? You want more money. How much? How much do you want?"

"I want you to leave me alone. If you want to talk to me, we'll do it when you're sober."

"I'm never drunk." Eyes ripe with venom, Gloria rapped the heel of her hand between Julia's breasts. "I'm never fucking drunk and don't you forget it. I don't need some slutty snitch Eve hired to tell me I'm drunk."

Temper snapped. Julia's hand swooped out and snatched a fistful of chiffon at Gloria's throat. "You touch me again, and—"

"Gloria." Paul's voice was quiet as he came down the path. "Aren't you feeling well?"

"No." She turned on tears as automatically as turning on a faucet. "I don't know what's wrong with me. I feel so weak and shaky." She buried her face against his jacket. "Where's Marcus? Marcus will take care of me."

"Why don't I take you into the house so you can lie down? I'll bring him to you."

"I have such a dreadful headache," she sobbed as Paul led her away.

He shot Julia a glance over his shoulder. "Sit" was all he said.

Julia folded her arms over her chest, and sat.

He was back in ten minutes, and dropped down beside her with a long sigh. "I don't believe I've ever seen the queen of the Gs sloshed before. You want to tell me what that was all about?"

"I haven't got a clue. But I intend to corner Eve at the first opportunity and find out."

Curious, he traced a finger down the nape of her neck. "Just what was it you were going to do if Gloria touched you again?"

"Slug her on her pointy little chin."

He laughed, squeezing her against him. "God, what a woman. Now I only wish I'd been ten seconds later."

"I don't enjoy altercations."

"No, I can see that. Eve, on the other hand, has set up multiple altercations in one star-studded evening. Shall I tell you what you've missed during your tour of the gardens?"

If he was trying to calm her down, the least she could do was give him a chance. "All right."

"Kincade has been waddling around looking fat and threatening, and failing to get Eve alone for a private chat. Anna del Rio, the designer? She's been telling catty stories about her hostess, hoping, I imagine, to offset whatever catty stories Eve intends to tell about her." He drew out a cigar. In the flare of his lighter his face looked tensed in opposition to the mild amusement in his voice. "Drake has been hopping around as though he had hot coals in his Jockeys."

"Maybe that's because I saw Delrickio and that other man in his office last week."

"Did you?" Paul expelled smoke slowly. "Well, well. Back at the ranch—Torrent is looking pitiful—more so after he and Eve had a little tête-à-tête. Priest is doing a lot of posturing and hearty laughing. While he and Eve were dancing, he was sweating."

"It sounds as though I should get back and see for myself."

"Julia." He stopped her from rising. "We need to talk about several things. I'll come by tomorrow."

"Not tomorrow," she said, knowing she was only procrastinating. "Brandon and I have plans."

"Monday then, while he's in school. That would be better."

"I have an appointment at eleven-thirty with Anna at her studio."

"Then I'll be there at nine." He rose, offering a hand to help her to her feet.

She walked with him toward the sound of music and laughter. "Paul, were you coming to my rescue with Gloria with handkerchiefs and sympathy?"

"It worked."

"Then we're even."

He hesitated only a moment before linking his fingers with hers. "Just about."

Chapter Sixteen

····

THE PARTY DIDN'T fizzle out until after three, though by then only a few diehards had remained, slopping up the last of the champagne and licking the beluga off their fingers. Perhaps they were the wise ones, greeting the oncoming day with bleary eyes, floating heads, and overfilled stomachs. Many of those who had left at a more conservative hour lost a night's sleep without the extras.

With a brocade smoking jacket wrapped around the enormous bulk that flirted gleefully with heart failure, Anthony Kincade sat up in bed smoking one of the cigars his doctors warned would kill him that much sooner. The boy he'd chosen to use that night lay sprawled among the silk sheets and feather pillows, snoring off a tidy dose of meth and a bout of brutal sex. Across his smooth, slender back a row of angry pink welts had risen.

Kincade didn't regret putting them there—the boy was paid well—but he did regret he'd had to settle for a substitute. All the time he'd whipped, all the time he'd driven himself, hard and cruelly into the boy, he'd dreamed of punishing Eve.

Bitch. Whore-bitch. He wheezed rustily as he shifted his mountainous flesh to reach for the glass of port beside the bed. Did she think she could threaten him? Did she think she could toy and tease and dangle exposure in front of his nose?

She wouldn't dare go public with what she knew. But if she did . . . His hand trembled as he slurped the wine. His eyes, nearly buried under the folds of sagging skin around them, glinted with venom. If she did, how many others might find the courage to walk through the door she'd opened? He couldn't allow it. Wouldn't.

He might be arrested, have to stand trial, even face prison.

It wouldn't happen. He wouldn't let it happen.

He drank, he smoked, he plotted. Beside him, the young prostitute murmured in his sleep.

♦ ♦ ♦ ♦

I~N~ Long Beach, Delrickio soaked in his whirlpool, letting the hot, jasmine-scented water beat over his tanned, disciplined body. He'd made love to his wife when he'd returned home. Sweetly, tenderly. His lovely Teresa now slept the sleep of the cherished.

God, he did cherish the woman, and hated the fact that while he'd steeped himself in her, he'd fantasized about Eve. Of all the sins he'd committed, this was the only one he repented. Even with what Eve was doing, what she was threatening to do, she couldn't kill the hunger in him. And that was his penance.

Fighting to keep his muscles from tensing again, he watched the steam rise to smoke up the slanted windows and block the stars. She had been like that to him, like steam smoking up his senses, blocking his sanity. Didn't she realize he would have kept her safe, happy, showered her with all the things a woman desired? Instead, she had spurned him, cut him out of her life with a finality and viciousness that had resembled death. And all because of business.

He forced his hand to relax and waited until the splinter of rage had been worked out of his heart. A man who thought with his heart made mistakes. As he had. It was his own fault that Eve had found out about some of the more unconventional parts of Delrickio Enterprises. Infatuation had made him careless. Still, he had believed, or made himself believe, that she could be trusted.

Then she had tossed Damien Priest in his face. She had looked at him, her eyes filled with disgust.

The former tennis player was a loose end that could easily be snipped at any time. But that would not make things right. It was Eve who could unravel his carefully woven cloak of respectability.

He would have to settle things, and he regretted it. But even before love came honor.

♦ ♦ ♦ ♦

G~loria~ D~u~B~arry~ cuddled beside her sleeping husband and let the tears stream down her face. She felt sick—too much liquor always upset her system. It was Eve's fault she'd overindulged and had come so perilously close to humiliating herself.

It was all Eve's fault. Hers and that nosy witch from back east.

They were going to see to it that she lost everything—her reputation, her marriage, maybe even her career. And all because of one mistake. One small mistake.

Sniffling, she stroked a hand over her husband's bare shoulder. It was solid, sturdy, like a quarter century of marriage. She loved Marcus so much. He took such good care of her. How often had he said she was his angel, his spotless, untarnished angel?

How could he understand, how could anyone understand, that the woman who made her career playing freckle-faced virgins had indulged in a torrid, illicit affair with a married man? That she had had an illegal abortion to rid herself of the result of that affair?

Oh, God, how could she ever have imagined herself in love with Michael Torrent? What was worse, much worse, was that while she'd been meeting him in dingy motels, he had been playing her father onscreen. Her father.

Having to come face-to-face with him tonight when he was old, half-crippled . . . frail. It disgusted her to think that she had once held him inside her. Terrified her. She hated him. She hated Eve. She wished they were both dead. Wallowing in self-pity, she wept into her pillow.

◆ ◆ ◆ ◆

MICHAEL TORRENT WAS used to bad nights. His body was so riddled with arthritis that he was rarely free of pain. Age and illness had hulled him out, leaving just enough flesh and nerve in the shell for misery. Tonight it was his mind, not his body, keeping him from the luxury of sleep.

He could curse the age that had ruined his body, sapped him of energy, robbed him of the comfort of sex. He could weep knowing he'd once been a king, and was now less than a man. All the memories of what he had been jabbed at him like hot needles that gave no peace to tired flesh. But that, all of that, was nothing.

Now Eve was threatening to take away the little he had left. His pride, and his image.

Perhaps he could no longer act, but he'd been able to sate that thirst with the legend. He was revered, admired, respected, thought of by fans and associates as a grand old man, the one-time king of the romantic era of Hollywood. Grant and Gable, Power and Flynn were dead. Michael Torrent, who had ended his acting career graciously playing wise old grandfathers, was alive. He was alive and they stood up and cheered for him whenever he granted an audience.

He hated the fact that Eve would tell the world that he had cheated his best and closest friend, Charlie Gray. For years Michael had used his clout to see that the studio hadn't given Charlie more than a sidekick role. He had gone out of his way to sneak behind Charlie's back and cuckold him with each one of his wives. How could he make anyone understand that it had been a game to him, a petty, childish game brought on by youth and envy? Charlie had been smarter, more skilled, and just plain nicer than Michael could ever hope to be. He hadn't meant to hurt Charlie, not really. After the suicide, guilt had eaten at him until he'd confessed it all to Eve.

He'd expected comfort, solicitude, understanding. She'd given him none of those things, but had settled into a cold rage. The confession had doomed their marriage. Now Eve would doom what was left of his life with a bitter humiliation.

Unless someone stopped her.

♦ ♦ ♦ ♦

SWEAT POPPED out on Drake's skin like bullets. Eyes wild, he wandered around his house, not nearly drunk enough to sleep. He was still fifty thousand short of the mark, and time was running out.

He needed to calm down, he knew he needed to calm down, but seeing Delrickio had scared him to the point of having his bowels turn to water.

Delrickio had talked to him politely, affectionately, and all the while Joseph had stood watching Drake with dispassionate eyes. It was as if the beating had never taken place—as if the threat it was meant to impart didn't exist.

That made it worse somehow, knowing whatever would be done to him would be done without passion, with the cold, clear head of business to be transacted.

How could he convince Delrickio that he had an inside track with Julia when everyone had seen her with Paul Winthrop?

There had to be a way to get to her, to the tapes, to Eve.

He had to find it. Whatever risks he took couldn't be worse than the risk of doing nothing.

♦ ♦ ♦ ♦

VICTOR FLANNIGAN THOUGHT of Eve. Then of his wife. He wondered how he could have gotten so tangled up with two such different women. Both had the power to destroy his life. One through weakness, one through strength.

He knew he was to blame. Even loving them, he had used them. Still, he had given them both the best he had—and by doing so had cheated all three of them.

There was no going back and fixing it, certainly no way to change what already was. All he could do was fight to keep it from unraveling.

And as he turned restlessly in the big, empty bed, he ached for Eve, and feared her. In much the same way he ached for and feared a single bottle of whiskey. Because he'd never been able to have enough of either.

However many times he had pulled himself away from both addictions, he was always dragged back. Though he had learned to hate the drink even as he thirsted, he could only love the woman.

His church wouldn't condemn him for draining a bottle, but they would for one night of love. And there had been hundreds of nights.

Even fear for his soul couldn't make him regret a single one of them.

Why couldn't Eve understand that whatever it did to him inside, he had to protect Muriel? After all these years, why was she insisting on exploding all the lies and secrets? Didn't she know she would suffer as much as he?

Rising, he turned away from the bed and walked to the window to stare at the lightening sky. In a few hours he would go to his wife.

He had to find a way to protect Muriel, and to save Eve from herself.

♦ ♦ ♦ ♦

IN HIS SUITE at the Beverly Wilshire, Damien Priest waited for the sun to rise. He didn't use liquor or drugs to dull his mind to sleep. He needed it awake, alert, so he could think.

How much was she planning to tell? How much would she dare make public? He wanted to believe that the party tonight had been orchestrated to make him panic. He hadn't given her the satisfaction. He'd laughed, swapped stories, slapped backs. Christ, he'd even danced with her.

How silkily she'd asked him how his sporting goods chain was doing. How malicious her expression had been when she'd commented on how well Delrickio was looking.

But he'd only smiled. If she'd hoped to make him afraid, she'd been disappointed.

He sat, staring out the dark window. And was very afraid.

♦ ♦ ♦ ♦

EVE SETTLED into bed with a long, satisfied sigh. As far as she was concerned, the night had been a tremendous success. Over and above the pleasure of watching a select few jump through hoops, she'd enjoyed watching Julia and Paul together.

There was an odd and sweet sort of justice in that, she thought as she let her eyes drift closed. And it was all about justice, wasn't it? That and a healthy dose of revenge.

She was sorry that Victor was still upset. He would have to accept that she was doing what Victor had to do. Perhaps he would before too much longer.

Feeling the huge, lonely bed around her, she wished with all her heart that he could have stayed with her tonight. Loving him would have capped off the evening, then they could have cuddled together and talked sleepily until sunrise.

There was still time for that. Eve closed her eyes tight and hung on to that one simple wish.

As she drifted off, she heard Nina come down the hall, move into her room to pace restlessly before shutting the door.

Poor girl, Eve thought. She worried too much.

♦ ♦ ♦ ♦

*B*Y NINE O'CLOCK Monday morning, Julia had stretched, curled, crunched, pumped, sweated, and steamed. Her body had been twisted, kneaded, pummeled, and rubbed. She left the main house carting her gym bag that contained her sweaty leotard and towel.

She was covered in less than attractive sweats, and tugged down the shirt as she passed Lyle lazily waxing the car outside the garage.

She didn't like the way he looked at her, or the fact that he always seemed to be doing something along the route the mornings of her workouts. As always, she greeted him with cool civility.

"Good morning, Lyle."

"Miss." He touched the brim of his cap in a move that seemed more suggestive than servile. "Hope you're not working too hard." He liked to imagine her in the gym, wearing something skimpy and spandex and sweating like a bitch in heat. "I sure wouldn't say you needed all that exercise."

"I enjoy it," she lied, and kept walking, knowing he watched her. She shook off the itch between her shoulder blades and reminded herself to keep the shades drawn in her bedroom.

Paul was waiting on the terrace, his feet propped on a chair. One quick glance had him grinning. "You look like you could use a tall cold one."

"Fritz," she said, and dug into the pocket of the gym bag for her keys. "He's working on my deltoids. My arms feel like two stretched-out rubber bands." After opening the door and tossing bag and keys on the kitchen table, she headed for the fridge. "He'd have been a star in the Spanish Inquisition. Today, while I was suffering on the slant board, he made me confess I like Devil Dogs and Ho-Hos."

"You could have lied."

She snorted, pouring a glass of juice. "Nobody can look into those big, sincere blue eyes and lie. You'd go straight to hell. Want some?"

"No, thanks."

By the time she'd drained the glass she felt nearly human. "I've got a little more than an hour before I have to change for my appointment."

Refreshed and ready for business, she set the empty glass on the counter. "What did you need to talk to me about?"

"A number of things." Idly, he ran his hand down the length of her ponytail. "The tapes, for one."

"You don't have to worry about them."

"Locking the house is a good precaution, Jules, but it isn't enough."

"I've done more. Come on." She led the way through the house to the office. On the journey he noted that she had vases and pots of flowers everywhere. A good many of the milky-white blooms from the party had found a home. "Go ahead," she invited him, pointing toward the desk drawer. "Take a look."

Paul opened the drawer to find it empty. "Where?"

It grated a little that he hadn't seemed surprised. "They're in a safe place. The only time I have any of them out is when I'm working. So . . ." She shut the drawer. "If anyone tried to poke around again, he or she would come up empty."

"If it's as harmless as that."

"What do you mean?"

"I mean someone might feel a bigger stake in all this." Watching her, he sat on the edge of the desk. "Take Gloria DuBarry's behavior the other night."

Julia shrugged. "She was drunk."

"Exactly—that itself is an anomaly. I've never seen Gloria so much as tipsy, much less sloppy drunk." He picked up a paperweight, a faceted globe of crystal that exploded with lights as he turned it. He wondered if Julia would do that—turn from cool and quiet to hot and explosive at the proper touch. "She was warning you off. Why?"

"I don't know. I don't," she insisted when he only continued to stare. "Her name hasn't come up in my sessions with Eve, except in passing. And today we talked about other things." Eve's scheduled trip to Georgia, Peter Jackson's buns, Brandon's upcoming test in social studies, and Julia's semiannual urge to whack off her hair. Eve had talked her out of it.

Blowing out a long breath, she dropped into the chair.

"Gloria seemed to think I was going to write something that threatened her reputation. She even offered to pay me off—though I think she'd have preferred to kill me off." When his eyes narrowed, she groaned. "For God's sake, Paul, I was being sarcastic." Then she laughed and leaned back, setting the chair rocking. "I can see you writing the scene now. Gloria DuBarry, dressed in the nun's habit she wore in *McReedy's Little Devils,* creeps up behind the intrepid biographer. I hope you put me in something scant and slinky after all these hours I've spent toning up the bod. She hefts a knife—no, too messy. Pulls a .22—no, too ordinary. Ah, she lunges forward and strangles her victim with her rosary beads." Steepling her fingers, she grinned over them. "How's that?"

"Not nearly as funny as you'd like it to be." He set the crystal aside. "Julia, I want you to let me listen to the tapes."

The chair snapped back. "You know I can't do that."

"I want to help you."

There was such strained patience in his voice, she couldn't resist reaching out to touch her hand to his. "I appreciate the offer, Paul, but I don't think I need any help."

He looked down to where her hand lay slender, delicate, on his. "If you did, would you tell me?"

Because she wanted to be sure to tell them both the truth, she waited a moment. "Yes." Then she smiled, realizing it wasn't so difficult, or so risky, to trust someone. "Yes, I would."

"At least I have an answer." He turned his hand over, gripping hers before she could pull away. "If you thought Eve needed help?"

This time there was no hesitation. "You'd be the first one I'd tell."

Satisfied, he put that part of the problem aside as he would a plot device needing time to brew. "Now I want to ask you something else."

Figuring the hard part was over, she relaxed. "And I keep thinking I'm going to get the interview."

"You'll get your turn. Do you believe I care about you?"

She couldn't say the question came out of left field, but that didn't make it any easier to handle the ball. "Right now I do."

The simple sentence told him much more than a yes or no. "Has everything in your life been so temporary?"

His hand was much too firm on hers, the palm rougher than was expected of a man who worked with words. While she could have resisted the hold, she couldn't resist his eyes. If it was impossible to lie to Fritz, it was useless to lie to Paul. Those eyes would see right through to the truth.

"I suppose, except for Brandon, it has."

"Is that the way you want it?" he asked, uneasy that it was so important he know.

"I haven't really thought about it." She rose, hoping to back away from an edge that seemed to be sneaking closer while she wasn't looking. "I haven't had to."

"Now you do." He cupped her face with his free hand. "And I believe it's time I did something to make you start thinking about it."

He kissed her, much as he had the last time, with too much passion, traces of anger, hints of frustration. He tugged her closer, continuing the rapid, reckless assault on her senses. To his pleasure he could feel, actually feel her skin warming as the blood raced close to the surface. Unbearably arousing was the faint taste of panic as her mouth opened for his.

He caged her hips between his thighs, his teeth nipping, nibbling at her lips, his tongue stroking between them. She heard her own groan of pleasure as he slipped his hands under her shirt to run them up and down her spine.

Her skin was going hot, then cold, shivering and sweating under his touch. But the fear was passing, too weak an emotion to compete with all the others he forced into her. Needs, so long ignored, rose up like a tidal wave to wash everything away. Everything but him.

She seemed to be floating, clinging to him as she glided inches above the floor. She could imagine herself drifting endlessly like this, steeped in sensation, weak—weak enough to be guided by someone else.

When he dipped his head to slick those hot kisses along her throat, she saw that she wasn't floating at all, but being led slowly out of the office, into the living room, to the base of the stairs.

That was reality. In the real world being led too often equaled surrender.

"Where are we going?" Was that her voice, that throaty, breathless murmur?

"This time, this first time, you need a bed."

"But . . ." She tried to clear her head, but his mouth skimmed back to hers. "It's the middle of the morning."

His laugh was quick and as unsteady as his pulse. He was half wild to get his hands on her, to feel her under him, to feel himself inside her. "God, you're sweet." Then his eyes flashed back to hers. "I want more, Julia. You've got one chance to tell me what you want." He tugged off her sweatshirt and let it drop at the top of the stairs. Beneath it she wore nothing but the lingering scent of soap and perfumed oils. "Do you want me to wait until sundown?"

She let out a little cry, part alarm, part delight as his hand closed over her. "No."

He had her back to the wall, letting those rough, clever hands do the seducing. His breath was heaving as if he'd scaled a mountain rather than a staircase. She felt it flutter hot over her throat, her cheek, into her mouth.

She was small and firm in his hands, and smooth as lake water. He knew he'd go mad if he didn't taste that soft, trembling flesh. "What do you want, Julia?"

"This." Her mouth moved frantically under his. And now it was she pulling him away from the wall and into the bedroom. "You." When she reached for the buttons of his shirt, her fingers were shaking. She fumbled, swore. God, she needed to touch him. Wherever this terrible hunger had come from, it was burning her up from the inside out. "I can't—it's been so long." Finally she let her clumsy hands drop and closed her eyes on the humiliation.

"You're doing fine." He'd nearly laughed, but he'd seen she'd had no idea what her frantic, inexpert attempts were doing to him. For him. "Relax, Julia," he murmured as he lay her on the bed. "The best things always come back to you."

The best she could manage was a small, panicked smile. His body was like iron over hers. "They say that about riding bikes, too, but I tend to lose my balance and fall off."

He traced his tongue along her jaw, stunned by the way her single quick tremor racked his system. "I'll let you know if you start to wobble."

When she reached for him again, he braceleted her wrists in his hand and made love to her fingers. Too fast, he berated himself as he watched her in the light that slanted through the blinds. He'd been rushing her, fueled by his own needs. She needed care, and patience, and whatever tenderness he had to give.

Something had changed. She wasn't certain what it was, but the mood had altered. The grinding in her stomach had become a quickening—every bit as exciting, but so much sweeter. His touch was no longer possessive, but experimental, fingers cruising over her. When he kissed her, the frustration was gone, and there was persuasion. Irresistible.

He could feel her relax, muscle by muscle, until she was like hot wax melting beneath him. He hadn't known that kind of surrender, that level of trust could make him feel like a hero.

So he wanted to give her more, show her more. Promise her more.

Slowly, his eyes on her face, he drew the band from her hair so that it fanned dark gold over the rose-colored spread. As her lips opened, he touched his to them, but softly, waiting for her to deepen that most basic and complex of contacts. When her tongue sought his, he sank in.

Arousal clouded her mind, racked her breathing. Though her fingers still trembled, she fought his buttons loose, letting out a long sigh of satisfaction as she felt his flesh slide over hers. With her eyes closed she thought she could hear his heartbeat vying with the pace of her own for speed.

A cloak of sensation covered her, a misty veil that allowed her to do as she wished with her mouth and hands, without hesitation or regret. Feed ravenously. Yes, she would. A soul that had known hunger for so long understood greed as well as abstinence. She wanted the feast.

Her lips, fully tempted, raced over his face, down his throat, as she filled herself with the rich animal flavor of man. He said something, fast and harsh, and she heard her own laugh, a laugh that ended on a gasp when he pressed desperately against her, center to center.

When his tongue flicked over the point of her breast, that sharp pleasure had her arching beneath him, body straining up as the vibrations sang through her. The scrape of his teeth, the sudden greed of his mouth, the glory of the ageless hunger for the taste of flesh. With a groan caught deep in her throat she pressed his head against her, demanding and offering what he had asked for.

More.

And this was a freedom, this heedless grasping of desires, that she had denied, even spurned, for so long.

The air around them was redolent with the perfume of the camellias in the bowl on her nightstand. Beneath them, the bed moaned as they tumbled over it. The sun creeping in through the blinds turned the light a warm and seductive gold. Whenever he touched her, that light would explode behind her heavy lids into fractured rainbows.

This was where he wanted her, climbing slowly toward the peak of passions. Clamping down hard on the need to take, he gave, he teased, he tormented—and was given the satisfaction of hearing his name erupt from her lips.

Her skin was smooth as silk, fragrant from the oils that had been worked so diligently into her muscles. Wanting all of it, he tugged the pants over her hips, groaning when he found her naked beneath the sweats.

Yet he found he could wait, still longer, contenting himself with the feel of those long, slim thighs under his hands. The taste of them against his lips. When he shifted, the slightest touch had her leaping over the edge where he'd held her, and soaring beyond.

The climax ripped through her, then left her stunned and dazed and staggered. After such a gentle introduction, the torrid pleasure was terrifying. And addicting. Even as she groped for him, he drove her up again and watched her eyes glaze over with passion, felt her body shudder from the thrill of it, heard her breath catch from the shock, expel from the glory.

As she went limp, he levered himself over her, his own body trembling as he waited for her heavy eyes to open, meet his.

He slid inside her. She rose to meet him. Iron into velvet. Merged, they moved together, the rhythm instinctive, ancient, beautiful. When her lids shuddered down again, her arms opened to bring him close. This time when she leapt off the edge, she took him with her.

♦ ♦ ♦ ♦

HE LAY QUIET, still steeped in her. The scent of her skin, heated with passion, drifted through his senses and merged with the fragile fragrance of the camellias. The light, shadowed by the blinds, seemed neither of day nor night, but of some timeless space hidden between. Captured in his arms, her body moved gently, softly, with each quiet breath she took. When he lifted his head he could see her face, the glow of passion still flushing it. He had only to kiss her mouth to taste those warm and sweet remnants of mutual pleasure.

He had thought he knew romance, understood it, appreciated it. How many times had he used it to seduce a woman? How often had he woven it cleverly into a plot? But this was different. This time—or this woman—had taken it all to another plane. He intended to make her understand that they would both go there together, again and again.

"I told you it would come back to you."

Her eyes opened slowly. They were huge and dark and sleepy. She smiled. It was no use telling him nothing had come back, because she had never experienced anything like what they had just shared.

"Is that similar to was it good for you?"

His grin flashed before he nipped her earlobe. "It's saying a lot more than that. In fact, I was just thinking that we could have a very productive day if neither of us moved from this spot."

"Productive?" She let her fingers comb through his hair, dance down his spine as he nuzzled her throat. She didn't feel like the cat who'd licked up the cream, but like the one who'd discovered a direct line to the cow. "Interesting, maybe. Enjoyable, certainly, but productive's another matter. My interview with Anna should—mmm—be productive." Lazily, she glanced toward the clock. On a quick cry, she struggled to get up, only to be held firmly in place. "It's eleven-fifteen. How can it be eleven-fifteen? It was only a little past nine when we—"

"Time flies," he murmured, more than a little flattered. "You'll never make it."

"But—"

"It'll take you the better part of an hour to get dressed and make the drive. Reschedule."

"Shit. This is completely unprofessional." She wiggled free and hauled open the drawer of the nightstand to search for the number. "It'll be my own fault if she refuses to give me another chance."

"I like you like this," he said as she dragged at the phone. "All hot and frazzled."

"Be quiet while I think." After pushing the hair out of her eyes, she punched in the number, then let out a gasp.

Paul merely grinned and continued to nibble on her toes. "Sorry. This is one particular fantasy I've got to fulfill."

"Now's hardly the time—" Pleasure arrowed in, had her head jerking back. "Paul, please. I have to . . . oh, God! What?" She fought to catch her breath as the receptionist repeated the standard greeting. "Yes,

I'm sorry." He was working on her other foot now, sliding his tongue over the arch. Jesus, who would have thought sensation could ripple out from there all the way to her hairline? "I—this is Julia Summers. I have an eleven-thirty with Ms. del Rio." He was up to her ankles now. Julia heard the blood roaring in her head. "I, ah, I need to reschedule. I've had a . . ." Hot, open-mouthed kisses along her calf. "An unexpected emergency. Unavoidable. Please give Ms. . . ."

"Del Rio," Paul supplied, then grazed his teeth over the back of her knee. Julia's fingers knotted in the tangled sheets.

"Give her my apologies, and tell her . . ." A trail of hot, wet kisses up her inner thigh. "Tell her I'll get back to her. Thank you."

The phone clattered to the floor.

Chapter Seventeen

♦♦♦♦

$\mathcal{D}$RAKE GAVE THE GUARD at the gate a cheery salute. As he drove through, he began digging at his thighs and grinding his teeth. Nerves had brought on an itchy, spreading rash that none of the over-the-counter creams and lotions he'd applied helped. By the time he'd arrived at the guest house he was whimpering and talking to himself.

"It's gonna be all right. Nothing to worry about. In and out in five minutes and everything's fixed up." Sweat trickled, turning his raw thighs into a blazing agony.

There were forty-eight hours left until his deadline. The image of what Joseph could do to him with those big cinder-block fists was enough to have him sprinting out of the car.

It was safe. At least he was sure of that. Eve was in Burbank filming, and Julia was off interviewing the witch Anna. All he had to do was walk in, dub the tapes, then walk out.

It took him nearly a full minute of rattling the doorknob to realize the place was locked. With the breath whistling through his teeth, he raced around the house, checking all the windows and doors. By the time he got back to his starting point, he was dripping with sweat.

He couldn't go away empty-handed. No matter how well Drake deluded himself, he knew he would never find the nerve to come back. It had to be now. Raking his fingers over his blazing thighs, he made it to the terrace in a stumbling run. He cast furtive glances over his shoulder as he picked up a small clay pot of petunias. The tinkle of breaking glass seemed as loud to him as the boom of an assault rifle, but the marines didn't come running in counterattack.

The pot dropped from his nerveless fingers to shatter on the terrace stones. Still watching his back, he reached in through the hole he'd made and tripped the latch.

Standing inside the empty house brought him a tingle of satisfaction and bolstered his courage. As he moved from kitchen to office, his stride was firm and confident. He was smiling when he opened the drawer. His eyes went blank for a moment, then he laughed to himself and pulled open another drawer. And another.

The smile had turned to a grimace as he continued to yank open the empty drawers and ram them shut again.

◆ ◆ ◆ ◆

JULIA COULDN'T REMEMBER ever having a single interview exhaust her as much as her session with Anna. The woman was like an LP run on 78. Julia had a feeling she might find some interesting and entertaining tidbits mired in the orgy of words Anna had indulged in—once she had the energy to review the tape.

She stopped in front of the house and sat in the car, eyes closed, head back. At least she hadn't had to push or pry to get Anna to open up. The woman gushed like water through a broken pipe, her mind on constant overdrive, and her stick-figure body never settled in one place for more than a few intense minutes. All Julia had had to do was ask what it was like to design wardrobes for Eve Benedict.

Anna had been off and running about Eve's outrageous and often unrealistic expectations, her impatient demands, her last-minute brainstorms. It was Anna—according to Anna—who had made Eve look like a queen in *Lady Love*. Anna who had made her sparkle in *Paradise Found*. There had been no mention, as there had been in Kinsky's and Marilyn Day's interviews that it had been Eve who had given Anna her first real break by insisting that she be used as costume designer on *Lady Love*.

The lack of gratitude reminded Julia of Drake.

It was beginning to rain when Julia sighed and climbed from the car. It was a fast, thin rain that looked as though it could go on for days. Like Anna, she thought as she dashed to the front door. Julia would have preferred to close the door on that particular tape as she would close the door against the chilling rain.

But as she searched out her keys, she knew that whatever her personal feelings, she would review the tape. If Anna came across as catty, spoiled, and ungrateful in the book, she had no one to blame but herself.

Wondering if she should make pork chops or chicken for dinner, Julia opened the door, and the scent of wet, crushed flowers poured out. The living room, which had been neat if not orderly, was now a jumble of overturned tables, broken lamps, torn cushions. In the moment it took her mind to register what her eyes were seeing, she stood, briefcase clutched in one hand, keys in the other. Then she dropped them both and walked through the destruction of what she had tried to make home.

Every room was the same—broken glass, overturned furniture. Pictures had been torn off the wall. Drawers had been broken. In the kitchen, boxes and bottles had been yanked out of cupboards so that their contents made an unappetizing stew on the tiled floor.

She turned and fled upstairs. In her room her clothes were strewn around the floor. The mattress had been dragged partially off the bed, the linens in torn and tangled knots. The contents of her dresser were scattered on top of it.

But it was Brandon's room that snapped the control she was desperately trying to cling to. Her child's room had been invaded, his toys, his clothes, his books, pawed through. Julia picked up the top of his Batman pajamas, and balling them in her hands, went to the phone.

"Miss Benedict's residence."

"Travers. I need Eve."

Travers answered that demand with a snort. "Miss Benedict's at the studio. I expect her around seven."

"You get in touch with her now. Someone's broken into the guest house and trashed it. I'll give her an hour before I call the police myself." She hung up on Travers's squawking questions.

Her hands were shaking. That was good, she decided. It was anger, and she didn't mind shaking with anger. She wanted to hold on to it, it and every other vicious emotion that pounded through her.

Very deliberately she went downstairs again, walking over the wreckage of the living room. She crouched in front of a section of wainscoting and pressed the hidden mechanism as Eve had showed her. The panel slid open, revealing the safe inside. Julia spun the dial, mentally reciting the combination. When it was open, she took inventory of the contents. Her tapes, her notes, the few boxes of jewelry. Satisfied, she closed it again, then went to the rain-splattered window to wait.

Thirty minutes later, Julia watched Paul's Studebaker slide to a halt. His face was set and expressionless when she met him at the door. "What the hell's going on?"

"Travers called you?"

"Yes, she called me—which is something you neglected to do."

"It didn't occur to me."

He was silent until he'd worked past the anger her remark caused. "Obviously. What's this about another break-in?"

"See for yourself." She stepped aside so that he could walk in ahead of her. Seeing it again brought on a fresh, red rage. It took everything she had to whip it down. Her fingers linked together until the knuckles were white. "First guess is that someone was upset when they couldn't find the tapes, and decided to tear the place up until they did." She nudged some broken crockery aside with her foot. "They didn't."

Fury, and the coppery flavor of fear in the back of his throat, had him whirling on her. His eyes were a blazing blue that had her backing up a step before she stiffened her spine. "Is that all you can think of?"

"It's the only reason," she said. "I don't know anyone who would do this because of a personal grudge."

He shook his head, struggling to ignore the twisting of his gut when he looked at a hacked cushion. What if he had found her like that—torn and tattered and tossed on the floor? His voice was cold as iron when he managed to speak again.

"So the tapes are safe, and that's that?"

"No, that is not that." She pulled her fingers apart, and as though that had been her only restraint, the fury she'd been strapping down broke loose. "They went into Brandon's room. They touched his things." Rather than nudging wreckage aside, she kicked at it, her eyes the color of the storm clouds that were shooting down that steady, driving rain. "No one, no one gets that close to my son. When I find out who did this, they'll pay."

He preferred the outburst to the cold control. But he was far from satisfied. "You said you'd call me if you had trouble."

"I can handle this."

"Like hell." He moved fast, grabbing her arms, shaking her before she could shoot out the first protest. "If it's the tapes someone's so desperate to get, they'll go through you next time. For Christ's sake, Julia, is it worth it? Is a book, a few weeks on the best-seller list, a five-minute spot on *Carson* worth all this?"

Every bit as livid as he, she jerked away, rubbing her arms where his fingers had dug in. The wind whipped up enough to beat the rain like impatient fingers against the glass. "You know it's more than that. You of all people should know. I have something of value to do with this. What I'll write about Eve will be richer, more poignant, more powerful than any fiction."

"And if you'd been home when they'd broken in?"

"They wouldn't have broken in if I'd been here," she countered. "Obviously, they waited until the house was empty. Be logical."

"Fuck logic. I'm not taking chances with you."

"You're not—"

"No, by Christ, I'm not." Cold fury had become hot as he heaved a table aside. More glass shattered, like thunder answering the rain. "Do you expect me to stand by and do nothing? Whoever was in here wasn't just looking for tapes, he was desperately trying to find them." He snatched up a mangled cushion and shoved it at her. "Look at this. Look at it, dammit. It might have been you."

It hadn't occurred to her, not for a second, and she resented that his words had the image leaping so vividly in her mind. She fought back a shudder and let the cushion fall to the floor. "I'm not a piece of furniture, Paul. Nor is it up to you to make decisions for me. Spending an afternoon in bed together doesn't make you responsible for my welfare."

Slowly, he clamped his hands on the lapels of her jacket. Anger and fear rode a thin blade of hurt that cut quick and deep. "It was more than an afternoon in bed, but that's another problem you'll have to deal with. Right now you're in the position where a fucking book is putting you at risk."

"And if I would ever have considered backing off from this work, this would have changed my mind. I will not run away from this kind of intimidation."

"Well said," Eve stated from the doorway. Her hair was wet, as was the cashmere sweater she'd tugged on so hastily after Travers's call. Her face was very pale as she stepped into the house, but her voice was strong and steady. "It appears we have someone running scared, Julia."

"What the hell is wrong with you?" Paul whirled on Eve with a rush of anger he'd never shown toward her. "Are you actually enjoying this? Lapping up satisfaction at the thought that someone would do this because of you? What have you come to, Eve, when your vanity, your attempt at immortality, is worth any price?"

Very carefully, she lowered herself to the arm of the damaged sofa, pulled out a cigarette, lighted it. Odd, she thought, she'd been sure Victor was the only man who could hurt her. How much sharper, how much deeper was the pain when it was stabbed into her by a man she thought of as her son.

"Enjoying it," she said slowly. "Do I enjoy seeing my property destroyed or having my guest's privacy invaded?" On a sigh, she blew out smoke. "No, I don't. Do I enjoy knowing that someone is so terrified at what I may tell the world that they would risk a foolish and futile move like this? Yes, by Christ, I do."

"It's not just you who's involved in this."

"Julia and Brandon will be taken care of." She tapped an ash carelessly on the rubble on the floor. With every beat of her heart her head pounded viciously. "Travers is seeing to guest rooms in the main house right now. Julia, you are both welcome to stay there as long as you like, or to move back here once we have made it habitable again." She glanced up, keeping her eyes and her voice carefully neutral. "Or, of course, you are free to abandon the project altogether."

In an unplanned gesture of alliance, Julia moved to Eve's side. "I have no intention of abandoning the project. Or you."

"Integrity," Eve said with a smile, "is an enviable trait."

"Blind stubbornness isn't," Paul retorted. He snapped his gaze to Julia. "It's obvious neither of you want or need my help."

Eve rose stiffly when he strode out of the house. In silence, she watched Julia look after him. "The male ego," Eve murmured as she put an arm around Julia's shoulders. "It's a huge and fragile thing. I always envision it as an enormous penis made of thin glass."

Despite her churning emotions, Julia laughed.

"That's better." Eve bent to pick up a shard of a broken vase, using it as an ashtray. "He'll be back, darling. Puffing and blowing in all likelihood, but he's too firmly hooked not to come reeling back." Smiling, she tapped the cigarette out, then, with a shrug, tossed it and the bit of porcelain into the rubble. "Do you think I can't tell you've been together?"

"I really don't think—"

"Don't think." Wanting a breath of fresh air, Eve moved to the open door. She liked the rain, the way it fell cool on her face. She'd come to the point where she appreciated life's little things. "I could see instantly what had happened between you. And that you've quietly, effortlessly, shuttled me out of first place in his affections."

"He was angry," Julia began. And because she was suddenly aware that her own head was pounding, she pulled her hair free of the pins.

"Yes, and rightfully so. I've put his woman in a difficult, perhaps dangerous position."

"Oh, come in out of that rain. You'll catch a cold." She bristled under Eve's amused glance. "And I'm my own woman."

"One must be." Obligingly, Eve stepped back inside. It relieved her to see youth standing there. Youth, courage, and temper. "Even when one belongs to a man, one must be one's own woman. However much you love him, or come to love him, hold on to yourself." The pain radiated so quickly, so sharply, she cried out and pressed the heel of her hand above her left eye.

"What is it?" Julia was at her side in an instant, taking her weight. On an oath, she half carried Eve to what was left of the sofa. "You're ill. I'll call a doctor."

"No. No." Before Julia could spring to a phone, Eve had her hand. "It's merely stress, overwork, delayed shock. Whatever. I often get headaches." She could nearly smile at the grim understatement. "If you'd get me a glass of water."

"All right. It'll take only a minute."

Once Julia had gone to the kitchen to search for an unbroken glass, Eve dug in her canvas bag for the pills. The pain was coming more often—as the doctors had said it would. It was becoming more vicious—again living up to the prediction. She shook out two pills, then forced herself to replace one. She wouldn't give in to the temptation to double the dose. Not yet. When Julia returned with the water, she'd replaced the bottle, and held the single pill in her palm.

Julia had also brought along a cool rag—and as she would have done for Brandon, stroked Eve's forehead with it as Eve swallowed the medication.

"Thank you. You have a very soothing touch."

"Just relax until you feel better." Where had all this affection sprung from? Julia wondered as she patiently sought to ease the pain. She smiled as Eve's hand reached for hers. Somewhere along the line a friendship had been formed, that woman-to-woman bond no man could possibly understand.

"You're a comfort to me, Julia. In more ways than one." The pain was almost tolerable now. Still, she sat with her eyes closed, letting the cool, competent touch soothe her. "I very much regret our paths were so late in crossing. Wasted time. Remember, I told you that's the only genuine regret."

"I like to think that no time's ever wasted. That things happen when they're meant to happen."

"I hope you're right." She fell silent again, sorting out the things she had left to do. "I arranged for Lyle to deliver Brandon straight to the main house. I thought you'd prefer that."

"Yes, thank you."

"It's little enough to make up for this disruption of your life." Stronger, more certain, she opened her eyes again. "You checked on the tapes."

"They're still there."

She only nodded. "I leave for Georgia at the end of the week. When I come back, we'll finish this, you and I."

"I still have several interviews left to do."

"There'll be time." She'd make sure of it. "While I'm gone, I don't want you to worry about this."

Julia cast a look around the room. "It's a little difficult not to."

"No need. I know who did this."

Julia stiffened, backed away. "You know. Then—"

"It was simply a matter of checking with the guard at the gate." Recovered, she rose and laid a hand on Julia's shoulder. "Trust me. I will take care of this matter."

◆ ◆ ◆

DRAKE TOSSED CLOTHES frantically into a suitcase. Neatly laundered and folded shirts were heaved in among shoes, belts, rumpled trousers.

He had to get away, and quickly. With less than five thousand to his name after a desperate and losing session at Santa Anita, and no tapes to bargain with, he didn't dare keep his appointment with Delrickio. So he would go somewhere Delrickio couldn't find him.

Argentina maybe, or Japan. He heaved argyle socks on top of swim trunks. It might be better if he went to Omaha first, laid low. Who the hell would look for Drake Morrison in Omaha?

His mother couldn't drag him out behind the barn for a beating anymore. She couldn't force him to prayer meetings or feed him bread and water to cleanse his body and soul of impurities.

He could stay there on the farm for a couple of weeks until he'd pulled himself together. And maybe he could finesse a few thousand out of his old lady. God knew she'd made enough off him—taking the money Eve had sent and pouring it into the farm, or into the church.

He deserved something, didn't he? From her. From Eve. After all, he was the only child. Hadn't he lived with crazy Ada for the first half of his life, and worked for Eve the second?

They owed him.

"Drake." He had his arms filled with socks and silk underwear. It all fluttered to the floor when Eve strolled in.

"How did you—"

She held up a key, jingling it. "You've often imposed on Nina to water your plants when you're out of town." She slipped the key into her pocket, daring him to comment, then sat on the bed. "Taking a trip?"

"I had some business come up."

"Abruptly." Her eyebrows shot up as she scanned the results of his frantic packing. "That's no way to treat a five-thousand-dollar suit."

The itching of his thighs had him grinding his teeth. "I'll have to have everything pressed when I get there."

"And where is there, dear?"

"New York," he said, considering it an inspiration. "You're my favorite client, Eve, but not the only. I have, ah, some details to iron out on a television deal."

She tilted her head to study him. "You must be very ruffled to lie so poorly. One of your best—perhaps your only—skill is your ability to lie with complete sincerity."

He wanted to show annoyance, but the panic shone through. "Listen, Eve, I'm sorry I didn't have the chance to fill you in on my plans, but I have obligations that don't center on you."

"Let's cut straight through the shit, shall we?" Her voice was pleasant. The expression on her face wasn't. "I know you broke into the guest house late this morning."

"Broke in?" Sweat streamed down his face. When he laughed, it came out as a croak. "Why the hell would I do anything like that?"

"Exactly my question. I have no doubt you were the one who broke in before and stole from me. I can't tell you how disappointed I am, Drake, that one of my few remaining blood relatives would find it necessary to steal."

"I don't have to take this from you." He slammed the suitcase shut. Unconsciously, he began to dig at his thighs. "Look around, Eve. Does it seem like I'd have to steal a few trinkets from you?"

"Yes. When a man insists on living well beyond his means, he opens himself up to larceny." She let out a weary sigh as she lit a cigarette. "Is it gambling again?"

"I told you I gave that up." His tone was almost indignant.

She blew smoke to the ceiling, then leveled her eyes back to his. "You're a liar, Drake. And unless you want me to go to the police with my suspicions, you'll stop being a liar as of this instant. How much are you down?"

He collapsed, folding like a house of cards under a child's whistling breath. "Eighty-three thousand, and interest."

Eve's lips thinned. "Idiot. To whom?"

He wiped his mouth with the back of his hand. "Delrickio."

She sprang up, snatching a shoe off the bed and heaving it at him. Whimpering, Drake crossed his arms over his face to protect it. "You goddamn simpering fool. I told you, I warned you. Fifteen years ago I pulled you out from under that slime. And again, ten years ago."

"I had a bad run."

"Asshole. You haven't had a good run in your life. Delrickio! Jesus Christ! He eats sniveling little wimps like you for breakfast." Furious, she tossed her cigarette on the carpet and ground it out before snatching Drake by the shirtfront. "You were after the tapes for him, weren't you? You fucking traitor, you were going to feed them to him to save your own skin."

"He'll kill me." His eyes and nose were running as he babbled up at her. "He'll do it, Eve. He's already had one of his goons give me a beating. He wants to listen to the tapes, that's all. I didn't figure it would hurt anything, and maybe he'd forgive part of the debt. I only—"

She slapped him, hard enough to snap his head back. "Pull yourself together. You're pathetic." She released him to pace the room while he dragged out a handkerchief to mop up his face.

"I panicked. Christ almighty, Eve, you don't understand what it's like, living with what he can do to me. All for eighty fucking thousand."

"Eighty fucking thousand you don't happen to have." Calmer, she turned back. "You betrayed me, Drake, my trust, my affection. I know your childhood was crap, but that's no excuse for turning on someone who tried to give you a chance."

"I'm scared." He started to weep again. "If I don't give him the money in two days, he'll kill me. I know it."

"And the tapes were to plug the dike. Well, too bad, darling, no dice."

"They don't have to be real." He struggled to his feet. "We could fake some, pass them off."

"And he'd kill you later for lying to him. Lies always surface, Drake. Believe me."

While he choked on the truth of that, his eyes darted around the room, afraid to settle anywhere. "I'm going to go away. Get out of the country—"

"You're going to stay right here and face the music like a man. For once in your pitiful life, you're going to deal with the consequences."

"I'll be dead," he said, lips quivering.

She pulled open her bag and took out a checkbook. She had come prepared, but that didn't diminish the anger, or the sadness. "One hundred thousand," she said as she sat and wrote. "That should take care of your debt, your interest."

"Oh. Oh, Christ, Eve." He fell at her feet, burying his face in her knees. "I don't know what to say."

"Don't say anything. Simply listen. You will take this check. You will not use one penny of it for gambling, but take the money to Delrickio."

"I will." Sheer delight transfigured his wet face. It gleamed like a converted saint. "I swear it."

"And this will be your final transaction with that man. If I ever hear of you doing business with him again, I'll kill you myself—in a way that even Delrickio would respect and admire."

His head bounced on his neck in enthusiastic nods. He'd promise anything, anything at all, and mean it—at least temporarily—for salvation.

"I would suggest that you seek therapy for your addiction."

"It's no problem. I'm through with it. I swear."

"As you have sworn before, but that's your business." Revolted, she pushed him aside and rose. The affection and hope she'd once had for this child of her sister was gone. She knew they would not be back. Once the disgust and anger faded, there might be pity. But nothing more. "I don't really give a shit if you waste your life, Drake. I've saved it for the last time. You're fired."

"Eve, you can't mean that." He struggled to his feet, using his most charming smile. "I fucked up, I admit it. It was stupid, and it won't happen again."

"Fucked up?" Nearly amused, she tapped her fingers against her bag.

"What a convenient expression, it covers so much ground. You broke into my home, you stole from me, you destroyed things I was fond of, and you invaded the privacy of a woman I am more than fond of, a woman I respect and admire, and who is a guest in my home." She threw up a hand before he could speak. "I'm not telling you you won't work in this town again, Drake. That's much too melodramatic and clichéd. But you won't work for me again."

His sense of relief and delight had faded. A lecture would have been one thing—a few threats he could have handled. But this kind of punishment was worse, and more permanent than a few licks with a belt behind the barn. He'd be damned if he'd stand for being whipped by a woman again.

"You've got no right to treat me this way, to toss me aside like I was nothing."

"I've got every right to fire an employee I find unsuitable."

"I've done good things for you."

Her brow arched at the minor audacity. "Then we'll consider the scales balanced. That check is all the money you'll ever see from me. Think of it as your inheritance."

"You can't!" He grabbed her arm before she could walk from the room. "I'm family, all you've got. You can't cut me out."

"Be assured I can. I've earned every nickel of what I have—something you couldn't possibly understand. What I have will go where I choose it to go." She yanked her arm free. "I don't reward betrayal, Drake, and in this case, I'm not even going to punish it. I've just given you back your life. Make something of it."

He rushed after her as she started out and down the steps. "You're not going to leave it all to that bastard Winthrop. I'll see you in hell first."

She whirled around at the base of the stairs. The look in her eyes had him freezing in mid-step. "You very likely will see me there. Until then, you and I are finished."

It wasn't going to happen. He sat down on the steps, holding his head in his hands as the slamming of the door reverberated. It couldn't happen. He'd make her see he couldn't be bought off with a lousy hundred grand.

Chapter Eighteen

♦ ♦ ♦ ♦

*B*RANDON SAT on the fourposter in the big, airy bedroom in the main house and watched his mother finish packing. "How come when ladies pack for the weekend and stuff, they have more junk than guys do?"

"That, my son, is one of the mysteries of the universe." She added another blouse, guiltily, to the garment bag. "Are you really sure you're not upset that you're not coming to London with me?"

"Heck no. I'm going to have lots more fun at the McKennas than you are talking to some old actor. They've got Nintendo."

"Well, Rory Winthrop can't compete with that." She zipped the bag, then checked her tote to see that all her toiletries and cosmetics were there. She shook her head as she tested the weight. Not a mystery at all, she thought. It was straight vanity. "CeeCee's going to be here any minute. Did we pack your toothbrush?"

"Yes, ma'am." He rolled his eyes. "You checked my bag twice already."

Because she was checking it again, she missed the look. "Maybe you should take an extra jacket. In case it rains." Or in case L.A. was suddenly swept by a snowstorm, floods, tornadoes. Earthquakes. Oh, Christ, what if there was an earthquake while she was gone? Struck with the fear and guilt that hit her whenever she left Brandon, she turned to look at him. He was bouncing gently on the bed and humming, his prized Lakers cap low on his head. "I'm going to miss you, baby."

He winced, as any self-respecting ten-year-old would when referred to as baby. At least they weren't in public. "I'll be okay and everything. You don't have to worry."

"Yes, I do. That's my job." She walked over to hug him, pleased when his arms came around her for a tight squeeze. "I'll be back by Tuesday."

"Are you going to bring me something?"

She tipped his head back. "Maybe I will." She kissed both his cheeks. "Don't grow too much while I'm gone."

He grinned. "Maybe I will."

"I'll still be bigger. Come on, let's get this show on the road." She picked up her briefcase—trying to remember if she'd checked to be sure she'd put her passport and tickets in the right compartment—slung the tote over one shoulder, the garment bag over the other. Brandon hoisted his well-stuffed gym bag, all the modern boy needed for a few days with friends.

It didn't occur to either of them to ring for a servant and have the bags carried down.

"I'm going to call every night, seven o'clock your time. That'll be right after dinner. I already put the name of the hotel and the phone number in your bag."

"I know, Mom."

She recognized impatience when she heard it, but didn't give a damn. A mother was entitled to behave this way. "You can call me there anytime if you need me. If I'm not in, the desk will take a message."

"I know what to do. It's just like when you go on tour."

"Yeah." But this time there would be an ocean between them.

"Julia." Nina hurried down the hall as they stopped at the base of the steps. "You shouldn't be carrying all that."

"I'm used to it. Really."

"It's fine." She was already pulling the garment bag from Julia's shoulder and setting it aside. "I'll have Lyle put your things in the limo."

"I appreciate it. You know, it's not really necessary for him to drive me to the airport." And it gave her the creeps. "I can—"

"You're Miss B.'s guest," Nina said primly. "And you're going to London on Miss B.'s business." That more than settled the affair in Nina's mind. She smiled down at Brandon. "It's going to be awfully quiet and boring around here the next few days, but I'm sure you'll have a great time with the McKennas."

"They're neat." He didn't think it was wise to add that Dustin McKenna had promised to teach him how to make rude noises with his armpit. Women just didn't understand that kind of thing. At the sound of the doorbell, he was streaking down the hall. "You're here!" he shouted at CeeCee.

"You bet. All aboard for three days of fun, excitement, and crowded bathrooms. Hi, Miss Soloman. Thanks for the day off."

"You deserve it." Her smile was absent as her mind leapt forward into what had to be done. "In any case, with everyone haring off here and there, there's little enough for you to do. Enjoy yourself, Brandon. Safe trip, Julia. I'll call Lyle and have him bring the car around."

"You behave." Julia walked forward to give Brandon a last crushing hug. "Don't fight with Dustin."

"Okay." He slung his gym bag over his shoulder. "Bye, Mom."

"Bye." She bit her lip as he marched outside.

"We'll take good care of him, Julia."

"I know." She managed a smile. "That's the easy part." Through the open door she saw the big black limo slide up behind CeeCee's Sprint. "I guess that's my cue."

While Julia headed for the airport in the bright Los Angeles sunshine, Eve stretched in bed and listened to the heavy drum of rain on the roof of the bungalow. There'd been no filming today, she thought, just a lot of long, lazy hours inside the cozy little cottage the producers had arranged to rent for the duration of location shooting.

She didn't mind a day off—under the circumstances. She stretched again, purring as a strong, wide-palmed hand stroked down her body.

"Doesn't sound like it's going to let up anytime soon," Peter commented, shifting so that he could roll her on top of him. It amazed him—and aroused him—how good she looked in the morning. Older, certainly, without her careful makeup. But the bones, the eyes, the pale skin, made age a minimal matter. "At this rate, we may be stuck inside all day."

Because she felt him pressed hard and hot against her, she slid up, then back to take him inside. "I think we can manage to keep busy."

"Yeah." His hands dug into her hips, urging her on as she began to rock. "I bet we can."

Eve arched up and back to let her body absorb all those delicious shock waves of pleasure. She'd been right about him being an intriguing lover. He was young, firm, energetic, and as innately aware of a woman's needs as his own. She appreciated sexual generosity in a man. It had been a bonus that by the time she had taken that last step and invited him to her bed, she had grown to like him.

And in bed . . . What woman her age wouldn't be gratified that she could excite so completely a man not yet forty? She knew he was lost in her—the ragged pace of his breathing, the glisten of sweat on his chest, the tremors that racked him as he streaked closer to climax.

Smiling, her head thrown back, she rode him hard, taking them both over that keen edge of pleasure.

◆ ◆ ◆ ◆

"*C*HRIST!" EXHAUSTED, Peter fell back on the bed. His heart was pumping like a jackhammer. He'd had other women, younger women, but never one so skilled. "You're incredible."

She slid out of bed to pluck a robe from the chair.

"And you're good. Very good. With luck you might get to incredible by the time you're my age."

"Honey, if I spent much time fucking like that, I'd be dead long before I got to be your age." He stretched like a long, lean tomcat. "And it would have been a short and happy life."

She laughed, pleased with him, and moved to the dresser to run a brush through her hair. He didn't, as so many younger men felt obligated to, dismiss her age. He didn't flavor sex with all those lies and flattery. She'd come to understand that what Peter Jackson said, he meant.

"Why don't you tell me how you feel about your short and happy life so far?"

"I'm doing what I want to do." He folded his arms under his head. "I guess I wanted to be an actor since I was about sixteen—got hooked on high school plays. Took drama in college and broke my mother's heart. She wanted me to be a doctor."

Her eyes met his in the mirror, then roamed lazily down his body. "Well, you've got the hands for it."

He grinned. "Yeah, but I really hate blood. And my golf game sucks."

Entertained, she set the brush aside and began to pat cream under her eyes. It soothed her, the sound of the rain, the sound of his voice. "So, shouldering aside the medical profession, you came to Hollywood."

"At twenty-two. I starved a little, snagged a few commercials." Because he could feel his strength coming back, he propped onto his elbows. "Hey, did you ever see me sell Blueberry Crunch Granola?"

Her eyes met his laughing ones in the mirror. "I'm afraid I missed it."

He took one of her cigarettes from the nightstand. "A stellar performance. It had grit, it had style, it had passion. And that was just the cereal."

She walked to the bed to share the cigarette with him. "I'll make sure the cook stocks it immediately."

"To tell you the truth, it tastes like something you dig off the floor in the forest. Speaking of food, why don't I fix us breakfast?"

"You?"

"Sure." He took the cigarette from between her fingers, put it between his lips. "Before I got my break in soaps, I moonlighted as a short-order cook. Swing shift."

"So you're offering to cook me bacon and eggs?"

"Maybe—if that keeps you interested."

Carefully, she took another drag. He was falling a little in love with her, she realized. It was sweet, and flattering, and if circumstances had been different, she might have let him. As it was, she needed to keep it simple. "I think I've shown I'm interested."

"But."

Her lips lightly brushed his. "But," she repeated. And that was all.

It was more difficult than he expected to accept those unspoken limitations. Difficult and surprising. "I guess a few days in Georgia's not such a bad deal."

Grateful, she kissed him again. "It's a great deal. For both of us. How about that breakfast?"

"Tell you what . . ." He bent forward to kiss her shoulder, enjoying not only the scent, the texture of her skin, but the sturdiness. "Why don't we take a shower, then you can watch me cook. After that I've got a great idea on how we can pass some time this afternoon."

"Do you really?"

"Yeah." He fondled her lightly, smiled. "We can go to the movies."

"To the movies?"

"Sure, you've heard of movies. That's where people sit down and watch other people pretend they're other people. What do you say, Eve? We'll catch a matinee, eat some popcorn."

She considered a moment, then realized it sounded like fun. "You're on."

♦ ♦ ♦ ♦

JULIA TOOK off her shoes and let her feet sink into the carpet in her room at the Savoy. It was a small, elegant suite, tastefully appointed. The bellman had been so scrupulously polite when he'd delivered her bags, he'd looked almost apologetic as he'd waited for his tip.

Julia wandered to the window to watch the river and let some of the travel weariness drain away. Nerves would take longer. The flight from L.A. to New York hadn't been so bad—as far as torture went. But from Kennedy to Heathrow—all those hours over the Atlantic—that had been a sheer and quiet hell.

But she'd gotten through it. And now she was in Britain. And she had the pleasure of reminding herself that Julia Summers was staying at the Savoy.

It still surprised her that she could afford such tony surroundings. But it was a good feeling, that surprise, telling her she hadn't forgotten what it was to earn, to climb, or to need.

The city lights winked at her on this March night. It was as if she were in someone else's dream, all that velvet darkness, the misty slice of moon, the shadow of water. And so warm here, so blissfully quiet. After one huge yawn, Julia turned away from the window, from the lights. Adventures would have to wait for the morning.

She unpacked only what she needed for the night, and was deep in her own dreams within twenty minutes.

◆ ◆ ◆ ◆

*I*N THE MORNING she stepped out of a cab in Knightsbridge and paid off the driver, knowing she was overtipping. She was equally sure, however, that she would never manage the British currency. She remembered to ask for a receipt—her accountant all but frothed at the mouth over her bookkeeping system—then stuck it carelessly in her pocket.

The house was everything she'd imagined. The enormous redbrick Victorian was sheltered by huge, gnarled trees. She imagined they would be beautifully shady in the summer, but for now, the wind rattled through their bare branches in a kind of Dickensian music that was oddly appealing. Smoke puffed from chimneys in thick gray wisps that were quickly tossed higher into the slate sky.

Though there were cars whizzing by on the street behind her, she could easily imagine the clop-clop of horses, the rattle of carriages, the cries of street vendors.

She moved through the little iron gate, up the cobbled path that cut through the winter-yellow lawn and up the sparkling white steps that led to a sparkling white door. Julia shifted her briefcase, annoyed that her palms were damp and chilled. There was no use denying it, she told herself, she was thinking of Rory Winthrop not so much as Eve's one-time husband, but as Paul's father.

Paul was six thousand miles away, and furious with her. What would he think, she wondered, if he knew she was here, not only pursuing the book, but about to interview his father? He wouldn't think kindly of it, she was sure, and wished there were a way to mesh his needs with hers.

She reminded herself that business came first, and pressed the doorbell. A maid answered within moments. Julia caught a glimpse of an enormous hall, all towering ceilings and tiled floors.

"Julia Summers," she said. "I have an appointment with Mr. Winthrop."

"Yes, ma'am, he's expecting you. Please come in."

The tile was a checkerboard of maroon and ivory, the ceilings graced with heavy brass-and-crystal chandeliers. To the right was a staircase that swept in a regal curve. Julia surrendered her coat to the waiting maid, then followed her past two George III hall chairs that flanked a mahogany table graced with a vase of hibiscus and one woman's glove of sapphire leather.

Instinctively she compared the sitting room with Eve's. This setting was certainly more formal, more steeped in tradition than Eve's airy, sun-drenched parlor. Hers shouted wealth and style. This murmured of old money and deep roots.

"Please make yourself comfortable, Miss Summers. Mr. Winthrop will be along directly."

"Thank you."

The maid moved almost soundlessly from the room, shutting the thick mahogany doors behind her. Alone, Julia walked to the hearth to hold her chilled hand out toward the leaping flames. The smoke smelled pleasantly of applewood, offering welcome and comfort. Because it reminded her a bit of her own fireplace in Connecticut, she relaxed.

The carved mantel above the fire was crowded with old photographs in ornate and highly polished silver frames. The maids, Julia was sure, would curse each time they had to fight the tarnish in all those curves and crevices.

She amused herself walking from one to the next, studying the dour-faced, stiff-shouldered ancestors of the man she had come to see.

She recognized Rory Winthrop, and caught a portion of his humor, in the black and white photo where he had posed in beaver hat and starched collar. The movie had been *Delaney Murders*, she recalled, and he'd played the ultra-proper, evilly deranged murderer with eye-glinting delight.

Julia wasn't content simply to look at the next picture. She had to pick it up, to hold it. To devour it. It was Paul, she was certain, though the boy in the portrait was no more than eleven or twelve. His hair was lighter, shaggier, and from the expression on his face, he'd been none too pleased to find himself bundled into a stiff suit and snug tie.

The eyes were the same. Odd, she thought, that even as a child he'd had those intense adult eyes. They weren't smiling, but looked back at her as if to say that he'd already seen, heard, and understood more than someone twice his age.

"Spooky little beggar, wasn't he?"

Julia turned, the portrait still clasped in her hand. She'd been so intent on it, she hadn't heard Rory Winthrop's entrance. He stood watching her, a charmingly crooked smile on his face, one hand casually dipped into the pocket of pearl-gray slacks. Physically he could have been taken for Paul's brother rather than father. His mahogany hair was full and swept back like a lion's mane. Rory allowed the gray only to dash the temples, where it added dignity rather than age. His face was as firm and as fit as his body. He, too, was no stranger to the fountain of youth offered by cosmetic surgeons. Besides the lifts and tucks, he had weekly treatments that included seaweed masks and facial massage.

"Excuse me, Mr. Winthrop. You caught me off guard."

"The best way to catch a beautiful woman." He'd enjoyed the fact that she stared. A man could preserve his face and body with care, diligence, and money. But it took a woman, a young one, to preserve the ego.

"Interested in my miniature rogues' gallery?"

"Oh." She remembered the portrait in her hand and returned it to the mantel. "Yes, it's very entertaining."

"That one of Paul was taken right after Eve and I were married. I didn't know what to make of him then any more than I do now. He mentioned you to me."

"He—" Surprise, pleasure, embarrassment. "Really?"

"Yes, I can't recall him ever mentioning a woman by name before. It's one of the reasons I was glad you could make this trip to see me." He crossed to her to take her hand in both of his. Up close, the smile that had devastated women for generations was very potent. "Let's sit by the fire, shall we? Ah, and here's our tea."

A second maid wheeled in the cart while they settled in two balloon-back chairs before the blaze. "I want to thank you for agreeing to see me, and on a weekend."

"My pleasure." He dismissed the maid with a friendly nod, then poured out himself. "I have to be at the theater by noon for the matinee, so I'm afraid my time's limited. Lemon or cream, dear?"

"Lemon, thank you."

"And do try these scones. Believe me, they're delightful." He took two, treating himself to a hefty portion of marmalade. "So, Eve's stirring up mischief with this book, is she?"

"You could say she's generated a great deal of interest and speculation."

"You're diplomatic, Julia." Again that quick, woman-melting smile. "I hope we'll be Julia and Rory. More comfortable that way."

"Of course."

"And how is my fascinating ex-wife?"

Though it wasn't blatant, Julia caught the affection in his tone. "I'd say she's as fascinating as ever. She speaks fondly of you."

He sipped his tea with a murmur of appreciation. "We had one of those rare friendships that grew warmer after lust cooled." He laughed. "Not to say she wasn't more than a little peeved at me toward the end of the marriage—with good cause."

"Infidelity often 'peeves' a woman."

His grin flashed, so much like Paul's, Julia couldn't prevent an answering smile. Direct women had always charmed him. "My dear, I'm the foremost expert on just how women react to infidelity. Fortunately, the friendship survived—in large part, I've always thought, because Eve is so tremendously fond of Paul."

"You don't find it odd that your ex-wife and your son are so close?"

"Not at all." He sampled a scone as he spoke, eating slowly, enjoying every morsel. It wasn't difficult for Julia to imagine he had enjoyed his women in much the same way. "Frankly, I was a poor father. I'm afraid I simply had no idea what to do with a growing boy. Now, in babyhood, you just stood by the crib now and again and cooed, or walked through the park pushing a pram, looking proud and rather smug. We had a nanny to deal with the less pleasant aspects of parenting."

Unoffended, he chuckled at her expression, then patted her hand before freshening the tea. "Julia dear, don't judge me too harshly. At least I admit my failings. The theater was my family. Paul had the misfortune to be born to two disgracefully selfish and extraordinarily gifted people who hadn't a clue about how to rear a child. And Paul was so terrifyingly bright."

"You make that sound like an offense rather than a compliment."

Aha, he thought, and covered his unrepentant grin by dabbing at his mouth with his napkin. The lady was smitten. "At the time I'd say the boy was more of a puzzle I hadn't the wit to solve. Now, Eve was quite natural with him. Attentive, interested, patient. I'll confess that through her Paul and I enjoyed each other more than we had before."

Making judgments again, Jules, she cautioned herself, and struggled to shift back into objective gear. "Would you mind if I turned on my tape recorder? It makes it easier for me to be accurate."

He hesitated for only a moment, then gestured his assent. "By all means. We want accuracy."

With a minimum of fuss, she set it on the edge of the tea table and switched it on. "There was quite a bit written about you and Eve, and Paul during the first year or so of your marriage. A kind of family portrait emerges."

"Family." Rory tested out the word, then nodded over his teacup. "It was an odd concept for me, but yes, we were a family. Eve wanted a family very badly. Perhaps because of what she felt she missed growing up. Or perhaps due to the fact she had reached the age when a woman's chemistry tricks her into yearning for prams and nappies, the patter of little feet. She had even convinced me that we should have a child of our own."

This new and fascinating information put Julia on alert. "You and Eve planned to have a baby?"

"My dear, Eve is a very persuasive woman." He chuckled and settled back. "We planned and strategized like two generals camped on the enemy line. Month after month, my sperm waged war on her ovum. The battles were not without their excitement, but we never achieved total victory. Eve went to Europe—France I believe, to see some specialist. When she returned, it was with the news that she could not conceive." He set his cup down. "I must say, she took what I knew was, for her, devastating news on the chin. No weeping and wailing or cursing God for Eve. She threw herself into her work. I know she suffered. She slept poorly, and all her appetites diminished for several weeks."

Objective? Julia asked herself as she stared into the leaping fire. Not a chance. Every sympathy was aroused. "You never considered adoption?"

"Odd that you should mention adoption." Rory's eyes narrowed as he thought back. "It was an option that occurred to me. I hated to see Eve fighting off the unhappiness. And to tell you the truth, she had gotten me stirred up about the idea of having another child. When I mentioned the possibility to her, she got very quiet. She even cringed, as if I had struck her. She said—how did she put it exactly? Rory, we've both had our chance. Since there's no going back, why don't we concentrate on moving forward?"

"Meaning?"

"I suppose I thought she meant that we had done our best to make a child, and had failed, so it was wiser to get on with our lives. That is what we did. As it happened, getting on with our lives eventually meant getting on with them separately. We parted amicably, even discussed doing another project together." His smile was a bit wistful. "Perhaps we will yet."

Eve might have been so interested in the story of Brandon's conception—the girl who had become pregnant unwillingly—because she herself had been a woman unable to become pregnant, Julia reflected. But this wasn't something Rory could answer. She led him back to an area he could discuss.

"Your marriage was considered a solid one. It was a shock to most people when it dissolved."

"We had a hell of a good run, Eve and I. But the curtain must come down on every performance sooner or later."

"You don't believe in 'until death do us part'?"

He smiled, wickedly charming. "My dear, I believe it, have believed it with a full heart. Each time I've said it. Now I'm afraid you'll have to excuse me. The theater is a man's most demanding mistress."

She turned off her recorder, then tucked it into her briefcase. "I appreciate your time, and your hospitality, Mr. Winthrop."

"Rory," he reminded her, taking her hand as they rose. "I hope this isn't good-bye. I'd be happy to talk with you again. The theater's dark tomorrow. Perhaps we could continue this over dinner."

"I'd like that, if it wouldn't interfere with your plans."

"Julia, a man's plans are meant to be changed for a beautiful woman." He lifted her hand to his lips. Julia was smiling at him when the sitting room doors opened.

"Smooth as ever, I see," Paul commented.

Rory kept Julia's tensed hand in his as he turned to his son. "Paul, what a delightful and ill-timed surprise. I don't have to ask what brings you."

Paul kept his eyes on Julia's. "No, you don't. Isn't there a matinee today?"

"Indeed there is." Rory stifled a laugh. It was the first time he'd seen that reckless hunger in his son's eyes. "I was just taking my leave of this charming lady. Now, I believe I'll have to pull rank and secure two tickets for tonight's performance. It would please me very much if you'd attend."

"Thank you. I—"

"We'll be there," Paul interrupted.

"Excellent. I'll have them delivered to your hotel, Julia. Now I'll leave you in what I'm sure are very capable hands." He started out, pausing beside his son. "At last you've given me the opportunity to say you have faultless taste. If it wasn't for Lily, old boy, I'd give you a hell of a run for her."

Paul's lips quirked, but when his father made his exit, the smile disappeared as well. "Don't you think traveling to London is a rather elaborate way to avoid me?"

"I'm doing my job." All nerves and annoyance, she picked up her briefcase. "Don't you think following me to London is a rather elaborate way to hold this conversation?"

"*Inconvenient* would be my word." He crossed the room with the kind of economic grace that reminded Julia of an expert hunter who'd caught the scent. Skirting the chair, he stopped to stand with her in front of the fire. It sizzled through a log and shot out a rain of angry sparks. "Why didn't you tell me you were coming to see my father?"

His words were as measured as his steps had been, she noted. Slow and patient. As a result, hers came out too quickly.

"It didn't seem necessary to tell you my plans."

"You're wrong."

"I see no reason to check with you."

"Then I'll give you one." He pulled her against him, crushing her mouth, jumbling her senses. The move was so violent, so unexpected, she didn't have time to protest. She managed, barely, to draw in a breath.

"That's not a—"

He covered her mouth again, cutting off her words, clouding her thoughts. On a throaty moan, she dropped the briefcase to hold him closer. In that instant when rational thought was overtaken by the senses, she gave him everything.

"Am I making myself clear enough?"

"Shut up," she muttered, wrapping her arms around his neck. "Just shut up."

He closed his eyes, outrageously moved by the way she rested her head on his shoulder. The gesture, the catchy little sigh she made, had him wanting to carry her off somewhere safe and quiet. "You worry me, Julia."

"Because I came to London?"

"No, because I came after you." He drew her back. He ran the back of his hand down her cheek. "You're at the Savoy?"

"Yes."

"Then let's go. I'd hate for one of my father's servants to walk in while I'm making love with you."

◆ ◆ ◆ ◆

THE BED FELT SAFE. The room was quiet. Her body was as fluid, as intoxicating as wine under his. Each shudder, each sigh he eased from her had his blood swimming faster. He'd kept the curtains wide when she would have closed them, to give himself the pleasure of watching her face in the thin winter sunlight.

He hadn't known there could be so much pleasure. It had surrounded him as he'd carefully, slowly, stripped her of the tidy business suit she wore, found the slither of silk beneath. It had pounded through him as he'd peeled that silk away, inch by erotic inch. She was there, delicate, mysterious, arousing, yielding with a sigh when he'd lowered her to the bed.

Now she was with him, slick, damp skin sliding over his, her breath trembling in his ear, her hands gentle, then greedy, then desperate. He could feel the needs vibrate from her, feel the wild excitement as he satisfied them one by one.

It was she who altered the pace, she who whipped up the speed until they were rolling over the bed in tangled, turbulent, titanic passion.

The bed was no longer safe, but full of dangerous delights. The room was no longer quiet, but echoing with whispered demands and broken moans. Outside, the weakening sun was swallowed up and rain fell in sheets. As gloom rushed into the room, he took her with a blind, ravenous hunger he feared would never be quenched.

And even when they lay quiet, wrapped close and listening to the rain, he could taste those little licks of hunger.

◆ ◆ ◆ ◆

"*I* NEED to call Brandon," Julia murmured.

"Mmmm." Paul shifted, fitting his body to hers and cupping her breasts. "Go ahead."

"No, I can't . . . I mean I can't call him while we're . . ."

He chuckled, nuzzling her ear. "Jules, the telephone service is an auditory one, not a visual one."

It didn't matter if she felt like a fool, she shook her head and eased away. "No, really, I can't." She looked at her robe, where it lay over the back of a chair three feet away. Noting her expression, Paul grinned.

"Want me to close my eyes?"

"Of course not." But it wasn't easy for her to walk to the robe, slip into it, knowing he was watching her.

"You're sweet, Julia."

She belted the robe, staring at her own hands. "If that's your way of saying I'm unsophisticated—"

"Sweet," he repeated. "And I've ego enough to be pleased you're not used to being in this position with a man." The need to ask her why that was true pulled at him, but he resisted, then glanced toward the rain driving at the windows. "I'd thought to show you a bit of London, but this doesn't seem to be the day for it. Why don't I go in the other room and ring up some lunch?"

"All right. Would you check for messages?"

She waited until he'd pulled on his slacks before she placed the call. Ten minutes later she walked into the parlor to see Paul standing by the window, lost in his own thoughts. She took what was for her a large step and went to him, wrapping her arms around his waist, pressing her cheek to his back.

"It's seventy-eight and sunny in L.A. The Lakers lost to the Pistons and Brandon went to the zoo. Where are you?"

He laid his hands on hers. "I was standing here wondering why I always feel like a foreigner in the place where I was born. We had a flat in Eaton Square once, and I'm told my nanny often took me for walks in Hyde Park. I don't feel it. Do you know I've never even set a book here? Whenever I come here, I expect to feel that click of recognition."

"It doesn't matter so much really. I don't even know where I was born."

"And it doesn't concern you?"

"No. Well, sometimes, because of Brandon." Wanting the contact, she nuzzled her cheek against his back. His flesh had cooled, and hers warmed it again. "But in the day-to-day way of things, I rarely think of it. I loved my parents, and they loved me. They wanted me." The way he brought her fingertips to his lips made her smile. "I suppose that's the biggest part of being an adopted child—knowing you were wanted that badly, that completely. It can be the most sturdy of bonds."

"I guess that's the way it is for Eve and me. I never really knew what it was to be wanted until I was ten, and she walked into my life." He turned, needing to see her face. "I wonder if you can understand, I never really knew what it was to want, until you."

His words caused something inside her to shift, to open, to yearn. More than his touch, more than his desire, those simple words broke down all the walls. "I . . ." She moved away. Seeing clearly into her own heart didn't make her less afraid. "I thought—I'd hoped," she corrected herself, "after I'd realized we might be together, like this, that I'd be able to handle it—well, the way I imagine men handle affairs."

Suddenly nervous, he thrust his hands into his pockets. "Which is?"

"You know, casually, enjoying the physical end of it without crowding in emotions or expectations."

"I see." He watched her move. The nerves weren't all his, he realized. Julia always moved when she was tense. "Is that the way you think I'm handling this?"

"I don't know. I can speak only for myself." She forced herself to stop, to turn and face him. It was easier with the width of the room between them. "I wanted to be able to take this relationship at face value, to enjoy it for what it was. Good sex between two adults who were attracted to each other." She made a concerted effort to take in one quiet breath and release it slowly. "And I wanted to be sure I could walk away when it was over, completely unscathed. The problem is I can't. When you walked in this morning, all I could think was how much I'd wanted to see you, how much I'd missed you, how unhappy I'd been because we were angry with each other."

She stopped, straightened her shoulders. He was grinning at her, rocking back and forth on his heels. In a minute she was sure he'd be whistling. "I'd appreciate it if you'd take that smug look off your face. This isn't—"

"I love you, Julia."

Numb, she lowered herself to the arm of a chair. If he'd jammed a fist into her solar plexus, he couldn't have taken her breath away more efficiently. "You—you were supposed to let me finish, and then say something about appreciating each moment for what it was."

"Sorry. Do you really think I jumped on the Concorde with hardly more than a change of underwear just so I could spend the afternoon in bed?"

She said the first thing that came to mind. "Yes."

His laugh was quick and deep. "You're good, Jules, but not that damn good."

Not quite sure how to take that, she angled her chin. "A few minutes ago you said—actually, it was more of a groan—that I was magnificent. Yes," she said, and folded her arms. "That was the word. *Magnificent.*"

"Did I?" Christ knew, she was. "Well, that's entirely possible. But even magnificent sex wouldn't have pulled me away from a very difficult stage of my book. At least not for more than an hour or so."

And that, she supposed, put her in her place. "Then why the hell did you come?"

"When you're mad, your eyes go the color of soot. Not a very flattering description, but accurate. I came here," he continued before she could think of a proper response, "because I was worried about you, because I was furious you went off without me, because I want to be with you if there's any kind of trouble. And because I love you so much I can barely breathe when you're not with me."

"Oh." Now that, she thought, very truly did put her in her place. "This wasn't supposed to happen." She stood up again to pace. "I had it all worked out, logically, sensibly. You weren't supposed to make me feel like this."

"Like what?"

"Like I can't live without you. Dammit, Paul, I don't know what to do."

"How about this?" He snatched her in mid-stride, nearly lifting her off her feet. The kiss did the rest. After a short, final struggle, she fell into it.

"I do love you." She held on tight to that, and to him. "I don't know how to deal with it, but I love you."

"You're finished dealing with things alone." He pulled her away enough so that she could see he meant everything he said. "Do you understand, Julia?"

"I don't understand anything. Maybe, for right now, I don't need to."

Content with that, he lowered his mouth to hers. The knock on the door had them both sighing. "I can send the waiter away."

She laughed, shaking her head. "No. Suddenly I'm starving."

"At least the champagne I ordered won't go to waste." He kissed her once, then again, lingeringly, as the knock sounded a second time.

When Paul admitted the waiter, she saw that he'd also ordered flowers, a dozen delicate pink roses just budding. She slipped one from the vase, holding it to her cheek as their lunch was set up.

"Two messages for you, Miss Summers," the waiter told her, offering the envelopes as Paul signed the check.

"Thank you."

"Enjoy your lunch," he said, adding a cheery smile at his tip.

"It feels decadent," Julia said when they were alone. "Champagne, romance, flowers, in the middle of the day in a hotel." She laughed as the cork popped. "I like it."

"Then we'll have to make it a habit." He lifted a brow as he poured. "Tonight's tickets?"

"Yes. Front row, center. I wonder how he managed it."

"My father can manage almost anything he wants to."

"I liked him," Julia continued as she ripped open the second envelope. "It isn't often you find the man so much like the image. Charming, urbane, sexy—"

"Please."

Her laugh was low and rich and delighted. "You're too much like him to appreciate it. I really hope we . . ."

She trailed off, going dead white. The envelope fluttered to the floor as she studied the sheet of paper in her hand.

TWO WRONGS DON'T MAKE A RIGHT.

Chapter Nineteen

♦♦♦♦

*P*AUL SET THE BOTTLE AND GLASS ASIDE so quickly that the champagne frothed over the lip. When he put both hands on Julia's shoulders to ease her into a chair, she folded into it as if the bones had melted out of her legs. The only sound in the room was the hum from the heater and the splat of sleet on the glass. He crouched beside her, but she didn't look at him, only continued to stare at the paper she held in one tensed hand, while her other pressed low on her stomach.

"Let it out," he ordered as his fingers began to rub at her shoulders. "You're holding your breath, Jules. Let it out."

The air escaped in a long, shaky stream. Feeling as though she'd just fought her way above a dragging current, she gulped another breath and forced herself to expel this one slowly.

"Nice going. Now, what is it?"

After a quick, helpless shake of her head, she handed the slip to him.

"Two wrongs don't make a right?" Curious, he glanced up again to study her. She was no longer white to the lips, which was some relief to him, but her hands had gripped together in her lap. "Do trite sayings usually send you into shock?"

"When they follow me six thousand miles, they do."

"Are you going to explain?"

They rose together, he to stand, she to pace. "Someone's trying to frighten me," she said, half to herself. "And it infuriates me that it's working. That's not the first little homily I've received. I got one a few days after we'd been in California. It was left on the stoop in front of the house. Brandon picked it up."

"The first afternoon I was there?"

"Yes." Her hair swung around her shoulders as she turned back to him. "How did you know?"

"Because you had that same baffled, panicky look in your eyes. I didn't like seeing it then. I like it less now." He ran the note through his fingers. "Did that note say the same thing?"

"No. 'Curiosity killed the cat.' It was like this one, a slip of paper inside an envelope." The initial sting of fear was fading rapidly into anger. It showed in her voice, in the way she walked off the emotion, her fisted hands jammed into the pockets of the robe, her strides lengthening. "I found another in my purse the night after the benefit, and a third one stuck in the pages of my draft right after the first break-in."

He handed her a glass of wine as she walked past him. If it couldn't be used for celebration or romance, he figured it might calm her nerves. "Now I have to ask why you didn't tell me."

She drank and kept on moving. "I didn't tell you because it seemed more appropriate for me to tell Eve. In the beginning I didn't tell you because I didn't know you, and then—"

"You didn't trust me."

The look she sent him was caught somewhere between embarrassment and righteousness. "You were against the book."

"I still am." He pulled a cigar out of the jacket he'd discarded earlier. "What was Eve's reaction?"

"She was upset—very, I think. But she hid it quickly and well."

"She would." He kept his thoughts on that to himself for the moment. Idly he picked up his own glass of champagne and studied the bubbles. They rushed crazily to the brim, full of verve and energy. Like Eve, he thought. And oddly, like Julia. "I don't have to ask your reaction. Why don't I ask what you think the notes mean?"

"I think they're a threat, of course." Impatience shimmered in her voice, but he merely lifted a brow and drank. "Vague, even foolish, but even worn-out phrases become sinister when they're anonymous and pop out of nowhere." When he remained silent, she pushed the tumbled hair away from her face. The move was sharp and impatient, and, he realized, the gesture would have come just as naturally to Eve. "I don't like the fact that someone's trying to gaslight me—don't laugh at me."

"Sorry, it was the expression. So apropos really."

She snatched the slip off the room service cart where Paul had laid it. "Getting this here, six thousand miles away from where the others were delivered means someone must have followed me to London."

He drank again, watching her. "Someone other than me?"

"It's obvious . . ." The words had come out in a rush, an angry rush, she realized. Now she trailed off, then let out a long breath. The room was between them again. Had she put the distance there, or had he? "Paul, I don't think you're sending me these notes. I never did. This is much too passive a threat for you."

He lifted a brow, then drank. "Was that meant to be flattering?"

"No, just honest." It was she who closed the distance, then lifted a hand to his face as if to smooth away the lines that had formed there in only the last few moments. "I didn't think it of you before, and I don't—couldn't—think it now."

"Because we're lovers."

"No, because I love you."

A ghost of a smile touched his mouth as he lifted his hand to cover hers. "You make it difficult for a man to stay annoyed, Jules."

"Are you annoyed with me?"

"Yes." Still, he pressed a kiss into the palm of her hand. "But I think we should work through the priorities. First, let's see if we can find out who left the message at the desk."

It irked that she hadn't thought of that before him. That was part of the problem—she wasn't thinking clearly. When he walked to the phone, Julia sat, reminding herself that if she intended to see this through—and she did—she would have to be not only calm but calculating. The next sip of champagne reminded her that she was drinking on an empty stomach. That was no way to keep the mind clear.

"The tickets were delivered by a uniformed messenger," Paul told her after he hung up. "The second envelope was left on the desk. They're checking, but it's doubtful anyone noticed who put it there."

"It could have been anyone, anyone who knew I planned to come here and interview your father."

"And who did know?"

She rose and walked to the cart to nibble. "I didn't make a secret of it. Eve, certainly. Nina, Travers, CeeCee, Lyle—Drake, I suppose. Then anyone who might have asked any of them. Isn't that what you did?"

Despite the circumstances, it amused him that she carried the dish of shrimp in lobster sauce with her as she paced, stabbing at it and forking it into her mouth as if she were refueling rather than dining. "Travers told me. I suppose the next question is what do you want to do about it?"

"Do about it? I don't see what there is to do but ignore it. I can't see me going to Scotland Yard." The idea, and the food, helped her disposition. Calmer, she set the nearly empty dish aside, then picked up the champagne. "I can see it now. Inspector, someone sent me a note. No, I can't say it was a threat really. More of a proverb. Put your best men on the case."

Normally he would have found her resilience admirable. Nothing was quite normal any longer. "You didn't find it so funny when you opened the envelope."

"No, I didn't, but maybe I should. Two wrongs don't make a right? How can I be bothered with someone who can't be any more original than that?"

"Odd, I thought it was clever." When he came to her, she saw that her attempt at humor had fallen well short of the mark. "If anyone caught the person who's sending them, it would hardly interest the police, would it? Harmless, even shopworn sayings. It would be hard to prove there was anything threatening about them. But we know differently."

"If you're going to tell me to give up the book—"

"I think I understand the futility of that one by now. Julia, don't block me out of this." He touched her, just a hand to her hair. "Let me listen to the tapes. I want to help you."

She couldn't turn away this time. It wasn't arrogance, it wasn't ego. It was love. "All right. As soon as we get home."

♦ ♦ ♦ ♦

EVEN WITH JULIA out of the country, Lyle found a lot to interest him in the comings and goings of the guest house. A cleaning crew had spent two full days on the place. Trucks had hauled away broken furniture, shattered glass, torn curtains. He'd taken a peek at the interior before the crew had arrived. It had looked as though someone had thrown one hell of a party.

He was sorry he'd missed it. Damn sorry. The name of the partygoer might have been worth a tidy sum. But that particular afternoon he'd been happily boinking the upstairs maid. He now considered the fact that that brief—but very gratifying—fuck had probably cost him several thousand.

Still, there were other ways to earn a living. Lyle had big dreams and a list of priorities. Right up top was a Porsche. Nothing impressed the babes more than a cool dude in a hot car. He wanted his own place, a beach house where he could sit on his deck and watch all those teeny bikinis and what was packed into them. He wanted a Rolex, too, and the wardrobe to go with it. Once he was set up, picking up classy women would be like swatting flies.

Lyle figured he was on his way. He could almost smell the sunblock and sweat.

He kept careful notes in his cramped handwriting. What was taken away from the guest house, what was brought in. Who made the deliveries. He'd even had a key made so he could move through the house at will. It had been a little dicier getting into the main house, but he'd chosen his time well and had managed to make a copy of Nina Soloman's phone log and appointment book.

Travers had nearly caught him sneaking into Eve's bedroom. Nosy, tight-assed bitch guarded the house like a junkyard dog. He'd been disappointed that Eve hadn't kept a diary or journal. That would have been worth big bucks. But he had found some interesting drugs in her bedside table, and some strange notes in her makeup drawer.

What the hell was she doing with notes that said stuff like "let sleeping dogs lie"? Lyle decided to keep the pills and the notes his own little secret until he could figure out what they might be worth.

It had been a cinch to get information from the guard at the gate, Joe. He liked to talk, and when you added a beer and some stories of your own, he got diarrhea of the mouth.

Even gone, Eve received lots of visitors.

Michael Torrent had been driven away after learning that Eve would be on location for the next couple of weeks. Gloria DuBarry had dropped by to see Eve, then had changed to Julia on learning Eve was away. She had driven herself, and according to Joe had been teary-eyed when she'd found no one at home.

A couple of paparazzi had tried to get through disguised as delivery men, but Joe had weeded them out. Joe's ability to sniff out press was revered among residents of Beverly Hills.

He'd admitted Victor Flannigan, then had let him out again less than twenty minutes later. Eve's agent, Maggie Castle, had gone in as well, and stayed twice as long.

Lyle gathered the information. He had what he considered a very professional report ready. Maybe he should go into P.I. work, he thought as he dressed for the evening. On TV those guys were always getting the chicks.

He chose a pair of black thong-style bikinis and gave his favorite member a quick pat. Some unsuspecting woman was going to get lucky tonight. He wiggled into black leather pants, then zipped a matching jacket over his tight red undershirt. Women, he knew, really went for a guy in leather.

He'd deliver his report, pick up the cash. Then he'd cruise a few clubs until he chose the lucky lady.

◆ ◆ ◆

JULIA HADN'T BEEN SURE what she'd think of Rory Winthrop's current wife. But whatever she'd been expecting, it wasn't that she would both like and admire Lily Teasbury.

Onscreen, the actress usually played the frothy, flighty heroine who suited her busty blond looks and guileless blue eyes. At first glance it was tempting to typecast her as someone who giggled and wriggled a lot.

It took Julia less than five minutes to revise her opinion.

Lily was a sharp, witty, ambitious woman who exploited her looks rather than being exploited by them. She was also very much at home in the traditional parlor of the Knightsbridge house, looking very cool, very British, and very wifely in a simple blue Givenchy.

"I wondered when you'd finally visit," she said to Paul as she served apéritifs. "We've been married three months."

"I don't get to London often."

Julia had been on the receiving end of that long, piercing look, and admired Lily for standing up under it with such apparent ease.

"So I'm told. Well, you've picked a miserable season for this visit. Is this your first visit to London, Miss Summers?"

"Yes, it is."

"A pity about all this sleet. Then again, I always think it's best to see a city at its worst—like a man—that way you can decide if you can really live with all the flaws."

Lily sat, smiled, and sipped her vermouth.

"That's Lily's subtle way of reminding me she knows all of mine," Rory put in.

"Not subtle at all," Lily said. She touched a hand to his briefly, but—Julia thought—with a great deal of affection. "It wouldn't do to be subtle when I'm about to be treated to reminiscences about one of the great love affairs of my husband's life." She beamed at Julia. "Don't worry, I'm not jealous, just avidly curious. I don't believe in jealousy, particularly over things past. As to the future, I've already warned Rory that if he becomes tempted to repeat his past mistakes, I won't be one to weep and wail and nag or run screaming to my solicitor." She sipped again, delicately. "I'll simply kill him quickly, cleanly, in cold blood, and without a moment's regret."

Rory laughed, then toasted his wife. "She terrifies me."

As the conversation flowed around him, Paul began to listen, to feel, with more interest. He wouldn't have believed it, but he began to think that something had clicked, something solid, between his father and the woman he had married. A woman younger than the man's only child—and one who, at first glance, had easily been dismissed as another of the big-breasted, pouty-lipped bimbos his father often dallied with.

But Lily Teasbury wasn't like any of the others. After he'd worked beyond an old and established resentment of one of his father's women, he watched with a writer's eye, listened with a writer's ear. He saw the subtle gestures, glances, heard the timbre of voices, a quick laugh. This, he realized with no little astonishment, was a marriage.

There was an ease and companionship that he had never sensed between his father and his own mother. There was a friendship he had seen in only one of his father's marriages. When Eve Benedict had been his wife.

When they went in for dinner, it was with a sense of relief and wonder. The relief came when he realized Lily would not fall into either of the two categories so many of Rory's women had. She would not pretend there was an instant familial relationship between them. Nor would she allude, privately, that she was open to a more intimate relationship.

His wonder came from the fact that his own instincts were insisting that his father might at long last have found someone he could live with.

Julia sampled the pressed duck and eased her left foot free of her shoe. There was a fire in the hearth behind Rory's back and a waterfall of crystal lights over their heads. The room with its tapestries and glinting display cabinets might have been dauntingly formal, but comfort seeped through by the way the two-pedestaled Regency table was left unextended, by the vase of fairy roses as a centerpiece, by the scent of applewood, and the quiet hiss of sleet. She slipped her other foot free.

"I haven't told you how wonderful you were last night," Julia said to Rory. "Or how much I appreciated your going to the trouble to send tickets."

"No trouble at all," Rory assured her. "I was delighted you and Paul would brave the elements and attend."

"I wouldn't have missed it."

"Do you enjoy *Lear*?" Lily asked her.

"It's very powerful, stirring. Tragic."

"All those bodies heaped up at the end—really all due to an old man's vanity and folly." She winked at her husband. "Rory's marvelous in the part, but I suppose I prefer comedy. It's as difficult to pull off, but at least when one crawls off the stage, it's with laughter ringing in one's ears rather than wails of lamentation."

Chuckling, Rory directed his comment to Julia. "Lily likes happy endings. Early in our relationship I took her to see *A Long Day's Journey into Night*." Rory forked up some wild rice. "Afterward, she told me that if I wanted to sit around for several hours absorbing misery, I'd have to do it with someone else. Next time around I took her to a Marx Brothers festival."

"So I married him." She reached over to touch her fingertips to his. "After I discovered he knew whole blocks of dialogue from *A Night at the Opera*."

"And I thought it was because I'm so sexy."

When she smiled at him, a tiny dimple winked at the left corner of her mouth. "Darling, sex is limited to bed. A man who understands and appreciates comic genius is a man you can live with in the morning." She leaned back again and fluttered her lashes at Julia. "Wouldn't you agree, dear?"

"Paul's never offered to take me anywhere but a basketball game," she said without thinking. Before she could regret it, Lily burst into delighted laughter.

"Rory, what a pathetic father you must have been if your son can't do better than a bunch of sweaty men tossing a ball at a hoop."

"I certainly was, but the boy always had his own ideas about everything, including the ladies."

"And what," Paul asked as he calmly continued to eat, "is wrong with basketball?" Since his gaze was leveled at Julia, she thought it prudent to give a noncommittal shrug. She looked amazingly beautiful when she was flustered, he thought. Her skin heated up, and she had that sexy way of nibbling on her bottom lip. He decided he'd be certain to nibble on it, and other areas, himself a little later.

"You wouldn't go with me," he reminded her.

"No."

"If I'd asked you to, say, a Three Stooges retrospective, would you have gone with me?"

"No." A smile tugged at her lips. "Because you made me nervous."

He reached across the table to toy with her fingers. "And if I asked you now?"

"You still make me nervous, but I'd probably risk it."

As he picked up his wine, he looked toward his father. "It seems my ideas work well enough. Lily, the duck is excellent."

"Why, thank you." She chuckled into her wine. "Thank you very much."

It wasn't until coffee and brandy were served back in the cozy sitting room that the subject of Eve Benedict was broached again. Julia was still casting around in her brain for the most tactful way to begin the interview, when Lily opened the door.

"I was sorry we weren't able to attend the party Eve gave recently. Surprised to be included in the invitation, and sorry to miss it." She tucked up her legs cozily, revealing their long length. "Rory tells me that she's always given incredible parties."

"Did you give many when you were married?" Julia asked Rory.

"Several actually. Small, intimate dinner parties, informal barbecues, glitzy soirees." He circled a hand in the air. His gold cuff links glinted in the firelight. "Your birthday party, Paul, do you remember?"

"It would be hard to forget." Because he understood it was an interview, he looked at Julia. He noted Lily had settled back to listen. "She hired circus performers—clowns, jugglers, a wire walker. Even an elephant."

"And the gardener nearly quit when he saw the state of the lawn the next day." Rory chuckled and swirled his brandy. "Living with Eve brought few dull moments."

"If you could use one word to describe her?"

"Eve?" He thought for a moment. *"Indomitable,* I suppose. Nothing ever held her back for long. I remember her losing a part to Charlotte Miller—a tough pill for Eve to swallow. She went on to play Sylvia in *Spider's Touch,* won in Cannes that year, and made everyone forget that Charlotte had even done a film at the same time. About twenty-five, thirty years ago it was becoming difficult to find good roles—actresses of a certain age were not courted by studios. Eve went to New York, plucked a plum in *Madam Requests* on Broadway. She ran with it for a year, won a Tony, and had Hollywood begging her to come home. If you'll look back at her career, you'll see that she's never chosen a bad script. Oh, there were some uneven ones in the beginning certainly. The studio pushed her and she had no choice but to follow. Yet in each one, even the poorest of them, her performance was that of a star. It takes more than talent, even more than ambition, to achieve that. It takes power."

"He'd love to work with her again," Lily put in. "And I'd love to see them do it."

"It wouldn't be awkward for you?" Julia asked.

"Not in the least. Perhaps if I didn't understand the business, it might be difficult. And if I weren't sure that Rory values his life." She laughed, rearranging those smooth, shapely legs. "In any case, I have to respect a woman who can remain friends, real friends, with a man she was once married to. My ex and I still detest each other."

"Which is why Lily hasn't left divorce as an option for me." Rory reached out to link his hand with hers. "Eve and I liked each other, you see. When she wanted out of the marriage, she went about it in a courteous, reasonable way. Since the failure was mine, I could hardly hold grudges."

"You say it was yours—because of other women."

"Primarily. I imagine my . . . lack of discretion where women are concerned is one of the reasons Paul's always been so cautious. Wouldn't you say?"

"Selective," Paul corrected his father.

"I was not a good husband, I was not a good father. The examples I set in each were less than admirable."

Paul shifted uncomfortably. "I did well enough."

"With little help from me. Julia's here for honesty. Aren't you?"

"Yes, but if I could say—as someone on the outside—I think you were a better father than you realize. From what I've been told, you never pretended to be anything but what you were."

His eyes warmed. "Thank you for that. I have learned that a child can benefit as much from bad examples as he can good ones. Depending on the child. Paul was always a bright one. Therefore he has been discriminating where the opposite sex is concerned, and he has little patience for the careless gambler. It was my lack of discrimination, and my carelessness that Eve finally tired of."

"I've heard you're interested in gambling. You own horses?"

"A few. I've always had luck in games of chance, perhaps that's why I've found it hard to resist a casino, a leggy Thoroughbred, the turn of a card. Eve didn't object to the gambling. She enjoyed a few games herself now and again. It was the people one tended to come into contact with. Bookies aren't normally the cream of society. Eve avoided most of the professional gamblers. Though several years after our divorce she did become involved with someone closely tied to the trade. That, too, was my fault, as I introduced them. At the time I didn't know myself how involved he was. Later, it was an introduction I came to regret."

"Gambling?" Though her instincts went on full alert, Julia took a casual sip of coffee. "I don't recall coming across anything in my research about Eve being involved with gambling."

"Not with gambling. As I said, Eve never had much interest in the delights of wagering. I suppose I couldn't call him a gambler. One isn't when the odds are always stacked in one's favor. The polite term, I suppose, would be *businessman*."

Julia glanced at Paul. The look in his eyes brought one name shooting into her mind. "Michael Delrickio?"

"Yes. A frightening man. I met him in Vegas on one of my more delightful hot streaks. I was playing craps at the Desert Palace. The dice were like beautiful women eager to please that night."

"Rory often refers to gambling in female terms," Lily put in. "When he's losing, he attaches very creative female terms to dice or cards." She gave him an indulgent smile before she rose to pour more brandy. "Such a filthy night out. Are you sure you won't have anything stronger than coffee, Julia?"

"No, really, thank you." Though impatient with the interruption, her voice was only mildly curious as she steered the conversation back. "You were telling me about Michael Delrickio."

"Hmmm." Rory stretched out his legs and cupped his snifter in both hands. Julia had time to think he looked the perfect English gentleman in repose—the fire crackling at his back, brandy warming in his hands. All that was missing was a pair of hounds to slumber at his feet. "Yes, I met Delrickio at the Palace after I had cleaned up at the tables. He offered to buy me a drink, professed to being a fan. I had nearly refused. Such interludes can often be uncomfortable, but I learned that he owned the casino. Or, more accurately, his organization owned it, and others."

"You said it was frightening. Why?"

"It was perhaps four A.M. when we had our drink," Rory said slowly.

"Yet he looked . . . well, like a banker taking a relaxed business lunch. I found him very articulate. He was indeed a fan, not just of mine, but of film. We spent nearly three hours discussing movies and the making of them. He told me he was interested in financing an independent production company, and would be in Los Angeles the following month."

He paused to sip and to think. "I ran into him again at a party Eve and I attended together. We were both unattached, Eve and I, and often escorted each other, one might say. In fact, Paul was living with Eve while he attended some classes in California."

"I was a sophomore at U.C.L.A.," Paul elaborated. With a small shrug he pulled out a cigar. "My father has yet to forgive me for turning down Oxford."

"You were determined to break family tradition."

"And you became an advocate of tradition only when I did."

"You broke your grandfather's heart."

Paul grinned around the cigar. "He never had one."

Rory straightened in his chair, ready to do battle. Just as suddenly, he fell back again with a laugh. "You're absolutely right. And God knows you were better off with Eve than with either your mother or me. If you'd buckled under and gone to Oxford, the old man would have done his best to make your life as bloody miserable as he tried to make mine."

Paul merely sipped his brandy. "I think Julia's more interested in Eve than in our family history."

With a smile, Rory shook his head. "I'd say the interest runs about neck-and-neck. But we'll concentrate on Eve for the moment. She was looking particularly stunning that night."

"Darling," Lily purred, "how rude of you to say so in front of your current wife."

"Honesty." He picked up Lily's hand and kissed her fingers. "Julia insists on it. I believe Eve had just returned from a spa of some sort. She was looking refreshed, regenerated. We'd been divorced several years by then and were back to being chums. We were both quite delighted by the fact that the press would make a great deal of our being seen together. In short, we enjoyed ourselves. We might have—forgive me, darling," he murmured to his wife. "We might have spent the night reminiscing, but I introduced her to Delrickio. The attraction was instant, the old cliché about lightning bolts, at least on his side. On hers, I'd say that Eve was intrigued. Suffice it to say that it was Delrickio who escorted her home. After that, I can only speculate."

"You haven't really answered the question." Julia set her empty cup aside. "Why was he frightening?"

Rory let out a little sigh. "I told you he'd said he was interested in a certain production company. It seemed the company wasn't interested in him, initially. Within three months of my introducing Delrickio to Eve, he—his organization—owned the company outright. There had been some financial setbacks, some equipment lost, some accidents. I learned through associates of associates that Delrickio had strong ties with . . . what does one call it these days?"

"He's Mafia," Paul said impatiently. "There's no need to skip around it."

"One hopes to be subtle," Rory murmured. "In any case, it was suspected—only suspected—that he had links with organized crime. He's never been indicted. I do know that Eve saw him discreetly for a few months, then she married that tennis player quite suddenly."

"Damien Priest," Julia supplied. "Eve mentioned that it was Michael Delrickio who introduced them."

"It's certainly possible. Delrickio knows a great many people. I can't tell you much about that particular relationship. The marriage was a short one. Eve never discussed the reasons for its abrupt ending." He sent a long look toward his son. "At least not with me."

◆ ◆ ◆

"*I* DON'T WANT to discuss Delrickio." The moment they entered the suite, Paul stripped off his jacket. "You've spent most of the evening interviewing. Give it a rest."

"You can give me an angle your father can't." Julia stepped out of her shoes. "I want your insight, your opinion." She could see the anger growing in him in the way he tugged off his tie—quick, tensed fingers dragging away the knot.

"I detest him. Isn't that enough?"

"No. I already know how you feel about him. I want to know how you came to feel that way."

"You could say I have an intolerance for crime lords." Paul toed off his shoes. "I'm funny that way."

Dissatisfied, Julia frowned as she drew the pins from her hair. "That answer would work if it weren't for the fact that I've seen you with him and know it's a personal intolerance rather than a general one." The pins jabbed into her palm. As she opened her hand and looked down at them, she realized that this kind of intimacy had become easy between them. The kicking-off-your-shoes taking-down-your-hair comfort between lovers. Another intimacy, that of the heart, was more elusive. The knowledge brought a dull edge of pain that was both anger and hurt.

Watching him, she tossed the pins on the table beside her. "I thought we'd come to the point where we trusted each other."

"It's not a matter of trust."

"It's always a matter of trust."

He sat, his face as stormy as hers was calm. "You're not going to let this go."

"It's my job," she reminded him. She walked to the windows to draw the drapes with one quick snap of her wrist and close out the storm. And to close them inside, so they were faced with only each other in the slant of gold from the lamp. "If you want to put this on a professional basis, fine. Eve can tell me anything I need to know about Michael Delrickio. I'd hoped to hear your point of view."

"Fine, my point of view is that he's slime oozing around in an Italian suit. The worst kind of slime because he enjoys being exactly what he is." His eyes glittered. "He profits from the miseries of the world, Julia. And when he steals, blackmails, maims, or kills, he lists it all under the tidy heading of business. It means no more and no less to him."

She sat, but she didn't reach for her tape recorder. "Yet Eve was involved with him."

"I think it would be accurate to say that she didn't realize precisely who and what he was before their relationship developed. Obviously, she found him attractive. He can certainly be charming. He's articulate, erudite. She enjoyed his company, and, I'd think, his power."

"You were living with her," Julia prompted.

"I was going to school in California and making my base with her. I didn't know how she'd met Delrickio until tonight." A small detail, he thought, that hardly mattered. He knew the rest, or enough of the rest. And now, due to her own tenacity, so would Julia. "He started coming around—for a swim, a game of tennis, dinner. She went to Vegas with him a couple of times, but for the most part, they saw each other at the house. He was always sending flowers, gifts. Once he brought in the chef from one of his restaurants and had him prepare an elaborate Italian dinner."

"He owns restaurants?" Julia asked.

Paul barely glanced at her. "He owns," he said flatly. "A couple of his men were around, always. He never drove himself or came unaccompanied." She nodded, understanding perfectly. Like the gates of Eve's estate. Power always exacted a price. "I didn't like him—didn't like the way he looked at Eve as though she were one of his fucking orchids."

"Excuse me?"

Paul rose and walked to the window. Restless, he tugged the drapes open a crack. The sleet had stopped, but there was a bitterness to the weather he could sense even behind the glass. One didn't always have to see ugliness to recognize it. "He grows orchids. He's obsessive about them. He was obsessive about Eve, hovering around, insisting on knowing where she was, with whom. She enjoyed that, mainly because she refused to account to him, and that would drive him crazy." He glanced back to see her smiling. "Amused?"

"I'm sorry, it's only that I'm—well, envious, I suppose, of the way she skillfully handles the men in her life."

"Not always so skillfully," he murmured, and didn't return the smile. "I walked in on an argument once when he was raging at her, threatening her. I ordered him out of the house, even tried to toss him out myself, but his bodyguards were on me like lice. Eve had to break it up."

Now there was no amusement, but a trickle of alarm and memory. Hadn't Delrickio said something about it being a pity Eve hadn't let him teach Paul respect? "You'd have been, what, about twenty?"

"About. It was ugly, humiliating, and illuminating. Eve was angry with him, but she was every bit as angry with me. She thought I was jealous—and maybe I was. I got a bloody nose, a few sore ribs—"

"They hit you?" she interrupted in a voice sharp with appalled shock. He had to grin.

"Babe, you don't train apes to play patty-cake. It could have been worse—a lot worse, as I was doing my best to get my hands around the bastard's throat. You might not have heard I have a sporadic affection for violence."

"No," she said calmly enough, even while her stomach churned. "I hadn't. Was this, ah, episode, the reason Eve broke it off with Delrickio?"

"No." He was tired of talking, tired of thinking. "As far as she was concerned, her relationship with him had nothing to do with me. And she was right." Slowly, as if he were stalking, he moved toward her. And, like all things hunted, she felt the quick tremor of alarm that kicked her heart rate from slow to racing. "Do you know how you look just now, sitting with your back straight in that chair, your hands neatly folded? And your eyes so solemn, so concerned?"

Because he made her feel foolish, she shifted. "I want to know—"

"That's the problem," he murmured, bending over to take her face in his hands. "You want to know when all you have to do is feel. What do you feel now when I tell you I can't think of anything but peeling you out of that proper little dress, of seeing if that perfume I watched you spray on hours ago is still clinging to your skin—just there—under the curve of your jaw."

As he ran his fingers along the line, she moved again. But rising was an error in judgment, only bringing her up hard against him. "You're trying to distract me."

"Damn right." He tugged down her zipper, chuckling as she tried to wriggle aside. "Everything about you has been distracting me from the moment I met you."

"I want to know," she tried again, then gasped as he jerked the dress down to her waist. His mouth was on her, and his hands, not gently, not seductively, but with a possessive fervor that edged toward frenzy. "Paul, wait. I need to understand why she ended it."

"It only took murder." His eyes blazed as he dragged her head back. "Cold-blooded, calculated murder for profit. Delrickio's money was on Damien Priest, so he eliminated the competition."

Horror widened her eyes. "You mean he—"

"Stay away from him, Julia." He dragged her against him. Through the thin silk she could feel the heat that poured from his flesh. "What I feel for you, what I might do for you, makes what I felt for Eve all those years ago nothing." He caught her hair in tensed, fisted fingers. "Nothing."

Even as she shuddered with excitement he pulled her to the floor and showed her.

Chapter Twenty

✦✦✦✦

$\mathcal{T}$UCKED INTO HER ROBE, Julia sipped a brandy. Her body was heavy with fatigue and sex. She wondered if this was what it might feel like to find herself tossed up on a dry shore after a wild battle with a violent sea. Drained, exhilarated, dazed, because she had survived the violence and the uncanny beauty of something so primitive and so ageless.

As her pulse leveled and her mind cleared, the word Paul had spoken before dragging her into that turbulent sea echoed in her head.

The word was *murder*.

She understood even though they sat close together on the sofa, the silence between them intimate, that this balance between them could be so easily skewed. However frenzied their mating, it was here, in the quiet after, while the air cooled and thinned again, where they needed to reach each other. Not just a hand linked with a hand, but again, that small, vital matter of trust for trust.

"As you were saying," she began, and made him smile.

"You know, Jules, some might call you focused. Others might consider you just a nag."

"I'm a focused nag." She laid a hand on his knee. "Paul, I need to hear this from you. If Eve has any objections to what you tell me tonight, it stops there. That's the agreement."

"Integrity," he murmured. "Isn't that what Eve said she admired in you?"

He touched her hair. They sat like that for a moment before he spoke again, quietly.

✦✦✦✦

$\mathcal{S}$HAKEN, Julia rose to pour more brandy. She'd said nothing throughout Paul's story of how Damien's competitor had died, Eve's suspicion it was murder—murder ordered by Delrickio.

"We never spoke of it again," Paul had ended. "Eve refused to. Priest went on to win the title, then retired. Their divorce caused some commotion for a while, but that died down. After a while I began to see why she had handled it that way. Nothing could have been proven. Delrickio would have had her killed if she'd tried."

Now, before trying to speak, she sipped and let the hot punch of liquor steady her voice. "Is this why you were against the bio? Were you afraid Eve would tell this story and put her life in jeopardy?"

Paul looked up at her. "I know she will. The right time, the right place, the right method. She wouldn't have forgotten; she wouldn't have forgiven. If Delrickio believes she's told you and you're contemplating printing it, your life won't be worth any more than hers is."

She watched him as she took the seat beside him. She would have to go carefully here. All the years she had been on her own, making her own decisions, following her own code made it difficult to explain herself. "Paul, if you had believed, really believed that going to the police would have brought justice, would you have walked away from it?"

"That's not the point—"

"Perhaps it's too late for points. It comes down to instinct and emotion, and that infinite gray area between right and wrong. Eve believes in what she's doing with this book. And so do I."

He grabbed at a cigar, struck viciously at a match. "Putting your life on the line for someone who's been dead for fifteen years doesn't make sense."

She studied his face, shadowed by the lamplight and smoke. "If I thought you believed that I wouldn't be here with you. No," she said before he could speak. "What's between you and me isn't just physical. I understand you, and I think I have right from the beginning. That's why I was afraid to let anything happen. Once before I let my actions be swayed by my feelings. I was wrong, but since the result was Brandon, I can't regret. This . . ." She laid a hand on his, slowly linking their fingers. "Is more, and less. More important, less superficial. I love you, Paul, and loving you means I have to trust my instincts, and respect my conscience—not only with you, but across the board."

He stared at the glowing tip of his cigar, more humbled by her words than he would have thought possible. "You don't leave me much room for arguments."

"I don't leave myself much room either. If I ask you to trust me, it means I have to trust you." She lifted her gaze from their joined hands to meet his eyes. "You haven't asked me about Brandon's father."

"No." He sighed. He would have to back away from his objections for now. It was possible but unlikely that he would have better luck with Eve. That Julia would volunteer to talk about Brandon's father meant they had scaled one more wall. "I didn't ask because I hoped you'd do exactly what you're about to do." He grinned at her. "And I was arrogant enough to be sure you would."

She laughed, a quiet, homey sound that made him relax. "I'm arrogant enough not to have told you if you had asked."

"Yeah, I know that too."

"It isn't as important as it once was to keep the circumstances private. It's become a habit, I suppose, and I've thought, still think, it's best for Brandon that it not be an issue. If he asks, and one day he will, I'll tell him the truth. I loved his father, the way a girl of seventeen loves, idealistically, rashly, romantically. He was married, and I regret the fact that I let my emotions gloss over the reality of that. At the time we became involved, he was separated from his wife—or so he said. I was all too eager to believe it and to delude myself that he would marry me and, well, sweep me away."

"He was older."

"Fourteen years."

"Someone should have tied his dick in a knot."

For a moment she stared, then the crudity of the remark issued in that smooth elegantly accented voice sent her off into peals of laughter. "Oh, my father would have liked you. I'm sure he would have said very much the same thing if he'd known." She kissed him, hard, then settled back as he continued to glare into the shadows. "I know it was more his responsibility than mine. But a girl of seventeen can be very persuasive."

Quietly, thoroughly, she told him about Lincoln, about the heedless rush of feelings that had pushed her into an affair, her fear of the resulting pregnancy, her grief at Lincoln's defection.

"I doubt I would change any of it. If I had it to do over again, I still wouldn't tell my parents and risk layering another level of hurt on my father. He thought of Lincoln as a son. And I certainly wouldn't have changed that awkward tumble on the couch, or there would be no Brandon." When she smiled, the expression was serene, confident. "He's given me the best ten years of my life."

Paul wanted to understand but couldn't get beyond the rage in his gut. She'd been a child, a child who had handled her responsibilities with more care and dignity than a man nearly twice her age.

"He doesn't stay in touch with you, or with Brandon?"

"No, and at this point of my life I'm glad of it. Brandon's mine."

"A pity," he said mildly. "It would be so satisfying to kill him for you."

"My hero," she said, and slipped her arms around him. "But not for me, Paul. That was yesterday. I think I have all I need today."

He cupped her face in his hands, his thumbs tracing the line of her jaw. "Let's make sure of it," he murmured, and kissed her.

Chapter Twenty-One

♦♦♦♦

$\mathcal{I}$T WAS SO GOOD to be home that Eve even looked forward to a session with Fritz. The fact was she'd missed the doses of sweat and strain more than she would ever admit to her trainer. She'd missed Travers's grousing, Nina's obsessive organization. Julia's company. It struck Eve, not altogether pleasantly, that she must at last be getting old if she had come to hoard in her heart like a miser the everyday things she'd once ignored.

The location shoot had gone well. Certainly better than she'd anticipated. She could credit Peter for much of that—not only for the bouts of good, solid sex, but for his patience and enthusiasm on the set, his sense of humor even when things were at their worst. Years before she might have made the mistake of stringing their affair out, of pretending, at least to herself, that she was in love with him.

Or, she certainly would have used whatever means at her disposal to tip him over into love with her. Good sense had prevailed, and they had agreed to leave the lovers in Georgia and come back to the West Coast as friends and colleagues.

Now, lowering thought, maturity offered perspective. She realized Peter reminded her of Victor, of the vital, charming, and talented man she had fallen so helplessly in love with. Of the man she still loved. Oh, God, she missed him. Of all her fears, the greatest was that they would waste what time they had left together.

Julia entered five minutes later. She was out of breath because she had hurried, had felt the need to hurry. The moment she saw Eve, bent low in a hamstring stretch, her tall, lush body unbelievably stunning in a snug sapphire leotard, she understood why. She had missed her, Julia thought. Missed Eve's acid comments, her stingingly honest memories, the outsize ego, the arrogance. All of it. She laughed to herself as she watched Eve switch her weight.

At that moment, Eve glanced up, caught Julia's smile, and returned it. Fritz looked over, his eyes moving from one woman to the other. His brows raised speculatively, but he said nothing. Something passed between them in the silence, unexpected by both. As Eve straightened, Julia felt an urge to walk to her and embrace, knowing she would be embraced in turn. Though she did cross the room, she only held out both hands, her fingers linking with Eve's in a quick, welcoming grip.

"So, how was the swamp?"

"Hot." Eve searched her face, pleased with what she saw there. Relaxation, a quiet contentment. "How was London?"

"Cold." Still smiling, Julia set her gym bag aside. "Rory sends his regards."

"Hmm. You know what I really want is an opinion on his new wife."

"I think she's perfect for him. She reminds me a bit of you." She swallowed a chuckle as incredulity shot into Eve's eyes.

"Darling, really. There's no one like me."

"You're right." The hell with it, she thought, and went with instinct, wrapping her arms around Eve in a tight, affectionate hug. "I missed you."

Now it was tears that glittered in Eve's eyes, quick, unexpected, and difficult to control. "I would have liked you with me. Your cool observations would have livened up the hours of boredom between takes. But I have a feeling you enjoyed the company in London."

Julia stepped back. "You knew Paul was with me."

"I know everything." Eve flicked a finger down Julia's jawline. "You're happy."

"Yes. Nervous, dazzled, but happy too."

"Tell me everything."

"Work," Fritz interrupted. "Talk while you work. You can't just exercise your tongues."

"You can't talk and do crunchies," Julia complained. "You can't even breathe and do crunchies." He only grinned.

By the time he put her on the weights, she was sheened with sweat, but she had her wind. Over his grunted instructions she told Eve about London, about Paul, about all the feelings that were bubbling inside. It was so easy she hardly thought about it. Years before, it had been impossible to talk to her mother about Lincoln. Now there was no shame, no fear.

There were a dozen times when she could have angled the conversation to Delrickio, but Julia felt it wasn't the time. And with Fritz in attendance, it wasn't the place. Instead, she tried what she thought would be a less sensitive area.

"I have an appointment with Nina's predecessor, Kenneth Stokley, this afternoon."

"Really? Is he in town?"

"No, he's still in Sausalito. I'm flying down for a few hours. Is there anything you'd like to tell me about him?"

"About Kenneth?" Eve pursed her lips as she finished her leg curls. "You might find him a difficult interview. Terribly polite, but not very expansive. I was very fond of him, and sorry when he decided to retire."

"I thought you'd had a disagreement."

"We did, but he was a top-notch assistant for me." She took a towel from Fritz and blotted her face. "He didn't have a very high opinion of my husband. Husband number four to be exact. And, I found it difficult to forgive Kenneth for being so right." She shrugged and tossed the towel aside. "We decided it would be best to sever our professional relationship, and, a frugal soul, he had more than enough to retire in style. Are you going alone?"

"Yes, I should be back by five. CeeCee's going to watch Brandon after school. There's a commuter flight that leaves at noon."

"Nonsense. You'll take my plane. Nina will arrange it." She waved a hand before Julia could speak. "It's just sitting there. This way you can come and go as suits you. That should appeal to that streak of practicality."

"Actually it does. Thank you. I'd also like to talk to you about Gloria DuBarry. She's been dodging my phone calls."

Eve bent down to rub at her calf, so her expression was veiled. But the hesitation, though brief, was obvious. "I wondered if you'd mention your little . . . altercation with her."

Julia lifted a brow. "It doesn't seem necessary. As you said, you know everything."

"Yes." She was smiling as she straightened, but Julia thought she detected a trace of strain. "We'll talk later, about Gloria and other things. I imagine if you try her again, she'll be more cooperative."

"All right. Then there's Drake—"

"Don't worry about Drake right now," Eve interrupted. "Who else have you interviewed?"

"Your agent, though we had to cut it short. I'm going to be talking with her again. I managed a brief phoner with Michael Torrent. He called you the last of the goddesses."

"He would," Eve muttered, and wished almost violently for a cigarette.

Julia grunted as her muscles trembled. "Anthony Kincade refuses, flatly, to speak to me, but Damien Priest was excessively polite and evasive." She rattled off a list of names, impressive enough to have Eve's brows rising.

"You don't let the grass grow under your feet, do you, darling?"

"I still have a ways to go. I'd hoped you'd help clear the path for me to Delrickio."

"No, that I won't do. And I'll ask you to give him a wide berth. At least for the time being. Fritz, don't wear the girl out."

"I don't wear out," he told Eve. "I build up."

Eve went off to shower while Julia suffered through power squats. By the time she was finished, Nina appeared.

"You're all set." Nina flipped open a notebook, then reached around to pluck a pencil from her hair. "The studio's sending a car for Miss B., so Lyle's at your disposal. The plane will be ready to go when you are, and a driver will be waiting on the other end to take you to your appointment."

"I appreciate it, but it isn't necessary to go to the trouble."

"No trouble." Nina checked off her list, then smiled. "Really, it's so much easier all around to have it all set up. Your flight might have been delayed, you could have trouble getting a cab and . . . oh, yes, your driver in Sausalito is from Top Flight Transportation. It's about a twenty-minute drive from the airport to the marina. Of course he'll be available to pick you up again at whatever time you decide."

"She's wonderful, isn't she?" Eve commented as she breezed back in. "I'd be lost without her."

"Only because you pretend you can't cope with details." Nina stuck the pencil back in her hair. "Your car should be out front. Shall I tell them to wait?"

"No, I'm coming. Fritz, my own true love, I'm so glad you haven't lost your touch." Eve gave him a long kiss that had him flushing down to his pecs.

"I'll walk out with you," Julia said, beating Nina to the punch by an instant. Nina hesitated, then gave way.

"I'll go get started on the half million phone calls I have to return. We'll expect you about seven, Miss B.?"

"If the gods are willing."

"I'm sorry," Julia began as they went out through the central court-yard. "I know that wasn't very subtle, but I wanted another minute."

"Nina's not easily offended. What is it you wanted to say that you wouldn't say in front of her, or Fritz?" She paused to admire the flame-colored peonies that were just about to bloom.

"Too much for a short trip to the car, but to begin with I think you should know. This was delivered to the desk of my hotel in London."

Eve studied the slip of paper Eve pulled out of her bag. She didn't have to open it to know, didn't have to read it. "Christ."

"It seems to me someone went to a lot of trouble to get it there. Paul was with me, Eve." She waited until Eve looked back at her. "He knows about the other notes as well."

"I see."

"I'm sorry if you feel I should've kept quiet about it, but—"

"No, no." She interrupted with a wave of her hand before her fingers moved unconsciously to rub at her temple. "No, maybe it's best this way. I still don't believe they're anything more than a nuisance."

Julia replaced the paper. The moment was probably all wrong, but she wanted to give Eve time to consider before she spoke again. "I know about Delrickio, and Damien Priest, and Hank Freemont."

Eve's hand fluttered to her side. The only sign of tension was the quick, instinctive clutching and releasing of her fist. "Well, that saves me from repeating the whole mess."

"I'd like to hear it from your view."

"Then you will. But we have other things to discuss first." She started walking again, past the fountain, the early roses, the thick islands of azaleas. "I'd like you to have dinner with me tonight. Eight o'clock." She turned inside to pass through the core of the main house. "I hope you'll come with an open mind, and an open heart, Julia."

"Of course."

She hesitated at the front door, then opened it and stepped into the sunlight again. "I've made mistakes and regret very few of them. I've lived with lies very comfortably."

Julia waited a moment, then chose her words carefully. "In the past few weeks I've come to wish that I'd accepted my own mistakes, and my own lies as well. It's never been my function to judge you, Eve. Now that I know you, I couldn't."

"I hope you still feel that way after tonight." She laid a hand on Julia's cheek. "You're exactly, exactly what I needed."

She turned, walking quickly to the car. Turmoil whirled around her. She barely acknowledged the chauffeur as he opened the door. Then everything fell quietly into place.

"I hope you don't mind," Victor said from the backseat. "I missed the hell out of you, Eve."

She slipped inside and into his arms.

◆ ◆ ◆ ◆

JULIA HAD DEVELOPED an image of Kenneth Stokley as a rather spare, graying man on the prim side. He would certainly have to be an organized individual to have worked for Eve. Conservative, she thought, to the point of being futsy. His voice had been cultured, smooth, and scrupulously polite.

Her first indication that she might be wrong about the image she'd conjured was the houseboat.

It was charming, romantic, a trim square of softly faded blue with gleaming white shutters. Blood red geraniums spilled lushly from snowy windowboxes. At the apex of a fanciful peaked roof was a wide sheet of stained glass. After a stare and a blink, Julia identified the portrait of a naked mermaid smiling seductively.

Her amusement at that faded a little when she took stock of the narrow swaying bridge that linked the boat to the dock and took off her shoes. At the midway point, she heard the passionate strains of *Carmen* soaring out of the open windows ahead. She was humming, doing her best to keep her rhythm harmonic with the sway of the bridge when the door opened.

He could have doubled for Cary Grant, circa 1970. Trim, silver-haired, tanned to a bronze sheen, and charmingly sexy in baggy white pants and a loose pullover of sky blue, Kenneth Stokley was the kind of man who had the saliva pooling in the mouth of any female with a heartbeat.

Julia nearly lost her balance, and her shoes, when he came out to help her.

"I should have warned you about my entranceway." He took the briefcase from her, then gracefully walked backward with her hand caught in his. "Inconvenient, I know, but it does discourage all but the most avid of vacuum cleaner salesmen."

"It's charming." She let out a little breath when her feet hit the more substantial wood of the deck. "I've never been on a houseboat."

"It's quite sturdy," he assured her while he made his own assessment. "And there's that possibility of being able to sail off into the sunset if the whim strikes. Do come in, my dear."

She stepped inside. Instead of the nautical decor of anchors and fishnetting she might have expected, she entered a sleek, elegant living area of low-slung sofas in vibrant tones of peach and mint. There was the warmth of teak and cherrywood and what was surely a gloriously faded Aubusson carpet. An entire wall was taken over by shelves of varying widths that were overflowing with books. Circular stairs wound tightly upward and bisected an overhanging balcony. The sun played through the mermaid and danced in rainbow colors on the pale walls.

"It's lovely," Julia said, and the astonishment as well as the appreciation in her voice made Kenneth smile.

"Thank you. One prefers to be comfortable after all. Please, sit down, Miss Summers. I was just making some iced tea."

"That would be nice, thanks." She hadn't expected to feel so at ease, but sitting on the cushy sofa, surrounded by books and *Carmen*, it was impossible to be otherwise. It wasn't until Kenneth had moved into the adjoining kitchen that she realized she had yet to put her shoes on again.

"I was sorry to miss Eve's little extravaganza recently," he told her, raising his voice to be heard over the music. "I'd taken a little trip down to Cozumel for some scuba diving." He came back in carrying an enameled tray with two green-hued glasses and a fat pitcher. Lemon slices and ice swam in the golden tea. "Eve always throws an unusual party."

Not Miss Benedict or even Miss B., Julia noted. "Are you still in touch with Eve?"

He settled the tray, handing her a glass before taking a seat across from her. "What you're asking, quite politely, is if Eve and I still speak. After all, in the strictest sense of the word, she did fire me."

"I was under the impression there was a disagreement."

His smile radiated good health and good humor. "With Eve life was filled with disagreements. In actual fact, it's much simpler to be associated with her now that I'm not in her employ."

"Do you mind if I record this?"

"No, not at all." He watched as she took out her tape recorder and set it on the table between them. "I was surprised to hear that Eve had instigated this book. Over the years the handful of unauthorized biographies annoyed her."

"That may be your answer. A woman like Eve would want to have the major part in the telling of her own story."

Kenneth lifted a silver eyebrow. "And the control of the telling."

"Yes," Julia said. "Tell me how you came to work for her."

"Eve's offer came at a time when I was considering changing jobs. She hired me away from Miss Miller and their competition forced Eve to offer me more money—a tidy bit more. There was the added incentive of having my own quarters. I must say I doubted Eve would be tedious, but I also knew her reputation with men. So I hesitated. It was vulgar, I suppose, to bring the fact up to her, and to state my requirements for a purely nonphysical relationship." He smiled again, fondly, a man cherishing memories. "She laughed, that big, lusty laugh of hers. She had a glass in her hand, I recall, a champagne flute. We were standing in the kitchen of Miss Miller's home where Eve had sought me out during a party. She picked another glass off the table, handed it to me, and then clinked crystal to crystal in a toast.

" 'Tell you what, Kenneth,' she said, 'you stay out of my bed, and I'll stay out of yours.' " He lifted his hand, palm out, fingers spread. "How could I resist?"

"And you both kept the bargain?"

If the question offended or surprised, he gave no sign. "Yes, we kept the bargain. I came to love her, Miss Summers, but I was never infatuated. In our own way, we forged a friendship, and sex was never involved to complicate matters. It would be dishonest to say that there weren't moments during the decade I worked for Eve that I didn't regret the bargain." He cleared his throat. "And, risking immodesty, I believe there were moments she regretted it as well. But it was a bargain we kept."

"You would have started as Eve's assistant about the time she married Rory Winthrop."

"That's right. A pity the marriage didn't work out. It seemed they were better friends than partners. Then there was the boy. Eve was devoted to him from the first. And though many would find the image difficult to focus, she made an excellent mother. I grew quite attached to Paul myself, watching him grow up."

"Did you? What was he like . . ." She caught herself. "I mean what were they like together?"

But he hadn't missed the first question, nor the look in her eyes when she'd asked it. "I take it you and Paul are acquainted."

"Yes, I've met most of the people who've been close to Eve."

When a man spent most of his life serving people, it became second nature to glean facts from gestures, tones, phrasing. "I see," he said, and smiled. "He's become quite a successful man. I have all of his books." He waved a hand toward the shelves. "I remember how he used to scribble stories, read them to Eve. They delighted her. Everything about Paul delighted her, and in turn he loved her without question, without reserve. They filled a void in each other's lives. Even when Eve divorced his father and ultimately married again, they remained close."

"Damien Priest." Julia leaned forward to set her glass back on the tray. "Paul didn't care for him."

"No one who cared about Eve cared for Priest," Kenneth said simply. "Eve was convinced that Paul's aloofness toward him stemmed from jealousy. The plain fact was that even at that age, Paul was an excellent judge of character. He had detested Delrickio on sight, and held Priest in the lowest contempt."

"And you?"

"I've always considered myself to be an excellent judge of character as well. Would you mind if we moved out to the deck above? I thought we'd have a light lunch."

♦ ♦ ♦ ♦

THE LIGHT LUNCH proved to be a small feast of succulent lobster salad, baby vegetables, and crusty bread lightly herbed, enhanced by a smooth, chilled Chardonnay. The bay spread below them, dotted with boats, sails puffed up by the breeze that smelled richly of the sea. Julia waited until they were toying with the fruit and cheese before she brought out her recorder again.

"From what I've already been told, I understand that Eve's marriage to Damien Priest ended acrimoniously. I've also been filled in on some of the details of her relationship with Michael Delrickio."

"But you would like my viewpoint?"

"Yes, I would."

He was silent for a moment, looking out over the water at a bright red spinnaker. "Do you believe in evil, Miss Summers?"

It seemed an odd question to come in the sunlight and gentle breeze. "Yes, I suppose I do."

"Delrickio is evil." Kenneth brought his gaze back to hers. "It's in his blood, in his heart. Murder, the destruction of hope, of will, are only a business to him. He fell in love with Eve. Even an evil man can fall in love. His passion for her consumed him, and, I'm not ashamed to admit, it frightened me at the time. You see, Eve thought she could control the situation as she had controlled so many others. This is part of her arrogance and her appeal. But one doesn't control evil."

"What did Eve do?"

"For too long she simply toyed with it. She married Priest, who struck a chord with her vanity and her ego. She eloped with him on impulse, partly to put a buffer between herself and Delrickio, who was becoming increasingly demanding. And dangerous. There was an incident with Paul. He had walked in on a scene where Delrickio was being physically threatening to Eve. When he attempted to intervene—hot-headedly, I should add—Delrickio's ubiquitous bodyguards took hold of him. God knows what damage they might have done to the boy if Eve hadn't prevented it."

Julia remembered the scene Paul had described to her. She stared, wide-eyed, at Kenneth. "You're telling me you were there. You saw it, saw that Paul might have been maimed, or worse. And you did nothing?"

"Eve handled it quite well, I assure you." He dabbed at his lips with a lemon-colored linen napkin. "I was superfluous as it happened, standing at the top of the stairs with a chrome-plated .32, safety off." He laughed a little and topped off the wineglasses. "When I saw it wouldn't be needed, I stayed in the shadows. Better for the boy's manhood, wouldn't you say?"

She wasn't sure what to say as she stared at the debonair gentleman whose silver hair ruffled dashingly in the breeze. "Would you have used it? The gun?"

"Without a moment's hesitation or regret. In any event, Eve married

Priest shortly after that. Exchanging evil for blind ambition. I don't know what happened at the U.S. Open; Eve never discussed it. But Priest won the tournament and lost his wife. She cut him completely out of her life."

"Then you weren't fired over Priest?"

"Hmm. That may well have been a part of it. Eve found it difficult to adjust to the fact that she had been wrong about him and I had been right. But there was another man, one who meant a great deal more to her, who indirectly caused the severing of our professional ties."

"Victor Flannagan."

This time he didn't bother to hide his surprise. "Eve's discussed him with you?"

"Yes. She wants an honest book."

"I had no idea how far she meant to go," he murmured. "Is Victor aware . . . ?"

"Yes."

"Ah. Well then, Eve's always had an affection for fireworks. Through two marriages, over thirty years, there's been only one man Eve Benedict really loved. His marriage, his tug-of-war with the church, his guilt over his wife's condition, made an open relationship with Eve impossible. Most of the time she accepted it. But other times . . . I remember once finding her sitting alone in the dark. She said: 'Kenneth, whoever said half a loaf is better than none wasn't hungry enough.' That summed up her relationship with Victor. Sometimes Eve got hungry enough to look for sustenance elsewhere."

"You disagreed?"

"With her affairs? I certainly thought she was throwing herself away, often recklessly. Victor loves her as deeply as she loves him. Perhaps that's why they cause each other so much pain. The last time we discussed him was shortly after her divorce plans became public. Victor came to the house to see her. They argued. I could hear them shouting all the way up in my office. I was working with Nina Soloman. Eve had brought her in, asked me to train her. I remember how embarrassed Nina was, how timid. She was far from the slick, confident woman you know today. At that point Nina was just a stray, a frightened little puppy who'd already felt the boot too many times. The shouting upset her. Her hands shook.

"After Victor stormed out, or was kicked out, Eve burst into the office. Her temper was far from over. She spewed out orders at Nina until the poor girl raced out of the room in tears. Then Eve and I had it out. I'm afraid I forgot my position long enough to tell her she'd been an idiot for marrying Priest in the first place, that she should stop trying to fill her life with sex instead of taking the love she already had. I said several other, probably unforgivable things, about her life-style, her temperament, and her lack of taste. When it was over, we both were quite calm again, but there was no going back to our former positions. I had said too much, and she had permitted me to say too much. I chose to retire."

"And Nina took your place."

"I believe Eve softened toward her. She felt tremendous compassion for the girl because of the ghastly things she'd been through. Nina was grateful, understanding that Eve had given her a chance many wouldn't have. All in all, it's worked out well for everyone."

"She still speaks of you fondly."

"Eve isn't one to bear a grudge against honest words, or honest feelings. I'm proud to say I've been her friend for nearly twenty-five years."

"I hope you don't mind, but I have to ask. Looking back, do you regret never being her lover?"

He smiled over the rim of his glass before he sipped. "I didn't say I was never her lover, Miss Summers, only that I was never her lover while in her employ."

"Oh." The humor in his eyes had her responding with a laugh. "I don't suppose you'd like to expand on that."

"No. If Eve chooses to, that's her business. But my memories are mine."

♦ ♦ ♦ ♦

JULIA LEFT feeling sleepy from the wine, relaxed from the company, and pleased with the day's work. During the brief wait in the terminal while her plane was readied, she labeled the tape and put a fresh one in her recorder.

A little ashamed of the weakness, she slipped two Dramamine on her tongue and washed the pills down at the water fountain. When she straightened she caught a glimpse of a man across the lobby. For a moment she thought he'd been watching her, but she told herself she was just being self-conscious as he turned a page in a magazine that apparently had his full attention.

Still, something about him nagged at her. There was something familiar about that sun-streaked mop of hair, the glossy tan, the casual beach-boy look.

She forgot it and him when given the signal to board.

She settled down, strapping in and gearing up for the short flight back to L.A. She thought that Eve would be amused to hear her impressions of Kenneth over dinner that evening.

And with any luck, she thought while the plane bumped down the runway for takeoff, this would be her last flight until the one that took her home.

Home, she thought, clinging to the armrests as the plane took to the air. There was part of her that yearned for the solitude of her own house, the routine of it, the simple fact of it. And yet, what would it be like to go back alone? To leave love now that she'd found it. What would happen to her relationship with Paul with him on one coast and her on another? How could there be a relationship?

The self-sufficient, independent Julia, single mother, professional woman, needed, and how she needed, someone else. Without Paul she would continue to raise Brandon, she would continue to write, she would continue to function.

Closing her eyes, she tried to picture herself going back, picking up where she had left off, moving quietly, solitarily, through the rest of her life.

And couldn't.

With a sigh she rested her head on the window glass. What the hell was she going to do? They'd discussed love, but not permanance.

She wanted Paul, she wanted a family for Brandon, and she wanted security. And she was afraid to risk the last for the possibility of the others.

She dozed, the wine and her own thoughts coaxing her to sleep. The first jolt awakened her, had her cursing herself for the instant streak of panic. Before she could order herself to relax, the plane veered sharply to the left. She tasted blood in her mouth from her bitten tongue, but worse, much worse, was the coppery flavor of fear.

"Stay in your seat, Miss Summers. We're losing pressure."

"Losing . . ." She forced back the first bubble of hysteria. The strain in the pilot's voice was enough to tell her screaming wouldn't help. "What does that mean?"

"We've got a little problem. We're only ten miles from the airport. Just stay calm and strapped in."

"I'm not going anywhere," Julia managed to say, and did them both a favor by putting her head between her knees. It helped the dizziness, almost helped the panic. When she forced herself to open her eyes again, she watched a sheet of paper slide out from under the seat as the plane dipped into a dive.

OUT, OUT, BRIEF CANDLE.

"Oh, Jesus." She snatched at the paper, crumbling it in her hand. "Brandon. Oh, God, Brandon."

She wasn't going to die. She couldn't. Brandon needed her. She willed the nausea back. The single overhead bin popped open, spilling out pillows and blankets. Over the prayers that spun inside her head all she could hear was the roar of the spitting engine and the pilot shouting into the radio. They were coming in, and coming in fast.

Julia righted herself and grabbed her notebook out of her briefcase. She felt the shudder as they dropped through a thin layer of clouds. Her time was running out. She scribbled a quick note to Paul, asking him to look after Brandon, telling him how grateful she was to have found him.

She swore richly when her hand began to shake too hard to hold the pencil. Then there was silence. It took her a moment to register it, and another longer moment to understand what it meant.

"Oh, my God."

"Fuel's gone," the pilot said between his teeth. "Engines are dead. We've got ourselves a good tail wind. I'm going to glide this baby right on in. They're ready for us."

"Okay. What's your name? Your first name."

"It's Jack."

"Okay, Jack." She took a deep breath. She'd always believed will and determination could accomplish almost anything. "I'm Julia. Let's get this thing on the ground."

"Okay, Julia. Now put your head between your knees, grip your hands behind your head. And say every fucking prayer you know."

Julia took one long last breath. "I already am."

Chapter Twenty-Two

◆◆◆◆

ƁETTER GUARD THE BALL," Paul panted as he feinted over Brandon's shoulder. The boy grunted and pivoted away, dribbling the ball with small hands and deadly concentration.

They were both sweating—he more than the boy. Age, he thought as he dodged Brandon's bony elbow, was a bitch. He had the kid on height and reach. So he was holding back. After all, it wouldn't be fair to—

Brandon ducked under Paul's arm and hit a lay-up dead on. Eyes narrowed, Paul rested his hands on his hips while he caught his breath.

"Tie score!" Brandon shouted, doing a quick dance that involved a lot of scraped-knee pumping and skinny-butt wiggling. "That's six-all, dude."

"Don't get cocky. Dude." Paul dabbed at the sweat that had dribbled through the bandanna he'd tied around his forehead. In a show of nonchalance, Brandon wore his Lakers cap jauntily backward. He grinned when Paul retrieved the ball. "If I'd put that hoop up to regulation height—"

"Yeah, yeah." Brandon's grin widened. "Big talk."

"Smartass."

Immensely flattered, Brandon let out a whoop of laughter at the muttered comment. He could see the answering grin in Paul's eyes. And he was having the time of his life. He still couldn't believe Paul had come over to see him—*him*—bringing a hoop, a ball, and a challenge for a game.

His enjoyment didn't lessen when Paul whizzed by him and sent the ball through the net in a nearly soundless swish.

"Lucky shot."

"My butt." Paul passed the ball to Brandon. He might have picked up the hoop on impulse. He might have bolted it over the garage door thinking Brandon would enjoy the opportunity to shoot a few baskets now and again. Even the one on one had been impromptu. The thing was, he, too, was having the time of his life.

Part of the visit that afternoon had been calculated. He loved the mother, wanted to be a part of her life—and the most important part of her life was her son. He hadn't been completely sure how he'd feel about the possibility of instant family, of taking another man's child into his heart and home.

By the time the score was ten to eight, his favor, Paul had forgotten all about that. He was just enjoying.

"All right!" Brandon waved a triumphant fist after he'd tipped another one in. His Bart Simpson T-shirt was plastered to his shoulder blades. "I'm right on your tail."

"Then get ready to choke on my dust."

"In your dreams."

Distracted by his own chuckle, Paul lost the ball. Like a hound after a rabbit, Brandon pounced on it. He missed his first shot, wrestled for the rebound, and hit the second.

When Paul's dust had settled, Brandon had edged him out, twelve to ten.

"I'm number *one!*" Brandon skipped over the concrete pad, arms stretched, fingers pointing to the sky.

Eyes narrowed, hands resting on his knees, Paul watched the victory lap and sucked in hot air. "I went easy on you. You're just a kid."

"Bull!" Cherishing the moment, Brandon ran a circle around him, his lightly tanned skin gleaming with sweat and bad Bart sneering. "I took it easy on *you*," he said. " 'Cause you're old enough to be my father." Then he stopped, embarrassed by what he'd said, shaken by his own longings. Before he could figure out how to retract it, Paul had him in a headlock and was making him scream with laughter as knuckles rubbed hard on the top of his head.

"Okay, big mouth. Two out of three."

Brandon blinked, stared. "Really?"

By God, Paul thought, he was falling for the kid all on his own. Those big, hungry eyes, that shy smile. All that hope, all that love. If there was a man alive who could resist that look, his name wasn't Paul Winthrop.

Paul gave him a big, evil grin. "Unless you're chicken."

"Me, scared of you?" He liked being held there, in a male embrace, smelling male smells, exchanging male taunts. He didn't try to wriggle out of Paul's hold. "No possible way."

"Prepare to lose. This time I'm going to demolish you. Loser buys the beer."

When Paul released him, Brandon raced to the ball. He was laughing when he saw his mother come out of the garden and onto the path. "Mom! Hey, Mom! Look what Paul put up. He said I could use it as long as we're here and everything. And I beat him first game."

She was walking slowly, had to walk slowly. That first comforting sheen of shock was melting away, leaving smears of fear behind. When she saw her child, his face grubby with dirt and sweat, his grin huge, his eyes excited, she broke into a run. She swooped him up, pressing him hard against her, burying her face against the damp and tender side of his throat.

She was alive. Alive. And holding her life in her arms.

"Jeez, Mom." He wasn't sure if he should be embarrassed or apologetic in front of Paul. He rolled his eyes once, showing that this was something he had to put up with. "What's the matter?"

"Nothing." She had to swallow, to force herself to relax her grip. If she started babbling now, she'd only frighten him. And it was over. All over. "Nothing, I'm just glad to see you."

"You saw me this morning." His puzzled look changed to astonishment when she released him to give Paul the same fierce, possessive hug.

"Both of you," she managed to say, and Paul could feel her heart thundering against his chest. "I'm just glad to see both of you."

In silence, Paul cupped her chin to study her face. He recognized the signs of shock, of stress, of tears. He gave her a long, soft kiss and felt her lips tremble against his. "Close your mouth, Brandon," he said mildly, bringing Julia's head to his shoulder to stroke her hair. "You'll have to get used to me kissing your mother."

Over Julia's shoulder he saw the boy's eyes change—wariness, suspicion. Disappointment. With a sigh, Paul wondered if he had the ability to handle both mother and son.

"Why don't you go inside, Jules? Get yourself something cold and sit down. I'll be with you in a minute."

"Yes." She needed to be alone. If she wasn't going to fall apart, she needed a few moments to herself to scrape together those flimsy rags of control. "I'll see if I can come up with some lemonade. You both look like you could use some."

Paul waited until she was well on her way before he turned back to the boy. Brandon's hands were stuffed into the pockets of his shorts. He was staring hard at the toes of his scuffed Nikes.

"Problem?"

The boy only shrugged his shoulders.

Paul mirrored the gesture before he walked over to the shirt he'd tossed off during the heat of battle. He took out a cigar then fought a brief battle with damp matches.

"I don't figure I have to explain to you the man-woman sort of thing," Paul mused aloud. "Or why kissing's so popular."

Brandon stared so hard at his shoes, his eyes nearly crossed.

"Nope. I didn't think so." Stalling, Paul drew in smoke, then exhaled. "I guess you should know how I feel about your mother." Brandon still said nothing, trapped in the silence of his own confusion. "I love her, very much." That statement at least had Brandon lifting his head to make eye contact. It wasn't, Paul noted, a particularly friendly look. "It might take you some time to get used to that. That's okay, because I'm not going to change my mind."

"Mom doesn't go out with guys and stuff very much."

"No. I guess that makes me pretty lucky." Christ, was there anything harder to face than a child's direct, unblinking stare? Paul blew out a long breath and wished he had something stronger than lemonade to look forward to. "Listen, you're probably wondering if I'm going to mess up and hurt her. I can't promise I won't, but I can promise I'll try not to."

Brandon was having a hard time even thinking about his mother in the way Paul was describing. She was, after all, first and last, his mother. It had never occurred to him that anything could hurt her. The possibility had the inside of his stomach jittering. To compensate, his chin shot out, much the way Julia's did. "If you hit her, I'd—"

"No." Paul was instantly in a crouch so that they were eye to eye. "I don't mean like that. Not ever like that. That is a promise. I mean hurt her feelings, make her unhappy."

The thought cued into something nearly forgotten that made Brandon's throat hurt and his eyes water. He remembered the way she had looked when his grandparents had died. And before, sometime in that misty before, when he'd been too little to understand.

"Like my father did," he said shakily. "He must have."

There the ground was too soft and unsteady for him to tread on. "That's something you'll have to talk to her about when you're both ready."

"I guess he didn't want us."

The man's hand cupped the boy's shoulder. "I do."

Brandon looked away again, over Paul's right shoulder. A bird zipped into the garden in a bright flash of blue. "I guess you've been fooling around, hanging around with me because of Mom."

"That's part of it." Paul took a chance and turned Brandon's face back to his. "Not all of it. Maybe I thought it'd go a little easier for me with Julia if you and I got along. If you didn't like me, I wouldn't have a shot. The thing is, I like hanging around you. Even if you are short and ugly and beat me at basketball."

He was a quiet child, and by nature an observant one. He heard the simplicity in Paul's answer, understood it. And, looking into the man's eyes, trusted it. His nerves settled, and he smiled. "I won't always be short."

"No." Paul's voice roughened even as he answered the smile. "But you'll always be ugly."

"And I'll always beat you at basketball."

"I'm going to prove you wrong there, a little later. Now, I think something's upset your mom. I'd like to talk to her."

"By yourself."

"Yeah. Maybe you could go over to the main house and charm some cookies out of Travers. Again."

Faint, embarrassed color stained Brandon's cheek. "She wasn't supposed to tell."

"She wasn't supposed to tell your mom," Paul said. "People tell me everything. And the thing is, Travers used to sneak me cookies too."

"Yeah?"

"Yeah." He rose then. "Give me about a half hour, okay?"

"Okay." He started off, then turned at the edge of the garden. A young boy with dirt on his face and scabs on his knees and the disconcertingly wise eyes of childhood. "Paul? I'm glad she didn't hang around with guys and stuff before now."

As compliments went, Paul couldn't remember better. "Me too. Now, beat it."

He listened to Brandon's quick, appreciative laughter, then turned toward the guest house.

Julia was in the kitchen, slowly, mechanically squeezing lemons. She'd slipped out of her suit jacket, stepped out of her shoes. The sapphire-colored shell she wore made her shoulders look very white, very soft, very fragile.

"I'm nearly finished," she said.

Her voice was steady, but he heard the underlying nerves. Saying nothing, he pulled her over to the sink to rinse her hands under cool water.

"What're you doing?"

He dried her hands himself with a dishtowel before he switched off the radio. "I'm going to finish it. Sit down, take a couple of deep breaths, and tell me what happened."

"I don't need to sit." But she did lean against the counter. "Brandon? Where's Brandon?"

"Knowing you, I thought you'd hesitate to let it loose in front of him. He's over at the main house for a while."

Apparently Paul Winthrop knew her much too well, much too quickly. "So Travers can sneak him cookies."

Paul glanced up as he added sugar. "What, have you got a hidden camera?"

"No, just a mother's primitive sensory skills. I can smell cookie breath at twenty paces." She managed a weak smile and finally did sit.

He pulled a wooden spoon from the rack and stirred. When he was satisfied, he filled a glass with ice and poured the tart drink over the cubes so that they crackled. "Was it the interview with Kenneth that upset you?"

"No." She took the first sip. "How did you know I was seeing Kenneth this afternoon?"

"CeeCee. When I came by to relieve her."

"Oh." She looked around blankly, just realizing CeeCee wasn't there. "You sent her home."

"I wanted to spend some time with Brandon. Okay?"

Struggling for calm, she sipped again. She hadn't meant to question him so sharply. "I'm sorry. My mind keeps going off on tangents. Of course it's okay. Brandon looked as if he was enjoying himself. I'm not much competition on the basketball court, and—"

"Julia, tell me what happened."

With a jerky nod she set the glass aside, then linked her hands on her lap. "It wasn't the interview. In fact, that went very well." Had she put the tape in the safe? Unconsciously she unlinked her fingers to rub them against her eyes. Everything seemed so fuzzy, from the time she had clasped her hands over her head. She started to get up, to go to him, but her legs wouldn't allow it. Funny that her knees would go weak now, when everything was all right again. The kitchen smelled of lemons, her son was sneaking cookies, and the faintest of breezes was nudging a tinkle out of the wind chimes.

Everything was all right again.

She started when Paul scraped back his chair and went to the refrigerator. He yanked out a beer, twisted the top, and drank deep.

"I'm not thinking straight," she said. "Maybe if I start at the beginning."

"Fine." He sat across the table from her, ordering himself to be patient. "Why don't you do that?"

"We were flying back from Sausalito," she began slowly. "I was thinking that I'd finished nearly all of the hard research, and that in a few weeks we'd be going home. Then I was thinking about you, and what it would be like to be there while you were here."

"Goddammit, Julia."

But she didn't even hear him. "I must have dozed off. I took drama-mine before the flight, and Kenneth served wine with lunch. Made me sleepy. I woke up when the plane . . . I might not have told you I'm afraid of flying. Well, it's not flying so much as being cooped up in there with no way out. And this time, when the plane started to buck, I told myself not to be a wimp about the whole thing. But the pilot said—" She wiped the back of her hand over her mouth. "He said we had a problem. We were going down so fast."

"Oh, sweet God." He was up, too terrified to realize how rough he was when he hauled her to her feet. His hands were moving over her, checking for injuries, making sure she was whole. "Are you hurt? Julia, are you hurt?"

"No, no. I think I bit my tongue," she said vaguely. She thought she remembered the taste of blood and fear in her mouth. "Jack said we were going to make it. The fuel—there was something wrong with the fuel line or the gauge. I realized it when it got so quiet. The engines shut down. All I could think of was Brandon. He'd been robbed of a father, and I couldn't bear to think of him being alone. I could hear Jack swearing, and the radio crackling with voices."

She was shaking now, hard and fast. He did the only thing he knew and picked her up off her feet to cradle her against him.

"I was so scared. I didn't want to die inside that damn plane." Her voice was muffled with her face pressed against his throat. "Jack yelled back for me to hang on. Then we hit. It felt like *I* was hitting the tarmac instead of the plane. Then we bounced—not like a ball. A rock—like a rock if rocks could bounce. I heard metal screaming, and the wind rush-ing in. There were sirens. We were fishtailing, like a car out of control on ice, and there were sirens. Then we stopped, we just stopped. I must have already unstrapped because I was getting up when Jack came back. He kissed me. I hope you don't mind."

"Not a damn bit."

"Good, because I kissed him back."

Still rocking her, Paul buried his face in her hair. "If I get the chance, I'll kiss him myself."

That made her laugh a little. "Then I got out, and I came back. I didn't want to talk to anyone." She sighed once, then twice before she realized he was holding her. "You don't have to carry me."

"Don't ask me to put you down for a while."

"No." She laid her head on his shoulder. Safe, secure, treasured. "In my whole life," she murmured. "No one's ever made me feel like you." When the dam burst, she turned her face to the curve of his throat. "I'm sorry."

"Don't be. Cry as long as you want."

He wasn't very steady himself as he carried her into the living room so he could sit on the sofa and hold her to him. Her sobs were already quieting. He should have known that Julia wouldn't draw out any bout of weakness.

And he could have lost her. That thought swam over and over in his mind, forming its own whirlpool of fear and rage. She could have been taken from him that quickly, that horribly.

"I'm all right." She straightened as far as he would permit to wipe the tears away with the backs of her hands. "It hit me, really hit me, when I saw you and Brandon."

"I'm not all right yet." The words were jerky. He closed his mouth over hers, not as gently as he might have wished. His fingers speared through her hair, closed into a fist. "How useless everything would be without you. I need you, Julia."

"I know." Her system settled, but she was content to stay cradled in his arms. "I need you too, and it's not nearly so hard as I thought it would be." She brushed her fingers over his cheek. How wonderful it was, how liberating, to know she could touch like that whenever the whim struck. And how liberating it was to trust. "There's more, Paul. You're not going to like it."

"As long as you're not going to tell me you've decided to elope with Jack." But she didn't smile. "What?"

"I found this under my seat on the plane." She got to her feet, yet even when she was no longer touching, she felt connected to him. She knew before she took the paper out of her skirt pocket and offered it, what he would be feeling.

Rage, that impotent, useless fear that went with it. And an anger that was different from rage, less combustible and more consuming. She gauged them all in his eyes.

"I'd say this is a little more direct," she began. "All the others were warnings. This . . . I guess we'll call it a statement."

"Is that what you'd call it?" He saw more than the words. She'd crushed the paper in a palm that had been damp with a fear and had smeared the type. "I'd call it murder."

She moistened her lips. "I'm not dead."

"Fine then." When he rose, his anger spilled over and lapped at her. "Attempted murder. Whoever wrote this sabotaged the plane. They meant for you to die."

"Maybe." She held up a hand before he could explode. "It seems more likely they wanted me to be scared. If they'd wanted me to die in a crash, why the note?"

Fury burned in his eyes. "I'm not going to stand here and try to reason out the criminal mind."

"But isn't that what you do? When you write about murder, aren't you always dipping into the criminal mind?"

The sound he made was somewhere between a laugh and a snarl. "This isn't fiction."

"But the same rules apply. Your plots are logical because there's always a pattern to the murderer's psyche. Whether it's passion or greed or revenge. Whatever. There's always motive, opportunity, and reasoning, however twisted. We have to use logic to figure this out."

"Fuck logic, Jules." His fingers closed over the hand she'd laid lightly on his chest. "I want you on the next flight to Connecticut."

She was silent for a moment, reminding herself he was being difficult only because he was frightened for her. "I thought about that. At least I tried to think about it. I could go back—"

"You damn well will go back."

She only shook her head. "What difference would it make? It's already started, Paul. I can't erase what Eve's told me— More, I can't erase my obligation to her."

"Your obligation ended." He lifted the paper. "With this."

She didn't look at it. Maybe it was a form of cowardice, but she wasn't going to test herself yet. "Even if that were true—and it isn't— going back east wouldn't stop it. I already know too much about too many people. Secrets, lies, embarrassments. Maybe this would stop if I kept quiet. I'm not willing to spend the rest of my life, the rest of Brandon's, on that kind of a maybe."

He hated the fact that part of him, the logical part, saw the sense of what she was saying. The emotional part simply wanted her safe. "You can announce, publicly, that you're abandoning the project."

"I'm not going to do that. Not only because it goes against my conscience, but because I don't think it would matter. I could take out an ad in *Variety,* in *Publishers Weekly,* in the *L.A.* and the *New York Times.* I could go back and pick up another project. After a few weeks, a few months, I might start to relax. Then there'd be an accident, and my son would end up an orphan." Her hand dropped away from his to curl at her side. "No, I'm going to see this through, and I'm going to see it through here, where I feel I have some leverage."

He wanted to argue, to demand, to drag her and Brandon both onto a plane and take them as far away as possible. But her reasoning made too much sense. "We go to the police with the notes, and with what we suspect."

She nodded. The relief that he was with her was almost as weakening as the fear. "But I think we'd have more plausibility after Eve gets the report on the plane. If they find proof of sabotage, it would go a long way to our being believed."

"I don't want you out of my sight."

Grateful, she held out both hands. "Me either."

"Then you'll go along with my staying here tonight?"

"Not only will I go along with it, but I'll personally turn down the bed in the guest room."

"The guest room."

She offered an apologetic smile. "Brandon."

"Brandon," Paul repeated, and drew her back in his arms again. Suddenly, she felt so small, so slight. So his. "Here's the deal. Until he gets used to it, I'll *pretend* to sleep in the guest room."

She thought it over, running her hands over his bare back. "I'm usually willing to compromise." Confused, she pulled away. "Where's your shirt?"

"You must have been nearly comatose not to've noticed my exceptional naked chest. The kid and I were playing ball, remember? It gets hot."

"Oh, right. Basketball. The hoop. There wasn't a hoop there before."

"She's coming back," Paul murmured, and kissed her. "I put it up a couple hours ago."

It was becoming easier and easier for her heart to melt. "You did it for Brandon."

"Sort of." He shrugged it off as he toyed with her hair. "I figured I'd dazzle him with my superior skills. Then he snuck up and beat me. The kid's tough."

Incredibly moved, she framed his face in her hands. "And I never thought, never imagined I could love anyone as much as I love him. Until you."

"Julia!" Nina rushed in through the kitchen door, bounding into the living room without a knock. It was the first time Julia had seen her truly frazzled. Her skin was pale, her eyes huge, the usually sleek crop of hair ruffled. "Oh, God, are you all right? I just heard." As Julia turned from Paul, Nina enveloped her in a trembling hug and the subtle scent of Halston. "The pilot called. He wanted to make sure you'd made it home all right. He told me . . ." She trailed off, tightening her hold.

"I'm fine. Now anyway."

"I don't understand it. I don't." She pulled back but kept her strong, businesslike hands firm on Julia's arms. "He's a top-flight pilot, and Eve's mechanic is the best in the business. I don't see how there could have been a problem like this."

"I'm sure we'll find out when they finish examining the plane."

"They're going to go over every inch of it. Every inch. I'm sorry." After letting out a shaky breath, she backed away. "I'm sure the last thing you need is me coming apart at the seams. It's only that when I heard, I had to see for myself that you weren't hurt."

"Not a scratch. You're right about Jack being a top-notch pilot."

"What can I do?" Nina summoned back her brisk efficiency. She glanced around the newly refurbished living area, pleased that Eve had allowed her to handle the decorating. "Fix you a drink? Draw you a bath? I could call Miss B.'s doctor. He'd come out and give you a tranquilizer so you could sleep."

"I don't think I'll need any help with that when the time comes, but thanks." Because she was steady again, Julia was able to laugh. "Actually, you look like the one who could use a drink."

"Maybe a seat," she said as she sank to the arm of the curvy sofa. "You're so calm."

"Now," Julia told her. "A few minutes ago it was a different story."

Nina shuddered, then rubbed the chill out of her arms. "The last time I flew we ran into a storm. I spent the most frightening fifteen minutes of my life at thirty-five thousand feet. I can't imagine it came close to what it was like for you."

"It's not an experience I'd like to repeat." She heard the kitchen screen door slam. "That's Brandon. I'd rather he didn't hear about this yet."

"Of course." Nina made herself get to her feet. "I know you wouldn't want to upset him. I'll go on back so I can waylay Eve and tell her about this calmly. Travers would blurt it out."

"Thanks, Nina."

"I'm glad you're all right." She gave Julia's hand a final squeeze. "Take care of her," she said to Paul.

"You can count on it."

She left by the terrace door, and was already smoothing her hair as she walked away. Julia turned to see Brandon watching from the kitchen doorway. There was a wary look in his eye, and a suspicious purple mustache over his lip.

"Why does he have to take care of you?"

"Just an expression," Julia told him. She narrowed her eyes. "Grape Kool-Aid?"

He covered most of his grin by swiping the back of his hand over his mouth. "Nehi. Travers had it opened and everything. I thought it would be rude not to drink it."

"I bet you did."

"A guy gets thirsty playing one on one," Paul put in.

"Yeah," Brandon tossed back at him, "especially when he wins."

"That does it, you little creep, you're on your own."

They exchanged what Julia thought were very manly looks before Brandon bounced into a chair.

"Are you okay and all? Paul said maybe you were upset or something."

"I'm okay," Julia told him. "In fact, I'm dandy. I might be persuaded to fix a few king-size Brandonburgers."

"Hey, cool. With fries and all?"

"I think I . . . oh, I forgot." She pressed a hand over her son's head. "I'm supposed to have dinner with Eve tonight. I promised." Because she felt his disappointment, she began to make adjustments. "Maybe I could call her and reschedule."

"Don't do it on our account." Paul winked at Brandon. "The brat and I can take care of dinner ourselves."

"Yes, but—"

But Brandon was interested. "Can you cook?"

"Can I cook? I can do better than that. I can drive to McDonald's."

"All right!" He bounded up, then remembered his mother and shot her a hopeful look. A trip to McDonald's meant all kinds of wonderful things. Including no cleaning up after dinner. "That's okay, isn't it?"

"Yeah." She kissed the top of his head, then smiled at Paul. "It's okay."

Chapter Twenty-Three

◆ ◆ ◆ ◆

A LONG, HOT BATH with fragrant oils, the creams, the lotions. Fifteen luxurious minutes fussing with powders and paints. By the time Julia slipped into the icy pink evening pants and draped jacket, she was completely recovered. So recovered, it amused her that Paul had insisted on walking her over to the main house.

"You smell incredible." He lifted her wrist to sniff, then lingered to nibble at it. "Maybe you'd like to join me in the guest room later."

"I might be persuaded." She stopped at the main door, turned, and linked her hands around his neck. "Why don't you start thinking of ways to persuade me?" Her lips touched his lightly, then she surprised and pleased them both by pouring herself into a long, breath-stealing kiss. "Now, go buy yourself a hamburger."

It felt as though the blood had drained from his brain straight to his loins. "Two things," he said. "Eat fast."

She smiled. "What's the second thing?"

"I'll show you when you get home." He started off, then called over his shoulders. "Eat real fast."

Laughing to herself, Julia knocked and decided she might set the world's record for gulping dinner. "Hello, Travers."

For once the housekeeper didn't grunt, but looked Julia over with what first appeared to be concern. It changed quickly to suspicion and annoyance. "You've got her upset."

"Eve?" Julia said as the door closed at her back. "I've upset Eve?" Then it struck her and she wasn't sure whether to laugh or swear. "About the plane? You can hardly blame me for almost being in a crash, Travers."

But apparently she could as she stomped back toward the kitchen after one sharp gesture toward the parlor.

"Always a pleasure chatting with you," Julia called after her, then made her way toward the parlor.

Eve was there, pacing the width of the room. Back and forth, an exotic beast in an elegant cage. Emotion washed in her wake, so strong, so intense, it was almost visible. Her eyes glistened, but the tears didn't fall until she looked over at Julia.

For once all her will deserted her. With a helpless shake of her head, she folded onto the sofa and began to weep.

"Oh, no, please." Julia was across the room like a shot, arms enfolding, voice soothing. Silk rustled as Eve turned into her. Their scents met, opposing notes that somehow harmonized into one exotic fragrance. "It's all right," Julia told her, the words as automatic, as comforting as her stroking hands. "Everything's all right now."

"You could have been killed. I don't know what I would have done." Moments after breaking down, she was struggling for composure. She drew back, wanting, needing to study Julia's face. "I swear to you, Julia, I never thought anyone would go this far. I knew they would try to stop me, but I never considered they would try to hurt you to do it."

"I haven't been hurt. I'm not going to be hurt."

"No. Because we won't go any further."

"Eve." Julia searched in her own pocket for a tissue and handed it over. "I've just been through all that with Paul. Stopping now won't make any difference, will it?"

She took the time to dab at the tears. "No." Slowly, feeling her age, she rose to go to the bar and poured a drink from the bottle of champagne that was already open and waiting. "You know more than you should." Her full red lips flattened. "That's my responsibility. My selfishness."

"My job," Julia countered.

Eve took a long sip before pouring a second glass for Julia. The girl had soft shoulders, she thought. Almost fragile in appearance, yet they were strong enough to support. "You don't want to stop?"

"I couldn't if I wanted to. And no, I don't." She accepted the glass Eve offered, then touched crystal to crystal. "I'm in for the duration."

Before Julia could drink, Eve gripped her wrist. Her eyes were suddenly very dry and very intense. "You may hate me before it's over."

The hold was so tight, Julia could feel the pulse in her wrist beat against that of Eve's thumb. "No, I couldn't."

Eve only nodded. She'd made her decision, for better or worse. The only thing left was to finish. "Grab the bottle, will you? We'll eat out on the terrace."

There were fairy lights strung through the trees and candles already glowing on the glass-topped table. The garden was hushed with dusk. Only the sound of air breathing through leaves and the music of water against water from the fountain. The gardenias were beginning to flower, and the sweet romance of their fragrance drifted everywhere.

"There's so much I need to tell you tonight." Eve paused as Travers came out with plates of stuffed mushrooms. "You may find it too much, all at once, but I feel I might have waited too long already."

"I'm here to listen, Eve."

She nodded. "Victor was waiting for me in the car this morning. I can't tell you how wonderful it was to be with him again, to know we were together, in our hearts. He's a good man, Julia. Trapped by circumstance, upbringing, religion. Is there a more difficult burden than trying to follow heart and conscience? Despite all the problems and pain, I've had more happiness with him than many women find in a lifetime."

"I think I understand." Julia's voice was like the shadows. Soft, comforting. "Sometimes you can love without the happy-ever-after. That doesn't make the story any less important, any less vital."

"Don't give up on your own happy-evers, Julia. I want them for you."

Travers trooped out with salads, frowned over the fact that Eve had barely touched her first course, but said nothing.

"Tell me what you thought of Kenneth."

"Well . . ." Realizing she was starving, Julia dived into the salad. "I'd have to say first that he wasn't what I expected. He was more charming, more relaxed, more sexy."

For the first time in hours, Eve was able to laugh. "Christ, yes. It used to irritate the hell out of me that the man could have so much sex appeal and be so prim about it. Always the proper word at the proper time. Except the last time."

"He told me." Her lips curved. "I'm surprised he escaped with his skin."

"It was nip and tuck. And he was right, of course, in what he said to me. Still, it's difficult for a man to understand what a woman goes through when she must be in second place. Even so, I've always known I could count on Kenneth for anything."

Julia listened to the rustle of air in the leaves, the first cooing of night birds as Eve stared into her wine. "Did you know he was at the top of the stairs the night Delrickio got out of hand, the night Paul was almost beaten?"

The green eyes flashed back up. "Kenneth?"

"Yes, Kenneth. At the top of the stairs with a loaded pistol, and apparently ready to use it. You're quite right when you say you can depend on him."

"I'll be damned." Eve set aside her fork, exchanging it for her glass. "He never said a word."

"There's more, if you want an opinion."

"I'd like yours."

"I think he's been in love with you most of his life."

Eve started to laugh it off, but Julia was watching her so quietly. Memories, scenes, half phrases, moments, passed through her mind so that her hand was unsteady when she set her glass down again. "God, how careless we are with people."

"I doubt he regrets a minute of it."

"But I do."

Eve was silent as Travers served the salmon. Inside her head was a cacophony of sound, voices hammering. Threats, promises. She was afraid she would say too much, afraid some things would never be said.

"Julia, did you bring your recorder?"

"Yes, you said there were things you wanted to tell me."

"I'd like to begin now." Eve made an elaborate pretense of eating while Julia set the tape. "You know my feelings now on many people. The way my life had wound with theirs. Travers and Nina coming to me from such destructive beginnings. Kenneth, whom I stole from Charlotte out of spite. Michael Torrent, Tony, Rory, Damien, all mistakes with different results. Michael Delrickio, who appealed to my vanity, my arrogance. Through him I lost Drake."

"I don't understand."

"It was Drake who broke into your house, who stole, who wanted the tapes."

"Drake?" Julia blinked against the flare of a match as Eve lit a cigarette.

"Perhaps it isn't entirely fair to blame Michael. After all, Drake was marred years before. But I prefer to blame him. He knew the boy's weakness for gambling. Hell, the boy's weakness for everything, and he used it. Drake was weak, he was calculating, he was disloyal, but he was also family."

"Was?"

"I've fired him," Eve said simply, "as my publicity agent, and as my nephew."

"That explains why he hasn't been returning my calls. I'm sorry, Eve."

She waved the sympathy away. "I don't want to dwell on Drake, God knows. My point is that all of the people in my life have had a certain amount of influence on it, and often on each other's as well. Rory brought me Paul, thank Christ, and that binds all three of us together. I suppose, if you're right about this Lily person, I'm connected to her too."

Julia couldn't help but smile. "You'd like her."

"Possibly." She shrugged it off. "Rory also brought me Delrickio, and Delrickio, Damien. You see how each character in a life story alters it, subtly or overtly? Without even one of the players, the plot might take a different turn."

"Would you say that Charlie Gray changed yours?"

"Charlie." Eve smiled wistfully into the night. "Charlie speeded up the inevitable. If I could go back, change one thing, it would be my relationship with Charlie. Perhaps if I'd been kinder, less self-driven, things would have been different for him. But you can't go back." Her eyes changed, darkened as they fixed on Julia's. "That's part of what I want to say tonight. Of all the people I've known, I've touched in my lifetime, there are two who have influenced it the most. Victor and Gloria."

"Gloria DuBarry?"

"Yes. She's outraged with me. Feels betrayed because I'm about to reveal what she considers her private hell. I don't do it for revenge, or vindictiveness. I don't do it lightly. Of all the things I've told you, this is the most difficult, and the most necessary."

"I told you from the beginning I wouldn't judge. I'm not going to start now."

"But you will," Eve said softly. "In the early part of Gloria's career, when she was playing young, innocent girls, giggling angels, she met a man. He was breathtaking to the eye, successful, seductive, and married. She confided in me, not only because we were friends, but because I'd once fallen under the same spell. The man was Michael Torrent."

"DuBarry and Torrent?" There were no two names that Eve could have linked together that would have surprised Julia more. "I've read everything I could find on both of them. There was never even a rumor."

"They were careful. I helped them be careful. Understand that Gloria was desperately in love. And she wasn't completely locked into her public image then. This would have been perhaps two years before she met and married Marcus. There was a wildness in her, a passion for life. One I'm sorry she's smothered so completely."

Julia could only shake her head. She could no more imagine Gloria DuBarry wild or passionate then she could imagine Eve leaping onto the table to do a quick tap dance.

Less.

"At that time Torrent would have been married to . . ." Julia did quick calculations. "Amelia Gray."

"Charlie's first wife, yes. Their marriage was rapidly sinking. It had a poor foundation. Michael's guilt. He had used all of his power and influence to keep Charlie out of lead roles and never learned to live with it."

Julia let out a long breath. If Gloria's illicit affair had been the left jab, this was the roundhouse. "You're telling me that Torrent sabotaged

Charlie's career? Christ, Eve, they were friends. Their partnership is a legend. And Torrent's become one of the most revered names in the industry."

"Become," Eve repeated. "He might have ended at the same place if he'd been patient and loyal. But he betrayed a friend out of his own fears. He was terrified that Charlie would overshadow him. He pressured the studio, as some stars could at that time, into boxing Charlie into the buddy characters."

"Did Charlie know?"

"He might have had suspicions, but he'd never have believed it. Michael also pleasured himself with Charlie's wives. He confessed it all to me not long after Charlie's suicide. That, plus excruciating boredom, is why I divorced him. He married Amelia, and somehow his guilt carried him through several years. Then he met Gloria."

"And you helped them? After what he'd done, with the way you must have felt about him?"

"I helped Gloria. Charlie was dead and she was alive. I was coming out of the disaster with Tony, and the intrigue of it all distracted me. They would meet at the Bel Air, but then, everyone with an illicit liaison did." She smiled a little. "Including me."

Intrigued, Julia cupped her chin on her open hand. "Wasn't it difficult, keeping the players straight? And think of how many bellhops were tipped into being millionaires."

Eve felt a layer of tension dissolve with her laugh. "It was a delicious time." There was appreciation in Julia's eyes. Interest, and no condemnation. Not yet. "Exciting."

"Sin usually is." The image was vivid. The glamorous, the famous, the passionate, playing hide-and-seek with gossip columnists and suspicious spouses. Temporary lovers having an afternoon romp—as much for the excitement of sin as the satisfaction of sex. "Oh, to have been a chambermaid," she murmured.

"Discretion was the byword of the Bel Air," Eve told her. "But, of course, everyone knew that was the place to go if you wanted a few hours of privacy with someone else's husband, or wife. And Amelia Gray Torrent wasn't a fool. Fear of discovery had Gloria and Michael holding their mating ritual at nasty little motels. My guest house wasn't completed yet, or I might have lent that to them. Still, they managed to do the deed well enough. Ironic that while they were tearing up the motel sheets, they were also filming a movie together."

"*The Blushing Bride,*" Julia remembered. "Jesus, he was playing her father."

"Ah, what Hedda and Louella might have done with that angle."

She couldn't help it, the idea had laughter bubbling out. "I'm sorry,

I'm sure it was intense and romantic at the time, but it's just sleazy enough to be funny. All that fatherly frustration and those daughterly pranks onscreen, then the two of them are rushing off to rent a room by the hour. Imagine if they'd gotten their lines mixed?"

Her tension fled long enough for Eve to chuckle into her wine. "Oh, Christ, it never even occurred to me."

"It would have been wonderful. The camera rolls in when he says: 'Young lady, I should put you over my knee and give you a good spanking.' "

"And her eyes glaze, her lips tremble. 'Yes, oh, yes, Daddy, please.' "

"Cut and print." Julia leaned back. "It would have been a classic."

"A pity neither of them ever had much of a sense of humor. They wouldn't be so crazed about it all still today."

Feeling good, Julia added wine to their glasses. "They can't really believe an affair all those years ago would shock people today. It might have been a scandal thirty years ago, but really, Eve, who'd give a damn now?"

"Gloria would—and her husband. He's a rigid sort. The kind who would have cheerfully cast the first stone."

"They've been married more than twenty-five years. I can't see him hauling her into divorce court for a past indiscretion."

"No, and neither can I. Gloria sees things differently. There's more, Julia, and while the rest might be hard for Marcus to shoulder, I think he will. But this will test him." She was silent a moment, knowing that her words would be like a snowball tossed down a long, steep hill. Before long, they would be too heavy to stop. "Just as the movie premiered, Gloria discovered herself pregnant, with Michael Torrent's child."

Julia's laughter stilled. This was a pain she understood too well. "I'm sorry. Finding yourself pregnant with a married man's child—"

"Gives you limited choices," Eve finished. "She was terrified, devastated. Her affair with Michael was already burning out. She'd gone to him first, of course, undoubtedly raging and hysterical. His marriage was ending, and, pregnancy or not, he wasn't about to tie himself into another."

"I'm sorry," Julia said again because it brought her own memories flashing by too clearly. "She must have been terrified."

"They were both afraid of the scandal, the responsibility, and of being stuck with each other for any appreciable length of time. She came to me. She had no one else."

"And you helped her, again."

"I stood by her, as a friend, as a woman. She'd already decided on an abortion. They were illegal in those days, and often dangerous."

Julia closed her eyes. The shudder came quickly, and from deep within. "It must have been horrible for her."

"It was. I found out about a clinic in France, and we went there. It was painful for her, Julia, not just physically. That choice is never easy for a woman."

"She was lucky to have you. If she'd been alone . . ." She opened her eyes again, and they were damp. Like wet gray velvet. "Whatever choice a woman makes, it's so hard to make it alone."

"It was a very sterile, very quiet place. I sat in a little waiting room with white walls and glossy magazines, and all I could see was the way Gloria had thrown her arms over her eyes, weeping, as they wheeled her away. It was very quick, and after they let me sit with her in her room. She didn't speak for a long time, hours really. Then she turned her head and looked at me.

" 'Eve,' she said, 'I know it was the right thing, the only thing, just as I know that nothing I ever do will hurt as much as this.' "

Julia brushed a tear from her cheek. "Are you sure it's necessary to publish this?"

"I believe it is, but I'm going to leave that decision in your hands, your heart, after you hear the rest."

Julia rose. She wasn't sure where the nerves had sprung from, but they were rippling just under her skin, like an itch she couldn't reach. "The decision shouldn't be mine, Eve. The judgment belongs to someone who was affected by the story, not an observer."

"You've never been just an observer, Julia, not from the moment you came here. I know you tried to be, that you would have preferred it that way, but it's impossible."

"Maybe I've lost my objectivity, and maybe I hope I'll write a better book that way. But it isn't my place to decide to include or delete something this intimate."

"Who better?" Eve murmured, then gestured to the chair. "Please, sit, let me tell you the rest."

She hesitated, but she wasn't sure why. Night had fallen quickly, leaving only the scatter of tiny lights and candleglow. Eve was haloed by the light, and an owl hooted from the shadows. Julia took her seat, and waited.

"Go on."

"Gloria went home. She picked up her life. Within a year she met Marcus and began a new one. That same year I met Victor. We didn't have our affair at discreet hotels or dingy motels. It wasn't a flash of passion, but a slow, steady flame that held us together. On other points, I suppose our relationship had many similarities with Michael and Gloria. He was married, and though his marriage was unhappy, we didn't make what we had public. I knew, though it's taken me years to accept, that we would never be a couple outside our own walls."

She looked around her now, while Julia remained silent. The backsplash of light from the kitchen window sprinkled over the geraniums. Moonlight slashed over the fuming water of the fountain and turned it to liquid silver. Around it all was a wall, closing her in, and others out.

"We loved here, in this house, and only a handful of people we both knew and trusted were ever included in our secret. I won't pretend I don't resent it, that I don't resent his wife, and at times resent Victor, for all that's been stolen from me. All the lies I've lived with. And one lie, one thing stolen most of all."

It was she who rose now, to walk toward the flowers, drinking in their fragrance deeply, as if she could find sustenance there that she hadn't found in the food on the table. This was the point, she knew. The point of it all, the point, once passed, she could never retreat from. Slowly, she walked back, but didn't sit.

"Gloria married Marcus one year after our trip to France. Within two months she was pregnant again, and deliriously happy. Weeks after that, I, too, was pregnant, and miserably unhappy."

"You?" Julia absorbed the jolt, then got to her feet to take Eve's hand. "I'm so sorry."

"Don't be." Eve tightened the grip. "Sit down with me. Let me finish."

Hands still linked, they sat together. The flame of the candle was between them, tossing light and shadow over Eve's face. Julia couldn't be sure what she was seeing. Grief, pain, hope.

"I was almost forty, and had long since given up on the notion of having children. The pregnancy frightened me, not only because of my age, but the circumstances. I wasn't afraid of public opinion, Julia, at least not for myself."

"It was Victor's," Julia murmured, understanding throbbing like a wound in her side.

"Yes, it was Victor's, and he was bound by law and church to another woman."

"But he loved you." Julia brought Eve's hand to her cheek a moment, in comfort. "How did he react when you told him?"

"I didn't tell him. I've never told him."

"Oh, Eve, how could you have kept it from him? It was his child as much as yours, and his right to know."

"Do you know how desperately he wanted children?" Eyes dark and bright, Eve leaned closer. "He had never, never forgiven himself for the loss of one. Yes, things might have changed if I'd told him. And I would have trapped him with me with that child as surely as she had trapped him with guilt, God, and grief. I couldn't, I wouldn't do it."

Julia waited while Eve shakily poured more wine. "I understand. I think I do," she corrected herself. "I never told my parents the name of Brandon's father for much the same reason. I couldn't stand the idea that the only reason he would be with me was because of a child conceived by accident."

Eve took one sip, then another. "The child was inside me, and I felt, always will feel, the choice was mine. I ached to tell him, to share it with him even for one day. But it would have been worse than a lie. I decided to go back to France. Travers was to go with me. I couldn't ask Gloria, couldn't even tell her when she was so cozily picking out names and knitting booties."

"Eve, you don't have to explain to me. I know."

"Yes, you would. Only a woman who had had to face that same choice would. Travers . . ." Eve fumbled with a match, then sat back gratefully when Julia lit it for her. "Travers understood as well." She blew out a stream of smoke. "She had a child, yet, at the same time, could never really have him. So, with Travers, I went back to France."

◆ ◆ ◆ ◆

NOTHING HAD ever seemed so cold, so without hope as the plain white walls of that examining room. The doctor had a gentle voice, gentle hands, gentle eyes. None of it mattered. Eve suffered through the required physical, dully answered all the necessary questions. She never took her eyes from that plain white wall.

That was what her life was like. Blank and empty. No one would believe that, of course. Not of Eve Benedict, star, movie goddess, the woman men craved and women envied. How could anyone understand that she would have given anything, at this single moment of her life, to be ordinary? The ordinary wife of an ordinary man having an ordinary child?

Because she was Eve Benedict, because the father was Victor Flannigan, the child could not be ordinary. The child could not even be.

She didn't want to wonder if it would have been a boy or girl. Yet she did. She couldn't afford to imagine what it would look like if she allowed those cells to grow, expand, become. Yet all too often she did imagine. And the child would have Victor's eyes. She would nearly collapse with love and longing.

There could be no love here, and certainly no longing.

She sat, listening as the doctor explained the simplicity of the procedure, as he promised little pain in his soft, soothing voice. She tasted her own tears as one slipped down her cheek and through her lips.

It was foolish, unproductive, this emotion. Other women had faced this same crossroads, and traveled it. If there was regret, she could live with it. As long as she knew the choice was the right one.

She didn't speak when the nurse came in to prep her. More gentle, competent hands, more quiet words of reassurance. Eve shuddered to think of the women without her funds and resources. Her sisters whose only solution to an impossible pregnancy was some shadowy back room.

She lay quietly on the gurney, felt only the quick sting of the needle. To relax her, she was told.

They wheeled her out. She watched the ceiling. In moments she would be in surgery. Then, in less time than it takes to talk about it, she would be out again, recuperating in one of the charming private rooms looking out on the distant mountains.

And she remembered the way Gloria had looked when she'd thrown her arm over her eyes.

Eve shook her head. The drug was making her sleepy, floaty, fanciful. She thought she could hear a baby crying. But that couldn't be. Her baby wasn't really a baby yet at all. And never would be.

She saw the doctor's eyes, those soft, sympathetic eyes over his surgical mask. She reached out for his hand, but couldn't feel it.

"Please . . . I can't . . . I want this baby."

◆ ◆ ◆

*W*HEN SHE AWAKENED, she was in bed, in one of those pretty rooms with the sun shooting slants of light through the blinds. She saw Travers sitting in the chair beside her. Though Eve made no sound, she was able to reach out.

"It's all right," Travers said, taking her hand. "You stopped them in time."

"You had the baby," Julia whispered.

"It was Victor's child, conceived in love. Rare and precious. And, as they wheeled me down that corridor, I realized what had been right for Gloria wasn't right for me. I'm not sure, if I hadn't gone through that with her, I'd have been able to make the right choice for myself."

"How did you have the child and keep it secret all these years?"

"Once I made the decision to bring the pregnancy to term, I made plans. I came back to the States, but to New York. I managed to interest some people into casting me in a Broadway play. It took time to find the right script, the right director and cast. And time was what I needed. When I was six months along, and no longer able to conceal my condition easily, I went to Switzerland, to a château I had had my lawyers buy. I lived there, with Travers, as Madame Constantine. Essentially, I disappeared for three months. Victor went wild trying to find me, but I lived quietly. At the end of my eighth month, I checked into a private hospital, this time as Ellen Van Dyke. The doctors were concerned. In those days it wasn't usual for a woman to have her first child at that age."

And alone, Julia thought. "Was it difficult, the pregnancy?"

"Tiring," Eve answered with a smile. "And difficult, yes, because I wanted Victor with me and couldn't have him. There were some complications. I didn't find out until a few years later that this would be my only child. I wouldn't be able to conceive again." She shook that aside. "Two weeks before my due date, I went into labor. A relatively short one, I was told, for a first baby. Only ten hours. It felt like ten days."

As women were over the pain and fears of childbirth, Julia was able to laugh. "I know. I was thirteen with Brandon. It felt like the rest of my life." Their eyes met over the flickering candles. "And the baby?"

"The baby was small, barely six pounds. Beautiful, the most beautiful thing. Pink and perfect, with big wise eyes. They let me hold her for a little while. That life that had grown in me. She slept, and I watched her sleep. I've never ached for Victor before or since as much as I did during that single hour of my life."

"I know." She covered Eve's hand with hers. "I wasn't in love with Lincoln. Not by the time Brandon was born, but I wanted him there. Needed him there. As wonderful as my parents were through it all, it wasn't the same. I'm glad you had Travers."

"I would have been lost without her."

"Can you tell me what happened to the baby?"

Eve stared down at their joined hands. "I had three weeks left in Switzerland, and then I was to go back and begin rehearsal on *Madam Requests*. I left the hospital and the child, because I felt it was best to sever the contact quickly. Best for me. My lawyers had several applications from prospective adoptive parents, and I screened them myself. I demanded that much control. Julia, I loved that child. I wanted the best for her."

"Of course you did. I can only imagine how much you suffered, giving her up."

"It was like dying. But I knew she was never going to be my child. My only choice was to make certain she had the best possible start. I chose her parents myself, and over the years, over my lawyers' disapproval, I had them send me reports on her progress."

"Oh, Eve, you could only have prolonged your own pain that way."

"No, no." The denial snapped out, urgent. "It reaffirmed that I'd done the right thing. She was everything I could have hoped. Bright and beautiful, strong, loving. She was much too young when she went through a similar kind of pain." Eve turned her hand over, gripping Julia's fingers with hers. "But she never buckled under. I've had no right to bring her back into my life. But just as I put her out of it, I've had no choice."

It wasn't the words so much as the look in Eve's eyes that had the breath backing up in Julia's lungs. They were hungry, fearful, and clear as glass. Instinctively she tried to jerk her hand free, but Eve held tight.

"Eve, you're hurting me."

"That's not what I want to do. But I have to."

"What are you trying to tell me?"

"I asked you to come here, to tell my story, because no one has more of a right to hear it than you." Her eyes held Julia's as unrelentingly as her hand. "You're my child, Julia. My only child."

"I don't believe you." She did jerk free now, scrambling up so quickly she sent the chair flying back. "What a despicable thing to try to do."

"You do believe me."

"No. No, I don't." She backed away another foot, raking both hands through her hair. She had to fight for each breath, fight it past the bitter anger in her throat. "How can you do this? How can you take advantage of me this way? You know I was adopted. You've made this all up, all of it, just to manipulate me."

"You know better than that." Eve got slowly to her feet, bracing one hand against the table for support. Her knees were shaking. "You know this is the truth." Their eyes met, held. "Because you feel it, you see it. I have proof if you need it. The hospitals records, the adoption documents, the correspondence with my attorneys. But you already know the truth. Julia . . ." She reached out, her own eyes filling as she watched her daughter's overflow.

"Don't touch me!" Julia screamed it, then closed her hands over her mouth because she was afraid she would go on screaming.

"Darling, please understand. I didn't do this, any of this to hurt you."

"Why then? Why?" Emotion after emotion layered inside until she thought she would explode from the weight of them. This woman, this woman who months before had been only a face on the screen, a name in a magazine, was her mother? Even as she wanted to shout out the denial, she looked at Eve, caught in a tower of moonlight, and knew. "You brought me here, involved me with your life, you played games with me, with everyone—"

"I needed you."

"You needed." Julia's voice slashed through Eve's like a blade. "You? The hell with you." Blind with grief, she shoved the table, sending it teetering over on its side. Crystal and china shattered. "Goddamn you. Do you think I should care? Do you expect me to run and embrace you? Do you think I should suddenly have this burst of love?" She dashed the tears from her face while Eve stood silent. "I don't. I detest you, I hate you for telling me, for everything. I swear I could kill you for telling me. Get out of here!" She whirled on Nina and Travers as they raced out of the house. "Get the hell out. This has nothing to do with you."

"Get back inside," Eve said quietly without looking at them. "Go back, please. This is between Julia and me."

"There's nothing between you and me," Julia managed to get out as a sob welled up in her throat. "Nothing."

"All I want is a chance, Julia."

"You had it," she snapped back. "Should I thank you for not going through with the abortion? Okay, thanks a lot. But my gratitude ends with the moment you signed the papers that gave me away. And why? Because I was inconvenient to your lifestyle. Because I was a mistake, an accident. That's all we are to each other, Eve. A mutual mistake." Tears choked her voice, but she pushed through them. "I had a mother who loved me. You could never replace her. And I'll never forgive you for telling me something I never wanted, never needed to know."

"I loved you too," Eve said with as much dignity as she could muster.

"That's just one more lie in a series of them. Stay away from me," she warned when Eve stepped forward again. "I don't know what I might do if you don't stay away from me." She turned, fleeing into the garden, running away from the past.

Eve could only cover her face with her hands, rocking back and forth against the pain. She went limply, like a child, when Travers came to lead her inside.

Chapter Twenty-Four

◆◆◆◆

*J*ULIA COULDN'T RUN from the anger, or the fear, or from the sense of loss and betrayal. As she rushed through the patchy moonlight, she carried all those things with her, along with a grief and confusion that swam sickly inside her stomach.

Eve.

She could still see Eve's face, those dark, fiercely intense eyes, the wide, unsmiling mouth. On a gasping sob, Julia brought her fingers to her own lips. Oh, God, oh God, the same shape, the same overfull bottom lip. Her fingers shook as she balled them into a fist and kept running.

She didn't notice Lyle standing on the narrow balcony over the garage, binoculars hanging around his neck, a pleased grin on his face.

She burst onto the terrace, her fisted hand pressed against her jittery stomach. Damp, her hand fumbled with the door before she cursed it, kicked it, then fought with the knob again. From inside, Paul swung it open, then caught her neatly by the elbows as she stumbled in.

"Whoa." He gave a quick laugh as he steadied her. "You must have missed me—" He cut himself off when he realized she was shaking. Tipping her head back by the chin, he saw the stricken look on her face. "What is it? Did something happen to Eve?"

"No." The lost, helpless expression changed to fury. "Eve's just fine, just fine and dandy. Why shouldn't she be? She's pushing all the buttons." She tried to jerk away, but he held firm. "Let me go, Paul."

"As soon as you tell me what's got you all worked up. Come on." He nudged her back outside. "You look like you could use some air."

"Brandon—"

"Is sound asleep. Since his room's on the other side of the house, I don't think anything you have to say out here will bother him. Why don't you sit down?"

"Because I don't want to sit. I don't want to be held or soothed or patted on the head. I want you to let me go."

He released her, holding his hands up, palms out. "Done. What else can I do for you?"

"Don't use that wry British tone. I'm not in the mood for it."

"All right, Jules." He rested a hip on the table. "What are you in the mood for?"

"I could kill her." She whipped up and down the patio, crossing from light into shadow then back into light. As she turned, she ripped one of the showy pink geraniums from its stem and shredded the blossom. The velvety shreds fluttered to the ground to be crushed and torn under her feet. "This whole thing, all of it, has been one of her famous maneuvers. Bringing me out here, taking me into her confidence, making me trust her—care for her. And she was sure—so fucking sure I'd fall right into the trap. Do you suppose she thought I'd be grateful, honored, flattered to be linked to her this way?"

He watched her throw the mangled stem aside. "I can't really say how she thought you'd feel. If you'd care to fill me in?"

She tossed up her head. For a moment she'd forgotten he was there. He stood, lazily leaning against the table, watching. Observing. They had that in common, she thought bitterly. There were those who stood and watched, recorded, reported, carefully noting how others lived, how they felt, what they said as they were tugged through life by fate's wily fingers. Only this time she was the one being manipulated.

"You knew." A fresh wave of rage crested inside her. "All this time, you knew. She never keeps anything from you. And you stood by and watched, waited, knowing she would do this to me. What role did she cast you in, Paul? The hero who calmly picks up the pieces?"

His patience was wearing thin. He pushed himself away from the table to face her. "I can't confirm or deny until you tell me what it is I'm supposed to have known."

"That she's my mother." Julia flung the words at him, tasting each bitter syllable on her tongue. "That Eve Benedict is my mother."

He hadn't even been aware of moving, but his hands had shot out to grip her arms. "What the hell are you talking about?"

"She told me tonight." She didn't jerk away. Instead, she grabbed two fistfuls of his shirt and leaned into him. "She must have thought it was time for a mother-daughter chat. It's been only twenty-eight years."

He gave her a quick, rough shake. Hysteria was rising in her voice, and he preferred the rage. "Told you what? Told you exactly what?"

Her head came up slowly. Though her grip on his shirt didn't lessen, she spoke calmly, clearly, as if explaining a particularly complex problem

to a slow-witted child. "That twenty-eight years ago she gave birth, se-
cretly, to a child in Switzerland. And having no place for that sort of
inconvenience, gave the child away. Me. She gave me away."

He would have laughed the thought aside if it hadn't been for the
desolation in her eyes. Her eyes . . . not the color, but the shape. Very
slowly, he moved his hands up into her hair. Not the shade, but the
texture. Her lips trembled. And the mouth . . .

"Good Christ." Still holding her, he stared at her face as if he'd
never seen it before. Perhaps he hadn't, he realized. How else could he
have missed the similarities? Oh, they were subtle, but they were there.
How could he have loved both of them, and not have seen, not have
known? "She told you this herself?"

"Yes, though I wonder she didn't have Nina jot it down in a memo.
'Tell Julia the secret of her birth over dinner. Eight o'clock.' " She broke
away then, turned her back on him. "Oh, I hate her for this. Hate her for
what she's stolen from me." She whirled back, her hair flying out, then
settling in a tangle on her shoulders. The trembling was past so that she
stood spear-straight in the cool white light of the moon while emotions
rolled off her like sweat. "My life, every moment of my life, changed in
the flash of an instant. How can anything be the same again?"

There were no answers. He was still reeling, fighting to take in the
single fact she'd shoved at him. The woman he'd loved most of his life
was the mother of the woman he wanted to love for the rest of it. "You're
going to have to give me a minute to take this in. I think I know how you
must be feeling, but—"

"No." The word erupted from her. Indeed, everything about her
was hot, on the point of boiling over. Her eyes, her voice, the fists held
rigidly at her sides. "You couldn't even come close. There were times as a
child I wondered. It's only natural, isn't it? Who were they, those people
who hadn't wanted me? Why had they given me up? What did they look
like, sound like? I made up stories—that they had loved each other desperately, but he'd been killed and left her destitute and alone. Or that
she'd died in childbirth before he could come back and save her, and me.
Lots of sweet, fanciful little stories. But I left them behind, because my
parents . . ." She lifted her hand to cover her eyes for a moment as the
pain ripped through her. "They loved me, they wanted me. Being
adopted wasn't something I thought about often. In fact, I'd forget about
it for long stretches of time because my life was so normal. But then it
would hit me again. When I was carrying Brandon, I wondered if she'd
been scared, like I was. Sad, and scared and lonely."

"Jules—"

"No, don't, please." She retreated instantly, hugging her arms tight against her body in defense. "I don't want to be held. I don't want sympathy or understanding."

"Then what?"

"To go back." Desperation snuck into her voice like a thief. "To be able to go back to before she started to tell me that story. To make her stop. To make her see this was one lie she should live with. Why couldn't she see? Why couldn't she see, Paul, that the truth would ruin everything? She's taken away my identity, scarred my memories, and left me rootless. I don't know who I am. What I am."

"You're exactly the same person you were an hour ago."

"No, don't you see?" She held her hands out, and they were empty. Like her heritage. "Everything I was was built on that one lie, and all the others that followed it. She had me in secret, under a name she'd borrowed from one of her scripts. Then she walked away, picked up her life exactly where she'd left off. She never even told . . ." The words shuddered to a halt, then began again on a husky whisper. "Victor. Victor Flannigan's my father."

That was the only thing that didn't surprise Paul. He took her hand, found it stiff and icy to the touch. He curled her fingers closed inside his as if to warm them. "He doesn't know?"

She could only shake her head. His face seemed pale in the moonlight, his eyes dark. Did he know? she wondered. Did he know he was looking at a stranger? "God, Paul, what has she done? What has she done to all of us?"

So he held her, despite her resistance. "I don't know what the consequences are, Julia. But I know whatever you're feeling now, you'll get through it. You survived your parents' divorce, their deaths, bringing Brandon into the world without a father."

She shut her eyes tight, hoping to erase the afterimage of Eve's face—with tears just beginning to spill out, leaving only hope and needs behind. "How can I look at her and not hate her, hate her for being able to live so easily without me?"

"Do you think it was easy?" he murmured.

"For her, yes." She pulled away to wipe impatiently at tears. The last thing she would feel now was sympathy. "Goddamn. I know what she went through. Disbelief, panic, misery—all the phases. Sweet Jesus, Paul, I know how much it hurts to find yourself pregnant and know the man you love, or think you love, will never make a family with you."

"Maybe that's why she felt she could tell you."

"Well, she was wrong." She was calming slowly, methodically. "I also know that if I had made the decision to give Brandon up, I would never push myself back into his life and make him wonder, make him question, make him remember all those doubts about not being good enough."

"If she made a mistake—"

"Yes, she made a mistake," Julia said on a hard laugh. "I'm it."

"That's enough." If she didn't want sympathy, he wouldn't give it. "At the very least, you know you were conceived in love. That's more than most people can be sure of. My parents have retained a polite revulsion for each other as long as I can remember. That's my legacy. You were brought up by people who loved you, and were conceived by people who continue to love each other. You can call that a mistake, but I'd swear you had the better bargain."

There were things she could have hurled back at him, hurtful things that rolled through her brain, then died of shame and self-disgust before they touched her tongue. "I'm sorry." Her voice was stiff, but no longer raw with pain. "There's no reason to take all this out on you, or to indulge in self-pity."

"I'd say there was plenty of reason for both. Will you sit down now, and talk to me?"

As she brushed away the last of the tears, she shook her head. "No, I'm all right, really. I hate to lose my temper."

"You shouldn't." To soothe himself as well as her, he combed her hair away from her face with his fingers. "You do it so well." Because it seemed right, he brought her back into his arms, resting his cheek against the top of her head. "You've had a rough night, Jules. Maybe you should get some rest."

"I don't think I can. I could use some aspirin, though."

"We'll get you some." He kept an arm around her as they walked back into the kitchen. There were lights, glowing cheerfully, and a buttery scent that made her think the hamburgers had been followed up by a bowl of popcorn. "Where's the aspirin?"

"I'll get them."

"No, I'll get them. Where?"

Because her mind felt as limp and achy as her body, she gave in and sat at the table. "Top shelf, left side of the stove." She closed her eyes again, listening to the sound of the cupboard door opening, closing, the sound of water hitting glass. On a sigh, she opened them again and managed what passed for a smile. "Tantrums always give me a headache."

He waited until she'd swallowed them. "How about some tea?"

"That'd be nice, thanks." Sitting back, she pressed her fingers to her temple, circling them slowly—until she remembered that was one of Eve's habitual gestures. With her hands clasped in her lap, she watched as Paul readied cups and saucers, rinsed out a porcelain pot in the shape of a donkey.

It was odd, sitting there while someone else handled the details. She was used to taking care of herself, solving the problem, mending the breaks. Now she knew it was taking all of her will, all of her energy to resist the need to lay her head down on the table and indulge in a bout of hot weeping.

And why? That was the question that dogged her. Why?

"After all this time," she murmured. "All these years. Why did she tell me now? She said she'd kept tabs on me all along. Why did she wait till now?"

He'd been wondering the same thing himself. "Did you ask her?"

She was staring down at her hands, shoulders slumped, eyes still damp. "I don't even know what I said to her. I was so blind with hurt and anger. My temper can be . . . ugly, which is why I try not to lose it."

"You, Jules?" he said lightly as he passed a hand over her hair. "An ugly temper?"

"Horrible." She couldn't bring herself to answer his smile. "The last time I went off was nearly two years ago. A teacher at Brandon's school had made him stand in the corner for over an hour. He was humiliated, wouldn't talk to me about it, so I went in for a conference. I wanted it straightened out because Brandon's just not a troublemaker."

"I know."

"Anyway, it turned out that they were making up Father's Day cards toward the end of the school year, and Brandon didn't want to make one. He, well, he didn't want to."

"Understandable." Paul poured boiling water over tea bags. "And?"

"And this teacher said he was expected to treat it as an assignment, and when he refused, she punished him. I tried to explain the situation, that Brandon was sensitive in that area. And with this tight-lipped sneer she said he was spoiled and willful and enjoyed manipulating others. She said if he wasn't taught to accept his situation, he'd continue to use his accident of birth—those were her words—accident, as an excuse not to become a productive member of society."

"I hope you slugged her."

"Actually, I did."

"No." Now he had to grin. "Really?"

"It's not funny," she began, then felt a bubble of laughter in her throat. "I don't remember hitting her exactly, though I recall a few of the names I called her as people came rushing in to pull me off her."

He picked up her hand, weighed it in his, then kissed it. "My hero."

"It wasn't nearly as satisfying as it sounds now. At the time I was sick and shaky, and she was threatening to sue. They calmed her down when the whole story came out. In the meantime, I pulled Brandon out of the school and bought the place in Connecticut. I wouldn't have him subjected to that kind of thinking, that kind of nastiness." She let out a long breath, then another. "I felt exactly the same way tonight. I know if Eve had come near me, I would have hit her first and been sorry about it later." Julia looked down at the cup he set in front of her. "I used to wonder where I got that streak of mean from. I guess I know."

"It scared you, what she told you tonight."

Julia let the tea slide into her system and soothe. "Yes."

He sat beside her, rubbing fingers at the base of her neck, knowing instinctively where the bulk of the tension would be lodged. "Don't you think she was scared too?"

Carefully, aligning the base of the cup with the rim of the saucer, she looked up. "I'm afraid I can't really think about her feelings yet."

"I love you both."

She saw now what she hadn't been able to see before. He'd been as shocked as she, and perhaps nearly as hurt. He was hurting still, for both of them. "Whatever becomes of all this, she'll always be more your mother than she could ever be mine. And, I guess, since we both love you, we'll all have to find a way to deal with it. Just don't ask me to be reasonable tonight."

"I won't. I will ask you something else." Taking her hands he drew her to her feet. "Let me love you."

It was so easy, so simple, to move into his arms. "I thought you'd never ask."

◆ ◆ ◆ ◆

*U*PSTAIRS, the bedroom was draped in shadows. She lit the candles while he drew the shades. Then they were alone in the half light, a lovers' light. She lifted her arms to him in a gesture of welcome, and of need.

He took her in, understanding without being asked that she needed to reaffirm her life, to take back her sense of self. So when she fit her body to his, tilted back her face, offered her mouth, he took gently, he took slowly, wanting her to remember every moment.

With long, moist kisses, he tasted, and her taste was the same. One firm, possessive stroke from waist to hip, and back. She felt the same. Nuzzling at her throat, he drank in her scent. Beneath that fragile perfume was the unmistakable essence of Julia. That, too, the same.

He would allow nothing to change between them.

The jacket slid smoothly from her shoulders. One tiny button at a time he unfastened her blouse, stepping back so he could see each inch of flesh exposed. That same excitement, that same clutching desire stirred in him as he parted the fabric, let it slip from her shoulders to the floor with a sensual whisper.

"You're all I've ever wanted," he told her. "Everything I've ever needed." He laid a finger on her lips before she could speak. "No, let me tell you. Let me show you."

He touched his mouth to hers, teasing, tempting, then taking her deep until she was drunk from the single kiss. All the while he was murmuring things, beautiful things, as his fingers moved lightly, competently, to undress her. The tension in her shoulders began to ease. The fluttering in her stomach changed from that hollow motion of stress to the warming movement of anticipation.

It was magic. Or he was. Here, with him, she could erase the past, forget tomorrow. There was only the everlasting now. How could he have known just how much she'd needed that? In the now there was the feel of tight muscles under her dancing fingers, the perfume of moon-dusted flowers, the first stirrings of hunger.

Lost in him, she let her head fall back, made soft, helpless sounds deep in her throat as his lips trailed down to cruise over her breast.

"Tell me what you like," he said, and his voice echoed inside her head. "Tell me what you want me to do to you."

"Anything." Her damp palms slid down his flesh. "Anything."

His lips curved once before he rolled his tongue over the heated point of her breast, caught it between his teeth on that delirious edge between pleasure and pain, drew it into his mouth—hot, firm, fragrant— to suck his fill.

He would take her at her word.

It was as if it were the first time she'd been with a man. She shook her head to try to clear it so that she could give back. But he was doing things to her, wild, wonderful, wicked things to her. She could only shudder at burst after burst of pleasure.

Her head lolled back as she struggled to gulp in air that was suddenly too thick. Her breasts were so heavy, the nipples so hot, that when he flicked his tongue there again, she cried out in astonishment at the good, hard orgasm he gave her.

"I can't." Dizzy, she braced her hands on his shoulders as he burned a line down her torso. "I have to—"

"Enjoy," he murmured, nipping at her quivering flesh. "You only have to enjoy."

He knelt in front of her, his hands gripping her hips to hold her in place while he dipped his tongue along the juncture of her thighs. He could feel each ripple of sensation that passed through her, and his body was hammered by the same dark delights that rocketed in hers.

She came again, and with a half sob clutched her fingers in his hair to drag him closer. Now her hips were moving, quick as lightning, urging him on. When his tongue speared inside her, she went rigid, stunned by the jolt of heat. Her knees went to jelly. She would have fallen if he hadn't grasped her hips and forced her upright.

Relentless, he drove her up again, his desire feeding greedily on hers. He wanted—wanted to know her system was a jumble of sensation, that her nerve endings sizzled to the touch, that her appetites matched his.

When he knew, when he was sure, he dragged her down to the floor with him and took her further. Showed her more.

He had to stop. She would die if he stopped. While they tumbled over the rug she clung to him, her body limp one instant, tense the next. She had thought they had given each other all there was long before this. Now she knew there was yet another level of trust. There, in the deep shadows of that room, there was nothing he could have asked of her, nothing she wouldn't have given willingly.

But before it was done, it was she who asked. She who would have begged. "Please, now. God, I need you now."

It was all he'd wanted to hear.

With his eyes on hers he brought them together, torso to torso. Slowly, watching the pleasure and confusion flicker in her eyes, he wrapped her legs around his waist. He filled her, inch by trembling inch, until he was plunged deep. Gasping, she reared back, accepting him, absorbing him, enjoying him.

When the first shudders had passed, she came back, bringing her lips to his even as they began to move together. Through the excitement, the passion, the clutching hunger, came a new sensation—one that settled and soothed and healed.

Lips curved, she held him close until there was nothing left but velvet darkness.

◆ ◆ ◆ ◆

*L*ATER, MUCH LATER, when she slept, he stood by the window, looking out at the single light he could see through the trees. Eve was awake, he knew, even as her daughter slept. How could he, a man so firmly tied to each of them, find the way to comfort both?

◆ ◆ ◆ ◆

*H*E WENT in the side door. Before he had crossed through the parlor with its scent of fading roses to start up the front stairs, Travers was there. She hurried down the hallway to him, rubber-soled slippers flapping.

"This isn't the time for visiting. She needs her rest."

Paul paused, one hand on the newel post. "She's awake. I saw the light."

"No matter. She needs her rest." Travers gave the belt of her terry-cloth robe a quick and audible snap. "She's not feeling well tonight."

"I know. I've spoken with Julia."

Like a fighter daring a punch, Travers stuck out her chin. "She left Eve in a terrible state. That girl had no right to say such things, shouting and breaking china."

"That girl," Paul said mildly, "had a hell of a shock. You knew, didn't you?"

"What I know is my own business." Lips folded tight on secrets, she jerked her head toward the top of the stairs. "Just like seeing to her's my business. Whatever you have to say can wait till tomorrow. She's had enough grief for one night."

"Travers." Eve came out of the shadows, down two steps. She was wearing a long, sleek silk robe in ripe red. Her face was an ivory oval above it. "It's all right. I'd like to speak to Paul."

"You told me you'd go to sleep."

Eve flashed her quick smile. "I lied. Good night, Travers." She turned away, knowing Paul would follow.

Because he respected loyalty, he spared the housekeeper a last look. "I'll see that she goes to bed soon."

"I'll hold you to it." With a final glance up the stairs, she walked away, terry cloth swishing, rubber flapping.

Eve waited for him in the sitting room adjoining the bedroom, with its plump cushions and low, inviting chairs. It held the evening's disorder—discarded magazines, a champagne glass with a few drops going flat and stale, tennis shoes carelessly kicked off, a slash of purple and scarlet that was the robe she'd tossed aside after her bath. Everything bright and vivid and alive. Paul looked at her, sitting in the midst of it all, and realized fully for the first time how much she was aging.

It showed in the hands that suddenly seemed too frail and thin for the rest of her body, in the fine lines that had crept stealthily back around her eyes since her last bout with the surgeon's knife. It showed in the weariness that coated her face like a thin, transparent mask.

She looked up, saw everything she needed to know on his face, and looked away again. "How is she?"

"Sleeping now." He took the chair across from her. It wasn't the first time he had come in here late at night to talk. The cushions were different, the pillows, the curtains. Eve was always changing things.

But much was the same. The scents that he had grown to love during childhood. Powders and perfumes and flowers—all the things that shouted this was a woman's room, and men were allowed only by invitation.

"How are you, gorgeous?"

The simple concern in his voice threatened to bring the tears back again, and she'd told herself she was through with them. "Angry with myself for doing such a poor job of it. I'm glad you were there for her."

"So am I." He said nothing more, knowing she would speak when she was ready, and without his prompting. And because his presence gave her comfort, she talked to him as she would have with a few others.

"I've carried this inside of me for nearly thirty years, the same way I carried Julia for nine months." Her fingers were drumming on the arm of her chair. As if even that whispering sound disturbed her, she stopped, letting them lay quiet. "In secret, in pain, and with a kind of despair no man could comprehend. I always thought as I grew older—hell, when I got old—that the memories would fade. The way my body changed, those movements inside my womb. The terrifying excitement of pushing her out of me and into the world. They don't." She shut her eyes. "God, they don't."

She took a cigarette from the Lalique holder on the table, then ran it through her fingers twice before lighting it. "I won't deny that I lived fully, richly, happily without her. I won't pretend that I grieved and mourned every day of my life for a child I held only an hour. And I never regretted doing what I did, but neither did I forget."

Her tone dared accusations, her eyes flared up at his, waiting for them. He only touched a hand to her cheek. "Why did you bring her here, Eve? Why did you tell her?"

Her fragile composure threatened to shred. She clutched at it, then at his hand. Then she released him, and continued. "I brought her here because there were loose ends in my life I wanted to . . . knot. It appealed to my sense of irony—maybe my vanity—that my daughter be the one to tie those knots." She blew out a stream of smoke. Behind its veil her eyes were full of power and purpose in a calm, pale fact. "And I needed the contact. I needed to see her, dammit. To touch her, to watch for myself what kind of woman she'd become. And the child, my grandchild, I wanted a few weeks to get to know him. If I go to hell for that sin, so be it. It's been worth more than most of the others I've committed."

"Did you tell her that?"

She laughed and crushed out the cigarette half finished. "She has a temper, and pride. I didn't have time to tell her much of anything before she clawed at me. With perfect justification. I'd reneged on the deal, after all. I'd given her away, and had no right to try to take her back."

She rose to walk to the window. In the black glass she saw her own reflection, like the ghost she felt herself becoming.

"But my God, Paul, the longer I was around her, the more I came to care for her. I could see pieces of myself in her, and pieces of Victor. I've never in my life felt such a need for another human being, unless it was a man. I've never known such a whole, unselfish love for anyone. Anyone else but you." She turned back, her eyes wet. "She was the child I couldn't have. You were the child I always wanted."

"And you were my mother, Eve. Julia had one of her own. She'll need time."

"I know." She turned away again, feeling the burden on her heart increase. "I know."

"Eve, why didn't you ever tell Victor?"

Weary, she laid her head on the glass. "I thought about it, then and a hundred times since. He might have left his wife, you know. He might have come to me, free. As much as he would have loved the child, I wonder if he would ever have forgiven me. I would never have forgiven myself for accepting him under those terms."

"Will you tell him now?"

"I think that should be Julia's choice." She glanced over her shoulder. "Does she know you're here?"

"No."

"Will you tell her?"

"Yes, I will."

"You love her."

Though it wasn't a question, he answered. "More than I knew I was capable of loving anyone. I want her, and Brandon. No matter what it takes."

Satisfied, she nodded. "Let me give you one piece of unsolicited advice. Let nothing stand in your way. Nothing. Least of all me." She held out her hands, waiting for him to stand and come to her to take them. "I have some things to see to tomorrow. Details. In the meantime, I'm trusting you to take care of her."

"I intend to, whether she likes it or not."

"Go back to her, then. I'll be fine." Eve lifted her face for his kiss, held on a moment longer. "I'll always be grateful I've had you."

"We've had each other. Don't worry about Julia."

"I won't. Now. Good night, Paul."

He kissed her again. "Good night, gorgeous."

When he had gone, she went directly to the phone and dialed. "Greenburg, this is Eve Benedict." She tossed back her head and picked up a cigarette. "Yes, goddammit, I know what time it is. You can charge me double whatever outrageous rates you lawyers charge. I need you here within the hour."

She hung up on his protest, then grinned. She felt almost like her old self.

Chapter Twenty-Five

♦♦♦♦

LESS THAN TWENTY-FOUR HOURS after Julia's plane accident, Paul arranged to meet with the pilot.

Jack Brakerman had worked for Eve more than five years, hooking the job through Paul himself. While doing research for a book that had involved smuggling, mayhem, and murder in the air, Paul had been impressed by Jack's knowledge and skill.

By the time it was finished, Paul had had enough material for two books, and Jack Brakerman had been able to quit flying cargo to take private passengers. His first client had been Eve.

Paul met him at a diner near the airport, where the food was greasy, the coffee hot, and the service prompt. The table was a circular slice of particle board coated with a sheet of linoleum that tried, unsuccessfully, to look like marble. Someone had paid for country on the juke, and Hank Williams, Jr., was moaning about the woman who done him wrong.

"Hell of a place, isn't it?" Jack pulled one of the miserly paper napkins out of its metal dispenser to wipe up the circles of wet left by the previous patrons' glasses. "Don't look like much, but they got the best goddamn blueberry pie in the state. Want a slice?"

"Sure."

Jack signaled the waitress and gave their order with a single gesture. He held up two fingers. Within minutes they were served thick wedges of pie along with mugs of steaming black coffee.

"You're right," Paul told him after the first bite. "It's great."

"I've been coming here for years, just for the pie. So tell me," Jack began over a hefty forkful. "You writing another book?"

"Yeah, but that's not what I want to talk to you about."

Jack nodded, took a wary sip of coffee, knowing it would be hot and strong enough to sear his stomach lining. "You want to talk about yesterday. I already filed the report. Looks like they're going to put it down to mechanical failure."

"That's the official story, Jack. What's your opinion?"

"Somebody fucked with the fuel line. Real slick, real professional. It looks like a mechanical failure. Hell, if it was somebody else's plane and I checked it out myself, I'd say the same. The line was stressed, sprung a leak. Dumped most of the fuel over the Sierra Madres."

Paul didn't want to think of the mountains and what the jagged, unforgiving peaks could have done to a sputtering plane. "But it isn't someone else's plane."

"That's right." Mouth full, he waved his fork for emphasis. "And I know my gear, Winthrop. Between the mechanic and me, we keep that bird in a-one condition. No way that line was fatigued, no fucking way it happened to spring a leak. Somebody messed with it, somebody who knew what to do and how to do it." He scooped up the last of the pie, swallowing it with a combination of pleasure and regret. "That's what my gut tells me."

"I'm willing to go with your gut, Jack. Now the question is what to do about it." Paul considered a moment. The juke had switched to K. D. Lang, and her mellow, masculine voice added a dash of class to the dreary diner. "Tell me exactly what you did yesterday after you landed in Sausalito."

"That's easy. I bumped around the lounge awhile, talked shop with some guys, had lunch with a couple other pilots. Julia said she'd be back by three, so I wound up the paperwork, cleared my flight plan. She was right on time."

"Yes," Paul said half to himself. "She's habitually prompt. Can you ask around, see if anyone noticed someone near the plane?"

"Already did. People don't notice much when they're not looking." Frowning, he scraped his fork over his plate, making patterns in the smear of purple juice. "You know the thing that hits me, whoever did this knew planes. He could have fixed it so we went down a lot quicker, say when we were over the bay with no place to go. The way it was done had the fuel leaking out, slow and steady. You following me?"

"Keep going."

"If he'd wanted us dead, there were a lot of other ways to fix it and still make it look like an accident. So, I gotta figure he didn't want us dead. Things could've gone wrong and we'd have been that way anyhow, so maybe he didn't give a shit one way or the other. But if we'd have bottomed out on fuel ten, fifteen minutes earlier, things would've been a lot dicier. He fixed it so I had enough juice to get close so a pilot good as me could bring her in."

"Sabotaging the plane was a scare tactic?"

"I don't know, Hoss, but if it was, it was a fucking bull's-eye." His round, pleasant face creased in a grimace. "I made so many bargains with God during the last five minutes that I'm in hock into the next life. And if it scared the sin out of me, I can tell you it left Julia pure as the driven snow." He eyed Paul's pie as he signaled for more coffee.

"Help yourself," Paul said, pushing the plate across the table.

"Thanks. It's easy to spot a nervous flier even when they're busy telling themselves they can handle it. She doesn't like being up there, not a bit, but she toughs it out without all the usual crutches—smoking, drinking, sleeping pills. When I had to tell her the situation, she was scared, scared right down to her shoes. Went so white I figured I was going to have a fainter on my hands, but she held on. No screaming, no crying, she just talked to me. She did everything I told her to do. You gotta admire that."

"I do."

"Somebody wanted to scare the lady, and scare her bad. I can't prove it, but I know it."

"I'm going to prove it," Paul told him. "You can take that to the bank."

◆ ◆ ◆ ◆

ℒYLE SHIFTED from foot to foot as he stood in Delrickio's living room. He didn't feel like sitting, not with the ice-faced goon watching his every move. Though he had to admire the dude's threads. Yes, indeed. He'd bet his next paycheck that coal-black crisply tailored suit was pure silk. And this guy was just an underling. It made him wonder how much the big guy himself pulled in every year.

Wanting to show his nonchalance, Lyle pulled out a cigarette. He'd taken out his genuine gold-plated Zippo when his watchdog spoke.

"Mr. Delrickio don't allow no smoking in this room."

"Yeah?" Lyle tried hard for a sneer as he clicked the lighter closed. "No sweat, man. I can live with them, I can live without them."

He was whistling under his breath when the phone on a dainty inlaid table rang. The guard answered it, grunted.

"Upstairs," he told Lyle after he'd replaced the receiver.

Lyle figured his brisk, unsmiling nod was Bogie-like. They'd already deflated his ego by patting him down the minute he'd pulled through the gates. He'd wished he'd been packing a gun. Wished he'd had one to pack. It would have made him seem tougher.

With what he figured he'd be paid for his information, he could buy himself an arsenal.

The guard knocked lightly on the door at the top of the stairs, then jerked his head in invitation, and Lyle walked through.

Delrickio gestured for Lyle to sit. "Good evening," he said mildly. "I believe we had agreed that I would contact you, when and if I chose."

The gentle, friendly voice had sweat springing to Lyle's palms. "Yes, sir, we did, but—"

"Then I must assume you felt compelled to go against my wishes."

A lump had formed in Lyle's throat the size and texture of a tennis ball. He swallowed gamely over it. "Yes, sir. That is, I came by some information I knew you'd want right away."

"And you couldn't find a telephone in working order?"

"I—that is, I thought you'd want to hear it face-to-face."

"I see." Delrickio let the silence drag out until Lyle had moistened his dry lips twice. "I find I must remind you that you were paid to observe, to pass along information, but not, as I recall, to think. However, I'll reserve judgment on whether you've thought well until after I hear what you've come into my home to tell me."

"Julia Summers was in a plane yesterday that nearly crashed."

At this outburst, Delrickio merely lifted his brows. Christ in heaven, how had he ever been deluded into believing this idiot could provide him with anything remotely useful? "You bring me information I already have. I'm never pleased to have my time wasted."

"They think the plane was fuck—tampered with," he corrected himself quickly. "I heard her and Winthrop talking. She was a mess when I picked her up at the airport. See, what I did was, I waited until they sent the kid along, and went in the house. I listened outside." Because Delrickio was tapping his fingers against the desktop, Lyle hurried on. "They think someone was trying to kill her. There was this note, and—"

He broke off when Delrickio raised a hand. "What note?"

"Something she found on the plane. From the way she talked, it wasn't the first one she'd gotten. He tried to talk her into leaving, but she wouldn't go."

"What did the note say?"

"I don't know." Lyle paled a bit and cleared his throat. "I didn't really see it. I only heard them talking about it." He wondered if he should bring up the notes he'd found in Eve's bedroom, and decided to bide his time.

"This is all very interesting, but hardly worth taking up my time on a beautiful morning."

"There's more." Lyle paused. Throughout the night, he'd gone over and over how he would play this card. "It's big, Mr. Delrickio, bigger than what you've been paying me for."

"Since I've been paying you for very little of interest, that makes no impression on me."

"I guarantee you, you'll want this. I figure it's worth a bonus. A fat one. Maybe even a permanent job. I got no intention of spending the rest of my life driving a car and living over a garage."

"Is that so?" Delrickio's distaste showed only briefly. "Tell me what you have, then I'll tell you what it's worth."

Lyle licked his lips again. He knew he was taking a chance, but the payoff could be incredible. Visions of cold money and hot women danced in his head. "Mr. Delrickio, I know you're a man of your word. If you promise me you'll pay me what the information is worth, I'll stand by that."

Stand or die, Delrickio thought with a weary sigh. "You have it."

Enjoying the drama of the moment, Lyle let silence hang. "Eve Benedict is Julia Summers's natural mother."

Delrickio's eyes narrowed, darkened. Angry color crept from his neck to cover his face. Each word he spoke was like an ice pick striking bone. "Do you think you can come into my house and tell me this lie, then walk out alive?"

"Mr. Delrickio—" Lyle's saliva dried to dust when he saw the small, lethal .22 in Delrickio's hand. "Don't. Christ, don't." He scrambled like a crab toward the back of the chair.

"Tell me that again."

"I swear it." Tears of terror leaked from his eyes. "They were on the terrace, and I was hiding in the garden, so I could find out anything you might want to know. Just like we agreed. And—and Eve, she started telling this story about Gloria DuBarry having an affair with that Torrent guy."

"Gloria DuBarry had an affair with Michael Torrent? Your fantasies grow." His finger caressed the trigger of the gun.

Terror made the .22 look like a cannon. "Eve said it. Jesus, why would I make it up?"

"You have one minute to tell me exactly what she said." Calmly, Delrickio glanced at the stately grandfather clock in the corner. "Begin."

Fumbling, stammering, Lyle blurted out everything he could remember, his wild eyes never leaving the barrel of the .22. As the story poured out, Delrickio's look became less intense and more speculative.

"So, Miss DuBarry aborted Torrent's baby." It was an interesting, potentially useful fate. Marcus Grant had a very successful business, and would probably object to having his wife's indiscretion come to light. Delrickio filed it away.

"How do you turn this information into Miss Summers being Eve's daughter."

"Eve told her, she told her about a year or so later she got knocked up by Victor Flannigan." Lyle's voice rose an octave effortlessly, like an opera singer practicing scales. "She was going to have an abortion, too, but changed her mind and had the kid. She gave it up for adoption. She told the Summers woman. Jesus, I swear she told her she was her mother. She even said she had papers, lawyer's stuff, to prove it." He was too terrified to move, even to wipe his running nose. "Summers went nuts, started screaming and throwing things. The other two—Travers and Soloman—came running out. That's when I went back to the garage, to watch. I could still hear her yelling, and Eve crying. Afterward Summers ran back to the guest house. I knew you'd want to know. I ain't lying, I swear it."

No, Delrickio thought, he wasn't clever enough to have made it all up, the clinic in France, the private hospital in Switzerland. He replaced the gun, ignoring the fact that Lyle covered his face with his hands and sobbed.

Eve had a child, he thought. A child she would undoubtedly want to protect.

Smiling to himself, he leaned back in his chair. Lyle was a revolting swine. But swine had their uses.

◆ ◆ ◆ ◆

JULIA HAD NEVER seen so much chintz in one place. Obviously Gloria had told the decorator to make her office cozy and old-fashioned. She'd gotten it. In spades. Frilly pink curtains with layers and more layers of flounce. Chairs so deep and cushy a small child could sink into them and never be seen again. Hooked rugs scattered over hardwood. Copper and brass pots overflowing with cute balls of yarn or dried flowers. Tiny tables crowded with miniature statuary. A dusting nightmare.

Everything was packed in and angled together so that the visitor was forced to pick through a country-motif obstacle course, shifting this way and that to avoid bumping a hip or stubbing a toe.

Then there were the cats. Three of them slept in a slant of sunlight, tangled around and over each other into one obscene ball of glossy white fur.

Gloria was seated at a small, curvy desk more suited to milady's boudoir than a working office. She wore a pale pink dress with full sleeves and a Quaker collar. In it she looked the picture of purity, good health, and goodwill. But nerves recognized nerves. Julia saw the stress in the bitten-down nails. Her own were a ragged mess after the hour she'd spent this morning agonizing over keeping this appointment or canceling.

"Miss Summers." With a warm, welcoming smile, Gloria rose. "Since you're right on time, you must not have had any trouble finding us."

"No trouble at all." Julia turned sideways to scoot between a table and a footstool. "I appreciate your agreeing to see me."

"Eve is one of my oldest and closest friends. How could I refuse?"

Julia accepted Gloria's invitation to sit. Obviously, the incident at Eve's party wasn't going to be mentioned. But they both knew it gave Julia the advantage.

"I received the message that you wouldn't be able to have brunch, but perhaps you'd like some coffee, tea?"

"No, nothing, thank you." She'd ingested enough coffee that morning to wire her for a week.

"So you want to talk about Eve," Gloria began in the voice of a cheerful nun. "I've known Eve for, goodness, it must be thirty years or so now. I confess, when we first met she terrified and fascinated me. Let's see, it was just before we began to work on—"

"Miss DuBarry." In a low voice directly opposed to Gloria's bubbly bright one, Julia interrupted. "There are a lot of things I'd like to talk to you about, a lot of questions I need to ask, but I feel we're both going to be uncomfortable until we get one point in the open."

"Really?"

The only thing Julia had been sure of that morning was that she would not play games. "Eve told me everything."

"Everything?" The smile stayed in place, but beneath the desk Gloria's fingers twisted together. "About?"

"Michael Torrent."

Gloria blinked twice before her expression settled into pleasant lines. If the director had ordered mild surprise and polite confusion, the actress would have nailed the first take. "Michael? Well, naturally, as he was her first husband, she would have discussed him with you."

Julia realized Gloria was a much more skilled actress than she'd ever been given credit for. "I know about the affair," she said flatly. "About the clinic in France."

"I'm afraid I'm not following you."

Julia picked up her briefcase to drop it on the dainty desk. "Open it," she said. "Look through it. No hidden cameras, no concealed mikes. Off the record, Miss DuBarry. Only you and me, and you have my word that anything you want kept in this room stays in this room."

Though shaken, she clung to the defense of ignorance. "You'll forgive my confusion, Miss Summers, but I thought you were here to discuss Eve for her book."

Anger, barely banked, flared again. Julia got to her feet and snatched the briefcase. "You know exactly why I'm here. If you're going to sit there and play the baffled hostess, we're wasting time." She started for the door.

"Wait." Indecision was its own agony. If Julia left now, this way, God knew how far the story would spread. And yet . . . and yet how could she be sure it hadn't already gone too far. "Why should I trust you?"

Julia searched for calm but couldn't find it. "I was seventeen when I found myself pregnant, unmarried, and alone. I'd be the last person to condemn any woman for facing that and making a choice."

Gloria's lips began to tremble. The freckles that had made her America's darling stood out in relief against her chalky skin. "She had no right."

"Maybe not." Julia came back to the chair, set her briefcase aside. "Her reasons for telling me were personal."

"Naturally, you'd defend her."

Julia stiffened. "Why?"

"You want to write the book."

"Yes," Julia said slowly. "I want to write the book." Need to write it. "But I'm not defending her. I'm only telling you what I know. She was greatly affected by what you went through. There was nothing vindictive or condemning in the way she related the story to me."

"It wasn't her story to tell," Gloria lifted her quavering chin. "Nor is it yours."

"Perhaps not. Eve felt . . ." Julia fumbled. Why did it matter what Eve felt? "Going through that with you altered her life, subsequent decisions she made."

The decision was me, she remembered. She was there, feeling all that pain, because of the misery Gloria had experienced thirty years before.

"What happened to you went beyond that clinic in France," Julia continued. "Because she stood by you through it, it changed her. Because . . . because it changed her, the lives of other people were changed as well."

Me, my parents. Brandon. When emotions threatened to choke her, she took two deep breaths. "It connects us, Miss DuBarry, in ways I can't begin to explain yet. That's why she told me. That's why she needed to tell me."

But Gloria couldn't see beyond the insular world she'd built so carefully. The world she saw tumbling around her shoulders. "What are you going to print?"

"I don't know. I really don't."

"I won't talk to you. I won't let you ruin my life."

Julia shook her head as she rose. She needed air. She needed to get out of that crowded room into the air, where she could think. "Believe me, that's the last thing I want to do."

"I'll stop you." Gloria sprang to her feet, shooting her chair back into the tangle of cats so that they shrieked in annoyance. "I'll find a way to stop you."

Had she already tried? Julia wondered. "I'm not your problem," she said softly and escaped.

But Eve was, Gloria thought as she crumpled back into her chair. Eve was.

◆ ◆ ◆ ◆

DRAKE FIGURED he'd given Eve enough time to cool off. After all, they were blood.

Right, he thought as he carried the dozen roses up to the door. He fixed on a charming smile, apologetic at the edges, and knocked.

Travers opened the door, took one look, and scowled. "She's busy today."

Interfering bitch, he thought, but chuckled and slipped inside. "Never too busy for me. Is she upstairs?"

"That's right." Travers couldn't prevent the smug smile. "With her lawyer. You want to wait, you wait in the parlor. And don't try slipping anything into your pockets. I'm on to you."

He didn't have the energy to be insulted. The wind had gone out of him at the word "lawyer." Travers left him standing stunned in the hallway, roses dripping out of his arms.

Lawyer. His fingers tightened involuntarily, but he didn't even feel the pierce of thorns. She was changing her fucking will. The cold-blooded bitch was cutting him out.

She wouldn't get away with it. Fury and fear sliced through him. He was halfway up the stairs at a dead run before he got himself under control.

This wasn't the way. Leaning against the banister, he took long, deep breaths. If he broke in there shouting, he'd only seal his fate. He wasn't going to let those millions slip through his fingers in blind anger. He'd earned them, by Christ, and he intended to enjoy them.

There was blood on his thumb. Absently he stuck it into his mouth to suck it clean. What was needed was charm, apologies, a few sincere promises. He ran a hand over his hair to tidy it as he debated whether to go up or wait downstairs.

Before he'd made up his mind which would be the most effective, Greenburg started down toward him. The lawyer's face was impassive, though the shadows under his eyes told of a lost night's sleep.

"Mr. Greenburg," Drake said.

The lawyer flicked his gaze over the flowers, up to Drake's face. His brow lifted briefly in speculation before he nodded and continued down. Stuffy old fart, Drake thought, and tried to pretend his insides weren't shaking. He checked his hair again, the knot of his tie, then started up with his best penitent expression on his face.

Outside Eve's office he straightened his shoulders. It wouldn't do to look too beaten. She'd have no respect for him if he crawled. He knocked quietly. When his knock went unanswered, he tried again.

"Eve." His voice held a gentle thread of remorse. "Eve, I'd like to—" He turned the knob. Locked. Forcing himself to be patient, he tried again. "Eve, it's Drake. I'd like to apologize. You know how much you mean to me, and I can't stand having this rift between us."

He wanted to kick the fucking door down and strangle her.

"I just want to find a way to make it all up to you. Not only the money—and I'm going to pay back every penny—but everything I said and did. If you'd only . . ."

He heard a door open, close quietly, down the hall. He turned hopefully, blinking a few tears into his eyes. Then he nearly ground his teeth when he saw Nina.

"Drake." Embarrassment shimmered off her in waves. "I'm sorry. Eve wanted me to tell you . . . She's awfully busy this morning."

"I'll only take up a few minutes."

"I'm afraid—Drake, I'm sorry, really, she just won't see you. At least not now."

He struggled to coat charm over anger. "Nina, can't you talk to her for me? She'll listen to you."

"Not this time." She put a comforting hand on his. "Actually, this isn't the time to try to mend fences. She had a disturbing night."

"She had her lawyer here."

"Yes, well . . ." Nina looked away, and missed the flash of venom in his eyes. "You know I can't discuss her private business. But if you'd take my advice, wait a couple of days longer. She isn't in a reasonable mood. I'll do what I can, when I can."

He thrust the roses into her arms. "Tell her I'll be back. That I'm not giving up."

He strode away. He'd be back all right, he promised himself. And he wouldn't give her a choice.

Nina waited until she heard the door slam before she knocked. "He's gone, Eve." Moments later she heard the lock click open, and entered.

"I'm sorry to dump the dirty work on you, Nina." Eve was already hurrying back to her desk. "I don't have the time or tolerance for him today."

"He left you these."

Eve glanced briefly at the roses. "Do whatever you like with them. Is Julia back yet?"

"No, I'm sorry."

"All right, all right." She waved that away. There was plenty to do before she spoke with her daughter again. "I want you to hold my calls, unless it's Julia. Or Paul. I don't want to be disturbed for at least an hour. Make it two."

"I need to talk to you myself."

"I'm sorry, darling, this isn't the time."

Nina looked at the flowers she held, then laid them on the desk. Near the edge was a stack of audio tapes. "You're making a mistake."

"If I am, it's mine to make." Impatient, she glanced up. "I've made my decision. If you want to hash it through, we will. But not now."

"The longer this goes on, the harder it will be to put things right again."

"I'm doing my damnedest to put things right." She crossed over to check the video camera she'd set on a tripod. "Two hours, Nina."

"All right." She left the flowers scattered over the desk like blood.

Chapter Twenty-Six

••••

$\mathcal{P}$AUL WAS SO IMMERSED in the scene he was writing, he didn't hear the phone ring; his machine picked up the call. But he heard Julia's voice.

"Paul, it's Julia. I just wanted—"

"Hi."

"Oh." Her thoughts scrambled. "You *are* there."

He glanced back at the screen of his word processor, at the cursor impatiently blinking. "More or less." Deliberately, he pushed back from the desk, taking the cordless phone with him as he walked out of the office and onto the circular deck. "Did you get some more sleep?"

"I . . ." She couldn't lie to him, even though she knew the only reason he'd left her was that she'd agreed to stay in bed through the morning without answering the phone. "Actually, I went ahead with the interview."

"You—" She winced as his anger erupted through the telephone line. "Goddamn, Julia, you promised to stay home. You had no business going out alone."

"I didn't promise, exactly, and I—"

"Close enough." He shifted the phone to his other ear and dragged a hand through his hair. "Where are you?"

"I'm in a phone booth in the Beverly Hills Hotel."

"I'm on my way."

"No. Dammit, Paul, stop playing Sir Gallahad a minute and listen. Just listen to me." She pressed her fingers to her eyes, hoping to dull the headache that worked behind them. "I'm perfectly all right. I'm in a public place."

"You're being stupid."

"All right, I'm being stupid." Eyes closed, she leaned her head back against the wall of the booth. She hadn't been able to shut the door, simply hadn't been able to pull it to and shut herself in the glass box. It forced her to keep her voice low. "Paul, I had to get out. I felt trapped in there. And I thought, I hoped, if I talked to Gloria, I'd get a clearer picture for myself."

Swallowing another oath, he rested a hip on the rail. Behind him he could hear the rush and tumble of waves against sand. "And did you?"

"Hell, I don't know. But I do know I have to talk to Eve again. I need a little more time to myself, then I'm going to go back and try."

"Do you want me to be there?"

"Would you . . ." She cleared her throat. "Would you wait until I call? CeeCee's taking Brandon to her place after school . . . to give me time to talk with Eve. I don't even know what I'm going to say, or how I'm going to say it. But if I knew I could call you when it's done, it would be easier."

"I'll be waiting. Jules, I love you."

"I know. Don't worry about me. I'm going to work it out."

"We're going to work it out," he corrected her.

After she hung up, she stayed where she was a moment. She wasn't sure she could go back yet, face Eve. There was still too much anger, too much hurt. How much time it would take to ease either of those emotions was uncertain.

Slowly, she walked back through the lobby, back outside, where the air was beginning to thicken with afternoon heat.

Like a shadow, the man she would have recognized from the airport, trailed behind her.

◆ ◆ ◆ ◆

DRAKE DECIDED he was finished with fucking around. No more Mr. Nice Guy. He was riled up enough to stand on the roof of his car without worrying about scratching the spiffy red paint. He didn't give more than a passing thought to ripping his Savile Row suit as he scrambled, awkwardly, on the wall of Eve's estate.

She thought he was stupid, he reflected grimly as he scraped his palms on stones. But he wasn't stupid. He'd been smart enough to detour through the house on his way out to switch off the main power of the security system.

Thinking ahead—that's right, he was thinking ahead. To his future. His belt buckle clinked against stone as he bellied his way over the wall. She couldn't have her goddamn secretary give him the old heave-ho. She was going to listen to what he had to say, and she was going to understand he meant business.

He landed with a grunt, his left ankle giving way so that he tumbled back into a hedge of Russian olives. The thorns raked over the back of his hands as he fought his way clear to his knees.

He was sweating hard, breathing hard. She wasn't going to cut him out. That one certainty was in his mind as he pushed himself up to limp toward the putting green. He was going to bring that single point home to her. With a vengeance.

♦ ♦ ♦ ♦

THE MAN shadowing Julia spotted the Porsche. He was circling the estate after watching Julia turn through the gates. He'd decided to spend the rest of the afternoon staked out down the block, in case she came out again.

It was a boring job, but the pay was good. A man tolerated a lot of inconveniences, like heat, tedium, and pissing in a plastic bottle, for six hundred a day.

When he recognized the Porsche, natural curiosity had him pulling up behind it. It was locked up tight, and was clean as a whistle except for a couple of scuff marks on the roof. Grinning, he hopped up and peered over the wall.

He was just in time to see Drake hobbling between the green and the tennis courts.

It took him only a moment to decide to hop the wall. When opportunity knocked, a smart man opened the door. He was bound to find out more inside than out. And the more he found out, the more he got paid.

♦ ♦ ♦ ♦

JULIA PULLED through the gates just as Gloria's Mercedes shot out. Without sparing her a glance, Gloria punched the gas and had her wheels screaming on asphalt.

"Nearly took off her bumper," Joe called out. He shook his head smiling through the window at Julia. "That lady drives worse than my teenager."

"She looked upset."

"Looked the same when she got here."

"Was she here long?"

"Nah." He worked a cherry Life Saver out of the roll, offered it to Julia, and at her murmured refusal popped it into his mouth. "Fifteen minutes maybe. People been coming and going all morning. I'da made a fortune if I was charging toll."

Because she knew he expected a smile, Julia accommodated him. "Is anyone with Eve now?"

"Don't think so."

"Thanks, Joe."

"No problem. You have a good day now."

Julia drove slowly, trying to decide whether to make the turn for the main house, or go on. She let instinct take her and followed the route to the guest house. She wasn't ready, she admitted. She needed a little more time, a little more space.

The moment she got out of the car, she turned toward the gardens, lost herself in them. Behind her a curtain twitched open, then back into place.

It was an indulgence, but only a small one, to sit on a stone bench and let her mind empty. With her eyes closed, she could absorb the sounds and smells of the garden. The low hum of bees, the rustle of birds among lush leaves. Oleander, jasmine, lilac, all those sweet fragrances mixed with the richer, deeper scent of earth freshly watered.

She'd always loved flowers. In the years she'd lived in Manhattan, she'd put geraniums on the windowsill every spring. Perhaps she'd inherited that love, that need for flowers from Eve. But she didn't want to think about that now.

As the minutes passed, she grew calmer. While her mind drifted, she began to toy with the broach she'd pinned to her jacket that morning. The broach her mother—the only mother she'd ever known—had left her. Justice. Both of her parents had devoted their lives to it. And to her.

She remembered so much—being driven to school on that first terrifying day, being held and rocked. The stories she'd been told at bedtime. The Christmas she'd been given the shiny two-wheeler with the white plastic basket on the front. And the pain, the confusion when divorce had separated the people she loved and depended on most of all. The way they had united in support of her during her pregnancy. How proud they'd been of Brandon; how they'd helped her finish her education. How painful it had been, and still was, to know she had lost both of them.

But nothing could dim her memories, or her emotions. Maybe that's what she'd been most afraid of. Afraid that if she'd known the circumstances of her birth, it would have diminished somehow that connection with the people who had raised her.

That wasn't going to happen. Steadier, she rose again. No matter what was said, no matter what transpired between her and Eve, nothing could change that bond.

She would always be Julia Summers.

Now it was time to face the rest of her heritage.

She started back to the guest house. Eve could come to her there, where they could have complete privacy. She stopped at the door to search through her bag for her keys. When was she going to learn not to drop them so carelessly into the black hole of her purse? When her fingers closed over them, she gave a little sigh of satisfaction. Her mind sketched out a vague plan as she unlocked the door.

She would treat herself to a glass of white wine, marinate some chicken for dinner, then call Eve. She wouldn't plan the conversation at all, but let it happen naturally. After it was over, she would call Paul. She could tell him everything, knowing he would help her sort it out.

Maybe they could take Brandon away for the weekend, just to relax, just to be together. It might be healthy to put a little distance between herself and Eve. After dropping her briefcase and purse on a chair, she started to turn toward the kitchen.

It was then Julia saw her.

She could only stare. Not even scream. It wasn't possible to scream when she'd stopped breathing. It passed hazily through her mind that it must be a play. Surely the curtain would come down any second, then Eve would smile that dazzling smile and take her bows.

But she wasn't smiling, or standing. She was sprawled on the floor, her magnificent body turned awkwardly on its side. Her pale face was propped on one outstretched arm, as if she'd settled herself down for a lazy nap. But her eyes were open. Wide and unblinking, their zest and passion drained.

Seeping darkly into the pretty rug in front of the low hearth was the blood that dripped from the gaping wound at the base of her skull.

"Eve." Julia took one stumbling step forward, then dropped to her knees to take Eve's cold hand in hers. "Eve, no." Frantic, she tried to lift her, to force the limp body to its feet. Blood soaked her shirt, smeared her jacket.

Then she screamed.

On her wild rush to the phone, she tripped. Still reeling with shock, she bent down to pick up the brass poker that lay on the floor. Blood glistened wetly on it. With a sound of revulsion, she tossed it aside. Her fingers trembled so badly she was sobbing by the time she managed to dial 911.

"I need help." Saying the words had her stomach heaving into her throat. She fought it back. "Please, I think she's dead. You have to help." Breath hitching, she listened to the dispatcher's soothing voice and instructions. "Just come," Julia demanded. "Come quickly." She forced out the address, then jangled the phone back onto the hook. Before she had time to think, she was dialing again. "Paul. I need you."

She couldn't say any more. As his voice buzzed through the receiver, she dropped the phone to crawl back to Eve. To take her hand.

♦ ♦ ♦ ♦

THERE WERE uniformed police at the gate when Paul got there. But he already knew. Unable to contact Julia again on the car phone while he'd raced from Malibu, he'd finally reached a hysterical maid at the main house.

Eve was dead.

He'd told himself it was a mistake, some kind of horrible joke. But his gut had known differently. All through the long, frustrating drive he'd fought to ignore that empty, clutching feeling in the pit of his stomach, that dry burning in his throat. The minute he pulled up at the gate, he'd known it was hopeless.

"I'm sorry, sir." The cop moved over to speak through the window of Paul's car. "No one's allowed through."

"I'm Paul Winthrop," he said flatly. "Eve Benedict's stepson."

With a nod, the cop turned away and pulled a walkie-talkie from his belt. After a brief conversation, he signaled the gate.

"Please drive directly to the guest house." He slid into the passenger's seat. "I'll have to go with you."

Paul said nothing, only started up the drive he'd cruised along countless times. He spotted more uniformed police walking over the estate slowly, fanned out like a search team. Searching for what? he wondered. For whom?

There were more cars, still more police surrounding the guest house. The air buzzed with the squawking from the radios. It rang with weeping. Travers was slumped onto the grass, sobbing into the apron she held to her face. And Nina, her arms around the housekeeper, her own face damp with tears, blank with shock.

Paul got out of the car and took one step toward the house before the cop stopped him.

"I'm sorry, Mr. Winthrop, you can't go in."

"I want to see her."

"Only official personnel allowed on the crime scene."

He knew the drill, goddammit, knew it every bit as well as this snot-nosed cop who'd barely begun to shave. Turning, he frosted the young officer with a single glance.

"I want to see her."

"Look, I'll, ah, check, but you're going to have to wait until the coroner gives the okay."

Paul yanked out a cigar. He needed something to take the taste of grief and waste out of his mouth. "Who's in charge here?"

"Lieutenant Needlemeyer."

"Where is he?"

"Around in back. Hey," he said as Paul started around. "He's conducting an investigation."

"He'll see me."

They were on the terrace, seated at the cheerful table, surrounded by flowers. Paul's gaze passed over Needlemeyer briefly, locked on Julia. Ice. Her face was so clear, so pale, so cold. She was gripping a glass in both hands, her fingers so tightly molded to it, they might have been glued.

And there was blood. On her skirt, on her jacket. Terror ripped through his grief.

"Julia."

Her nerves were stretched so tight, the sound of her name had her leaping up. The glass flew out of her hands to shatter on the tiles. For an instant she swayed as the air went thick and gray. Then she was racing toward him.

"Paul. Oh, God, Paul." The trembling started again the moment his arms came around her. "Eve" was all she could say. And again. "Eve."

"Are you hurt?" He wanted to yank her back, to see for himself, but couldn't force his arms to loosen their grip. "Tell me if you're hurt."

She shook her head, gulping in air. Control. She had to take back some control now or she'd never find it again. "She was in the house when I got home. In the house, on the floor. I found her on the floor. Paul, I'm sorry. I'm so sorry."

Paul looked over her shoulder. Needlemeyer hadn't moved, but sat quietly, watching. "Do you have to do this now?" Paul demanded.

"Always the best time."

They knew each other, had known each other for more than eight years, and had become friends through Paul's research.

Frank T. Needlemeyer had never wanted to be anything but a cop. He'd never looked like anything but a graduate student—one who majored in party. Paul knew he was nearly forty, but his baby face showed no sign of age. Professionally, he had seen just about all the ugliness humanity had to offer. Personally, he'd weathered two miserable marriages. He'd come through it without a line, without a gray hair, and with the stubborn confidence that things could be made right if you kept hacking away at wrong.

And because they knew each other, Frank understood how much Eve Benedict had meant to Paul. "She was a hell of a woman, Paul. I'm sorry."

"Yeah." He wasn't ready for sympathy, not yet. "I need to see her."

Frank nodded. "I'll arrange it." Then let out a quiet breath. Obviously the woman Paul had told him about the last time they'd tossed back a few was Julia Summers. How had he described her? Frank flipped through his memory of Paul, tipping back a long-neck beer, grinning.

"She's stubborn, likes to be in control. Probably comes from having to raise a kid on her own. Got a great laugh—but she doesn't laugh enough. Irritates the hell out of me. I think I'm crazy about her."

"Yeah, yeah." Bleary with drink, Frank had grinned back. "But I want to hear about her body. Start with her legs."

"Amazing. Absolutely amazing."

Frank had already noted Paul had been right about those legs. But right now it looked as if Julia Summers's legs weren't going to hold her up for long. "Would you sit down, Miss Summers? If you don't have any objection, Paul can stay while we talk."

"No, I . . . please." She gripped Paul's hand.

"I'm not going anywhere." He took the seat beside her.

"Okay, now we're going to start right at the beginning. Do you want some more water?"

She shook her head. More than anything, she wanted to get this over with.

"What time did you get home?"

"I don't know." She took a long, steadying breath. "Joe. Joe at the gate might remember. I'd had an appointment this morning with Gloria DuBarry. After, I drove around . . ."

"You called me about noon," Paul prompted her. "From the BHH."

"Yes, I called you, then I drove around some more."

"Do you drive around like that often?" Frank asked.

"I had things on my mind."

Frank watched the look pass between her and Paul, and waited.

"I got here just when Gloria was leaving, and—"

"Miss DuBarry was here?" Frank interrupted.

"Yes, I guess she was here to . . . to see Eve. She was pulling out of the gate as I drove up. I talked to Joe for a few minutes, then I parked my car in front of the house. I didn't want to go in yet. I . . . ." She dropped her hands into her lap, gripped them together. Saying nothing, Paul covered them with his own. "I walked to the gardens and sat on a bench. I don't know how long. Then I went to the house."

"Which way did you go in?"

"The front. I unlocked the front door." When her voice broke, she pressed her hand to her mouth. "I was going to get some wine, going to marinate some chicken for dinner. And then I saw her."

"Go on."

"She was lying on the rug. And the blood was . . . I think I went to her, tried to wake her up. But she . . ."

"Your call to 911 came in at one twenty-two."

Julia shuddered once, then settled. "I called 911, then I called Paul."

"What did you do then?"

She looked away, away from him, away from the house. There were butterflies floating above the columbine. "I sat with her until they came."

"Miss Summers, do you know why Miss Benedict would have been in the guest house?"

"Waiting for me. I—we were working on the book."

"Her biography," Frank said with a nod. "During the course of time you've been working with her, did Miss Benedict indicate to you that someone might wish her harm?"

"There were a lot of people who were unhappy about the book. Eve knew things." She stared down at her hands, then into his eyes. "I have tapes, Lieutenant, tapes of my interviews with Eve."

"I'd appreciate it if you'd let me have them."

"They're inside." In a quick, convulsive movement her fingers tightened on Paul's. "There's more."

She told him about the notes, about the break-in, the theft, the plane. As she talked, Frank took short, scattered notes and kept his eyes on her face. This was a lady, he thought, about to snap and determined not to.

"Why wasn't the break-in reported?"

"Eve wanted to handle it herself. Later, she told me that it had been Drake—her nephew Drake Morrison—and that she'd dealt with him."

Frank jotted down the initials D.M., circled them. "I'll need the notes."

"I have them—with the tapes—in the safe."

His brow lifted slightly, his own sign of interest. "I know this is tough on you, Miss Summers, and there isn't a hell of a lot I can do to make it easier." Out of the corner of his eye he saw one of the uniforms come to the kitchen door and signal. "After you've had a chance to settle a bit, I'll need you to come down, give a formal statement. I'd also like to take your prints."

"Christ, Frank."

He shot Paul a look. "It's standard. We need to match any of the prints we come up with on the scene. Pretty obvious yours'll be there, Miss Summers. Eliminating them will help."

"It's all right. Whatever it takes, I'll do. You need to know . . ." She fought grimly to keep her breath from hitching. "She was more than a subject to me. Much more than that, Lieutenant. Eve Benedict was my mother."

♦ ♦ ♦ ♦

*W*HAT A FUCKING MESS.

Frank wasn't thinking about the crime scene. He'd been on too many to allow himself to be overly affected by the aftermath of violent death. He hated murder, despised it as the darkest of sins. But he was a cop, first and last, and it wasn't his job to philosophize. It was his job to find a firm grip on the slippery rope of justice.

It was his friend he was thinking about as he watched Paul stand over the draped body. As he watched him reach down to touch the dead face.

Frank had cleared the room, and the forensic boys weren't too happy. They still had their dusting and vacuuming to do. But there were times you bent the rules. Paul was entitled to a couple of minutes alone with a woman he'd loved for twenty-five years.

He could hear movement upstairs, where he'd sent Julia with a policewoman. She needed to change, to gather up whatever personal items she and her kid would need. No one without a badge would be coming inside this house for some time.

Eve still looked beautiful, Paul reflected. Seeing that helped somehow. Whoever had done this hadn't been able to take her beauty from her.

She was too pale, of course. Too still. Shutting his eyes, he struggled over another raw wave of grief. She wouldn't want that. He could almost hear her laugh, feel her pat his cheek.

"Darling," she would say. "I packed more than enough into one life, so don't shed any tears for me. Now, I expect—hell, I demand that my fans weep copiously and gnash their teeth. The studios should shut down for a goddamn day of mourning. But I want the people I love to get stinking drunk and have one hell of a party."

Gently, he slipped her hand into his, raised it to his lips for the last time. "Bye, gorgeous."

Frank laid a hand on his shoulder. "Come on out back."

With a nod, Paul turned away from her. God knew he needed the air. The moment he stepped onto the terrace, he took a big gulp of it.

"How?" was all he said.

"Blow to the base of the skull. Looks like the fireplace poker. I know it doesn't help much, but the coroner thinks death was instantaneous."

"No, it doesn't help." He stuffed impotent fists into his pockets. "I'm going to need to make arrangements. How soon will you . . . when will you release her to me?"

"I'll let you know. I can't do any better than that. You're going to have to talk to me, officially." He pulled out a cigarette. "I can come to you, or you can come downtown."

"I need to take Julia away from here." He accepted the cigarette Frank offered, leaned into the flame of the match. "She and Brandon will stay with me. She's going to need some time."

"I'll give her what I can, Paul, but you've got to understand. She found the body, she's Eve's long-lost daughter. She knows what's in here." He lifted the bag full of the tapes he'd taken from the safe after Julia had given him the location and combination. "She's the best lead we've got."

"She may be the best lead you've got, but she's hanging together by a very thin thread. Stretch it much more, and it's going to snap. For God's sake, give us a couple of days."

"I'll do what I can." He blew smoke from between his teeth. "It's not going to be easy. Reporters are staking out the place."

"Fuck."

"You said it. I'm going to keep the business of Julia's relationship with Eve under wraps for as long as I can, but that's going to bust loose too. When it does, they'll be on her like fleas." He glanced up as Julia stepped through the doorway. "Get her out of here."

◆ ◆ ◆ ◆

*P*ANTING, Drake shoved through the door, then locked it behind him. Thank Christ, thank Christ, he thought over and over as he rubbed shaking hands over his clammy face. He'd made it home. He was safe.

He needed a drink.

Favoring his ankle, he hobbled through the living room to the bar and snatched a bottle at random. A quick twist of the top and he was drinking Stoli. He shuddered, gulped oxygen, and guzzled some more.

Dead. The queen was dead.

He gave a nervous giggle that ended on a racking sob. How could it have happened? Why had it happened? If he hadn't gotten away before Julia had come back . . .

Didn't matter. He shook even the possibility away, then pressed a hand to his spinning head. The only thing that mattered was that nobody had seen him. As long as he kept calm, played it smart, everything was going to be dandy. Better than dandy. She couldn't have had time to change her will.

He was a rich man. A fucking tycoon. He raised the bottle again in toast, then dropped it to the ground on his rush to the bathroom. Clinging to the john, he vomited up sickness and fear.

◆ ◆ ◆ ◆

*M*AGGIE CASTLE HEARD the news in one of the coldest ways—a phone call from a reporter asking for reaction and comment.

"You slimy son of a bitch," she began, leaning forward in her buttery leather swivel chair. "Don't you know I can have your ass for pulling a stunt like this." She slammed the phone down with relish. With a pile of scripts to review, contracts to revise, and phone calls to return, she didn't have time for warped jokes.

"Fucking jerk," she said mildly, and eyed the phone with dislike. Her stomach rumbled, distracting her, and she pressed a calming hand to it. Starving to death, she thought. She was starving to death and would have cheerfully killed for a big fat roast beef on rye. But she was going to fit into that size ten she'd plunked down three thousand for, and the Oscars were less than a week away.

She dealt out a trio of eight-by-ten glossies like playing cards and studied the sultry faces. She had to decide which one to send to read for a plum part in a new feature under development.

Tailor-made for Eve, she mused. Sighed. If Eve had been twenty-five years younger. The hell of it was, even Eve Benedict couldn't be young forever.

Maggie barely glanced up as her door opened. "What is it, Sheila?"

"Ms. Castle . . ." Sheila stood in the doorway, one hand gripping the knob, the other braced on the jamb. "Oh, God, Ms. Castle."

The trembling tone had Maggie's head jerking up. Her half glasses slid down her nose. "What? What is it?"

"Eve Benedict . . . She's been murdered."

"That's bullshit." The anger came first so that she reared out of her chair. "If that asshole's called again—"

"The radio," Sheila managed to say, fumbling in her skirt pocket for a tissue. "It just came over the radio."

Still fueled by fury, Maggie snatched up the remote and aimed it at the television. By the time she'd flipped the channels twice, she hit the bulletin.

"Hollywood, and the world, is shocked this afternoon by the death of Eve Benedict. The perpetually glamorous star of dozens of films was found on her estate, the apparent victim of homicide."

Eyes glued to the set, Maggie lowered herself slowly into her chair. "Eve," she whispered. "Oh, God, Eve."

♦ ♦ ♦ ♦

LOCKED IN his office miles away, Michael Delrickio stared at the television, dully watching the pictures flicker. Eve at twenty, bright, vivid. At thirty, sultry, sensational.

He didn't move. He didn't speak.

Gone. Wasted, finished. He could have given her everything. Including life. If she'd loved him enough, if she'd believed in him, trusted him, he could have stopped it. Instead, she had scorned him, defied him, detested him. So she was dead. And even in death she could ruin him.

♦ ♦ ♦ ♦

GLORIA LAY in her darkened bedroom, a chilled gel mask over her swollen eyes. The Valium wasn't helping. She didn't think anything would. No pills, no ploys, no prayers would ever make things right again.

Eve had been her closest friend. She hated that she couldn't erase the memories they'd shared, the value of their woman-to-woman intimacy.

Of course she'd been hurt, angry, fearful. But she'd never wanted Eve dead. She'd never wanted it to end like this.

But Eve was dead. She was gone. Beneath the soothing mask, tears streamed. Gloria wondered what would become of her now.

♦ ♦ ♦ ♦

IN HIS LIBRARY, surrounded by the books he'd loved and collected over a lifetime, Victor stared at a sealed bottle of Irish Mist. Whiskey, he thought, the way the Irish made it, was the best way to get drunk.

He wanted to get drunk, so drunk he wouldn't be able to think, or feel, or breathe. How long could he stay that way? he wondered. One night, one week, one year? Could he stay that way long enough so that when he came to himself again, the pain would be over?

There would never be enough whiskey, there would never be enough time for that. If he was cursed to survive another ten years, he'd never outlive the pain.

Eve. Only Eve could stop the pain. And he would never hold her again, never taste her, never laugh with her or sit quietly in the garden and just be with her.

It wasn't supposed to be this way. In his heart he knew it could have been changed. Like a bad script, poorly written, the ending could have been revised.

She'd left him, and this time there could be no reconciliation, no compromise, no promises. Now all he had were memories, and empty days and nights to relive them.

Victor lifted the bottle, flung it against the wall, where it exploded. Choking against the ripe smell of whiskey, he covered his face with his hands and cursed Eve with all his heart.

♦ ♦ ♦ ♦

ANTHONY KINCADE GLOATED. He rejoiced. He laughed out loud. As he greedily stuffed pâté-smeared crackers into his mouth, he kept his gaze fixed on the television. Each time a channel segued back to regular programming, he switched, searching for a fresh bulletin, a recap of the news.

The bitch was dead, and nothing could have made him happier. It was only a matter of time now before he dealt with the Summers woman and got back the tapes Eve had taunted him with.

His reputation, his money, his freedom, they were safe now. Eve had gotten exactly what she'd deserved.

He only hoped she'd suffered.

♦ ♦ ♦ ♦

*L*YLE DIDN'T KNOW what the hell to think. He was too scared to bother. The way he figured it, Delrickio had iced Eve—and he was connected to Delrickio. Sure, he'd only been doing some snooping, but men like Delrickio never went down. They made sure someone went down for them.

He could run, but he was damn sure he couldn't hide. He didn't figure his alibi about sleeping off a fat joint all afternoon would hold much water with the cops.

Goddamn, why had the broad gone and gotten herself wasted now? If she'd waited a few weeks, he'd have been long gone, his pockets fat, his road clear. Just his luck. His fucking luck.

Naked, he sat on the bed, dangling a beer between his knees. He'd have to come up with a tighter alibi. He drew on the beer, racked his poor brain, then grinned. He had the five big ones Delrickio had planted on him. If he couldn't buy an alibi with a couple of grand—and his famous, tireless dick, life wasn't worth living.

♦ ♦ ♦ ♦

*T*RAVERS WOULDN'T BE comforted. Nina tried, but the housekeeper wouldn't eat, she wouldn't rest, she wouldn't take a sedative. She simply sat on the terrace, looking out at the garden. She wouldn't even come inside, no matter how Nina coaxed or prodded.

The police had been all through the house, poking into drawers, running their cop hands over Eve's personal belongings. Contaminating everything.

Through her own swollen, red-rimmed eyes, Nina watched her. Did the woman think she was the only one in pain? Did she think she was the only one who was sick and scared and uncertain?

Nina spun away from the terrace doors. Christ, she needed someone to talk to, someone to hold. She could pick up the phone, dial one of dozens of numbers, but everyone she was close to would ask about Eve. After all, Nina Soloman's life had begun the day Eve Benedict had taken her in.

Now Eve was gone, and she had no one. Nothing. How could it be that one person should have such an affect on another? It wasn't right. It wasn't fair.

She walked over to the bar and fixed herself a stiff bourbon. She grimaced at the taste. It had been years since she'd drunk anything stronger than white wine.

But the taste didn't bring back ugly memories. Instead, it soothed and strengthened. She drank again. She was going to need all the strength she could muster to get through the next few weeks. Or the rest of her life.

Tonight. She would concentrate on getting through just this one night.

How was she going to sleep here, in this big house, knowing that Eve's bedroom was down the hall?

She could go to a hotel—but she knew that wouldn't be right. She would stay, she would get through the first night. Then she would think about the next. And the next.

♦ ♦ ♦ ♦

When Julia fought off the weight of the sedative, it was after midnight. There was no disorientation, no instant when she convinced herself it had all been some terrible dream.

She knew, the moment she regained consciousness, where she was, and what had happened.

She was in Paul's bed. And Eve was dead.

Aching, she turned, wanting to feel him, to press herself against warmth and life. But the space beside her was empty.

She pushed herself up and out of bed, though her body felt too light, her head too hazy.

She remembered that they had driven over to pick Brandon up—at her insistence. She couldn't have stood it if he'd heard from the television. Still, she hadn't been able to tell him everything, only that there'd been an accident—a pitiful euphemism for murder—and that Eve had been killed.

He'd cried a little, his natural emotion for a woman who had been kind to him. Julia wondered how and when she would find the way to tell him that woman had been his grandmother.

But that was for later. Brandon was sleeping, safe. Perhaps a little sad, but safe. Paul was not.

She found him on the deck, looking out to the sea that plunged in black waves onto black sand. For a moment she thought her heart would break. He was silhouetted in the moonlight, his hands thrust deep into the pockets of the jeans he must have pulled on when he'd left her alone in bed.

She didn't have to see his face, his eyes. She didn't have to hear his voice. She could feel his grief.

Uncertain if she would help him more by going to him, or staying away, she stood where she was.

He knew she was there. From the moment she'd stepped into the doorway, her scent had carried to him. And her sorrow. For most of the night he'd been doing what needed to be done, automatically. Making the necessary calls, screening others. Eating the soup she'd insisted on heating, browbeating her into taking the pills that would help her rest.

Now he didn't even have the strength to sleep.

"When I was fifteen, just before my sixteenth birthday," he began, still watching the water roll dark toward the sand. "Eve taught me to drive. I was here on a visit, and one day she just pointed to her car. A goddamn Mercedes. She said 'Get in, kid. You might as well learn to drive on the right side of the road first.'"

He pulled a cigar from his pocket. The flare of the match etched the misery on his face, then plunged it into shadows again.

"I was terrified, and so excited my feet were shaking on the pedals. For an hour I drove all over Beverly Hills, bucking, stalling out, bumping over curbs. I nearly creamed a Rolls, and she never blinked. Just threw her head back and laughed."

The smoke burned his throat. He threw the cigar over the rail, then leaned on it. "God, I loved her."

"I know." She went to him and put her arms around him.

In silence, they held on to each other, and thought of Eve.

Chapter Twenty-Seven

◆ ◆ ◆ ◆

THE WORLD GRIEVED. Eve would have enjoyed it. She copped the front page of *People* along with a six-page spread.

Nightline dedicated an entire segment to her. Eve Benedict festivals preempted regular programming on nearly every channel. Including cable. The *National Enquirer* was screaming that her spirit haunted the back lot of her old studio. Enterprising street people were selling T-shirts, mugs, and posters faster than they could be manufactured.

One day before the Oscars, and Hollywood was draped in black glitter. How she would have laughed.

Paul tried to bury his grief, imagining her reaction to the tributes—tacky and triumphant. But there were so many things, countless things, that reminded him of her.

And there was Julia.

She moved through each day, doing what needed to be done, her energy constant and practical. Yet there was a haunted desperation in her eyes he couldn't ease. She'd given her statement to Frank, spending hours at the station going over every detail she remembered. Her seamless control had torn only once—the first time Frank had played back one of the tapes. The moment she'd heard Eve's rich, husky voice, she'd bolted to her feet, excused herself, and dashed away to be violently ill in the ladies' room.

After that, she managed to sit through every replay, corroborating the tape with her own notes, adding the date, the circumstance of the interview, the mood, her own interpretation.

And during those three miserable days, she and Brandon had stayed in Malibu while Paul had made arrangements for the funeral.

Eve hadn't wanted the simple. When had she ever? Her instructions had been left for Paul in the hands of her lawyers, and had been crystal-clear. She'd bought the lot—prime real estate, she'd called it—nearly a year before. Just as she'd chosen her own coffin. A gleaming sapphire blue lined in snowy white silk. Even the guest list with predetermined seating arrangements had been included, as if she'd planned the ultimate party.

The music had been chosen, as well as the musicians. Her burial dress had been selected—a glittery emerald evening gown she had never worn in public. Its debut was a grand one.

Of course she'd insisted her hair be styled by Armando.

On the day of her funeral, Eve's public lined the streets. They crowded the entrance of the church, some weeping, some snapping pictures, necks straining as people fought for a glimpse of the mourning famous. Video cameras hummed. Wallets were stolen, and occasionally someone fainted. It was, as she would have appreciated, a production number. Only the crisscrossing spotlights were missing from this particular premiere.

The limos arrived, ponderously disgorging their gilded cast. The rich, the famous, the glamorous, the grieving. The best designers were shown off in basic black.

The crowd gasped and murmured as Gloria DuBarry stepped out, leaning heavily on her husband's sturdy arm. Her Saint Laurent was accented by a heavy veil.

There were more murmurs, and a few chuckles, as Anthony Kincade heaved himself out of a limo, his bulk sausaged obscenely into a black suit.

Travers and Nina passed through the lines buffered by anonymity.

Peter Jackson kept his head down, ignoring the giddy fans who called out his name. He was thinking about the woman he had spent a few sultry nights with, and how she'd looked on a rainy morning.

A cheer went up as Rory Winthrop stepped out. Unsure how to respond, he assisted his wife from the car, then waited for Kenneth to join them on the curb.

"Christ, it's a circus," Lily muttered, wondering if she should turn her back or her best side to the ubiquitous cameras.

"Yes." With a grim smile, Kenneth scanned the crowd, plunging and pressing against the police barricade. "And Eve's still the ringmaster."

Turning from him, Lily supported her husband by slipping a hand through his arm. "Are you all right, darling?"

He could only shake his head. He could smell his wife's exotic perfume, sense the firmness of her guiding arm. The cold shadow of the church seemed to reach out for them with dead hands. "I feel mortal for the first time in my entire life." Before they could climb the stairs, he spotted Victor. There was nothing he could say, no words that would even touch the grief so clear in the other man's eyes. Rory leaned closer to his wife. "Let's get this bloody show started."

Julia knew she could get through it. Knew she had to. She clung to an outer calm, but her insides churned with fear of the ritual. Was this rite to honor the dead or entertain the living? When the limo drew up to the curb, she closed her eyes quickly, tightly. But when Paul reached down for her hand, her fingers were firm and dry. She had a bad moment when she saw Victor at the entrance to the church. His gaze flicked over her, then away.

He didn't know, she thought, and her fingers convulsed into a fist. He didn't know how intimately they had shared the woman they had come to bury.

Too many people, she thought on a flare of panic. There were too many people, all of them too close, and pressing closer. Staring, calling out. She could smell them, the hot flesh, the hot breath, the shimmery energy that came from the combination of grief and vivid excitement.

The trembling began again, and she started to pull back when Paul slipped an arm around her waist. He murmured something, but she couldn't hear it over the buzzing in her ears. There was no air here. She tried to tell him that, but he was sweeping her up the steps and inside.

Now there was music, not the ponderous moan of an organ, but the clear, sweet strains of a violin, melded with the elegant notes of a flute. The church was packed, flowers and people. Yet the thick air seemed to part, to cool. The somber garb of those who had come to Eve's last party was offset by the jungle of blossoms. No funeral wreaths for Eve. Instead, there were oceans of camellias, mountains of roses, sweeps of magnolias heaped like snowdrifts. The scene had both glamour and beauty. At center stage, where she had spent most of her life, was the glossy blue casket.

"How like her," Julia murmured. The panic had fled. Even under the pall of sadness she felt a bright, beautiful admiration. "I wonder that she never tried her hand at directing."

"She just has." It wasn't very difficult to smile. Paul kept his arm around Julia's waist as they began the long walk to the front of the church. He noted tears and solemn eyes, but as many sharp glances, studied poses. Here and there clutches of people were murmuring among themselves. Projects would be discussed, deals would be made. In Hollywood, no opportunity could be missed.

Eve would understand, and approve.

Julia hadn't intended to go up to the coffin, take her last look, say the last good-bye. If it was cowardice, she accepted it. But when she saw Victor staring down at the woman he loved, his big hands clenched, his broad shoulders slumped, she was unable to simply slide into the pew.

"I need to . . ."

Paul only nodded. "Do you want me to go with you?"

"No, I . . . I think I should go alone." The first step away from him was the hardest. Then she took another, and another. When she was beside Victor, she searched her heart. These were the people who had made her, she thought, the woman who slept so beautifully against the white silk. The man who watched her sleep with grief-ravaged eyes. Perhaps she couldn't think of them as parents, but she could feel. Going with her heart, she laid a hand on his.

"She loved you, more than she loved anyone else. One of the last things she told me was how happy you had made her."

His fingers convulsed on Julia's. "I never gave her enough. Never could."

"You gave her more than you realize, Victor. To so many others she was a star, a product, an image. To you she was a woman. *The* woman." She pressed her lips together, hoping what she was doing, what she was saying, was right. "She once told me her only real regret was waiting until after the movie was finished."

He turned then, looking away from Eve to the daughter he didn't know he had. It was then Julia realized she had inherited her father's eyes—that deep, pure gray that could go from smoke to ice as colored by emotion. The knowledge had her taking a quick step back, but his hand was already coming down to cover hers.

"I'm going to miss her, every moment of the rest of my life."

Julia let her fingers link with his and led him to the pew where Paul was waiting.

♦ ♦ ♦ ♦

THE LINE of cars sedately cruising to Forest Hills streamed like a black ribbon for miles. Inside the individual cars some grieved deeply. Others cuddled in the cool lushness of the rented limos mourned in an abstract, general way, as people do when they hear on the late news that a celebrity has died. They mourned the passing of a name, of a face, of a personality. It wasn't an insult to the person behind the face, but a tribute to its impact.

Some were simply grateful to have been included in the guest list. For surely such an event would warrant plenty of print space. This, too, was not an insult. It was simply business.

There were others who grieved not at all, who sat in the silent cave of the big, smooth car holding pleasure in their hearts as dark and shiny as the gleaming paint that glinted in the sunlight.

In some ways, this, too, could be considered a tribute.

But Julia, who stepped out of the car to make the short walk to the gravesite fit none of these categories. She had already buried her parents, already taken that long, difficult step from daughter to orphan. And yet, moving with her with each step, was a deep, dragging ache. Today she would bury another mother, face yet again her own ultimate mortality.

As she stood, smelling grass, earth, and the heavy curtain of flowers, she blocked out the present and let her mind travel back into the past.

Laughing with Eve beside the pool, drinking a little too much wine, speaking much too frankly. How had it been that she had been able to say so much to Eve?

Sweating together as Fritz whipped them into shape. Grunted curses, breathless complaints. The odd intimacy of two half-naked women trapped in the same cage of vanity.

Shared secrets, candid confidences, unwrapped lies. How easy it had been to forge a friendship.

Isn't that what Eve had wanted? Julia asked herself. To ease her into friendship, to make her care, to force her to see Eve as a person, whole, vulnerable. And then . . .

What did it matter? Eve was dead. The rest of the truth, if there was a rest, would never come out.

Julia mourned, even as she wondered if she could ever forgive.

♦ ♦ ♦

"SHIT." Frank scrubbed his hands over his face. His job was pushing at him from all angles. He saw only one route, and it led straight to Julia Summers.

All of his professional life, Frank had relied heavily on instinct. A good gut hunch could guide a cop through the labyrinth of suspects, evidence, procedure. Never in his career could he remember his instincts being so dramatically opposed to the facts.

They were all in front of him, in the fat file he'd been building over the past three days.

Forensic reports, autopsy, the typed and signed statements of the people he or one of the other detectives had interviewed.

And the timing, the goddamn timing couldn't be ignored.

Both the housekeeper and the secretary had seen Eve Benedict a few minutes before one P.M. on the date of the murder. Gloria DuBarry had left moments before, after a short private conversation with Eve. Julia Summers had arrived at the gate at approximately one, had chatted with the guard, then had gone inside. The emergency call from the guest house had been logged in at one twenty-two.

Julia had no alibi for that vital length of time, that vital twenty-two minutes, when, according to the evidence, Eve Benedict had been murdered.

The hook on the brass fireplace poker had impaled the base of her neck. That wound and the blow had resulted in death. Julia Summers's fingerprints were the only ones found on the poker.

All the doors had been locked except the main entrance, which Julia had admitted to opening herself. No keys had been found on Eve's body.

Circumstantial, certainly, but damning enough, even without the addition of the argument described in both statements.

Being told she was Eve Benedict's illegitimate daughter had apparently sent Julia Summers into a wild rage.

"She was screaming, threatening," he read from Travers's statement. "I heard her shouting and came running out. She shoved over the table so that the china broke all over the tiles. Her face was pale as a sheet and she warned Eve not to come near her. Said she could kill her."

Of course, people said that kind of thing all the time, Frank thought, digging at an itch at the back of his neck. It was just their bad luck when somebody died hard on the heels of them using the common little phrase.

Trouble was, he couldn't think about luck. And with the pressure from the governor all the way down to his own captain, Frank couldn't afford to let instinct sway him from the facts.

He was going to have to bring Julia in for questioning.

♦ ♦ ♦ ♦

THE LAWYER CLEARED his throat as he scanned the room. Everything was exactly as Eve had requested it. Greenburg wondered if she could have known when she had demanded he put everything through so quickly that her time would be short.

He pulled himself up. He wasn't a fanciful man. Eve had been in a hurry because she had always been in a hurry. The ferocity with which she had approached this new will was the same she had shown for everything. The changes had certainly been brutally simple. That was another quality Eve could assert when the mood struck.

When he started to speak, everyone in the room fell silent. Even Drake, in the process of pouring another drink, paused. When the statement began with the routine list of bequests to servants and charities, he continued to pour. Over the silence was the sound of liquid hitting crystal.

The personal bequests were specific. To Maggie, Eve left a particular pair of emerald earrings and a triple rope of pearls, along with a Wyeth painting the agent had always admired.

For Rory Winthrop, there was a pair of Dresden candlesticks they had purchased during their first year of marriage, and a volume of Keats.

Gloria began to sob against her husband's shoulder when she heard she had inherited an antique jewelry box.

"We were in Sotheby's, years ago," she said brokenly. Guilt and grief waged a vicious war inside her. "And she outbid me for it. Oh, Marcus."

He murmured to her while Greenburg again cleared his throat and continued.

To Nina she had left a collection of Limoges boxes and ten thousand dollars a year for every year she had been in Eve's employ. To Travers she left a house in Monterey, the same financial bequest, and a trust fund for her son that would see to his medical needs for his lifetime.

To her sister, who hadn't attended the memorial or the reading, Eve left a small block of rental units. Drake was mentioned only in passing, as having received all of his inheritance during her lifetime.

His reaction was predictable, predictable enough to bring grim smiles to some of those seated in the room. He spilled his drink, infusing the room with the smell of expensive whiskey. His gasp of disbelief was accented by the tinkle of ice cubes as they dropped from his glass onto the glossy surface of the bar.

While those in the room watched with varying degrees of interest or disgust, he flew into a rage that traveled the spectrum from swearing, to whining, to babbling, and back to swearing.

"Goddamn bitch." He nearly choked on the air he dragged into his lungs. His face was the unhealthy color of an eraser faded by sunlight. "I gave her years, nearly twenty fucking years of my life. I won't be cut off this way. Not after everything I did for her."

"Did for her?" Maggie gave a hoarse laugh. "You never did anything for Eve except lighten her bank account."

He took a step forward, nearly drunk enough to consider hitting a woman in front of witnesses. "All you ever did was leech your fifteen percent. I was family. If you think you're going to walk out of here with emeralds or anything else while I get nothing—"

"Mr. Morrison," the attorney interrupted. "You are, of course, free to contest the will—"

"Fucking-a right."

"However," he continued with unruffled dignity. "I should tell you that Miss Benedict discussed her wishes with me quite specifically. I also have a copy of a videotape she made, less conventionally stating those wishes. You will find contesting this document very expensive, and less than fruitful. If you wish to do so, you'll still have to wait until I finish with today's procedure. To continue . . ."

There was a bequest for Victor that included her collection of poetry and a small paperweight described as a glass dome enclosing a red sleigh and eight reindeer.

"To Brandon Summers, whom I find charming, I leave the sum of one million dollars for his education and entertainment to be set in trust until his twenty-fifth birthday, when he will be free to do whatever appeals to him with whatever sum remains."

"That's fucking ludicrous," Drake began. "She leaves a million, a goddamn million to some kid? Some snotty brat kid who might as well have come off the street."

Before Julia could speak, Paul had risen. The look on his face had her blood going cold. She wondered how anyone could survive being on the receiving end of that ice-edged glance.

Threats were expected. A quick, nasty fistfight wouldn't have surprised. Hell, it would have been enjoyed. Even Gloria had stopped whimpering to watch. But Paul, his eyes flat and hard and level, spoke only one sentence.

"Don't open your mouth again."

He said it quietly, but no one could have missed the barbed and ready edge beneath the words. When he took his seat again, Greenburg merely nodded, as if Paul had given the correct answer to a particularly thorny question.

"The rest," he read, "including all real and personal property, all assets, all stocks, bonds, revenue, I leave to Paul Winthrop and Julia Summers, to be shared between them in whatever manner they see fit."

Julia heard nothing else. The lawyer's droning voice couldn't penetrate the buzzing in her ears. She could see his mouth move, see his dark, sharp eyes on her face. There was a tingling in her arm, as if it had fallen asleep and the blood was fighting its way back into circulation with its little pinpricks of annoyance. But it was only Paul's hand as he gripped her.

She rose to her feet without being aware. Blindly, her feet reaching for the floor like a drunkard's, she stumbled out of the room and onto the terrace.

There was life there, the vibrant hues from the flowers, the insistently cheerful call of birds. And air. She could pull it into her lungs, feel it stream in, then out again as if it, too, had color and texture and sound. She drew more in, greedily, then felt the stab of pain slice through her stomach.

"Take it easy." Paul's hands were on her shoulders, his voice low and soft in her ear.

"I can't." The voice she heard sounded much too thin, much too wobbly to be hers. "How can I? It isn't right that she should have given me anything."

"She thought it was right."

"You don't know the things I said to her, how I treated her that last night. And beyond—for God's sake, Paul, she owed me nothing."

He caught her chin, forced her to look at him. "I think you're more afraid of what you feel you owe her."

"Mr. Winthrop. Excuse me." Greenburg nodded at both of them. "I realize this is a difficult day for you, for all of us, but there is one more item Miss Benedict asked me to see to for her." He held out a padded envelope. "A copy of the tape she made. Her request was for you, both of you, to view this after the reading of the will."

"Thank you." Paul accepted the bag. "She would have appreciated your . . . efficiency."

"No doubt." The barest wisp of a smile touched his thin face. "She was quite a woman—annoying, demanding, opinionated. I'll miss her." The smile faded as if it had never been. "If you need me for anything, please don't hesitate to call. You may have questions about some of the properties or her portfolio. And when you're ready, there will be some paperwork for you to look over. My condolences."

"I'd like to take Miss Summers home shortly," Paul told him. "But we'll want to go inside and have some privacy when we view this. Could I leave you to—to secure the premises?"

Something twinkled in his eyes that might have been amusement. "It would be a pleasure."

Paul waited until they were alone on the terrace again. Through the glass doors Greenburg had closed at his back came the sounds of heated voices and bitter tears. The old man was going to have his hands full, he thought, then looked at Julia. Her eyes were dry again, her face composed. But her skin was so pale he wondered if his fingers would pass right through it, straight to the grief, if he touched her now.

"It might be best if we went up to Eve's room to take a look at this."

Julia stared at the package he held. Part of her, the part she recognized as a coward, wanted to turn away, to go pick up Brandon and run back east. Couldn't she, if she tried hard enough, convince herself it had all been a dream. From the first phone call, the first meeting with Eve, right up to this moment?

She brought her gaze up, met his eyes. Then he would have been a dream as well. Then he would have to be a dream as well, everything they'd shared and built. All those fragile new hopes would be blown away like dust.

"All right."

"Give me a minute." He pressed the tape into her hands. "Go on in around the other side of the house. I'll be right there."

It wasn't easy to go in, to open the door and enter the room where Eve had slept and loved. It smelled of flowers, flowers and polish, and that smoldering woman scent Eve had always carried with her.

Travers had tidied, of course. Compelled, Julia trailed her fingers over the thick satin of the sapphire bedspread. She'd chosen a coffin of the same color, Julia remembered, snatching her hand back. Was that for irony, or for comfort?

Closing her eyes, she rested her brow against the cool wood of the carved bedpost. For a moment, just a moment, she let herself feel.

No, it wasn't death that surrounded her here. Only the memories of life.

When Paul joined her, he didn't speak. Over the past few days he had watched her grow more and more delicate. His own grief was like a small wild animal in his gut that kept clawing and chewing and ripping. Whatever form Julia's grief took, it was slowly, insidiously sucking the life and strength from her. He poured them both a brandy, and when he spoke, his voice was deliberately cool and detached.

"You'll have to snap out of it soon, Jules. You're not doing yourself or Brandon any good walking around in a trance."

"I'm fine." She took the snifter, then passed it from hand to hand. "I want it over. All the way over. Once the press gets a hold of the terms of the will—"

"We'll deal with it."

"I didn't want her money, Paul, or her property, or—"

"Her love," he finished. He set his glass aside to pick up the envelope. "The thing about Eve is that she always insisted on having the last word. You're stuck with all of them."

Her fingers whitened on the bowl of the glass. "Do you expect that since I've known for a week that she was my mother, I should feel an obligation, an immediate bond, gratitude? She manipulated my life before I was born, and even now, even when she's gone, she continues to manipulate it."

He ripped the envelope open, slid the tape out. "I don't expect you to feel anything. And if you learned anything about her over the past couple of months, you know that she wouldn't expect you to feel." He shoved the tape into the VCR, keeping his back to her, while the jagged teeth of his own anguish snapped at him. "I can do this alone."

Damn him, she thought, damn him for forcing her to feel this bright flush of shame. Rather than speak, she sat on the pillow-plumped daybed, lifted the brandy to her lips. He joined her, but when he sat, there was much more distance between them than a few inches of cushion.

A flick of the remote, and Eve was filling the screen as she had filled so many others during her life. Misery clamped around Julia's heart like an iron fist.

"Darlings, I can't tell you how delighted I am that you're together.

I'd hoped to do this with a bit more ceremony, and on film, certainly, rather than videotape. Film's so much more flattering."

Eve's rich laugh seeped into the room. On the screen, she reached for a cigarette, then leaned back in her chair. She'd done her own makeup carefully, camouflaging the shadows under her eyes, the strain around her mouth. She wore a fuchsia man-styled shirt with a standing collar. It took Julia only an instant to realize she had been wearing that shirt when she'd been sprawled on the bloody rug.

"This little gesture may become unnecessary if I find the courage to speak to both of you face-to-face. If not, please forgive me for not telling you about my illness. I found the tumor a flaw I wanted to keep to myself. Another one of those lies, Julia. This one not entirely selfish."

"What does she mean?" Julia murmured. "What is she talking about?"

Paul only shook his head, but his body had tensed.

"When I got the diagnosis, prognosis, and all those other *nosises,* I went through all those stages I'm told are quite typical. Denial, anger, grief. You know how I detest being typical. Being told you have less than a year to live, less than that to function, is a humbling experience. I needed to do something to offset that. I needed to celebrate life, I suppose. My life. So I got the idea to do the book. Making clear what I had been, what I had done, not only for the ever-hungry public, but for myself. I wanted my daughter, a part of myself, to tell the story." Her eyes sharpened as she leaned into the camera. "Julia, I know how upset you were when I told you. Believe me, you have every right to hate me. I won't offer excuses. I can only hope that between then and now, when you're watching this, that we've come to some sort of understanding with each other. I didn't know how much you would mean to me. How much Brandon . . ." She shook her head and dragged deep on the cigarette. "I won't become maudlin. I'm counting on there being wailing and gnashing of teeth at the announcement of my death. And by this time there should have been enough of it.

"This time clock in my brain . . ." She smiled a little as she rubbed her fingers over her temple. "Sometimes I swear I can hear it ticking away. It forced me to face my mortality, my mistakes, and my responsibilities. I'm determined not to leave this world with regrets. If we haven't mended our fences, Julia, then at least I have the comfort of knowing we were friends for a time. And I also know you'll write the book. If you've inherited any of my stubbornness, you may not speak to me again, so I've taken the precaution of making the other tapes. I'm quite sure I haven't left out anything of importance."

Eve crushed out her cigarette, seemed to take a moment to gather

her thoughts. "Paul, I don't have to tell you what you've meant to me. For twenty-five years you gave me the unconditional love and loyalty I didn't always deserve. You'll be angry, I know, that I didn't tell you about my illness. It may be selfish of me, but an inoperable brain tumor is a personal thing. I wanted to enjoy the time I had left without being watched, or coddled, or worried over. Now, I want you to remember how much fun we had. You were the only man in my life who never caused me a moment's pain. My last bit of advice to you is if you love Julia, don't let her wriggle away from you. She may try. I've left you both the bulk of my estate not only because I love you, but because it will complicate your lives. You'll have to deal with each other for some time to come."

Her lips trembled once; she controlled them. Her eyes gleamed with tears. Emeralds washed with rain. "Damn you both, give me more grandchildren. I want to know that you've found what always eluded me. Love that can be celebrated not only in the shadows, but in the light. Julia, you were the child I loved but couldn't keep. Paul, you were the child I was given and was allowed to love. Don't disappoint me."

She tossed her head back, sent them one last, vivid smile. "And it wouldn't hurt if you named the first girl after me."

The tape flickered off, turned to snow. Julia took another long drink of brandy before she managed to speak. "She was dying. All this time, she was dying."

In one abrupt move, he switched off the tape. Eve had been right. He was angry, furious. "She had no right to keep it from me." Fists clenched, he sprang to his feet to pace the room. "I might have been able to help. There are specialists, holistic medicine. Even faith healers." He stopped, dragging a hand through his hair as he realized what he was saying. Eve was dead, and it hadn't been a brain tumor that had killed her. "It hardly matters, does it? She made that tape for us to watch after she'd died quietly in some hospital bed. Instead . . ." He looked toward the window, but saw the Eve sprawled on the rug.

"It matters," Julia said quietly. "All of it matters." She set her glass aside and rose to face him. "I'd like to talk to her doctor."

"What's the point?"

"I have a book to write."

He took a step toward her, then stopped himself. His fury was much too ripe and ready to risk touching her. "You can think of that now?"

She saw the bitterness, heard it. There was no way she could explain that writing it, making it important, was the only way she knew to pay Eve back for the debt of her birth. "Yes. I have to think of it."

"Well." He pulled out a cigarette, lighted it slowly. "If they can crank it out within the year, you can cash in on her murder and have yourself the hit of the decade."

Her eyes went blank. "Yes," she said. "I certainly hope so."

Whatever he might have said, whatever venom rose up in his throat, was swallowed at the sound of the brisk knock on the door. The moment he turned from her to answer, Julia's face crumbled. She pressed the heel of her hand between her brows and fought to hold on until she could find a moment alone.

"Frank."

"Sorry, Paul, I know it's a rough day." Frank stood on the threshold. Because his business was official, he didn't step inside, but waited to be asked. "Travers told me that you and Miss Summers were up here."

"We're in the middle of something. Can it wait till later?"

"I'm afraid not." He glanced over Paul's shoulder, then lowered his voice. "I'm bending some rules here, Paul. I'm going to make it as easy as I can, but it's not good."

"You've got a lead?"

Frank stuffed his hands into his pockets. "Yeah, you could say that. I need to talk to her, and I'd rather go through it only once."

There was a tension at the back of his neck, a sharp and disturbing sensation that made him want to shut the door and refuse. When he hesitated, Frank shook his head. "You'll only make it worse."

Julia had regained her composure. She turned, her face calm, and nodded at Frank. "Lieutenant Needlemeyer."

"Miss Summers. I'm sorry, but I'm going to need to ask you some more questions."

Her stomach muscles twisted at the thought, but she nodded again. "All right."

"It's going to have to be downtown."

"Downtown?"

"Yes, ma'am." He took a card from his pocket. "I'm going to have to read your rights, but before I do, I want to advise you to call a lawyer. A good one."

Chapter Twenty-Eight

••••

$\mathcal{I}$T WAS LIKE being trapped in a maze in some vicious amusement park. Each time she thought she had found her way out, she would stumble around a corner and smash against another blank, black wall.

Julia stared at the long mirror in the interrogation room. She was reflected there in her black funeral suit, her face too pale against the crisp linen as she sat at the single table on a hard wooden chair. She could see the smoke that was stinging her nostrils curling up toward the ceiling in a soft blue haze. The trio of coffee cups whose brew smelled as bitter as it tasted. And the two men in shirtsleeves, with badges hooked to their pockets.

Testing, she moved her fingers, steepling them, interlinking them. And watched the reflections do the same.

Which woman was she? she wondered. Which woman would they believe?

She knew there were other faces on the opposite side of that glass, staring back at her. Staring through her.

They had given her a cup of water, but she couldn't seem to swallow. They kept the room too warm, a few degrees warmer than comfort. Beneath her dark suit her skin was damp. She could smell her own fear. Sometimes her voice shook, but she clamped down on the rising bubbles of hysteria until it was steady again.

They were so patient, so tenacious with their questions. And polite, so very polite.

Miss Summers, you did threaten to kill Miss Benedict?

Did you know she'd changed her will, Miss Summers?

Miss Summers, didn't Miss Benedict come to see you on the day of the murder? Did you argue again? Did you lose your temper?

No matter how often she answered, they would wind their way around until she had to answer again.

She'd lost track of time. She might have been in that small, windowless room for an hour, or a day. Occasionally, she would find her mind wandering, simply going away.

She wanted to be certain that Brandon got his supper. She had to help him study for a geography test. While her brain took these short trips into the simple and the ordinary, she answered.

Yes, she had argued with Eve. She had been angry and upset. No, she couldn't remember exactly what she had said. They had never discussed the changes in the will. No, never. She might have touched the murder weapon. It was hard to be sure. No, she hadn't been aware of the details of Eve's will. Yes, yes, the door had been locked when she'd arrived home. No, she wasn't aware if anyone had seen her after she'd passed through the gates.

Again and again she went over her movements on the day of the murder, picking her way carefully through the maze, treading on her own footsteps.

◆ ◆ ◆ ◆

JULIA STRUGGLED to divorce her mind from her body through the booking procedure. She stared straight ahead when she was ordered, blinked at the flash of light as her picture was taken for the files. She turned her profile.

They'd taken her jewelry, her bag, her dignity. All she had to cling to now were the shreds of pride.

They led her to the cell where she would wait until her bail was set and paid. Murder, she thought dizzily. She had just been booked for second degree murder. She'd made some horribly wrong turn in the maze.

At the clang of the metal doors, panic ripped through her. She nearly screamed out, then tasted blood as she bit through her bottom lip. Oh, God, don't put me in here. Don't lock me inside this cage.

Gasping for breath, she sat on the edge of the bunk, clasped her hands in her lap, and held on. She would swear the air stalled when it reached the bars. Someone was swearing, low, foul obscenities rattled off like a laundry list. She could hear the whine of junkies, the bitching of hookers. Someone was crying, low, pitiful sobs that echoed endlessly.

There was a sink bolted to the wall opposite the bunk, but she was afraid to use it. Though nausea rolled sickly in her stomach, she choked it back rather than crouch over the stained toilet.

She would not be sick. And she would not break.

How soon would the press find out? She could write the headlines herself.

EVE BENEDICT'S DAUGHTER ARRESTED
FOR HER MURDER
ABANDONED DAUGHTER'S REVENGE
THE SECRET THAT ENDED EVE'S LIFE

Julia wondered if Eve would have appreciated the publicity, then pressed a hand to her mouth to hold back a wild burst of laughter. No, not even Eve, with all her skill at manipulation, with all her clever ways of maneuvering the players in her own script, could have foreseen this kind of irony.

When her hands began to shake, she went back to the bunk, pushing herself into the corner. With her knees up tight against her chest, she lowered her head to them and shut her eyes.

Murder. The word swam through her mind. When her breath began to hitch, she squeezed her eyes tighter. Behind her eyes the scene played out as it had been described to her in the interrogation room.

Arguing with Eve. The fury building. Her hand closing over the gleaming brass poker. One desperate violent swing. Blood. So much blood. Her own scream as Eve crumpled at her feet.

"Summers."

Julia's head jerked up. Her eyes were wild and blinked furiously to focus. Had she fallen asleep? All she knew was she was awake now, and still in the cell. But the door was open, and the guard was standing just inside.

"You made bail."

◆ ◆ ◆ ◆

*P*AUL'S FIRST impulse when he saw her was to rush over and hold her against him. One look told him she might crack like eggshells in his hand. More than comfort, he thought she needed strength.

"Ready to go?" he said, and slipped a hand into hers.

She didn't speak until they were outside. It shocked her that it was still daylight. Cars were stretched along the road as commuters battled their way home to dinner. Hours before, only hours ago in the soft blue morning, they had buried Eve. Now she was accused of causing that death.

"Brandon?"

He caught her arm when she swayed, but she kept walking, as if she hadn't noticed her own weakness.

"Don't worry. CeeCee's handling everything. He can stay the night with them, unless you want to go pick him up."

God, she wanted to see him. To hold him. To smell him. But she remembered the glimpse of her own face when they'd let her dress. Her face was white, her eyes shadowed. And there was terror in them.

"I don't want him to see me until I've . . . until later." Confused, she stopped by Paul's car. It was funny, she thought, now that she was outside again, out of that cage, she didn't know what to do next. "I should—I should call him. I'm going to need to explain . . . somehow."

She swayed again so that when he caught her he could all but pour her into the car. "You can call him later."

"Later," she repeated, and let her eyes close.

She didn't speak again, so he hoped she slept. But as he drove he could see the way her hand would go from limp in her lap to clenched. He'd been prepared for tears, for outrage, for fury. He wasn't sure any man could prepare himself for this kind of dangerous fragility.

When she smelled the sea, she opened her eyes. She felt drugged, as if she'd awakened from a long illness. "Where are we going?"

"Home."

She pressed a hand to her temple, as if she could press reality back in. "To your house?"

"Yes. Is that a problem?"

But when he glanced over, she'd turned away so that he couldn't see her face. He braked too hard when he pulled to a stop up in front of the house. They both jerked forward, snapped back. By the time he'd slammed out of his door, she was already standing.

"If you don't want to be here, just tell me where you want to go."

"I have nowhere to go." Eyes stricken, she turned to face him. "And no one to go to. I didn't think you'd . . . bring me here. Want me here. They think I killed her." Her hands shook so badly she dropped her bag. After she crouched to pick it up, she couldn't find the strength to stand again. "They think I killed her," she repeated.

"Julia." He reached for her, but she pulled back.

"Please don't. Don't touch me. I won't be able to hold on to whatever pride I have left if you touch me."

"The hell with that." He gathered her up, into his arms. The first sobs began to rack her body as he carried her inside.

"They put me in a cell. They kept asking me questions, over and over, and they put me in a cell. They locked the door and left me there. I couldn't breathe in there."

Even as his mouth tightened into a grim line, he murmured reassurances. "You need to lie down for a while. Rest for a while."

"I kept remembering the way she looked when I found her. They think I did that to her. God, they're going to put me back in there. What's going to happen to Brandon?"

"They're not going to put you back in there." After he laid her on the bed, he took her face in his hands. "They're not going to put you back in there. Believe it."

She wanted to, but all she could see was that small, barred space, and her trapped inside. "Don't leave me alone. Please." She gripped his hands, her tears burning her eyes. "Touch me. Please." She pulled his mouth down to hers. "Please."

Comfort wasn't the answer. Quiet reassurances and gentle strokes couldn't sear away the desperation. It was passion she needed, fast and fulminating, rough and ready. Here, with him, she could empty her mind, fill her body. She groped for him, her eyes still wet with shock and terror, her body arching against his as she tugged at his clothes.

There were no words between them. She wanted no words; even the softest of them could make her think. For this brief space of time she wanted only to feel.

He forgot about easing her fears. There was no fear in the woman who rolled over the bed with him, her avid mouth and seeking fingers shooting arrows of pleasure into him. Every bit as desperate as she, he tore at her clothes to find her. That hot, damp skin vibrating under his hands, the wild, wanton scent of desires, the seductive scent of woman.

The light poured into the room, touched with the first flames of sunset. She rose over him, her face no longer pale, but flushed with life. She gripped his wrists, brought his hands to her breasts. With her head thrown back she sheathed him, taking him deep, surrounding him.

Her body went rigid, then shuddered as she came. With her eyes on his, she brought his palm up to press a kiss to it. Then with a cry that was both despair and triumph, she rode him fast, and hard, as if she were riding for her life.

♦ ♦ ♦ ♦

SHE SLEPT for an hour in dreamless exhaustion. Then reality began to creep into her defenses, shooting her from sleep to full wakefulness. Biting off a cry of alarm, she sat up in bed. She'd been certain she would find herself back in the cell. Alone. Locked in.

Paul rose from the chair where he'd been sitting, watching her, and moved to the bed to take her hand. "I'm right here."

It took her a moment to fight for her breath. "What time is it?"

"It's early yet. I was just thinking I'd go down and make some dinner." He caught her chin in his hand before she could shake her head. "You need to eat."

Of course she did. She needed to eat and sleep and walk and

breathe. To do all of those normal things to prepare herself for the abnormal. And there was something else she had to do.

"Paul, I need to tell Brandon."

"Tonight?"

To fight off the weepy feeling, she looked away, toward the window and the roar of the sea. "I should have gone to him right away, but I wasn't sure I could handle it. I'm afraid he might hear something, see something on television. I have to explain it to him, prepare him for it myself."

"I'll call CeeCee. Why don't you take a long, hot shower, down a couple of aspirin? I'll be downstairs."

She plucked at the sheets as he walked to the door. "Paul . . . thank you. For this, and before."

He leaned against the jamb. He folded his arms, lifted a brow. And his voice took on that oh-so-British and very amused tone. "Are you thanking me for making love with you, Jules?"

Uncomfortable, she shrugged. "Yes."

"Well then, I suppose I should say you're quite welcome, my dear. Be sure to call on me again. Anytime."

By the time she heard him starting down the stairs she was doing something she hadn't been sure she'd be capable of doing again. She was smiling.

◆ ◆ ◆ ◆

THE SHOWER HELPED, as did the few bites she could manage of the omelette Paul served. He didn't expect conversation. That was something else she owed him for. He seemed to understand that she needed to think through what she would say to her son. How she would tell her little boy that his mother was being accused of murder.

She was pacing the living room when she heard the car drive up. With her hands gripped together she turned to Paul. "I think it would be best if—"

"You talked to him alone," he finished. "I'll be in my office. Don't thank me again, Jules," he said as she opened her mouth. "It might not go so easy on you this time."

As he headed up the stairs, he let out one quiet, vicious oath.

Braced, Julia opened the door. There was Brandon, his backpack slung over his shoulder, grinning up at her. He managed to keep himself from bursting out with all the things he'd done that day. He remembered what she'd done. She'd gone to a funeral, and her eyes were sad.

From behind him, CeeCee reached out a hand for Julia's. The unspoken sign of support, of belief, had the back of Julia's throat stinging.

"You just call," CeeCee said. "Just tell me what you need."

"I . . . thank you."

"Call," CeeCee repeated, then gave Brandon's hair a quick tousle. "See you, kid."

"Bye. Tell Dustin I'll see him in school."

"Brandon." Oh, God, Julia thought. She'd been so certain she'd been prepared. But he was looking up at her, his face so young, so full of trust. She closed the door behind her and led him around to the deck. "Let's stay out here for a minute."

He knew all about death. She'd explained it to him when his grandparents had died. People went away, up to heaven like angels and stuff. Sometimes they got really sick, or had an accident. Or they got all sliced up like the kids in the *Halloween* video he and Dustin had snuck out of bed to watch on the VCR a couple of weekends before.

He didn't like to think about it very much, but he figured his mom was going to talk to him about it again.

She kept holding his hand. Tight. And she was looking out into the dark to where you could just see the white foam of water run up on the sand. The lights were on in the house behind them so he could see her face, and the way the wind caught at the long blue robe she wore.

"She was a nice lady," Brandon began. "She used to talk to me, and ask me about school and stuff. And she'd laugh at my knock-knock jokes. I'm sorry she had to die."

"Oh, Brandon, so am I." She drew a deep breath. "She was a very important person, and you'll be hearing a lot of things about her—at school, on TV, in the papers."

"They say things like she was a goddess, but she was a real person."

"Yes, she was a real person. Real people do things, make decisions, mistakes. They fall in love."

He shifted. She knew he was at the age when talk of love made him uncomfortable. Ordinarily, it would have made her smile. "Eve fell in love a long time ago. And she had a baby. Things couldn't be worked out between her and the man she loved, so she had to do what she thought was best for the baby. There are a lot of good people who aren't able to have babies of their own."

"They adopt them, like Grandma and Granddad adopted you."

"That's right. I loved your grandparents, and they loved me. And you." She turned, crouching down to cup his face in her hands. "But I found out, just a few days ago, that the baby Eve gave away was me."

He didn't recoil in shock, but shook his head as if trying to shake her words into order. "You mean Miss B. was your real mom?"

"No, Grandma was my real mom, the person who raised me and loved me and cared for me. But Eve was the woman who gave birth to me. She was my biological mother." With a sigh, Julia brushed a hand through his hair. "Your biological grandmother. You became very important to her once she got to know you. She was proud of you, and I know she wishes she'd had time to tell you that herself."

His lip quivered. "How come if you were her baby she didn't keep you? She had a big house and money and everything."

"It isn't always a big house and money, Brandon. There are other reasons, more important reasons, for making a decision like that."

"You didn't give me away."

"No." She laid her cheek on his and the love was there, as strong and steady as it had been when he'd been growing in her womb. "But what's right for one person isn't always right for another. She did what she felt was right, Brandon. How can I be sad about it when I got to belong to Grandma and Granddad?"

With her hands resting on his shoulders, she sat back on her heels. "I'm telling you all this now because there's going to be talk. I want you to know that you've got nothing to be ashamed of, nothing to be sorry for. You can be proud that Eve Benedict was your grandmother."

"I liked her a lot."

"I know." She smiled and led him over to the bench that was built into the rail. "There's more, Brandon, and it's going to be very hard. I need you to be brave, and I need you to believe that everything's going to be all right." She waited, her eyes on his, until she could be sure she could say it calmly. "The police think I killed Eve."

He didn't even blink. Instead, his eyes filled with hot anger. His little mouth firmed. "That's stupid."

Her relief came out in a laugh as she rested her cheek on his hair. "Yes. Yes, it is stupid."

"You don't even kill spiders. I can tell them."

"They're going to find out the truth. It may take a little time though. I might have to go to trial."

He buried his face at her breast. "Like with Judge Wapner?"

When he trembled she began to rock him, as she had when he'd been just a baby, restless with colic. "Not exactly. But I don't want you to worry, because they will find out."

"Why can't we just go away? Why can't we just go home?"

"We will. When it's all over, we will." She wrapped herself around him. "I promise."

◆ ◆ ◆ ◆

IN HIS BEDROOM where he'd crawled away to drink and sulk, Drake prepared to make a phone call. He was damn glad the bitch was up to her neck in trouble. Nothing could please him more than having his *cousin* going to the block for murder.

But even with her out of the way, there was Paul standing between him and all that money. Maybe there was no way for him to break the will, no way for him to rake in the inheritance he'd worked for.

But there was always an angle. He'd been saving this one.

He sipped Absolut straight and smiled when the connection rang through. "It's Drake," he said without preamble. "You and I need to get together. . . . Why? Well, that's simple. I have some information you're going to want to pay me for. Like what you were doing sneaking into the guest house and searching through dear Cousin Julia's notes. Oh, and another matter the police might be interested in. Such as the fact the security system was shut off the day Eve was murdered. How do I know?" He smiled again, already counting the money. "I know all sorts of things. I know Julia was in the garden that day. I know someone else went into the guest house where Eve was waiting, then came out alone. All alone."

He listened, smiling at the ceiling. God, it was good to be in charge again. "Oh, I'm sure you have lots of reasons, lots of explanations. You can make them to the cops. Or . . . you can convince me to forget all about it. A quarter million would go a long way to convincing me. For now. Reasonable?" he said with a laugh. "Shit yes, I'll be reasonable. I'll give you a week to come up with it. One week from tonight. Let's make it midnight. It has such a nice ring. Bring it here. All of it, or I go straight to the D.A. and save my poor cousin."

He hung up, then decided to pick a name out of his little black book. He felt like celebrating.

◆ ◆ ◆ ◆

*R*USTY HAFFNER WAS looking for an angle of his own. Most of his life he'd been playing the odds, and though in a final count he'd lost more than he'd gained, he figured he was still in the game. He'd been bullied into the Marine Corps by his father the day after he'd graduated from high school. He'd slipped and slithered through his enlistment, avoiding dishonorable discharge by the skin of his pearly whites.

But he'd learned how to pump out the 'Sir, yes, sirs,' how to kiss whatever ass was most important and wriggle out of trouble.

He'd been bored with his current job, and would have ditched it. If the money hadn't been so good. Getting paid six big ones a week to watch a woman had been hard to turn down.

But now old Rusty was wondering if there was a way to butter his bread a little thicker on the other side.

Over a late night snack of blueberry yogurt, Rusty watched the eleven o'clock news. It was all there. Julia Summers, the classy babe he'd been shadowing for weeks. And wasn't it a kick in the head to discover that she was Eve Benedict's daughter? That she was the prime suspect in the old broad's murder? And, most interesting of all to Rusty P. Haffner, she was about to inherit a large chunk of an estate rumored to be over fifty million.

A classy babe like Summers would be very grateful to someone who could help her out of her mess. A lot more grateful than six hundred a week. Grateful enough, Rusty figured as he licked his spoon, to set a man up for life.

Could be his current client would be pissed enough to cause some trouble. But for, say, two million—cash—Rusty could deal with trouble.

Chapter Twenty-Nine

◆ ◆ ◆ ◆

SWEATY, INVIGORATED, AND PLEASED with the world in general, Lincoln Hathoway breezed into the kitchen from his morning jog. The Krups coffeemaker was just beginning to brew, and he checked his watch. Six twenty-five. On the dot.

If there was one thing he and Elizabeth, his wife of fifteen years, agreed on, it was symmetry. Their life ran along very smooth lines. He enjoyed being one of the most respected criminal lawyers on the East Coast, and she enjoyed being the wife and hostess of a successful man. They had two bright, well-mannered children who had known nothing but affluence and stability. A decade before they'd run over a little rough ground, but had smoothed it out again with barely a ripple. If the years had settled into a routine that edged toward bland, that was just the way they wanted it.

As always, Lincoln took down his mug that read LAWYERS DO IT IN THEIR BRIEFS—a gag gift his daughter, Amelia, had given him on his fortieth birthday. He would drink his first cup of the day alone, catching the morning news on the kitchen TV before going up to shower. It was a good life, Lincoln thought as he switched on the set. The newscaster was announcing a surprise development in the Eve Benedict murder.

The mug Lincoln held slipped out of his fingers and shattered. Hot black Columbian coffee ran like a river over the glossy white tiles.

"Julia." Her name whispered through his lips as he groped for a chair.

◆ ◆ ◆ ◆

SHE SAT ALONE, curled into a corner of the couch. The notepad she'd tried to write on was held limply in her hands. She'd told herself to make a list, her priorities. What had to be done.

She needed a lawyer, of course. The best she could possibly afford. It might mean taking out a second mortgage on her home. Even selling it. Eve's money—had she wanted to consider it—couldn't apply. As long as she was suspected of causing Eve's death, she wouldn't be allowed to benefit from it.

Death benefits. She'd always found that an awkward term. No more so than now.

She had to arrange for Brandon to be taken care of. During the trial. And after, if . . . It wasn't time to think of *if.* She had no family. There were friends, many of whom had tried to reach her already. But to whom could she possibly give her child?

It was there her list had stopped, because at that point she could go no further.

Every few minutes the phone would ring. She would hear the machine click on, and Paul's voice would inform the caller that no one was available. Interspersed with the reporters were the concerned. CeeCee, Nina, Victor. God, Victor. When she heard his voice, she shut her eyes. Did he know? Did he suspect? What could they possibly say to each other now that wouldn't cause more pain?

She wished Paul would get back. She wished he would take longer so that she could just be alone. He had told her only that he'd had things to do. He hadn't told her what they were, and she hadn't asked.

He'd driven Brandon to school himself.

Brandon. She had to make arrangements for Brandon.

When the phone rang again, she continued to ignore it. But it was the urgency in the voice that had her listening, then recognizing, then staring.

"Julia, please, call me as soon as possible. I've canceled my appointments for the day and arranged to stay home. I just heard, on the news, this morning. Please get back to me. I can't tell you how . . . Just call. The number here is . . ."

Slowly, hardly aware she had risen and crossed the room, she lifted the receiver. "Lincoln. It's Julia."

"Oh, thank God. I wasn't even sure they'd given me the right number. I pulled all the strings I could manage at L.A.P.D."

"Why are you calling me at all?"

It wasn't bitterness he heard, but puzzlement. It made the shame almost unbearable. "Because you're about to face a murder trial. I can't believe it, Julia. Can't believe they have enough evidence for trial."

His voice was the same, she realized. Neat and precise. For reasons she couldn't fathom, she wondered if he still had his underwear pressed. "They seem to think they do. I was there. My fingerprints are on the weapon. I'd threatened her."

"Jesus Christ." He ran a hand through his smooth blond hair. "Who's representing you?"

"Greenburg. He was Eve's lawyer. Actually he's looking for someone else. He doesn't practice criminal law."

"Listen to me, Julia. Don't speak to anyone. Do you hear me? Don't speak to anyone."

She nearly smiled. "Shall I hang up, then?"

He'd never understood her humor and plunged straight on. "I'm going to get the first plane out I can. I'm a member of the California Bar, so there's no problem. Now, give me the address where you're staying."

"Why? Why would you come here, Lincoln?"

He was already formulating his reasons and excuses to his wife, to his colleagues, to the press. "I owe you," he said tightly.

"No. You don't owe me anything." She was holding the phone with both hands now. "Do you realize, does it even occur to you that you haven't asked about him? You haven't even asked about him."

In the silence that followed, she heard the door close. Turning, she saw Paul watching her.

"Julia." Lincoln's voice was quiet, utterly reasonable. "I want to help you. Whatever you think of me, you know I'm the best. Let me do this for you. And for the boy."

The boy, she thought. He couldn't even say Brandon's name. She rested her head in her hand a moment, struggling to get beyond emotion. Lincoln had said one thing that was perfectly true. He was the best. She couldn't afford to let pride stand in the way of freedom.

"I'm in Malibu," she said, and gave him the address. "Good-bye, Lincoln. Thank you."

Paul said nothing, waited. He didn't know what he felt. No, he thought, he did. When he had walked in and realized who was on the phone it had felt exactly like being shot. Now he was bleeding inside.

"You heard," she began.

"Yes, I heard. I thought we agreed you wouldn't answer the phone."

"I'm sorry. I had to."

"Naturally." He rocked back on his heels. "He ignores you for ten years, but you had to answer his call."

Unconsciously she rubbed a hand on her stomach where the muscles were beginning to knot. "Paul, he's a lawyer."

"So I've heard." He walked to the bar but thought it best to stick with mineral water. A drink now would be like tossing gasoline onto a fire. "And of course he's the only lawyer in the country who's qualified to take your case. He's going to streak out here on his silver briefcase and save you from the clutches of injustice."

"I can't afford to turn down help from any quarter it's offered." She pressed her lips together, needing to keep her voice calm. There was a terrible urge gnawing inside her to rush past him and fling open the door. "Maybe you'd think more of me if I'd spit in his eye. Maybe I'd think more of myself too. But if they send me to jail, I'm not sure I'll survive it. And I'm afraid, I'm very afraid for Brandon."

He set his glass aside before he crossed to her. His hands were gentle as they skimmed up and down her arms. "Tell you what, Jules. We'll let him work his legal magic. And when it's all over, we'll both spit in his eye."

She wrapped her arms around him, pressing her cheek to his. "I love you."

"It's about time you mentioned that again." He tipped her face up to kiss her, then drew her toward the couch. "Now, sit down while I tell you what I've been up to."

"Up to?" She tried on a smile, wondering if they could possibly have a normal conversation.

"Playing detective. What mystery writer isn't a frustrated detective? Have you eaten?"

"What? Paul, you're jumping subjects."

"I've decided we're going to talk in the kitchen. Over food." He rose, grabbing her hand and pulling her behind him. "It's distracting watching you drop pounds while I'm talking. I think Brandon left some peanut butter."

"I'm going to have a peanut butter sandwich?"

"And jelly," he told her as he took out a jar of Skippy. "Listen, it's loaded with protein."

She didn't have the heart to tell him she wasn't hungry. "I'll fix them."

"They're my speciality," he reminded her. "Sit down. When I'm facing a murder charge, you can pamper me."

Now she did manage to smile. "It's a deal." She watched him slather the bread, wondering if he remembered that first morning he'd met Eve. With a little sigh, she looked past him, to the jade plant on the windowsill. Did he realize that it had been dying when she and Brandon had moved in? A little water, a little plant food, and it was thriving again. It took so very little to sustain life.

She smiled again at the plate he set in front of her. Like peanut butter and jelly, and someone to love.

"You didn't cut it into triangles."

He lifted a brow. "Real men don't eat cut sandwiches. It's wussy."

"Thank God you told me, or I might have continued to cut Brandon's and humiliated him." When she picked it up, jelly squirted cheerfully out the sides. "So, how have you been playing detective."

"What we call legwork." As he sat, he reached over to tuck her hair behind her ear. "I talked to Jack, the pilot. He'll swear that in his expert opinion, the fuel line was tampered with. It may not be much, but it could prove that something was going on, something outside, threatening you. Maybe Eve as well."

She made herself eat, made herself hope. "All right. I think it could be very important to convince the police that someone was sending threats—because of the book. The tapes. I don't understand why if they've listened to the tapes they can think I . . ." She shook her head. "No way to prove anyone but myself and Eve knew what was on them."

"The phrase is *reasonable doubt*. That's all we need. I went to see Travers," he added. Here, while he wanted to be honest, he also wanted to choose his words with care. "She's still a wreck, Jules. She'd wrapped her whole life around Eve—what Eve had done for her, for her son."

"And Travers believes I killed her."

He stood to get them both something to drink. Chablis was the first that came to hand, and he figured it would go just fine with peanut butter. "At this point she needs to blame someone. She wants that someone to be you. The thing about Travers is that very little could go on in that house without her being aware. The fact that Eve could have kept her illness from everyone, including Travers, is only a testament to Eve's skill and determination. Someone else was on the estate that day. Someone else was in the guest house. Travers is our best bet for finding out who."

"I only wish . . . I wish she could understand that I didn't mean the things I said that night." Her voice thickened as she picked up her glass, set it down again without drinking. "That I never wanted that to be Eve's last memory of me. Or mine of her. I'll regret that for the rest of my life, Paul."

"That would be a mistake." He put a hand over hers, squeezed it lightly. "She brought you out here so that each of you could get to know the whole person. Not by one incident, a few hot words. Julia, I went to see her doctor."

"Paul." She linked her fingers with his. At the moment every touch, every point of contact seemed so precious. "You shouldn't have done that alone."

"It was something I wanted to do alone. She was diagnosed right after Thanksgiving last year. At the time, she had told us she wasn't in the mood for turkey or pumpkin pie and was going off for a week or two to the Golden Door to be pampered and revitalized." He paused here to battle his own emotions. "She checked into the hospital for the tests. Apparently, she'd been having headaches, blurred vision, mood swings. The tumor was . . . well, to put it simply, it was too late. They could give her medication to take the edge off the pain. She could go on normally. But they couldn't cure it."

His eyes flicked up to hers. In them she could see the dark, depthless well of grief.

"They couldn't stop it. She was told she had a year at best. She went directly from there to a specialist in Hamburg. More tests, the same result. She must have made her mind up about what she was going to do right away. It was early December when she told Maggie and me about the book. About you. She wanted to finish out her life, and keep those she loved from knowing how little time she had."

Julia looked toward the little jade plant, thriving in its patch of sun. "She didn't deserve to be robbed of what was left."

"No." He drank, a silent toast. Another good-bye. "And she'd be bloody pissed if whoever killed her got away. I'm not going to let that happen." He touched his glass to Julia's in a show of partnership that made her throat sting. "Drink your wine," he told her. "It's good for the soul. And it'll relax you so it's easier for me to seduce you."

She blinked back the tears. "Peanut butter and jelly, and sex, in one afternoon. I don't know if I can take it."

"Let's check it out," he said, and pulled her to her feet.

♦ ♦ ♦ ♦

*H*E HOPED she would sleep for an hour or two, and left her in the bedroom with the shades drawn against the sun, the ceiling fan spinning away the heat.

Like most storytellers, Paul could formulate a plot anywhere—in the car, waiting in the dentist's office, at a cocktail party. But he had found over the years that his best structuring was done in his office.

He'd set up the room as he'd set up his home. To suit himself. The airy space on the second floor was where he spent most of his time. One wall was all glass, all sky and sea. Those who didn't understand the process didn't believe he could be working when he simply sat, staring out, watching the change in light and shadow, the swoop of laughing gulls.

To compensate for the discomfort of tearing a story out of his head and heart, Paul had made his working space a celebration of comfort. The side walls were lined with books. Some for research, some for pleasure. Twin ficus trees thrived in heavy stone pots. One year Eve had invaded his inner sanctum and had hung tiny red and green balls on their slim branches to remind him that deadline or not, Christmas would come.

He'd embraced the computer age, and worked on a clever little PC. And still scribbled notes on odd scraps of paper he often lost. He'd had a top of the line stereo hooked up, certain he would enjoy composing with a background of Mozart or Gershwin. It had taken him less than a week to admit that he detested the distraction. He kept a small refrigerator stocked with soft drinks and beer. When he was on a roll, it might be eighteen hours before he'd open the door and stumble bleary-eyed out of the office, and into reality.

So it was there he went to think of Julia, and the puzzle of proving her innocence.

He sat in his chair, tipped back, and cleared his mind by staring at the sky.

If he were searching for a plot, an ordinary one, she would be the perfect murderer. Calm, collected, and wrapped much too tightly. Reserved. Repressed. Resistant to change. Eve had come along and exploded the tidy, ordered life she had built for herself. The seething temper had ripped its way through that snug outer layer of control, and in a blind moment of rage and despair, she had struck out.

The prosecution might play it that way, he thought. Tossing in several millions in inheritance for extra incentive. Of course, it would be difficult for them to prove that Julia had known about the will. Yet, it might not be so difficult to convince a jury—if it went to a jury—that Julia had been in Eve's confidence.

The aging and ailing movie queen searching for a lost past, the love of a child she'd given up. They could cast Eve as the vulnerable victim, facing her illness bravely and alone and desperately seeking to bond with her daughter.

Eve would sneer and call it crap.

Matricide, he mused. A very ugly crime. And he thought the D.A. would settle very happily for murder two.

He lighted a cigar, closed his eyes, and ran through his mind the reason the scene didn't work.

Julia was incapable of murder. That was, of course, his opinion, and hardly an adequate defense. Better to focus on outside forces and basic facts than his own emotions.

The notes. They were a fact. He had been with Julia when she had received one. There had been no feigning that shock and fear. The prosecution might argue that she was the daughter of an actress, and had once aspired to the stage herself. But he doubted even Eve could have delivered a performance like that cold.

The plane had been tampered with. Could anyone seriously believe she would have risked her life, risked making her child an orphan, just for effect?

The tapes. He had listened to the tapes, and they were volatile. Which secret would have been worth Eve's life?

There was no doubt in Paul's mind that she had died to preserve a lie.

Gloria's abortion. Kincade's perversions. Torrent's ambitions. Priest's greed.

Delrickio. With all his heart Paul wanted to believe Delrickio had been responsible. But he couldn't make the pieces fit. Could a man who so coolly dealt out death lose control and kill so recklessly?

It had almost certainly been a crime born of the moment. Whoever had done it couldn't have been sure when Julia would return, or if the gardener might have passed by a window on his way to prune roses.

That didn't account for the security. No one but the staff had been inside the gates. And yet, someone had come in.

Paul asked himself what he would do if he'd wanted to confront Eve, alone, without anyone knowing. It wouldn't have been difficult to visit openly, then leave, making a quick trip to shut off the power on the alarms. Double back. Face her down. Lose control.

He liked it. He liked it very much, except for the minor fact that the alarms had been on when the police had checked them.

So he would talk to Travers again, and Nina, and Lyle. And everyone else, down to the lowliest dust chaser on the estate.

He had to prove that someone could have gotten inside. Someone frightened enough to send notes. Someone desperate enough to kill.

On impulse he picked up the phone and dialed. "Nina. It's Paul."

"Oh, Paul. Travers said you'd been by. I'm sorry I missed you." She glanced around her office, at the cardboard boxes she was meticulously packing. "I'm in the process of putting things in order, moving my own things out. I'm renting a house in the Hills until . . . well, until I can think what to do next."

"You know you can stay as long as you like."

"I appreciate that." She groped in her pocket for a tissue. "I'm worried about Travers, but I can't bear staying, knowing Miss B. won't come flying in with some new impossible demand. Oh, God, Paul, why did this have to happen?"

"That's something we need to figure out. Nina, I know the police have questioned you."

"Over and over," she said with a sigh. "And now the D.A. He seems certain I'll have to testify in court, about the argument. About Julia."

He heard the way her voice changed, tightened. "You think she did it, don't you?"

She looked down at the tattered tissue, tossed it away and picked up a fresh one. "I'm sorry, Paul, I understand you have feelings for her. But yes, I don't see any other explanation. I don't think she planned it. I don't even think she meant it. But it happened."

"Whatever you think, Nina, you may be able to help me. I'm trying out a little theory. Can you tell me who came to see Eve the day she was killed. Even the day before."

"Oh, God, Paul."

"I know it's hard, but it would help."

"All right then." Briskly, she dried her eyes, tucked away the tissue, then reached for the date book not yet packed. "Drake was here, and Greenburg. Both Maggie and Victor were by the evening before. Oh, and you, of course. Travers mentioned you'd come to see Eve, so I jotted it down in her book."

"Always efficient, Nina." He toyed with another possibility. "Did Eve have anything going with the chauffeur?"

"Lyle?" For the first time in days, Nina really laughed. "No! Miss B. had too much class for his kind. She liked the way he looked with the car. That was it."

"One more thing. The day it happened. Did you have any trouble with the alarms. Anybody check them?"

"The alarms? No, why should there have been trouble?"

"Just tapping all the bases, Nina. Listen, let me know when you're settled. And don't worry about Travers. I'll look after her."

"I know. I'll keep in touch. Paul . . . I'm sorry," she said lamely. "Sorry about everything."

"So am I." He hung up, still wondering. He made the next call more slowly, more deliberately, then waited to be put through to Frank.

"Only got a minute, Paul. Things are hopping."

"Julia?"

"Mostly. She's got some big gun coming in from back east."

"Yes, I know."

"Oh, yeah, guess you do. Anyway, he wants every goddamn scrap of paper we've got on the case. He casts a pretty big shadow, even out here, so the D.A.'s making sure we've got everything all nice and tight. He's already got some stiff-necked P.I. looking over our shoulders."

"Hathoway works fast."

"Yeah." He lowered his voice. "So the D.A.'s working faster. He wants this one, Paul, bad. It's got it all—money, power, glitz, scandal. It's going to give him some great press."

"Tell me something, Frank. Is there any way you can check if the security system had been turned off that day?"

Frank frowned and pushed through his papers. "It was on when we did our check."

"But could it have been turned off earlier, then turned on again?"

"Christ, Paul, you're spitting in the wind." When he got no response to that, Frank muttered under his breath. "Okay, I'll talk to a couple of the electronics boys, but I don't think you've got a shot."

"Then give me another. Are you going to talk to the chauffeur again?"

"Studly Doright? What for?"

"Hunch."

"Shit, spare me from mystery writers." But he was already making a note. "Sure, I can give him another shake and rattle."

"I'd like to tag along when you do."

"Sure, why the hell not? What do I need a pension for when I can live on good deeds?"

"And one more thing."

"Fire away. You want me to turn over the files to you? Lose some evidence? Badger a witness."

"I'd appreciate it. While you're about it, why don't you check the airlines? See if anyone connected with Eve took a quick trip to London last month. Around the twelfth."

"No problem. That should only take me, oh, about ten or twenty man-hours. Any particular reason?"

"I'll let you know. Thanks."

And now, Paul thought as he hung up the phone, he'd wait for the answers, stir them around and see if he had a workable plot.

Chapter Thirty

♦ ♦ ♦ ♦

$\mathcal{I}$T WAS A LONG TRIP from Philadelphia to L.A. Even flying first class didn't eliminate jet lag and travel fatigue. But Lincoln Hathoway looked as though he had just stepped out of his tailor's. His navy gabardine suit with its subtle chalk stripes showed nary a wrinkle. His hand-sewn shoes shone like a mirror. His blond, conservatively cut hair was perfectly in place.

Paul liked to think it was the seamless correctness that had him detesting the man on sight.

"Lincoln Hathoway," he said, extending a manicured hand. "I'm here to see Julia."

It pleased Paul that his own palm was gritty with sand. "Paul Winthrop."

"Yes, I know." Not that he recognized him from his book jackets. Lincoln didn't have time to spare on popular fiction. But he'd had his secretary gather every clipping available on Julia from the last six months. He was aware of who Paul was, and his relationship with both victim and accused. "I'm pleased Julia has somewhere discreet to stay until we work this all out."

"Actually, I've been a bit more worried about her peace of mind than discretion." He gestured Lincoln inside, deciding he would thoroughly enjoy detesting him. "Want a drink?"

"Some mineral water with a twist would be fine, thank you." Lincoln was a man who formed opinions quickly. It was often necessary to gauge a jury by little more than appearance and body language. He summed Paul up as wealthy, impatient, and suspicious, and wondered how he might use those qualities if the case went to trial. "Mr. Winthrop, how is Julia?"

Suddenly the epitome of the aloof Brit, Paul turned and offered the glass. "Why don't you ask her yourself?"

She was standing in the doorway, a lean, dark-eyed child tucked protectively under her arm. Ten years, Lincoln thought, had changed her. She no longer radiated enthusiasm and trust, but composure and caution. The fawn-colored hair that had once swung free was now swept back from a face that had fined down and become elegant.

He looked at the boy, hardly aware that the four of them were standing, silent and tensed. He searched for some sign, some physical trait that would have run from him into the child he'd never seen, or wanted. That was human nature, and his own ego.

But he saw nothing of himself in the slight-framed, tousel-haired child. And it relieved him, swept away the traces of guilt and apprehension that had snuck into him during the flight west. The boy was his— Lincoln had never doubted it—but was not his. His world, his family, his conscience were safe in that brief moment it took him to look, appraise, and reject.

Julia saw it all—the way his gaze landed on Brandon, hovered fleetingly, then dismissed. Her arm tightened around her son to shield him from a blow he couldn't have felt. Then relaxed. Her son was safe. Any lingering doubts that she should tell him his father's name faded away. His father was dead, to both of them.

"Lincoln." Her voice was as cool and reserved as the nod of greeting she offered. "It was good of you to come so far so quickly."

"I'm only sorry about the circumstances."

"So am I." Her hand slid over Brandon's shoulder to rest at the tender nape of his neck. "Brandon, this is Mr. Hathoway. He's a lawyer who used to work with Granddad a long time ago. He's come out to help us."

"Hello." Brandon saw a tall, stiff-looking man with shiny shoes and that dopey aren't-you-a-big-boy expression some adults put on whenever they were introduced to a kid.

"Hello, Brandon. I don't want you to worry, we're going to take care of everything."

He couldn't stand it. In another moment Paul was certain he would deck the man for being so detached. "Come on, kid." Paul held out a hand. Brandon took it willingly. "Let's go upstairs and see what kind of trouble we can get into."

"Well then . . ." Lincoln took a seat, not even glancing around as Brandon clattered up the stairs. "Why don't we get started?"

"It really didn't mean anything to you, did it?" she said quietly. "Seeing him didn't mean a thing."

He lifted his fingers to the perfect Windsor knot in his tie. He'd been afraid she'd manufacture some sort of scene. Of course, he was prepared for it. "Julia, as I told you years ago, I can't afford to entertain an emotional bond. I'm very, very grateful you were mature enough not to go to Elizabeth, regret you were too stubborn to accept any financial help I offered, and pleased that you've achieved the kind of success where you don't require it. Naturally, I feel I owe you a great deal, and am deeply, deeply sorry that you find yourself in a position where you require my services."

She began to laugh—not the thin, edgy laugh of hysteria, but a full, rich chuckle that had Lincoln baffled. "I'm sorry," she said as she dropped into a chair. "You haven't changed. You know, Lincoln, I wasn't sure what I would feel, seeing you again. But the one thing I didn't expect was nothing." She let out a little sigh. "So, let's shovel away the gratitude, and do what has to be done. My father had the greatest respect for you as a lawyer, and since his opinion weighs heavily with me, you'll have all my cooperation, and for the time it takes to put things right, my complete trust."

He merely nodded. Lincoln appreciated good, solid sense. "Did you kill Eve Benedict?"

Her eyes flashed. He was surprised to see such deep and volatile anger spark so quickly. "No. Did you expect me to admit it if I had?"

"As the daughter of two of the best attorneys I've ever worked with, you already know it would be foolish to lie if you want me to represent you. Now then . . ." He took out a blank legal pad and a black Mont Blanc pen. "I want you to tell me everything you did, everyone you spoke with, everything you saw on the day Eve Benedict was murdered."

She went through it once, then again. Then, led by his questions, a third time. He made few comments, only nodded from time to time as he jotted down notes in his neat, precise hand. Julia got up only once to refill his glass, and to pour one of her own.

"I'm afraid I haven't had much time to acquaint myself with the evidence against you. Naturally, I notified the D.A., and the investigating officer that I would be your attorney of record. I was able to secure a copy of certain reports from the prosecutor before I came here, but only glanced at them in the cab."

He paused, folding his hands in his lap. She remembered he had always had that same quiet, tidy manner. It, plus the sadness in his eyes, had first attracted a romantic, impressionable teenager to him. Now, though the gestures were the same, the sadness had been replaced by shrewdness.

"Julia, are you certain you unlocked the door to enter the house that afternoon?"

"Yes, I had to stop and look for my keys. Ever since the break-in I'd been much more careful about locking up."

His eyes remained level, his voice even. "Are you quite sure?"

She started to respond, then stopped and sat back. "Do you want me to lie, Lincoln?"

"I want you to think very carefully. Unlocking a door is a habit, an automatic sort of motion that one might assume one did. Particularly after a shock. The fact that you told the police you unlocked the front door, and all of the other doors were locked from the inside when they arrived on the scene, is very damning. There were no keys on the body, no extra keys found around the house. Therefore, either the door was unlocked to begin with or someone, someone with a key, let Eve in."

"Or someone took Eve's key after they killed her," Paul said from the stairs.

Lincoln glanced up. Only the faintest tightening around his mouth revealed any irritation at the interruption. "That is, of course, one angle we can try to pursue. Since the evidence points in the direction of a crime of passion and impulse, it may be difficult to convince a judge that someone was in the house with Eve, killed her, then had the presence of mind to take the key and lock up."

"Then again, that's your job, isn't it?" Paul walked over to the bar. His fingers moved to the bourbon, backtracked, and settled on club soda. The temper he was holding back didn't need the kick of liquor.

"It's my job to give Julia the best possible defense."

"Then I'm sorry to make it more difficult for you, Lincoln, but I unlocked the door, with my key."

He pursed his lips and reviewed his notes. "You don't mention touching the murder weapon, the fireplace poker."

"Because I don't know if I did or not." Suddenly weary, she dragged a hand through her hair. "Obviously I did or my fingerprints wouldn't have been on it."

"They might if you'd built a fire within the last week or two."

"I hadn't. The nights have been pleasant."

"The weapon was found several feet from the body." He took a file out of his briefcase. "Are you up to looking at some pictures?"

She knew what he meant, and wasn't sure of the answer. Bracing herself, she reached out. There was Eve, crumpled on the rug, her face still so breathtakingly beautiful. And the blood.

"From this angle," Lincoln was saying, "you see the poker is lying over here." He leaned forward to touch a finger to the print. "As if someone had thrown it there, or perhaps dropped it after backing up from the body."

"I found her like that," Julia whispered. Her own voice was muffled by the roaring in her head, the quick, deadly illness in her stomach. "I went to her, took her hand. I think I said her name. And I knew. I got up, stumbled. I picked it up—I think—it had her blood on it. And on my hands. So I threw it down because I had to do something. Call someone." She thrust the picture away and rose unsteadily to her feet. "Excuse me, I have to say good night to Brandon."

The moment she'd rushed up the stairs, Paul turned on him. "Did you have to do that to her?"

"Yes, I'm afraid so. And worse before it's over." In an economic move, Lincoln turned over a page on his pad. "The prosecuting attorney is a very determined, very capable man. And like all men elected to office, ambitious and aware of the value of a celebrity trial. We'll have to show a plausible alternative from every scrap of physical evidence he has. We're also going to stuff reasonable doubt down the throats of not only a judge, a jury if it comes to that, but the public at large. Now I realize you and Julia have a personal relationship—"

"Do you?" With a slow, grim smile, Paul sat on the arm of a chair. "Let me spell it out for you, counselor. Julia and Brandon belong to me now. Nothing would give me greater pleasure than to break several small, vital bones in your body for what you did to her. But if you're as good as I've heard, if you're her best chance to get through this, then whatever you ask me to do, I'll do."

Lincoln relaxed his grip on his pen. "Then I'd suggest the first thing be we forget about what happened between Julia and me more than a decade ago."

"Except that," Paul said, and smiled again. "Try again."

Lincoln had seen more pleasant smiles on felons he'd seen convicted. "Your personal feelings about me will only hurt Julia."

"No. Nothing's going to hurt her again. Including you. If I'd thought differently, you wouldn't have walked through the door." With his eyes still on Lincoln's he pulled out a cigar. "I've worked with scum before."

"Paul." Julia spoke quietly as she came downstairs again. "That won't help."

"Clearing the air always helps, Julia," he contradicted her. "Hathoway knows that while he has all of my disgust, he also has all my cooperation."

"I came here to help, not to be judged for a mistake I made over ten years ago."

"Be careful, Lincoln." Julia rounded on him before she could stop herself. "That mistake is upstairs, sleeping. I'm accepting your help not only for my own sake, but for his. He's been fatherless all his life. I can't bear to think of him losing me too."

Only a faint flush rising up from his knotted tie to his cheeks indicated she'd hit any mark. "If we can all keep our personal feelings out of this, we have a much better chance of seeing that doesn't happen." Satisfied the subject was settled, he moved on. "You both knew the deceased, were privy to the workings of her household, her friendships, her enemies. It would be helpful if you told me everything you could about those close to her. Anyone who stood to gain by her death, financially, emotionally."

"Besides me?" Julia said.

"Perhaps we'll start with you, and Mr. Winthrop. Just a brief sketch, if you will. I've arranged for a suite at the Beverly Hills Hotel, where I'll be working. Meyers, Courtney, and Lowe have agreed to lend me two of their clerks, and my own secretary will be flying out tomorrow." He checked his watch, which he'd already changed to West Coast time, frowned. "We'll need more in-depth interviews once I've set up. First thing Monday I'll petition for a postponement of the arraignment."

"No." Chilled, Julia began to rub her hands over her arms. "I'm sorry, Lincoln, but I can't stand the idea of dragging this out."

"Julia, I'll need time to structure your defense. With luck, we can keep this from going to trial."

"I don't mean to be difficult, but I have to get it over with. Postponements only give more time to sensationalize. Brandon's old enough to read the paper, see the newscasts. And I . . . to be frank, I can't stand much more waiting."

"Well, we have the weekend to think about it." Or, Lincoln decided, to turn her around to his way. "For now, tell me about Eve Benedict."

◆ ◆ ◆ ◆

*B*Y THE TIME Lincoln left it was nearly two A.M., and Paul had developed a grudging respect for his thoroughness. He might have found the attorney's organization and neatness irritating. Lincoln always turned over a new sheet of paper for each change of topic, he ate the brownies Julia served with coffee using a fork, and not once during the long, repetitive evening did he loosen his tie.

But Paul had also noted that Lincoln's eyes had sharpened when told about the notes, and that a look of pure pleasure had come into them when Delrickio's connection had been explained.

When he left, he didn't look like a man who had been up for nearly twenty-four hours straight, and had bid them good night as politely as if they'd just enjoyed a friendly dinner party.

"I suppose it's none of my business." Paul shut the door and turned back to Julia. She braced, resenting the fact that she would have to explain herself again, remember again. "But I just have to know." He walked over to her, brushed the hair from her face. "Did he hang up his clothes and fold his socks before you made love?"

The giggle surprised her, the comfort she found when she rested her head on his shoulder didn't. "Actually, he folded his clothes and rolled his socks."

"Jules, I have to tell you, your taste has improved." A quick, nipping kiss, and he picked her up to carry her toward the stairs. "And after you've had about twelve hours sleep, I'll prove it to you."

"Maybe you could prove it to me now, and I'll sleep later."

"A much better idea."

♦ ♦ ♦

EVEN PUTTING BRANDON on the plane, knowing he was tucked away thousands of miles from the eye of the storm, didn't console her. She wanted her child back. She wanted her life back.

She met with Lincoln every day, sat in the suite he'd booked and drank black coffee until she was certain she could feel it burning a hole in the center of her gut. She talked to the detective he'd hired—another intrusion in her life, another person to pry apart the tenuous threads on what had been her privacy.

It was all so ordered—the files, the law books, the busy ringing of the phones. The unbroken efficiency of it began to lull her. Until she saw a headline, heard a broadcast. Then she was tossed back into the fear of it being her name, her face, her life under the public microscope. And her fate in the hands of justice, whose blindness was not always a boon for the innocent.

Paul kept her from going over that thin edge. She didn't want to lean. Hadn't she promised herself that she would never depend on anyone for her happiness, for her security, for her peace of mind? Yet, just the fact that he was there gave her the illusion of all three. And because she was terrified it was an illusion, she backed away, quietly slipping inches of distance between them until there was a foot, a foot until there was a yard.

He was exhausted himself, discouraged by the fact that his connections at the precinct weren't bringing him any closer to the truth. Frank had let him come along when he'd questioned Lyle again, but the former chauffeur had refused to budge on his story to see, hear, and speak no evil.

The fact that Drake's finances were in a mess didn't implicate him in Eve's death. More, the fact that she had given him a large amount only weeks before she was killed worked in his favor. Why would he kill the golden goose?

Paul's single interview with Gloria had only made things worse. With tears and trembling, she admitted to arguing with Eve on the day of the murder. Guilt poured out along with the words. She had said terrible things, then had left in a rage, speeding home to confess the entire business to her shocked husband.

At almost the same moment Julia had discovered Eve's body, Gloria had been weeping in her husband's arms, and begging for forgiveness.

Since Marcus Grant, the housekeeper, and the curious pool man had all heard the sobbing Gloria at one-fifteen, and the drive from estate to estate couldn't be managed in under ten minutes, it was impossible to tie her to the murder.

Paul still felt the book was the key. When Julia was out of the house he would listen to the tapes over and over again, trying to find the one phrase, the one name that would open the door.

When she came home, wired from another session of rehearsing her testimony with Lincoln, she heard Eve's voice.

"He directed with a whip and a chain. I've never known anyone to use less finesse and get more results. I thought I hated him—did, actually, throughout the movie. But when McCarthy and his slimeball committee went after him, I was outraged. That was the main reason I joined Bogie and Betty and the others in their trip to Washington. I've never had any patience with politicking, but, by Christ, I was ready to fight tooth and nail then. Maybe we did some good, maybe not, but we had our say. That's what counts, isn't it, Julia? Making sure you're heard goddamn loud and goddamn clear. I don't want to be remembered as someone who sat on the sidelines and let other people clear the way."

"She won't be," Julia murmured.

Paul turned from his desk. He'd been listening so intently, he almost expected to see Eve sitting there, telling him to light her cigarette or open a bottle.

"No, she won't." He switched off the tape to study Julia. In the past week, she'd rarely let him see that pale, haunted look. It was there, always there, just beneath the mask of control. But whenever that mask began to crack, she closed in on herself and away from him. "Sit down, Julia."

"I was going to make some coffee."

"Sit down," he repeated. She did, but on the edge of the chair, as if she would spring up any moment if he got too close. "I got a subpoena today. I'm going to have to testify at the hearing tomorrow."

She didn't look at him, but focused on a point somewhere between them. "I see. Well, that isn't unexpected."

"It's going to be rough on both of us."

"I know. I'm sorry. Actually, I was thinking, as I was coming back this afternoon, that it might be best, easier, if I moved to a hotel—until this is all over. My living here is giving the press a lot of ammunition, and only adding more strain to an already impossible situation."

"That's bullshit."

"That's fact." She rose, hoping for a graceful exit. She should have known better. He only stood and blocked her way.

"Just try it." Eyes narrowed and dangerous, he wrapped his hands around her lapels and yanked her forward. "You're here for the long haul."

"Did it ever occur to you that I might want to be alone?"

"Yeah, it occurred to me. But I'm part of your life, and you can't shut me out."

"I may not have a life," she shouted. "If they bind me over for trial tomorrow—"

"You'll deal with it. We'll deal with it. You're going to trust me, goddamn you. I'm not a ten-year-old boy you have to protect. And I'm sure as hell not some spineless prick who'll let you carry the whole load while I run off to my own tidy life."

Her eyes went to smoke. "This has nothing to do with Lincoln."

"The hell it doesn't. And don't ever compare us in that sharp little brain of yours again."

Her face wasn't pale now, nor was her breath even. The flash of temper meant more to him than a dozen words of love. "Let go of me."

He lifted a brow, knowing the gesture was derisive. "Sure." He released her, stuffed his hands into his pockets.

"This has nothing to do with Lincoln," she said again. "And it has nothing to do with you. It's me. Get that through your surplus of testosterone. I'm the one whose life is on the line in that courtroom tomorrow. You can beat your chest and howl all you want, that's not going to change. I haven't got that many choices left, Paul, and if I want to walk out of that door, that's just what I'll do."

"Try it," he invited her.

Incensed, she whirled around. He caught her before she'd reached the stairs. "I told you to let me go."

"I haven't finished beating my chest or howling." Because he was dead sure she'd take a swing at him, he cuffed her hands behind her back. "Hold it. Dammit, Jules." Faced with a tumble down the stairs, he shoved her back against the wall. "Look at me. Just look. You're right about choices." With his free hand he forced her head up. "Do you want to walk away from me?"

She stared into his eyes and saw that he would let her. Maybe. And if she turned away now from this, from him, she would always regret it. Survivors lived with their mistakes. Hadn't Eve told her that? But there were some you couldn't afford to make.

"No." She pressed her mouth to his, felt the heat and the strength. "I'm sorry. I'm so sorry."

"Don't be sorry." His kiss grew more avid, more needy. "Just don't walk away from me."

"I'm so scared, Paul. I'm so scared."

"We're going to make it right. Believe it."

For a moment she could.

♦ ♦ ♦ ♦

DRAKE WAS FEELING like a million dollars. Or at least a quarter million. Within twenty-four hours he'd have the cash in his hand and the world at his feet. He was dead sure Julia would go to trial, and, with any luck, be convicted. Once that happened—and with money in the bank—he figured it wouldn't be too hard to get his piece of Eve's estate. He resented Paul getting half, but he could live with it. With a good lawyer Drake was sure he could cop Julia's share.

The law wouldn't let her touch it. And anyway, where she was going, she wasn't going to need it.

All and all, things had worked out fine.

Pleased with himself, he turned the stereo on blast and settled down with a racing form. By the weekend he was going to have a nice little stake to take to Santa Anita. He'd play it conservative, but with a few thousand on the nose of the little filly he had a tip on, he could finesse that first payment into the big time.

Of course, his backer didn't know it as only a first payment. Drake hummed along with Gloria Estefan and figured he could milk his source for plenty over the next year or two. By then, his inheritance should come in. After that, he was taking off. Riviera, Caribbean, the Keys. Anywhere where the beaches, and the women, were hot.

He picked up a glass of champagne. The Dom Pérignon was an early celebration. He had a date to meet a sexy little number at Tramp, but the action wouldn't start for an hour or two.

Christ, he felt like dancing. While he tried out a little conga, wine sloshed over his fingers. Gleefully, he licked it off.

He thought about ignoring the doorbell when it rang, then chuckled to himself. It was probably the lucky lady of the evening. Who could blame her for wanting to start things off early? Instead of meeting at the club, they would get things going here and now.

When the bell rang again, he brushed his hand over his hair, and on a whim unbuttoned his shirt. He had the champagne glass in his hand when he answered the door. Though it wasn't tonight's lucky winner, he toasted his guest.

"Well now. I didn't expect to see you until tomorrow. But that's fine. Just so happens I'm open for business. Come on in. We'll do this over a glass of champagne."

Grinning to himself, he led the way back to the bottle. It looked like he wasn't celebrating early after all. "What do you say we drink to dear Julia?" He poured a second glass right to the rim. "Dear cousin Julia. Without her, we could both be standing in some deep shit."

"Maybe you'd better check your own shoes."

Drake turned, thinking that a great joke. He was still laughing when he saw the gun. He never felt the bullet that plowed between his eyes.

Chapter Thirty-One

· · · ·

SPECTATORS AND PRESS crammed together on the courtroom steps. Julia's first test of the day would be to walk through them. Lincoln had instructed her on how to do that. To walk briskly, but not to appear hurried. Not to bow her head—it looked guilty. Not to keep her head back too far—it looked arrogant. She was to say nothing, not even the ubiquitous "no comment," no matter what questions where hurled at her.

The morning was warm and sunny. She'd prayed for rain. Rain might have kept some of the curious and accusing inside. Instead, she climbed out of the limo into a cloudless southern California day. With Lincoln on one side and Paul on the other, she moved into the wall of people who wanted her story, her secrets, or her blood. Only the fear that she might stumble and be swept away by them helped her ignore the painful clenching in her stomach, the uncontrollable trembling of her legs.

Inside there was more air, more space. She shuddered off the nausea. It would be over soon. Over and behind her. They would believe her, they had to believe her. Then she would be free to start her life again. Free to take that one slim chance on making a new life.

It had been years since she'd been in a courtroom. From time to time during summer vacation, she'd been allowed to watch her mother or father work a jury. They hadn't seemed like her parents then, but larger than life. Actors on a stage, gesturing, manipulating, strutting. Perhaps that was where she'd gotten that first spark to take to the stage herself.

But no, she thought. That had come through the blood. That had come through Eve.

At a signal from Lincoln, Paul leaned closer, took both of Julia's hands in his. "It's time to go in. I'll be sitting right behind you."

She nodded, her fingers creeping up to touch the brooch she'd pinned to her lapel. The scales of justice.

The courtroom was jammed. Among the faces of strangers she saw the familiar. CeeCee sent Julia a quick, encouraging smile. Beside her niece, Travers sat rigid, her face set and fierce. Nina stared down at her linked fingers, unwilling or unable to meet Julia's eyes. Delrickio, flanked by his steely-eyed guards, studied her impassively. Gloria's eyes gleamed with tears as she twisted a handkerchief in her hands and huddled under her husband's protective arm.

Maggie, her lipstick chewed off until it left only a thin line of red around her mouth, looked up, then away. Kenneth leaned over her to murmur to Victor.

It was that look, that tortured, grieving look that had Julia faltering. She wanted to stop, to scream out her innocence, her rage, and her terror. She could only move forward and take her seat.

"Remember," Lincoln was saying, "this is only a preliminary hearing. It's to determine if there's enough evidence for a trial."

"Yes, I know," she said quietly. "It's only the beginning."

"Julia."

She tensed at Victor's voice and made herself turn. He'd aged. In a matter of weeks the years had caught up with him, pulling down the skin under his eyes, digging lines deep around his mouth. Julia put a hand on the rail that separated them. It was the closest she believed either of them could come to reaching out.

"I don't know what to say to you." He pulled air into his lungs and let it trickle out. "If I had known, if she had told me . . . about you, things would have been different."

"Things weren't meant to be different, Victor. I would have been sorry, very sorry, if she had used me to change them."

"I'd like to—" Go back, he thought. Thirty years, thirty days. Both were equally impossible. "I couldn't stand behind you before." He looked down, lifted his hand, laid it on hers. "I'd like you to know I'll stand behind you now. And the boy, Brandon."

"He's—he's missed having a grandfather. When this is over, we'll talk. All of us."

He managed a nod before his hand slid away from hers.

"All rise!"

A buzzing filled her ears when the courtroom rose to its feet. She watched the judge stride in, take his place behind the bench. Why, he looks like Pat O'Brien, she thought foolishly. All ruddy and round and Irish. Surely O'Brien would know the truth when he heard it.

The D.A. was a wiry, energetic-looking man with sideburns of gray on his close-cropped hair. Obviously he didn't take the warning about sun exposure seriously, for his tan was deep and smooth, making his pale blue eyes gleam in contrast.

He had the voice of an evangelist. Without hearing the words, Julia listened to it rise and fall.

Reports were placed in evidence. Autopsy, forensic. The pictures, of course. As Julia watched the prosecutor present them, the image of Eve sprawled on the rug froze in her mind. The murder weapon. The suit Julia had worn that was streaked with a rusty-looking stain that was dried blood.

She watched the experts take the stand, then step down. Their words didn't matter. Lincoln obviously thought differently because he would rise and object from time to time, and he chose his own carefully in cross-examination.

But the words didn't matter, Julia thought. The pictures said it all. Eve was dead.

When the D.A. called Travers, she shuffled up to the stand as she had shuffled her way up and down the hallways of Eve's home. As if she were reluctant to expend the energy it took to lift one foot, then the other.

She'd scraped her hair back and was wearing a plain, working-class dress of unrelieved black. She clutched her purse with both hands and stared straight ahead.

Even when the prosecutor led her gently through the early questions, she didn't relax. Her voice only became more harsh as she explained her relationship with Eve.

"And as a trusted friend and employee," the prosecutor continued. "Did you have occasion to travel with Miss Benedict to Switzerland in . . ." He reviewed his notes before he stated the date.

"Yes."

"What was the purpose of this trip, Ms. Travers?"

"Eve was pregnant."

The statement caused a ripple of murmurs through the spectators until the gavel was struck.

"And did she have a child, Ms. Travers?"

"Your honor." Lincoln rose to his feet. "The defense is ready to stipulate that Miss Benedict had a child, which she gave up for adoption. And that the child is Julia Summers. The state need not waste the court's time proving what has already been established."

"Mr. Williamson?"

"Very well, your honor. Ms. Travers, is Julia Summers Eve Benedict's natural daughter?"

"She is." Travers flicked one brief, hate-filled glance in Julia's direction. "Eve agonized over that adoption, did what she thought was best for the child. She even kept tabs on her over the years. It upset her something fierce when the girl got herself pregnant. Said she couldn't bear to think about her going through all that she'd been through herself."

Lincoln leaned toward Julia. "I'm going to let her go on. It establishes a bond."

"And she was proud," Travers continued. "Proud when the girl started writing books. She used to talk to me, 'cause there was nobody else who knew."

"You were the only one aware that Julia Summers was Eve Benedict's biological daughter?"

"No one knew but me."

"Can you tell us how Miss Summers came to live on Miss Benedict's estate."

"It was that book. That cursed book. I didn't know then how she got the idea in her head, but nothing I said talked her out of it. Said she was scooping up two birds. She had a story to tell, and she wanted time to get to know her daughter. And her grandson."

"And did she tell Miss Summers the truth of their relationship?"

"Not then, not for weeks after she'd come. She was afraid how the girl would react."

"Objection." Lincoln rose smoothly to his feet. "Your honor, Miss Travers couldn't know what was in Miss Benedict's mind."

"I knew her," Travers tossed back. "I knew her better than anybody."

"I'll rephrase, your honor. Miss Travers, were you a witness to Miss Summers's reaction when Miss Benedict told her of their relationship?"

"They were on the terrace, having dinner. Eve had been nervous as a cat. I was in the parlor. I heard her shouting."

"Her?"

"Her," Travers spat out, pointing at Julia. "She was screaming at Eve. When I ran out, she'd shoved the table over. All the china and crystal were smashed. There was murder in her eyes."

"Objection."

"Sustained."

"Miss Travers, can you tell us what Miss Summers said during this incident?"

"She said don't come near me. And I'll never forgive you. She said . . ." Travers aimed that black, furious look at Julia. "She said I could kill you for this."

"And the next day Eve Benedict was murdered."

"Objection."

"Sustained." The judge looked faintly censorious. "Mr. Williamson."

"Withdrawn, your honor. No further questions."

Lincoln was clever on cross. Did the witness believe that everyone who said "I could kill you" in anger meant it literally? What kind of a relationship did Eve and Julia establish over the weeks they'd worked together? During the argument, which was born out of natural shock, did Julia try to strike or harm Eve in any physical way?

He was clever, but Travers's conviction that Julia had killed Eve seeped through.

Nina took the stand, looking chic and efficient in a rose-colored Chanel. She gave her observations on the argument. Lincoln thought that her doubt, her uncertainty, was more damaging than Travers's testimony.

"That same night, Miss Benedict summoned her attorney to the house."

"Yes, she insisted he come right away. She wanted to change her will."

"You knew this."

"Yes. That is, after Mr. Greenburg arrived, Eve asked me to take the changes down in shorthand, and transcribe them. I'd witnessed her other will, and it was no secret that she'd left the bulk of her estate to Paul Winthrop, with a generous provision for her nephew, Drake Morrison."

"And in this one?"

"She bequeathed a trust to Brandon, Julia's son. After the other bequests, she left the rest to Paul and Julia."

"And when did Mr. Greenburg return to have Miss Benedict sign the new will?"

"The next day, the next morning."

"Do you know if anyone else was aware of Miss Benedict's change of heart?"

"I really can't say for sure."

"You can't say, Miss Soloman?"

"Drake came by, but Eve wouldn't see him. I know he saw Mr. Greenburg leave."

"Did she see anyone that day?"

"Yes, Miss DuBarry was by. She left just before one o'clock."

"Did Miss Benedict make plans to see anyone else?"

"I . . ." She pressed her lips together. "I know that she phoned the guest house."

"The guest house where Julia Summers was living?"

"Yes. She told me to keep her afternoon clear. That was right after Miss DuBarry left. Then she went into her bedroom to call the guest house."

"I didn't talk to her," Julia whispered urgently to Lincoln. "I never talked to her after that night on the terrace."

He only patted her hand.

"After the phone call?"

"She seemed upset. I don't know whether she reached Julia or not, but she was only in her room for a minute or two. When she came out, she told me she was going down to talk to Julia. She said . . ." Her troubled eyes darted to Julia, then back to the prosecutor. "She said they were going to have it out."

"And what time was this?"

"It was just one o'clock, perhaps a minute or two past."

"How can you be sure?"

"Eve had given me several letters to type. As she was leaving, I went into my office to start them, and I looked at my desk clock."

Julia stopped listening for a while. If her body couldn't get up and walk away, at least her mind could. She imagined herself back in Connecticut. She'd plant flowers. She would spend a week planting them if she wanted. She'd get Brandon a dog. That was something she'd been thinking about for quite a while, but she'd put off going to the pound to choose one, afraid she'd want to take them all.

And a porch swing. She wanted a porch swing. She could work all day, then in the evenings, when things were quiet, she could sit and swing and watch night fall.

"The state calls Paul Winthrop to the stand."

She must have made some sound. Lincoln put a hand on hers under the table and squeezed. Not in comfort, but in warning.

Paul answered the opening questions briefly, weighing his words, his eyes on Julia's.

"Would you tell the court the nature of your relationship with Miss Summers?"

"I'm in love with Miss Summers." The faintest of smiles touched his lips. "Completely in love with Miss Summers."

"And you also had a close personal relationship with Miss Benedict."

"Yes, I did."

"Didn't you find it difficult to juggle relationships with two women, women who were working closely together? Women who were in actuality mother and daughter."

"Your honor!" Lincoln, the picture of righteous indignation, sprang to his feet.

"Oh, I'd like to answer that one." Paul's quiet voice cut through the uproar of the courtroom. His gaze had veered from Julia to pin the D.A. "I didn't find it difficult at all. Eve was the only mother I'd ever known. Julia is the only woman I've ever wanted to spend my life with."

Williamson folded his hands at his waist, tapped his index fingers together. "Then you had no problem. I wonder if two dynamic women would have found it so easy to share one man."

Heat flashed in those pale blue eyes, but his voice was cool and disdainful. "Your implication is not only idiotic, it's revolting."

But he need not have spoken. Lincoln was already objecting over the courtroom buzz.

"Withdrawn," Williamson said easily. "Mr. Winthrop, were you present during the argument between the deceased and Miss Summers?"

"No."

"But you were on the estate."

"I was in the guest house, watching Brandon."

"Then you were present when Miss Summers returned, directly after the scene on the terrace."

"I was."

"Did she describe her feelings to you?"

"She did. Julia was upset, shocked, and confused."

"Upset?" Williamson repeated, rolling the word around on his tongue as if testing its taste. "Two witnesses have stated that Miss Summers left the terrace in a rage. Are you saying that in a matter of moments that rage had cooled so that she was merely upset?"

"I'm a writer, Mr. Williamson. I choose my words carefully. *Rage* is not the term I'd use to describe Julia's state when she returned to the guest house. *Hurt* would be closer to the mark."

"We won't waste the court's time with semantics. Did you receive a phone call from Miss Summers on the day of the murder?"

"I did."

"At what time?"

"About one-twenty P.M."

"Do you recall the conversation?"

"There wasn't a conversation. She could barely talk. She told me to come, to come right away. That she needed me."

"That she needed you," Williamson repeated on a nod. "Don't you find it odd that she would have found it necessary to make a phone call when her mother was lying dead only a few feet away?"

When court recessed from one to three, Lincoln tucked Julia away in a small room. There was a plate of sandwiches, a pot of coffee, but she touched neither. She didn't need his constant rehearsing, refining, to remind her that she would take the stand herself when court resumed.

Two hours had never gone more quickly.

◆ ◆ ◆ ◆

"THE DEFENSE CALLS Julia Summers to the stand."

She rose, well aware of the stares and murmurs behind her. Reaching the witness box, she turned and faced those stares. She raised her right hand and swore to tell the truth.

"Miss Summers, were you aware when you came to California that Eve Benedict was your natural mother?"

"No."

"Why did you come across country to live on her estate?"

"I had agreed to write her biography. She wanted to give her complete cooperation to the project, as well as maintain some control. We decided that my son and I would stay on her estate until the first draft was completed and approved."

"During the course of this project, did Miss Benedict share portions of her private life with you?"

Sitting by the pool, sweating in the gym. Eve in a vivid robe squatting on the floor building a space port with Brandon. The image flashed by quickly, stinging her eyes. "She was very frank, very open. It was important to her that the book be thorough. And honest," Julia murmured. "She didn't want any more lies."

"Did you have occasion to tape conversations with her, and with people closely connected with her, personally and professionally?"

"Yes. I work from taped interviews and notes."

He walked back to his desk to pick up a box of tapes. "Are these copies of those taped interviews you conducted from January of this year?"

"Yes, those are my labels."

"I'd like to offer these tapes into evidence."

"Your honor, the state objects. These tapes contain the deceased's opinions and recollections, her personal observations on individuals. And their authenticity cannot be substantiated."

Julia let the argument roll around her. She didn't see the point in bringing the tapes into it. The police had listened to the originals, and nothing they had heard had swayed them.

"I'm not going to allow the tapes at this hearing," the judge decided. "Since Mr. Hathoway cannot establish their direct bearing on the accused's defense. My listening to Miss Benedict's memoirs at this time would only cloud the issue. Proceed."

"Miss Summers, during the course of conducting these interviews, did you receive certain threats?"

"There were notes. The first one was left on the porch outside the house."

"Are these the notes you received?"

She glanced down at the papers in his hands. "Yes."

He questioned her about Eve's reaction to them, about the plane flight back from Sausalito, about the argument, her feelings, and at last her movements on the day of the murder.

Her answers were calm, brief, as she'd been instructed.

Then she faced the prosecutor.

"Miss Summers, was anyone present when you received these notes?"

"Paul was there when I received the one in London."

"He was present when it was handed to you?"

"It was delivered to my room, my hotel room, with a room service tray."

"But no one saw who delivered it, or when."

"It was left at the front desk."

"I see. So anyone might have left it there. Including yourself."

"Anyone could have. I didn't."

"I find it difficult to believe that anyone would feel threatened by such inane phrases."

"Even the inane is threatening when it's anonymous, particularly when Eve was relating to me volatile and sensitive information."

"These anonymous notes weren't found in your possession, but in the deceased's dressing table."

"I gave them to her. Eve wanted to deal with them herself."

"Eve," he repeated. "Let's talk about Eve, and volatile information. Would you say you trusted her?"

"Yes."

"That you had grown fond of her?"

"Yes."

"And that you had felt violated, betrayed by her when she revealed that you were the child she had borne out of wedlock, in secret, then had given up for adoption?"

"Yes," she said, and could almost hear Lincoln wince. "I was stunned, and hurt."

"You used the word *manipulated* that night, did you not? You said she had manipulated your life."

"I felt that way. I'm not sure what I said."

"You're not sure?"

"No."

"Because you were too enraged to think clearly?"

"Objection."

"Sustained."

"Were you angry?"

"Yes."

"Did you threaten to kill her?"

"I don't know."

"You don't know? Miss Summers, do you often have trouble recalling your words and actions during violent incidents?"

"I don't often have violent incidents."

"But you have had them. Didn't you once attack a teacher for correcting your son?"

"Your honor, really!"

"I'm merely establishing the defendant's temperament, your honor. Her previous incidents of physical outbursts."

"Overruled. The defendant will answer."

It should have been funny. Julia wondered if years from now she'd see the humor in it. "I once struck a teacher who had belittled and mortified my son for not having a father." She looked directly at Lincoln. "He didn't deserve to be punished for the circumstances of his birth."

"As you felt you had been? Did you feel belittled and mortified by Miss Benedict's revelation?"

"I felt she had taken away my identity."

"And you hated her for that."

"No." She lifted her eyes again, found Victor's. "I don't hate her. I don't hate the man she loved enough to conceive me with."

"Two witnesses have sworn, under oath, that you screamed out your hate for your mother."

"At that moment I did hate her."

"And the next day, when she came to the guest house, came to—in her own words—have it out with you, you picked up the fireplace poker, and, fueled by that hate, struck her down."

"No," she whispered. "I did not."

◆ ◆ ◆ ◆

She was bound over for trial, on the strength of the physical evidence. Bail was set for five hundred thousand.

"I'm sorry, Julia." Lincoln was already writing a note to his law clerk. "We'll have you out within the hour. I guarantee you a jury will acquit."

"How long?" Her gaze flew to Paul's as handcuffs were snapped over her wrists. She heard the quiet metallic clicks and thought of the cell door, locking into place. "Brandon. Oh, God, call Ann, please. I don't want him to know."

"Just hold on." He couldn't reach her, couldn't touch her. Could only watch while they took her away. He dragged Lincoln around by the collar. The violence in his eyes only reflected the tip of the emotion in his heart. "I'll post bail. You get her the hell out. Do whatever you have to do to keep her out of a cell. Understand?"

"I don't think—"

"Just do it."

◆ ◆ ◆ ◆

THE CROWDS WERE still there when they released her. She walked through the dream, wondering if she'd already died. She could still feel the coldness the handcuffs had left at her wrists.

But there was the limo. Eve's limo. But not Lyle, she thought dazedly. A new driver. She slipped inside. It felt clean, cool, safe. Eyes closed, she heard the sound of liquid hitting glass. Brandy, she realized, when Paul pressed the snifter into her hand. Then she heard his voice, as cool as the interior of the limo.

"Well, Julia, did you kill her?"

Fury punched through the shock so fast, so hot that she was hardly aware of snapping up, of dragging the sunglasses off and tossing them on the floor. Before she could speak he had his hand firm on her chin.

"You keep that look on your face." His voice had changed, roughened. "I'll be damned if I'm going to sit by and watch you let them beat you. It's not just your life you're fighting for."

She jerked away and used the brandy to calm her. "No sympathy?"

The muscles in his jaw worked as he drained every drop in his own snifter. "They cut me in half when they took you away. Is that enough for you?"

She shut her eyes again. "I'm sorry. It doesn't do any good for me to swipe at you."

"Sure it does. You've stopped looking like you'd melt through the floorboards." He put a hand to the back of her neck to rub away the tension. Her fingers were twisting in her lap as she battled her own nerves. Slender fingers, he thought, with the nails bitten viciously down to the quick. Gently, he lifted them, touched them to his lips.

"Do you know what first attracted me to you?"

"The fact that I pretended not to be attracted to you?"

The way her lips curved made him grin. Yes, she would fight. No matter how fragile her hold, she would fight. "Well, there was that—that intriguing sense of distance. But even more was the way you looked that first time, walking into Eve's parlor. There was a look in your eyes."

"Jet lag."

"Shut up and let me finish." He touched his mouth to hers, felt her relax fractionally. "It said, quite clearly, I don't like chatty little dinner parties, but I'm going to get through it. And if anyone here takes a punch at me, I'll punch them right back."

"You did, I recall."

"Yeah, I did. I didn't like the idea of the book."

She opened her eyes then and looked into his. "Whatever happens, I'm still going to write it."

"I know." Because he could see tears were threatening, he kissed her eyes closed, then pulled her against his shoulder, where her head could rest. "Now take five. We'll be home soon."

◆ ◆ ◆ ◆

THE PHONE WAS ringing when they walked in the door. By tacit agreement, they both ignored it. "I think I'll take a shower," Julia said. She was halfway up the stairs when the phone machine clicked on.

"Julia Summers." The voice was friendly, amused. "Well, maybe you're not back from the big day yet. Do yourself a favor and give me a call. The name's Haffner, and I've got some interesting information for sale. You might want to know who else was snooping around on the estate the day Eve Benedict went down."

She froze, one hand on the banister. When she turned, Paul was already picking up the phone and punching it to speaker.

"The number here's—"

"This is Winthrop," Paul interrupted. "Who the hell are you?"

"Just an interested bystander. I saw you and pretty Julia leave the courthouse. Tough break."

"I want to know who you are and what you know."

"And I'm more than glad to tell you, friend. For a price. I think, say, two hundred and fifty thousand, cash, ought to cover my expenses."

"What am I paying for?"

"You're paying for reasonable doubt, and I can deliver. That's all you need to keep that sexy lady out of a cage. You bring half the money and the lady up to the HOLLYWOOD sign, nine o'clock. Then if you want me to talk to the cops, or a judge, you deliver the other half. I'll be all yours."

"The banks are closed."

"Oh, yeah, ain't that a bitch. Well, I can wait, Winthrop. Can she?"

Paul looked over. Julia was standing a foot away, straight as a spear. Her eyes were locked on his. In them was something he hadn't seen for days. It was hope.

"I'll get it. Nine o'clock."

"And we'll just leave the cops out of it for now. I smell one, I'm gone."

Her eyes followed the receiver as Paul replaced it. She was almost afraid to speak, afraid to say the words. "Do you think—could he have really seen someone?"

"Someone else was there." Before he could pull his thoughts together, the phone rang again. "Winthrop."

"Paul, it's Victor. I wanted to know . . . is she all right?"

Paul looked at his watch. "Victor, how much cash can you get your hands on in the next two hours?"

"Cash? Why?"

"For Julia."

"Dear God, Paul, she's not going to run."

"No. I don't have time to explain. How much can you get?"

"In an hour or two? Forty, maybe fifty thousand."

"That'll do. I'll be by to get it. No later than eight."

"All right. I'll make some calls."

Julia pressed her fingers to her mouth, then dropped them in a helpless gesture. "Just like that," she said. "No questions, no conditions. I don't know what to say."

"You will when the time comes. I can bring it up to a hundred thousand out of my automatic teller. What about your agent? Can she wire you the rest?"

"Yes. Yes." She felt the tears as she picked up the phone. Not of fear this time, but of desperate hope. "Paul, I'm going to pay you back. I don't mean just the money."

"Let's do it. And make it fast, I want to call Frank."

"The police? But he said—"

"He'll stay downwind." There was something in Paul's eyes as well. Excitement. The dark and dangerous kind. "No way I'm going to hand over this cash, then watch the guy walk. Not after he waited and watched you go through hell. Make the call, Jules. We've got a trap to spring."

◆ ◆ ◆

HAFFNER LIT a cigarette, then leaned up against the bar of the big white "H." He liked it up there. It was a nice, quiet place to do business. He kicked aside an empty can of Diet Coke and wondered how many babes had opened the gates of paradise right here on this spot.

The lights were twinkling on in the basin below. But up there, if you waited long enough, if you were quiet enough, you might hear a far-off coyote call to the moon that had just begun to rise.

Haffner thought he might just take his profits and go on a camping trip. Yosemite, Yellowstone, Grand Canyon. He'd always gotten a kick out of nature. And he'd have earned a vacation, mostly honestly. Expert witnesses got paid all the time. It just so happened his fee was stiff.

He heard the car engine and tramped out his cigarette, moving away from the sign and into the shadows. If Winthrop or the lady tried to pull anything, he's slip back to where he'd hidden his car and be gone.

They came in silence, walking close. The satchel in Paul's hand had Haffner grinning. Smooth as silk, he thought. Smooth as fucking silk.

"He's not here."

The strain in Julia's voice almost made Haffner feel sorry for her. "He'll be here."

She nodded, her head twisting this way and that. "Maybe we should have called the police. It's dangerous, coming up here alone."

"All he wants is the money," Paul said soothingly. "Let's play it his way."

"Good thinking." Haffner stepped toward them. He threw up a hand to shield his eyes from Paul's flashlight, and chuckled. "Aim it low, son, no need to blind me."

"Haffner?"

"That's my name. Well, well, Julia. Good to see you again."

She slid her hand inside her purse as she studied him. "I know you. I've seen you."

"Sure you have. I've been following you for weeks. A little job for a client. I'm a P.I. Well, used to be."

"In the elevator, outside of Drake's office. And in the airport at Sausalito."

"Good eye, honey."

"Who are you working for?" Paul demanded.

"Who *was* I working for? My services are no longer required, seeing as Eve's dead and Julia here's up to her pretty neck."

Paul gripped Haffner's cotton shirt, ripping seams. "If you had anything to do with Eve's murder—"

"Hold it, hold it. You think I'd be here if I did?" He held out both hands, still grinning. "All I did was some shadowing for an interested party."

"Who?"

Haffner thought it over. "Seeing as I'm not on the payroll anymore, it couldn't hurt to tell you. Kincade, Anthony Kincade. He wanted me to keep a real close eye on you, Julia. The book you and Eve were working on had him sweating bullets."

"The notes," she said. "He was sending the notes."

"I don't know anything about any notes. He wanted you tailed, wanted to know everyone you talked to. Bought me some real nice surveillance equipment, so I was able to listen in on some of the interviews. Juicy stuff. That's a real kicker about DuBarry having an abortion. Who'd have thought? I followed you after you left her house. You were pretty erratic that day, Julia. Musta had a lot on your mind. Then I drove around the estate, and—" He paused, grinned. "I'll be glad to tell you all about that. After I see the money."

Paul shoved the satchel at him. "Count it."

"Come on, friend." Haffner set the case on a rock and popped it open. After pulling out a penlight, he shined it over the stacks of bills. Manna from heaven. "I trust you. After all, we're just doing each other a little favor."

"You said you saw someone else on the estate that day," Julia prompted. "How could you have gotten in? Joe was at the gate."

"Guys like me aren't usually invited through gates in Beverly Hills." Enjoying himself, Haffner pulled out a roll of fruit-flavored candy. He crunched down on one. Julia smelled oranges. "I spotted a car by the wall. Made me curious. So I climbed up on the roof, took a peek over, and guess what I saw?" He looked from Julia to Paul. "No guesses? I saw Drake Morrison limping his way across the putting green. Hell, imagine having a putting green right in your yard."

"Drake?" Julia clutched at Paul's hand. "You saw Drake?"

"He was a mess," Haffner continued. "Guess he'd taken a tumble going over the wall. These executive types aren't athletic."

"What about the alarm?" Paul asked.

"Couldn't say. But stands to reason he'd taken care of it or he wouldn't have chanced going over. Seeing as the way was clear, I hopped over after him. Figured Kincade might pay big for some inside information. I couldn't get too close, seeing as it's pretty open there. He was heading for the house, the big house, then he pulled up short, tried to hide himself behind a palm tree, like he was watching somebody. Then he changed direction, went toward the little house. I couldn't get too close myself 'cause he was diddling around, looking for a place where he could get close to a window. Then he jerks back, starts running like demons are after him. I had to dodge into some bushes. I figured I'd take a look in myself, but before I could get close enough, you drove up." He nodded at Julia. "I saw you get out of the car, walk into the garden. I figured I'd better get out before somebody turned the security back on."

"You saw me." Julia shoved Paul aside to get to Haffner herself. "You saw me. You knew I was telling the truth, and you didn't say a word."

"Hey, I'm here now. And you come up with the other half, I'll sing to the D.A. in three-part harmony. Besides, I can only tell them like I saw it. For all I know, you doubled back out of the garden and whacked the lady."

She slapped him, hard enough to have him lose his footing and ram against the rock. "You know I didn't kill her. You know Drake saw whoever did. And you waited until I was desperate enough to sell my soul."

Haffner swiped a hand over his mouth as he got to his feet. "Keep it up and I'll tell the D.A. you tried to bribe me to alibi you. You're nothing to me, lady. So be nice, or I might decide against doing my civic duty."

"Civic duty, my ass," Paul said. "Did you get enough, Frank?"

"Oh, more than." Frank stepped into the clearing, smile beaming.

"Son of a bitch." Haffner took one step forward before Paul caught him with a right to the jaw.

"I couldn't have said it better."

"Rusty? Rusty Slimeball Haffner?" Frank said pleasantly as he hauled Haffner to his feet. "I remember you. Do you remember me? I'm Lieutenant Francis Needlemeyer, and you're under arrest for extortion, withholding evidence, and being a general pain in the ass. I'll read you your rights in just a minute." After clamping on the cuffs, Frank took out a walkie-talkie. "I've got a load of shit for you to pick up."

"On the way, Lieutenant. By the way, the reception was loud and clear."

Chapter Thirty-Two

◆ ◆ ◆ ◆

THE D.A. WANTS MORRISON quick, fast, and in a hurry."

Frank was whistling as they stepped from the driveway to the walk leading to Drake's house. "You get ahold of your lawyer?"

"Yes." Julia wiped her damp hands on her slacks. "He's probably harassing your captain by now. Lincoln said you wouldn't let Paul and me go with you to pick up Drake."

"I can't help it if you just showed up." He winked at Paul. "The thing is, I figure Morrison will break down quicker faced with you."

"I'd prefer to break him down myself," Paul muttered. "Piece by piece."

"You do that. But wait until after we get his statement. Christ, how does he stand the music up that loud?" Frank pushed the bell, then hammered his fist on the door.

"The bastard saw who killed her." Paul's fingers tightened on Julia's until she winced. "Eve gave him everything that was decent in his life, and he didn't give a damn. He used her dead just like he used her alive. For money."

"He might have had a better shot of getting a hefty share of the estate if Julia were convicted." Still whistling under his breath, Frank hammered again. "Now he's going to face an obstruction-of-justice charge. The bastard's in there. The car's here. The lights and music are on. Morrison!" he bellowed. "This is the police. Open the door." He slanted a glance at Paul.

Understanding, Paul put a hand on her back. "Julia, go wait in the car."

She understood as well and shook off his nudging hand. "Like hell."

Frank merely sighed. "Stand back." He kicked the door three times before the hinges gave. "Losing my touch," he said to himself, then drew his gun. "Keep her out here until I say different."

The moment Frank was inside, Julia batted Paul's restraining arms away. "Do you think I'm going to stand out here and wait? He knows who killed her." Violently, she shook her head. "Paul, she was my mother."

He wondered if she knew this was the first time she'd accepted it. With a nod, he took her hand. "Stay close to me."

The music switched off abruptly, so when they stepped into the foyer, they stepped into silence. Paul swept a look up the steps, angling his body so that Julia was shielded behind it.

"Frank?"

"Back in here. Shit. Keep her out."

But she was already in. For the second time violent death stared back at her. He was on his back, where he had fallen. Shattered crystal was scattered on either side of him. The smell was blood and flat champagne—a party gone horribly wrong.

◆ ◆ ◆ ◆

"*I* NEED TO KNOW." An hour later Julia was sitting in Paul's living room, calmed through sheer will. She watched Lincoln's face as she spoke. "Do they think I killed him?"

"No. There's no motive. Once they establish the time of death, it's doubtful there would be opportunity. At this point, it looks professional."

"Professional?"

"One shot, very clean. We'll know more in a day or two."

"A day or two." Unsure how she could get through even an hour or two, she pressed her fingers to her eyes. "He could have cleared me, Lincoln. He's dead, and all I can think of is that if we'd had a couple of days, he could have cleared me."

"He may still. With Haffner's statement, and the fact that Drake was murdered, the case against you is looking very shaky. It proves that someone else was on the estate, that the alarm system was inoperable. Haffner also corroborates the fact that you went into the garden instead of the house. And that someone, probably Eve, was already inside. Drake wouldn't have been looking through the window, wouldn't have been frightened enough to run away if the house had been empty."

Cautious, she closed her hand lightly over the thread of hope. "If we still have to go to trial, that's what you'll use."

"If we still have to go to trial, yes. It's more than enough for reasonable doubt, Julia. The D.A. knows it. Now I want you to get some sleep."

"Thank you." She rose to walk him to the door, and the phone rang. "I'll get it," she said to Paul.

"Let it ring."

"If it's a reporter, I'll have the satisfaction of hanging up. Hello?" Her eyes went quietly blank. "Yes, of course. Just a moment. Lincoln, it's your son."

"Garrett?" He'd already taken a step forward when the shame flooded through him. "My, ah, family decided to fly out for a few days. The children have spring break."

When she didn't respond, he took the receiver. "Garrett, you made it. Yes, I know the flight was delayed. It's good to hear your voice." He laughed, and deliberately turned his back on the room. On Julia. "Well, it's only just past eleven out here, so you're not really up that late. Yes, we're going to see a ball game and Disneyland. Tell your mother and sister I'm heading back to the hotel right now, so wait up. Yes, yes, very soon. Good-bye, Garrett."

He hung up, cleared his throat. "I'm sorry. I'd left this number for them. Their flight was delayed in St. Louis, and I was a bit concerned."

She met his wary eyes levelly. "That's perfectly all right. You'd better get back."

"Yes. I'll be in touch."

He let himself out, hurriedly, Julia thought. "It's ironic, isn't it?" she said when she and Paul were alone. "That boy is only a few short months younger than Brandon. When Lincoln found out I was pregnant, he was so terrified of what would happen that he ran straight to his wife. You could say I saved his marriage, and am in part responsible for Brandon's half brother's birth. He sounded like a very bright, well-mannered boy."

Paul's cigar broke in half as he crushed it out. "I'd still be more than happy to rub Hathoway's face against a concrete wall for you. For an hour or two anyway."

"I stopped being angry. I'm not even sure when. But he's still running." She walked over to fold herself into Paul's lap. "I'm not running anymore, Paul, and I do know when that stopped. It was that night, in London, when we sat up so late, and I told you everything. All the secrets I didn't think I'd ever tell a man." She moved in, letting her lips toy with his. "So I don't think I want you to rub his face against concrete." With a sigh, she trailed kisses down his throat. "Maybe you could just break his arm."

"Okay." His arms tightened so suddenly around her, she gasped. "We're going to be all right," he murmured against her hair.

They fell asleep like that, cuddled on the couch, tangled together, and fully dressed. The knock on the door at a little after six had them jerking awake and blinking at each other.

They went into the kitchen. Frank took a seat while Julia put a skillet on the range. "I have some good news and some bad news," he began. "The bad news is the D.A.'s not ready to drop the charges."

Julia said nothing, only pulled a carton of eggs out of the refrigerator.

"The good news is the investigation's been blown wide open again. Haffner's statement is working in your favor. We need to check out some points, prove the connection to Kincade. It would have been nice if old Rusty had taken a look in the window himself, since Morrison isn't going to be telling anyone what he saw that day. But the fact that they were there at all throws a pretty heavy wrench in the works. The biggest factors against you were the timing, and the fact that everyone else inside had an alibi. If we buy Haffner's story, both those factors are wiped."

"If," Julia repeated.

"Listen, the creep would like to recant. He's pretty pissed that you set him up, but he also knows the score. It's going to be tougher on him if he isn't cooperative. Now, the D.A.'d like to blow his statement apart, but it hangs together. Once we establish that he was being square about working for Kincade, about following you, the D.A.'s going to have to swallow the rest. Morrison was on the estate at the time of the murder, he saw something, now he's dead." He gave a sigh of appreciation as Paul set a mug of coffee in front of him. "We're working on getting his phone records. It'd be interesting to see who he talked to since the murder."

They were talking about murder, Julia thought. And the bacon was sizzling, coffee was steaming. Just outside the window a bird was perched on the deck rail, singing as though its life depended on it.

Three thousand miles away, Brandon was in school, tackling fractions or taking a spelling test. There was a comfort in that, she realized. In knowing that life went on in its steady, unhurried cycle even while hers spun inside the whole on a skewed orbit.

"You're working awfully hard to help me pull out of this." Julia set the bacon aside to drain.

"I don't like working against my gut." Frank had added just enough milk to his coffee to keep it from scalding his tongue. He sipped and let the hot caffeine slide into his system. "And I've got this personal resistance to seeing anybody get away with murder. Your mother was a terrific lady."

Julia thought of both of them. The dedicated lawyer who had still found time to bake cookies or fix a hem. The dynamic actress who had grabbed at life with both hands. "Yes, she was. How do you want your eggs, Lieutenant?"

"Over hard," he said, smiling back at her. "Hard as a rock. I picked up one of your books. The one on Dorothy Rogers. You had some amazing stuff in there."

Julia broke eggs into the skillet and watched the whites bubble. "She'd had some amazing experiences."

"Well, for someone who interrogates people for a living, I'd like to know your trick."

"There's no trick, really. When you talk to people they never forget you're a cop. Most of what I do is just listening, so they get caught up in their own story and forget all about me, and the tape recorder."

"If you ever marketed those tapes, you'd make a fortune. What do you do with them after you've finished?"

She flipped the eggs over, quietly pleased when the yolks held firm. "File them. The tapes aren't much good without the stories that connect them."

Paul set his own mug down with a clatter. "Wait a minute."

Turning, a platter piled with food in her hand, Julia watched him rush out of the kitchen.

"Don't worry." Frank rose to take the platter from her. "I'll eat his share."

Five minutes later, Paul was calling from the top of the stairs. "Frank, I want you to take a look at this."

Grumbling, Frank piled more bacon on his plate and took it with him. Julia was right behind, a mug of coffee in each hand.

Paul was in his office, standing in front of the television, watching Eve. "Thanks." He took a mug from Julia, then nodded at the set. "Jules, I want you to listen carefully to this."

". . . I've taken the precaution of making the other tapes . . ."

He hit freeze, turned to Julia. "What other tapes?"

"I don't know. She never gave me any tapes."

"Exactly." He kissed her, hard. She could feel his excitement sing through his fingertips as they pressed into her shoulders. "So where the hell are they? She made them between the time you last saw her and the time she was murdered. She didn't give them to Greenburg. She didn't give them to you. But she meant to."

"She meant to," Julia repeated, lowering herself into a chair. "And she'd come to the guest house to see me, to wait for me."

"To give them to you. To erase all the rest of the lies."

"We went through that place, top to bottom." Frank set his plate aside. "There weren't any tapes except the ones in the safe."

"No, because someone had taken them. Someone who knew what was on them."

"How could anyone have known?" Julia looked back to the set, to the frozen image of Eve. "If she made them that night, or the next morning? She never left the house."

"Who came in?"

Frank pulled out his notebook, flipped pages. "Flannigan, her agent, DuBarry. She might have told any of them something they didn't want to hear."

Julia turned away. She couldn't face the possibility it could have been Victor. She'd already lost a mother twice. She wasn't sure she could survive losing another father. "Eve was alive after each of them left. How could they have come back without Joe knowing?"

"The same way Morrison got in," Frank mused. "Though it's tough swallowing the idea that someone else came over the wall."

"Maybe they didn't." With his eyes on Eve, Paul ran a hand over Julia's hair. "Maybe they didn't have to worry about getting in, or getting out. Because they were always inside. They were with her because they were expected to be with her. Someone she cared enough about to explain what she was doing."

"You're reaching for one of the servants," Frank muttered, and began flipping pages again.

"I'm reaching for someone who lived on the estate. Who didn't have to worry about security. Someone who followed her from the main house to the guest house. Someone who could kill Eve in the heat of the moment, and Drake in cold blood."

"You've got your cook, your gardener, your assistant gardener, a couple of maids, the driver, housekeeper, secretary. They've all got a pretty snug alibi for the time of the murder."

Impatience shimmered like heat waves. "Maybe one of them manufactured an alibi. It fits, Frank."

"This isn't one of your books. Real murder's messier, the pieces don't fit so neat."

"They always make the same picture. Haffner said she came out of the house, that Morrison changed direction and went straight for the guest house. He didn't stop by the garage, which though I'd love to nail the little slime, probably eliminates Lyle. And I think we're looking for someone close to her. Someone who knew Julia's pattern, so the notes could get through."

"Haffner might have passed the notes," Julia mused.

"Why would he bother to deny it? He told us everything else. I want to know who followed you to London—and to Sausalito."

"I went over the manifests for the London flights, Paul. I already told you I couldn't find a connection."

"Have you got a list of the names?"

"In the file."

"Be a pal, Frank, have them faxed here."

"Christ." Then he looked at Julia's face, at the television screen that was filled with Eve. "Sure, sure, why not? I'm tired of carrying around a badge anyway."

It was worse somehow, Julia thought. Waiting. Waiting while Frank made the phone call, while Paul smoked and paced. Waiting for technology to kick in and send them another slim hope. She watched the sheets click out, hundreds of names. There was only one that would matter.

They developed a routine. She would study one sheet, hand it to Paul. He would pore over another, pass it to Frank. She felt an odd jolt seeing her own name, mixed among so many strangers. And there was Paul's, on the Concorde. He'd been impatient to get to her, she thought with a small smile. He'd been angry, pushy, demanding. By the time they'd flown back together, he'd been everything.

Rubbing her tired eyes, she took another sheet. In her methodical way she tried to study and absorb each name, put a face, a personality with it.

Alan Breezewater. Middle-aged, balding, a successful broker.

Marjorie Breezewater. His pleasant wife who enjoyed a ripping game of bridge.

Carmine Delinka. A boxing promoter with delusions of grandeur.

Helene Fitzhugh-Pryce. A London divorcee returning from a shopping spree on Rodeo Drive.

Donald Frances. A young, upwardly mobile ad executive.

Susan Frances. Donald's attractive, British-born wife who's working her way up in television production.

Matthew John Frances. Their five-year-old son, excited about visiting his grandparents.

Charlene Gray. Julia yawned, shook her brain clear and tried to concentrate. Charlene Gray.

"Oh, God."

"What is it?" Paul was already at her shoulder, fighting back the urge to snatch the sheet from her hand.

"Charlie Gray."

Scowling, Frank looked up from his own sheet. The whites of his eyes were streaked with red. "I thought he was dead."

"He is. He committed suicide in the late forties. But he had a child, a baby. Eve told me she didn't know what had happened to it."

Paul had already homed in on the name. "Charlene Gray. I think it's a little late to think of coincidence. How do we find her?"

"Give me a couple of hours." Frank took the sheet and two slices of cold bacon with him and headed for the door. "I'll call you."

"Charlie Gray," Julia murmured. "Eve cared very deeply for him, but he cared more. Too much more. She broke his heart when she married Michael Torrent. He gave her rubies, and her first screen test. He was her first lover." The chill shivered down her arms. "Oh, God, Paul, could his child have killed Eve?"

"If he'd had a daughter, how old would she be now?"

Julia circled her fingers over her temples. "Early to mid-fifties." Her motion stopped. "Paul, you don't seriously believe—"

"Do you have a picture of him?"

Her hands were beginning to shake. And it was excitement. "Yes, Eve gave me hundreds of snapshots and studio stills. Lincoln has everything."

Paul started to pick up the phone, then let out an oath. "Wait." He turned to the shelf along the wall, running his fingers along the titles of video cassettes. *"Desperate Lives,"* he murmured. "Eve's first picture— starring Michael Torrent and Charles Gray." He gave Julia's hand a quick squeeze. "Let's watch a movie, baby."

"Yeah." She managed to smile. "But hold the popcorn."

She held her breath as well as he took Eve's tape out of the machine, slipped in the copy of the old movie. Muttering to himself, he fast-forwarded through the FBI warning, the opening titles.

Eve was in the first scene, strutting her way down a sidewalk that was supposed to be New York. A flirty hat was perched over one eye. The camera zoomed in, caught that young, vibrant face, then panned down as Eve bent, swiveled, then ran a finger slowly up the seam of her stocking.

"She was a star from the first reel," Julia said. "And she knew it."

"Tell you what. We'll watch this all the way through on our honey-moon."

"On our—"

"We'll get into that later." While Julia was trying to decide if she'd just received a proposal, Paul zipped through the film. "I want a close-up. Come on, Charlie. There." On the single triumphant word he hit the freeze. Charlie Gray, his hair slicked back, his mouth quirked in a self-deprecating grin, looked back at them.

"Oh, my God, Paul." Julia's fingers dug into his shoulder like wires. "She has his eyes."

Mouth grim, Paul flicked off the set. "Let's go talk to Travers."

◆ ◆ ◆ ◆

DOROTHY TRAVERS SHUFFLED from room to room in the empty house, chasing dust, polishing glass, building hate.

Anthony Kincade had killed any chance she might have had for believing in a healthy relationship with a man. So she had focused all her love on two people. Her poor son who still called her Mommy, and Eve.

There hadn't been anything sexual in her love for Eve. She'd been done with sex before Kincade had been done with her. Eve had been sister, mother, daughter to her. Though Travers was fond of her own family, having Eve cut out of her life left her with such pain she could tolerate it only by coating it with bitterness.

When she saw Julia walk into the house, she lurched forward, hands extended and curled like claws. "Murdering bitch. I'll kill you for showing your face here."

Paul caught her, struggled her beefy arms back. "Stop it. Dammit, Travers. Julia owns this house."

"I'll see her in hell before she steps foot in it." Tears gushed out of her eyes as she fought to free herself. "She broke her heart, and when that wasn't enough, she killed her."

"Listen to me. Drake's been murdered."

Travers stopped struggling long enough to catch her breath. "Drake. Dead?"

"He was shot. We found him late last night. We have a witness who saw him, here, on the estate the day Eve was killed. Travers, the security had been shut off. Drake climbed over the wall."

"You're trying to tell me that Drake killed Eve?"

He had her attention now, but loosened his hold only slightly. "No, but he saw who did. That's why he's dead."

Travers's gaze scraped back to Julia. "If she could kill her own mother, she could kill her cousin."

"She didn't kill Drake. She was with me. She was with me all night."

The lines around Travers's face only deepened. "She's blinded you. Blinded you with sex."

"I want you to listen to me."

"Not while she's in this house."

"I'll wait outside." Julia shook her head before Paul could protest. "It's all right. It'll be better that way."

When Julia had closed the door behind her, Travers relaxed. "How could you sleep with that whore?" The minute Paul released her she groped in her pocket for a tissue. "I thought Eve meant something to you."

"You know she did. Come in here and sit down, we need to talk." Once he had settled her in the parlor, he crouched at her feet. "I need you to tell me about Charlie Gray's daughter."

Something flashed in Travers's eyes before she lowered them. "I don't know what you're talking about."

"Eve knew. She trusted you more than anyone. She would have told you."

"If she trusted me, why didn't she tell me she was sick?" Overwhelmed with grief, she buried her face in her hands. "That she was dying."

"Because she loved you. And because she didn't want what time she had left to be marred with pity or regrets."

"Even that was taken from her. That little bit of time."

"That's right. I want whoever took that from her to pay every bit as much as you. It wasn't Julia." He gripped her hands before she could push him away. "But it was someone she loved, someone she'd taken into her life. She found Charlie's daughter, didn't she, Travers?"

"Yes."

Chapter Thirty-Three

◆ ◆ ◆ ◆

THE SUN WAS BOUNCING off the deep blue water of the pool. The ripples caused by the fountain that still fed it widened, and spread and vanished. Julia wondered who would swim there again. If anyone would shuck off their suit, stand under that rush of water, and laugh.

She had an urge to do it herself, quickly, while she was alone, to pay homage to someone she had loved very briefly.

Instead, she watched a hummingbird, a small bright missile, flash above the water, then hover and drink from a vivid red petunia.

"Julia."

The smile that had started to curve her lips froze. She felt her heart leap and lodge in her throat. Very slowly, very carefully, she relaxed the fingers that had tensed into fists, and calling on whatever skill had passed from Eve's blood to hers, turned to face Charlie Gray's daughter.

"Nina. I didn't realize you were here. I thought you'd moved out."

"Almost. I just had a few more things to pack up. It's amazing how much you accumulate in fifteen years. You've heard about Drake."

"Yes. Why don't we go inside? Paul's here."

"I know." Nina let out a quick breath that caught like a sob. "I heard him and Travers. She didn't realize I'd come in earlier and gone upstairs. None of this should have happened. None of it." She reached into her buff-colored envelope bag and pulled out a .32. Sun hit chrome and dazzled. "I wish I could have found another way, Julia. I really do."

Finding herself facing a gun brought on more anger than fear. She didn't consider herself invincible. A part of her mind acknowledged that the bullet could rip through her, cut off her life. But the way the threat was offered, the incredible politeness of it, buried any thought of caution.

"You can stand there and apologize to me as if you'd forgotten a luncheon date. Sweet Jesus, Nina, you killed her."

"It wasn't something I planned." Her tone was only mildly irritated as she pressed a hand between her breasts. "God knows I did everything I could to reason with her. I asked, I pleaded, I sent the notes to try to scare her. When I saw that wasn't going to work, I sent more notes to you. I even hired someone to tamper with the plane."

Somewhere in the garden, a bird began to sing. "You tried to kill me."

"No, no. I know what a good pilot Jack is, and my instructions were very specific. It was meant to scare you, to make you see how important it was that the book research stopped."

"Because of your father."

"Partly." Her lashes lowered, but Julia could still see the glint of her eyes through them. "Eve ruined his life, ended his life. I hated her for that for a long time. But it became impossible to keep hating her when she did so much to help me. I cared very, very deeply for Eve, Julia. I tried to forgive her. You have to believe me."

"Believe you? You murdered her, then were willing to stand back and watch me hang for it."

Nina's mouth firmed. "One of the first things Eve taught me was survival. Whatever the price, I'm going to get through this."

"Paul knows, and Travers. The police are already checking on Charlene Gray."

"I'll be gone long before they link her to Nina Soloman." She glanced back at the house, satisfied that Paul and Travers were still talking. "I haven't had much time to work this out, but there seems to be only one way."

"Killing me."

"It has to look like suicide. We'll take a walk down to the guest house. Returning to the scene—the police ought to like that. You'll write a note confessing to killing Eve, and Drake. This is the gun I used. It isn't registered or traceable to me. I can promise to make it quick. I was trained by the best." She gestured with the gun. "Hurry along, Julia. If Paul comes out, I'll have to kill him too. Then Travers. You'll have a regular bloodbath laid at your door."

The hummingbird streaked from the blossom, bulleted over the water. It was that vibrant flash of red, and the unexpected rage leaping at her that had Nina stumbling back a pace, had her first shot going wide. Thrust forward by a blind, titanic fury, Julia rammed into her, striking out with a force that threw them both off balance and into the pool.

Tangled together, they plunged to the bottom. Buoyancy had them surfacing as they kicked and clawed and gagged on water. Julia didn't hear her own howl of rage as her hair was viciously pulled. The pain dimmed her vision, sharpened her fury. For an instant she saw Nina's face, diamond glints of water sprinkled over it. Then her hands clamped around Nina's throat and squeezed. Her lungs gulped in air automatically before she was dragged under again.

Through the veil of water she could see Nina's eyes, the wild panic in them. She had the satisfaction of watching them snap closed as her fist made a slow sweep through the water to plow into Nina's stomach. Her own head rapped hard against the bottom, forcing her to clamp her teeth on the need to cry out. Lights danced behind her eyes as she twisted and shot her leg out to kick vulnerable flesh. Scratches and bruises were ignored, but the ringing in her ears, the burning in her chest, had her fighting her way back to the surface for more air.

Shouts and screams echoed in her head as she dived forward, catching hold of Nina's blouse as Nina tried to thrash her way to the side. Water dripped from Julia's cheeks, ran from her eyes. She didn't know when the sobs had begun. "Bitch," she said between her teeth. Swinging back, she rammed fist into face, then yanked her up by the hair to hit her again.

"Stop. Come on, baby, stop." Struggling to tread water and hold on to her, Paul grabbed at her arm. "She's out cold." He hooked an arm under Nina's chin to keep her from sinking under. "She scratched you. Your face."

Julia sniffed and wiped at the mix of water and blood. "She fights like a girl."

He wanted to laugh at the chilly derisiveness in her voice. "Travers is calling the cops. Can you get to the side on your own?"

"Yeah." The moment she had, she began to retch.

Without a backward glance, Paul left Nina unconscious on the pool apron and went to Julia.

"Get rid of it," he said quietly, holding her head in his trembling hands. "You swallowed more than your share. That's a girl." He stroked and soothed as her choking turned to labored breathing. "That's the first time I've seen you in action, champ." He pulled her up against him and just held on. "Bloody amazon. Remind me not to tick you off."

Julia sucked in air and felt it burn her ravaged throat. "She had a gun."

"It's okay." His hold on her tightened spasmodically. "I've got it now. Let's get you inside."

"I'll take her." Grim-faced, Travers swooped down on Julia with a huge bath towel. "You watch that one. You come with me now." She wrapped her big arm around Julia's waist. "I'm going to get you some dry clothes and fix you a nice cup of tea."

Paul wiped the water from his face and watched Travers lead Eve's daughter into the house. Then he rose to see to Charlie's.

♦ ♦ ♦ ♦

SWATHED IN one of Eve's flowing silk robes, bolstered by tea spiked with brandy, Julia rested against the pile of pillows Travers had plumped around her.

"I haven't felt so pampered since I was twelve and broke my wrist roller skating."

"It helps Travers deal with the guilt." Paul stopped pacing to light a cigar.

"She doesn't have anything to feel guilty about. She believed I'd done it. Christ, there were moments I almost believed it myself." She shifted, winced.

"You should let me call the doctor, Jules."

"The paramedics already cleared me," she reminded him. "Scratches and bruises."

"And a gunshot wound."

She glanced down at her arm where it was bandaged just above the elbow. "Gosh, Rocky, it's just a scratch." When he didn't smile, she reached out her hand. "Really, Paul, it's a graze, just like in the movies. The little bite she landed on my shoulder hurts worse." Grimacing, she touched it gingerly. "I just want to stay right here, with you."

"Shove up," he ordered, sitting by her hip when she made room. He took her hand between both of his, then brought it to his lips. "You sure know how to scare the life out of a man, Jules. When I heard that gunshot, I lost five years."

"If you kiss me, I'll do my best to give them back to you."

He bent down to her, intending to keep the kiss light. But she wrapped her arms around him, drew him in. With a low sound of desperation he hauled her against him and poured all of his needs, his gratitude, his promises into that one meeting of lips.

"Hate to interrupt," Frank said from the doorway.

Paul didn't glance around, but brushed his mouth over the scratches on Julia's cheeks. "Then don't."

"Sorry, pal, it's official. Miss Summers, I'm here to inform you that all charges against you have been dropped."

Paul felt her shudder. Her hand had fisted against his shirt as he looked up at Frank. "Sure, after she collared the killer for you."

"Shut up, Winthrop. And to offer an official apology for the ordeal you've experienced. Can I have one of those sandwiches? I'm starved."

Paul glanced at the plate of cold cuts Travers had left on the table. "Take it to go."

"No, Paul." Julia pushed him away far enough to sit up. "I need to know why. I have to know what she meant by some of the things she said. She's talked to you, hasn't she?"

"Yeah, she talked." Frank bent over to build a huge sandwich of chilled ham, salami, chicken breast, topped with three cheeses and thick slices of beefsteak tomatoes. "She knew we had her. Got anything to drink with this?"

"Try the bar," Paul told him.

Impatient, Julia got up to fetch him a soft drink herself. "When she talked about killing me, she said she'd make it quick. That she'd been taught by the best. Do you know who she meant?"

Frank took the bottle she offered and nodded. "Michael Delrickio."

"Delrickio? Nina was involved with Delrickio?"

"That's how Eve met her," Paul said. "Sit down. I'll tell you what Travers told me."

"I think I'd better." Unconsciously she took the chair under Eve's portrait.

"It seems Nina's background wasn't quite what she'd led you to believe. It hadn't been poor, but it had been abusive. Her father had left her mother a sizable bequest. But it wasn't enough to buy off hate. Nina's mother took out that hate on the child—physically, emotionally. And there was a stepfather for a while. All of that was true. What she left out was the fact that her mother tried to poison her against Eve, telling Nina how she'd betrayed Charlie, caused his death. When Nina left home at sixteen, she was very confused, very vulnerable. She worked the streets for a while, then went to Vegas. She worked a floor show and turned tricks. That was where she met Delrickio. She'd have been about twenty then, sharp as a tack. He saw potential and began using her as a hostess for his more important clients. They had an affair that went on for several years. Somewhere along the line she fell for him. She didn't want to entertain his clients anymore. She wanted a straight job, and some sort of commitment from him."

"The lady showed real poor taste," Frank said over a mouthful of sandwich. "And poor judgment. Delrickio kept her in Vegas, and when she caused a scene, he had one of his boys teach her a lesson. That quieted her down for a while. The way she tells it, she still had a thing for him, couldn't let go. She found out he was boffing some other babe and she went after her, cut her up some. Delrickio liked her initiative, and strung her along."

"Then Eve came into the picture," Paul put in. He stroked a hand up and down Julia's arm, slowly, rhythmically, as if he were afraid to break contact. "This time it was Delrickio who fell hard. When Nina wouldn't shake loose, he had some of his muscle try to convince her. Eve got wind of it, and since she'd just found out—through Priest—how far Delrickio would go, she went to see Nina herself. Nina was in the hospital, pretty racked up, and the whole thing spilled out of her."

"And when Eve found out she was Charlie's daughter," Julia said quietly, "she brought her here."

"That's right." Paul looked up at the portrait. "She gave Nina a fresh start, friendship, had Kenneth train her. And for all the years in between, Eve lied for her. When Eve decided she wanted to clean up the lies, that she wanted the truth to be part of her legacy, Nina panicked. Eve promised she would wait until she trusted you before she told you everything, but she felt Charlie deserved honesty. And she reasoned with Nina that she was a symbol of how far a woman could come."

"Nina couldn't handle it," Frank continued. "She liked the image she'd developed. The cool, competent career woman. She didn't want all of her upper class contacts to know she'd been a whore for a Mafia don. She didn't plan to kill Eve, not consciously, but when she found out she'd put the whole story down on tape and was going to give it to you, she snapped. The rest is easy."

"She followed Eve down to the guest house," Julia murmured. "They argued. She picked up the poker, hit her. Nina would have been scared then, but very organized. She'd have wiped her prints off the weapon, taken the keys—because she'd have remembered how I'd fought with Eve the night before."

"She heard you drive up," Frank told her. "Saw you walk into the garden. That's when she decided to throw suspicion on you. She got the hell out. She was the one who turned the security back on. It scared her when she found the main switch off. She figured it would complicate things, so she turned it on again and went back to work. Oh, and she made sure to call down to the kitchen, so Travers and the cook would know she was busy transcribing letters."

"But she didn't know Drake had seen her." Julia leaned back and closed her eyes.

"He tried to blackmail her." Frank shook his head as he built another towering sandwich. "She could afford the money, but not the loose end. With him dead and you heading for prison, she knew she was away free. Travers was so loyal to Eve that she would never have told anyone about Nina's background—and she'd have no reason to."

"I heard them," Julia remembered. "The night of Eve's party I heard someone arguing. Delrickio and Nina. She was crying."

"Seeing him again didn't do much for Nina's state of mind," Frank put in. "She still loved the sleaze. He told her she could prove it by getting Eve to stop the book. She must have really started to crack that night. I got to figure some of her mother's poison was still swimming around in her system. When she couldn't stop Eve one way, she stopped her another."

"It's funny." Julia said half to herself. "It all began with Charlie

Gray. He gave Eve her start. His was the first story she told me. And now it ends with him."

"Don't spill that sandwich on the way out, Frank," Paul murmured, and gestured to the door.

"What? Oh, yeah. The D.A. notified Hathoway," he said as he rose. "He said to tell Julia to call if she had any questions. He was taking his son to a ball game. See you around."

"Lieutenant." Julia opened her eyes. "Thank you."

"My pleasure. You know, I never noticed before how much you look like her." He took another huge bite of the sandwich. "She sure was one fine-looking lady." He went out, eating.

"You okay?" Paul asked.

"Yes." Julia drew a deep breath. It still burned a little, but it reminded her she was alive, and free. "Yes, I'm fine. Do you know what I'd like? I'd like a very tall glass of champagne."

"That's never a problem in this house." He walked over to the refrigerator behind the bar.

Rising, she walked over to stand on the opposite side of the bar. Eve's robe slid off one shoulder. While she watched Paul, Julia adjusted it, smoothed it—her fingers lingering for a moment as if she were touching an old friend. Though he smiled a little at the gesture, he said nothing. She wondered if he had noticed that Eve's scent still clung to the silk.

"I have a question."

"Fire away." Paul ripped the foil off a bottle and began untwisting the wire.

"Are you going to marry me?"

The cork exploded out. Paul ignored the froth spilling over the side, and watched her. Her eyes were cautious, the way he liked them best. "You bet."

"Good." She nodded. Her fingers slid down the silk until her hands linked together on the bar. Wherever she had come from, wherever she was going, she was her own woman first. "That's good." Steadying herself, she took another long breath. "How do you feel about Connecticut?"

"Well, actually—" He paused to pour two glasses. "I've been thinking it's time for a change of scene. I hear Connecticut's got a lot going for it. Like fall foliage, skiing, and really sexy women." He offered her a glass. "You figure you've got enough room to put me up?"

"I can just squeeze you in." But when he started to touch his glass to hers, she shook her head. "Ten-year-old boys are noisy, demanding, and have little respect for privacy."

"Brandon and I already have an understanding." Comfortable, he leaned against the bar. He caught her scent, and only her scent. "He thinks my marrying his mother is a pretty good idea."

"You mean you—"

"And," Paul continued, "before you start worrying about me dealing with the fact that I'm not his natural father, I'll remind you that I found my mother when I was ten." He laid a hand over hers. "I want the package, Jules—you and the kid." He brought her hand to his lips, pleased when she spread her fingers to caress his cheek. "Besides, he's exactly the right age to baby-sit when we start giving him brothers and sisters."

"Okay. The deal's two for one." She clicked her glass against his. "You're getting a hell of a bargain."

"I know."

"So are we. Are you going to come around here and kiss me?"

"I'm thinking about it."

"Well, think fast." She laughed and held out her arms for him. He scooped her up and kissed her beneath the portrait of a woman who had lived with no regrets.

About the Author

NORA ROBERTS was the first writer to be inducted into the Romance Writers of America Hall of Fame. The *New York Times* bestselling author of such novels as *Sweet Revenge* and *Divine Evil,* she has become one of today's most successful and best-loved writers. Nora Roberts lives with her family in Maryland.